D0463961

MOON-KISSED PROMISES

MOON-KISSED PROMISES

Sylvie F. Sommerfield

KENSINGTON BOOKS

KENSINGTON BOOKS are published by

Kensington Publishing Corp.
850 Third Avenue
New York, NY 10022

ISBN 0-8217-5308-8

First Pinnacle Paperback Printing: May, 1993
First Kensington Hardcover Printing: September, 1995

Printed in the United States of America

Introduction

This book was written especially for all the wonderful fans who read *Moonlit Magic* and took the time to write to me.

All the letters expressed their enjoyment of *Moonlit Magic*, but all of them presented the same question: What happened to Michael Cord?

It seems that Michael Cord, the brother of the hero Trace Cord in *Moonlit*, caught the fancy of most of the readers . . . as he did mine. He seemed to come alive for me as I wrote.

In answer to the thousands of requests I've received, I finally sat down and created Michael's story. It follows Michael from the moment *Moonlit* ends.

His story is unique, and the more I wrote about him the more I liked him. I hope you enjoy reading *Moon-Kissed Promises* as much as I enjoyed writing it.

I should love to hear your reaction to *Moon-Kissed Promises*. Drop me a line at 2080 W. State St., Westgate Plaza Suite 9, New Castle, PA 16101. Let me know how you feel about the adventures of Michael Cord and Hannah, the love of his life.

With this book I send you my thanks for all your heart-warming responses, and my hope that it brings you some hours of pleasure.

—Sylvie Sommerfield

Prologue

Nevada-California Border
1869–70

The huge, black engine stood still, spewing smoke, seeming to be straining to move. The stack, firebox, and steam dome were painted black. The rest of the train exhausted the colors of the rainbow. The wheels and pilot were a vivid vermilion red. The boiler rose high with the railroad's name, "The Starett line," scripted in flowing ribbon and surrounded by curlicues of gold. The outside of the cab was exquisite with gold scrollwork, and underneath the window was a painting in natural colors of a bengal tiger stalking some unseen prey in a jungle as green as emeralds. The nameplate, set well forward on the boiler, spelled *Tiger* in great circus-type letters; another jungle painting appeared on the side of the headlight, and, as a final effect, the American flag flew from a pole atop the pilot.

The engine had come far from St. Louis, and the rails that were being laid just a few miles ahead were the silver ribbons on which it traveled.

The man who had dreamed of building his railroad line from St. Louis to San Francisco stood beside the engine now. Though his gaze was on the distance where antlike figures scurried about laying rail foot by foot, his concentration was focused on the tall, lean man who stood beside him.

This man wore a dark shirt and gray pants that whispered of rebel affiliations. His wide-brimmed hat was set low over piercing blue eyes, one of which was covered by a black patch. A short beard covered the lower part of his face, masking a strong, square chin.

As he paced a few steps back and forth, a pronounced limp bore evidence of past violence. It seemed to him he had been fighting one kind of war or another for as long as he could remember. His voice was crisp and firm, as if he was well used to command.

"I've got to go, and you know it, Max. It's not my choice. I'd rather stay with you until you lay the final rail. It was good news when you decided to push on to San Francisco instead of stopping in Sacramento. I was looking forward to that, and to seeing the ocean. I'd certainly like to stay . . . but the men who trail me are dangerous. They wouldn't hesitate to kill you or any of your men if they got in the way."

"There's enough of our men to get rid of the problem," Maxwell said.

"There's never enough men to get rid of that kind. I know," his voice grew bitter. "I'm one of them."

"Stop it, Michael," Maxwell said gruffly. "If you were one of that kind, it wouldn't matter to you how many stood between you and them, or how many died." His voice grew gentle. "Don't you think it's time you stopped running, boy?"

"Max, there's three this time. But there will be more and more, and I can't keep standing against them because one day one of them will be lucky."

"And you're not the surrendering kind."

"Not when it means killing again. I thought after the war I was done with it. But I wasn't." Before Maxwell could answer, a small Chinese man of unestimable age came to stand beside him. His eyes ere filled with the same sorrow as Maxwell's.

"Mistah Mikel," he said, in soft, lilting intonations. "You have many friends, stand beside you. One cannot fight devil by running. Sometimes harder to fight than run away."

"You calling me a coward, Lee Chu?" Michael asked with a little laugh.

Lee Chu, confidant of Maxwell Starett for so many years neither remembered exactly how many, looked at Michael with shock.

"Oh, no Mistah Mikel, you no coward. Maybe . . . too brave. Maybe worry about wrong things. Maybe already you run too far. Maybe . . . you lose yourself and never find again."

"He's right. Michael, you have friends here."

"Friends I don't want to see dead."

Maxwell sighed. They had been having this argument for two days and it was as useless now as it was before.

"What are you going to do?"

"I figured to get myself lost in one of the mining camps. There's hundreds of them, and nobody will ask any questions of me there."

Maxwell cast a quick glance at Lee Chu, who remained inscrutable. Then he turned his head to look at Michael Cord. He felt a kind of bitter, silent misery seep through him and knew it was reflected from Michael himself.

He remembered hiring Michael's brother, Trace Cord, what seemed like a lifetime ago. Trace had helped lead the railroad as far as Colorado where problems had struck when they were searching for a way through Roaring Fork Valley. Michael had come at the height of the problem and helped them. Trace married Jenny Graham, the girl who had fought their right of way so hard. They decided to return to the Cord plantation in Georgia. Michael, unable to return with the brother he missed so deeply, decided to go on with the railroad in Trace's place. Maxwell now knew that Michael had been driven by a past he seldom spoke about. A few friends in camp, Maxwell, and Lee Chu—those were the only ones Michael had confided in, besides his brother, of course.

"Michael, it's a waste of your life to be lost like that. You deserve more."

"Don't give me opinions about what you don't know. I think I left my life back there at Gettysburg. What's left," he shrugged, "is not really worth worrying about wasting. The best I can do with it is make sure it doesn't get anyone else killed."

"I wish you'd change your mind."

"I can't. I need to move faster than you're able to. By the time they catch up with the tracks, I'll be gone. You go on to San Francisco. Maybe I'll look you up sometime, when it's safer."

Maxwell knew there was no use in arguing more. Michael intended to go, and Maxwell wanted to part as friends. He extended his hand to Michael, who took it in a firm grip.

"What about Trace . . . and your sister, Allison? Are you at least going to contact them? You know they'll be writing to me in San Francisco. At least let them know where you are."

"Don't you think someone might learn about my family soon? Come around there asking questions? It's better they don't know where I am. That way no one gets hurt."

"Except you."

Michael remained silent. He removed his hat and used the crook of his arm to wipe the sweat from his brow. Then he replaced the hat and again he turned to look at Maxwell.

"Thanks for the ride, Max. I'll see you one day."

"I wish you'd promise me that."

Michael laughed a humorless laugh. "I wish I could. Good luck. Open a bottle of champagne for me when you celebrate in San Francisco."

"The hell I will. I'll save the bottle for you to open."

"Fair enough." Michael walked a short distance away, then Maxwell's voice stopped him.

Michael turned to look at him.

"What about Hannah?" The name hung between them like a thick, dark wall. Maxwell could see the fleeting look of pain before it was forcefully camouflaged.

"Don't be a fool, Max," he said softly. "Hannah least of all. She's a rose that needs to bloom in someone's garden—someone who can protect her and give her a good life. That's not me. That's not the kind of life I could give her. I wouldn't drag her into my life. I wouldn't do that to her."

He turned and walked away, and Maxwell stood in silence. There was nothing more he could say. Nothing that would turn Michael from the path he had chosen. Maxwell prayed silently that whatever powers there were would find a way to reach Michael Cord before he was lost in a way that was worse than death.

* * *

The rails moved slowly and methodically toward San Francisco and completion. It had been almost three weeks since Michael had left. There had been no sign of the men he'd said were coming, but Maxwell knew that meant little. They knew Michael had ridden with him and he was reasonably sure they were watching his camp.

The next morning proved him right. They rode into his camp at sunup.

He knew them, and he knew what they were up to. He sensed it in the way they rode, the guns that hung low on their hips. But he was still unprepared for the dead-cold eyes and the aura surrounding them that promised death to anyone who got in their way. He stood and waited until they stopped their horses close to him.

"Morning, gentlemen," Maxwell said. He could have been a lot less pleasant, but he wanted no trouble with these men . . . and he didn't want to give them what they wanted.

"You Maxwell Starett?" one questioned.

"Yes, I am. Who might you be?"

"My name's Jonas Holt," He waited for a minute as if he expected Maxwell to know the name. He was disappointed. "But my name's not your concern. Another name is more important to me. I'm looking for a gent, calls himself Michael Cord."

"I know him. He used to work for me. Quit a couple of weeks ago."

The men exchanged a look, then Jonas spoke again. "A couple of weeks ago? Why did he just up and do that?"

Maxwell knew they didn't believe him. "I don't know. Came to me one morning and just said he was quitting."

"Where did he go?"

"I don't know that, either."

"For the boss, you don't know much."

"Man works for me, his work time's mine. His private life is his own. I don't ask questions about it."

"I don't suppose you'd mind if we looked around?"

"Help yourself. I don't make a habit of lying. You'll find out he's gone like I said."

Jonas looked at him for a long moment as if debating what to do, then turned to one of the other men. "Let's ride on, he isn't here."

"But Jonas . . ." Logan protested.

"Shut up," Jonas snapped. "He isn't here." He threw Maxwell a deadly smile. "Which way did he ride?"

Maxwell pointed in the direction Michael had taken, hoping they would mistrust him enough not to believe him.

"If he's pointin' that way, sure as hell Cord's gone the other way," Logan said.

"Unless," Jonas said quietly, watching Maxwell, "that's exactly what he wants us to believe. No, we'll go exactly where the boss told us to. I'm real sure an upstanding man like him wouldn't lie to us. Come on, let's go."

Maxwell was angry at himself. Trying to be clever he had pointed them directly at Michael. He just hoped the time he had given Michael and the opportunity to get as lost as he had planned on was enough. How could one man fight those three?

"Jesus, Lee Chu, what have I done?" he asked as he watched them ride away.

"You have tlied your best to be fliend. Mistah Mikel, he would understand this. Sometime, fate wiser than man."

"Fate couldn't be so cruel as to let those varmints catch up with Michael. Not after what he's been through already."

"Maybe they no kill . . . maybe fate will end Mistah Mikel's reasons to run. Then . . . he can find home."

"Maybe. I hope you're right. I just don't see how—"

"Wisdom come with gleat age," Lee Chu grinned. "You too young yet."

"Come on then, you old fox. See if we have enough wisdom to get this track laid."

"Good . . . good. We go. You no worry. Fate older than you."

Maxwell chuckled and they both returned to work.

The three men sat around the campfire that night. They had traveled some distance away from the railroad camp.

"Jonas, why are you so sure we ain't on the wrong trail?"

Jonas smiled. "Because that railroad boss was one of Cord's

friends. He was trying to be clever, and he was counting on us being so dumb we'd just figure he was lying to us. No, we're on his trail all right."

"He's led us on quite a chase," Logan King complained. "When I get my hands on him I'm gonna plug him right between the eyes."

"Don't be too anxious, Logan. When we catch up with him you'll get your chance. But you know his reputation. He's got a fast gun. Killed a few that thought they were faster than he was. He proved them wrong."

"He's fast maybe," Hammond Gordon said arrogantly, "but he ain't met up with the right gun yet."

"Yeah, well, get some sleep now. We'll hit the trail early."

"Where we headed?"

"He's gonna try and lose himself. In one of the mining towns somewhere, I'd say. We just want to make sure he doesn't get *too* lost."

They rolled into their blankets and slept . . .

They were saddled and riding when the first rays of sun touched the horizon.

Chapter One

Michael had ridden at a steady pace. He wanted to put as much distance between him and the rail line before night fell. He had no idea when the men who had trailed him for so long would approach the camp. He hoped they would wait and watch for a while, at least long enough for him to put enough space between them that he could effectively vanish.

How often, in the years since the war ended, had he run from this ugliest part of his past? How often must he continue to do it before they gave up and let the tragedy be put to rest? he refused to let himself relive the past for the time he rode. But when night fell and he had to stop, it was a different matter. He cared for his horse, built a fire, and ate . . . then the night, memories, and dead dreams loomed before him.

He lay on his back, resting against his saddle, close to the low-burning fire. A soft breeze whispered through the trees and occasional night sounds came to him. The night was a miracle of beauty. It was also empty and lonely, sensations he had experienced more often than he cared to remember.

He tried desperately to hold the good memories of a happier time. The days when he, Trace, and Allison had grown up on Fallen Oaks. Picnics and barbeques, dances and parties. Pretty girls and no cares. It had been a fairy-tale time, which had all too soon been brought to an end by a cannon at Fort Sumter.

He, like all other young men, had met the challenge of the war with laughing enthusiasm. At twenty-two, he was three years younger than Trace, and filled with an exuberant confidence.

He had always been a laughing boy, prone to mischievous tricks, yet filled with a gentle warmth. now, a few short years later, he felt as old as the rolling hills that surrounded him.

At first the novelty of military life was exciting. The first real battle destroyed that excitement very effectively. He'd killed a man, and, after that, the taste of war became bitter.

Four battles later he had been brutally wounded. He'd lost the sight of one eye. After only eight short months he found himself in a wicked battle. He received a fierce wound high on his right thigh and was taken prisoner at the same time. Medical facilities in a Yankee prison camp were poor, and he came very close to losing his leg. It had left him with a limp he would never lose.

Then the war ended and he came home. Home to emptiness. Another man, Reid Anderson, was in charge of supervising Fallen Oaks with the assistance of Marsh and Amanda, who told him all that had happened. His parents were dead. Trace and Allison were gone. He could not settle comfortably at Fallen Oaks because he worried about the rest of his family. So he set out to find them.

He knew the railroad was to begin at St. Louis, and he went there. That was where he ment Marie Trent . . . and that was where he also met Scott Merrell, the son of Senator Thomas Merrell. The senator was a powerful man who wielded it like a scepter. He doted on his one and only son, had spoiled him beyond help. Scott was an arrogant young man who was sure his father's wealth, power, and position put him beyond anyone's touch.

St. Louis was a lusty, brawling town at that time, the starting place for all who moved west, and the war's end saw a lot of people on the move. Michael was one of the displaced and unhappy. He was also fast with the gun he wore, which was necessary to face the harshness of the vast untamed territory beyond the Mississippi.

For a while Michael enjoyed the festive atmosphere of St. Louis, and he enjoyed it all even more with Marie, a very pretty girl with gold-blond hair and violet eyes.

For the first time in a long time he could laugh. They laughed together and after a while began to fall in love ... but Scott Merrell wanted Marie, too. At first he only tried to steal Marie from Michael, but, when that didn't work he made subtle threats that slowly turned vicious and mean ... then dangerous.

Everyone seemed to sense what was happening, but no one would speak against the wealthy senator's handsome son.

Then one moonlit night, the inevitable happened. Michael and Marie had gone for a walk. A few kisses and embraces found them quite unaware of anyone else until Scott spoke.

"Get away from her, you saddle tramp," he snarled.

Both Michael and Marie were startled enough to move apart. Michael could see at once that Scott had been drinking and that the gun he held was new and very, very real.

He tried to be calm. "Come on, Scott, there's no sense to this."

"I think it's time you got out of town," Scott said arrogantly.

"And I'm supposed to just run because you say so," Michael laughed. "You're not big enough to do it. Why don't you go someplace and sober up."

"I intend to see that you take my advice," Scott said threateningly, and that was when the two men stepped from the shadows behind Scott. Now Michael was shaken. Three to one were pretty high odds and Marie was holding his arm. From the way her hands were shaking, he knew she was terrified.

"Scott ..." Her voice was more controlled than her body. "I tried to tell you last night—" He never let her finish.

"He's not for you, Marie. He's nothing but a drifter. I can give you more than he can."

"It has nothing to do with money, Scott," she protested. "You can't just buy anything you want."

Michael had cautiously disengaged his arm and moved one step away from Marie. He had to have his hand free. He saw the look in Scott's eyes and knew none of this would ever be settled by words. He was frightened for Marie, and this was one time he wished she were anywhere else but beside him.

Scott and his two friends edged closer, and Michael could see the guns they wore beneath their jackets, tucked into their belts. They didn't mean to rough him up as he'd first thought—they meant to kill him! He knew he couldn't reach for his gun with

Marie standing so close to him. He began to sweat. Now an innocent life hung in the balance. Scott was drunk enough that he
didn't understand—or maybe didn't care—that Marie was so
close. Was he fool enough to believe that Marie would fall into
his arms if Michael was dead? One of the men who stood beside
Scott finally spoke.

"He ain't fast enough to take you, Scott boy. Look at him sweat.
He's scared of you."

Suddenly Michael knew. Scott was being pushed by these two
men and so drunk as not to be realistic. Obviously they had been
working on him for some time. Michael could see the feverish
glow in Scott's eyes . . . A fanatic's look.

"Scott, don't be a damned fool," Michael said angrily. But he'd
said the wrong thing at the wrong time.

He knew Scott was going for his guns. "Don't! Don't!" he
shouted. But it was too late for that. He knew he could beat Scott,
but he didn't count on the love Marie had for him. It all happened
too fast for him to stop.

Marie thought she might be able to stop the reckless and deadly
move Scott was going to make. She didn't love him, in fact, she
felt very sorry for him, but she didn't want him to die. She stepped
between them, arms outstretched toward Michael at the same
time Scott drew his gun and fired. At his first flicker of movement
Michael had gone for his gun as well.

Scott's bullet hit Marie, who crumpled at Michael's feet. But
Michael's bullet found its mark, too. Scott Merrell lay dead. The
two men who had pressured Scott into all this knew the import
of what had happened. Michael knelt beside Marie, but it was too
late to help. When he looked up the two men were gone . . . and he
knew where. Knew, too, that his hours of life would be numbered if
he remained in St. Louis.

He took Marie's body back to her family and tried as best he
could to explain. Maybe he reached their understanding . . . but
he couldn't reach his own guilt. He just had to carry it with him,
and it became worse when he tried to face the furious grief and
anger of the senator. He wasn't sure why he even had to try to
explain . . . maybe to exorcise the heavy burden of guilt. In any
case, he failed in every way. He was stunned by the extent of his
failure when Thomas Merrell coldly told him that leaving town

was the best thing he could do. He hadn't known the depth of
the hatred that followed.

He'd only been gone from St. Louis a week when the first of
them caught up with him. Michael killed him and rode away. Two
weeks later there was another. Young, mean, and fast with a gun.
Michael killed *him.* He moved faster, trying to outrun his past
and, for a while, when he was caught up in Trace and Jenny's
problem, he'd thought he'd succeeded. But he hadn't.

He couldn't go home with Trace and Jenny because he knew
he'd be taking his problem with him and the last thing he could
bear was to let the past touch those he loved. Those he loved . . .

Hannah came unbidden into his mind. He'd tried from the
first moment he'd seen her to close the doors of his heart against
her. He'd done well, except for moments like this when his defenses were at their lowest ebb. When she crept inside the barriers
. . . then he remembered.

At the same time Michael found his family he also discovered the
dilemma in which they were caught. Trace was facing opposition
in getting the railroad a right of way. Michael had felt it better
to remain incognito, not to let anyone know he was Trace and
Allison Cord's brother. Eventualloy he had used his reputation
as a fast gun to ally himself temporarily with the people who
opposed Trace.

In the process of learning about the Grahams, especially Jenny
Graham the girl who opposed Trace so valiantly, he had also run
across the Marshall family.

The Marshalls, close friends of the Grahams, were owners of a
nearby ranch. They, as many of the others in the valley, did not
know the man they trusted was planning to possess their land
before the railroad came, and that he intended to make a fortune
from their property.

Michael had made tentative contact with the Marshalls, just to
warn them about their connection between the railroad and the
ranchers. He'd become aware of Hannah that very first meeting.
Compared to her sweet innocence, he somehow felt jaded and
dirtied by the life he lived. He'd denied her then because he'd
recognized his own vulnerability.

But fate had seen things differently. He had rescued her from a brutal attempt at rape and had been alone with her in the wilderness it was as vivid tonight as it had been that night so long ago.

Michael had made camp in a thick stand of woods outside the town, where he would be free to move about. When he'd rescued Hannah he had brought her there, planning to keep her so the man who ordered the kidnapping would not know his plan had failed.

Those few days had nearly been his undoing, for he did the thing he knew was forbidden. He had fallen in love.

. . . He'd prodded the fire with a stick, still unaware that she had wakened. But after a few minutes he sensed her intense scrutiny. His defenses had risen in the only way they could. He chuckled at her defiant innocence.

"What are you staring at, child?"

"I'm not staring," she quickly replied, surprised that he could know what she was doing without turning his head. "And I'm not a child."

Then he had laughed outright and rose to walk to her side. He squatted down near her.

"What were you doing out here alone?"

"I was on my way to see Mrs. Carter."

"And your father, with all the trouble that's been around, let you go alone? You shouldn't have been allowed."

"I'm allowed to do as I wish," she said sharply.

"Don't get upset, little one," he requested with a grin.

"Stop treating me like I'm six!" she said, her anger surfacing.

"Would you rather I treated you the way your friend was planning on doing?"

The reminder of the man who had assaulted her caused her to sit up quickly and search about her. Fear was rampant on her face. She even forgot that her dress was torn and she was revealing much of her body. Michael's smile had faded and he had reached out for her blanket to wrap about her.

"Don't worry," he said gruffly. "He's dead."

she had shivered at the deadly cold tone of his voice and the matter-of-fact way he spoke of death.

"Oh," she said weakly. Then she had looked at him with emerald eyes that seemed to pierce the wall he was building between them.

"Don't worry, I don't molest children."

"I'm not a child!"

"What are you, eighteen . . . nineteen?"

"Twenty!"

He looked at her and grinned.

"Well . . . nearly twenty," she added lamely.

"How near?"

"Almost."

"Near nineteen?"

"Almost."

"You're eighteen," he chuckled.

"Well," she cried defensively. "You're not much older."

His smile had faded as he reached out to touch her hair. "I'm a hundred years older than you, little one,' he said gently, "a hundred long, hard years."

She was a defiant child with a lot of courage, and she was beautiful. He'd cautioned himself over and over that she was not for him. He had too many troubles, and he knew he would have to move on. He had too many debts to pay and there was no room for a woman in his life.

But he had almost lost that calm control one night a short time later. He'd gotten her a dress to replace the torn one so no questions would be asked of her when she returned home. He'd made the mistake of tossing it to her, and the blanket covering her fell away. In the glow of firelight he could not miss the creaminess of her exposed flesh.

"Change your clothes," he had said. she had stepped out of the light of the fire to change, and even though he could not see her, he had sensed her. When she had stepped back into the light of the fire she stepped just as casually past his defense.

"I knew I was right, little one. You do look pretty in green. It matches your big green eyes."

"Are you laughing at me?" she asked suspiciously.

"I'm sorry. I didn't mean to upset you."

"You didn't upset me." Her voice was soft. "I'm not a foolish child. Please don't treat me like one." She was too close. She was too vulnerable

and sweet. He was tired and his control was not at its best. He knew it was wrong, but he reached to draw her forbidden softness into his arms. Their lips met gently. He had been lonely too long and had been hurt too deeply. Suddenly the realization of what he was doing exploded in his mind. He was actually trying to seduce a child whose experience amounted to nothing in comparison to his. They had gazed at each other helplessly, for both were still within the grip of an amazing force. A force he could not allow to overcome him.

"Little girls shouldn't play with fire. You might just get burned," he laughed in an effort to drive her away with anger. But she didn't respond as he expected.

"My dear man of mystery," she said. "I don't know which of us is afraid of fire, me . . . or you."

It had been a challenge given by a woman who had never tasted love, and he had known it. He wanted to save her from the hurt he knew he would eventually inflict on her.

"This is not a game you should be playing. You're a sweet girl. Find a nice boy and settle down. Don't look for adventure. It's not fun when you find it."

She had wanted to reach past the barriers but he had not let her.

They had sat across the fire from each other eating and talking. He refused to meet her eyes, for he knew it would be too easy to get lost there. They had laughed . . . because neither could cry.

He remembered his last words to her before he left.

"You're one of the most beautiful women I have ever known. You have a loving heart. I don't want you to waste it. I want you to forget me, for my life is something you could not live with. One day someone will come along who is right for you. When that happens he'll be a very lucky man. Hannah, forgive me, for we could never have a life together . . . not like you know it, and I won't drag you into mine."

"I'll never forget you," she had whispered. It filled him now, in his loneliness and his bitter hunger. "I will never forget you" . . . and he would never forget her.

Eventually he had turned Hannah over to the care of his sister Allison. But he could not turn out her memory so easily. He gazed at the dying fire and saw her face. If he lay back and looked at the stars he saw the glimmer of her eyes. There was no way to elude the whispering fingers of memory, so for this one night he allowed them. He allowed the dreams of what might have been. He allowed the forbidden touches and gentle kisses and let them lead him into dreams. Tomorrow he must face reality.

Michael had left the railroad at the California border and had ridden with the early-morning sun over his right shoulder. He'd made a decision. if the men behind him knew the railroad was on its way to California, they might believe, because of the rush for gold, that he might be heading there, too. So he had decided to find a mining city somewhere in Nevada. He followed the Carson River northward and skirted Empire city by nightfall. He didn't enter the city at all even though it was well populated. His instincts—or some sense of urgency—told him to move on. He camped outside the city and moved on with the next light.

He traveled slowly, letting the hours and days drift away. He didn't have a destination. He no longer cared where he was going, only about putting distance between him and the long talons of the past. If a voice somewhere deep inside him warned him that he could not run away he did his best to ignore it. He didn't want to think about it. In fact, he didn't want to think about much of anything. Too many thoughts led to despair.

He did allow Hannah into his mind because she was the only sanity he knew. She was forbidden to him, but nothing could stop his dreams. Those were beyond the touch of any law, moral or legal. It was Hannah who gave him the strength to move through each day. Without her, he might have found solace in waiting for the enemy and letting a gunfight put an end to it all.

At Daton he crossed the river and headed toward Silver City. The Comstock lode had lured men to the Nevada territory. Fabulously rich silver and gold mines caused men to dream of millions of dollars. Despite the hazards of crumbling rock, stifling air, and scalding water, the miners still drove their shafts more than a half mile down into the earth.

Development of this huge body of silver caused Nevada to become a state in 1861, pumping much-needed financing into the federal government and giving President Lincoln additional support in Congress.

Michael knew the history of the place and expected Silver City to be booming enough so that he could get lost in it. He entered the town late in the evening, the time he'd always found best for his purposes. At night, those on the street had either been celebrating too much or were on their way to do so and paid little attention to a newcomer. Any genteel residents were already behind closed doors. It was about as safe as he could make it. . . . But it was never *really* safe and he knew it. At first view he sensed the town might still be a bit too small and too tame to let him hide there successfully.

He knew he would have to leave, but he was tired. Tired of the saddle, of sleeping in the wild, and of his own cooking. He would stay for a couple of days, then decide where to go. He could hope, he thought in wry amusement, that his followers would not be close enough to find him within those two days. The way he felt right now, he was going to find himself a bed whether they found him or not.

Silver City was a collection of rough buildings: an assortment of stores, a church, post office, a newspaper office, and a small hospital. The Sutter House, one of the two hotels in town, was located in the very center of town. After seeing that his house would be boarded and well cared for during his short stay, he walked up the three steps and entered the hotel.

The lobby contained a large desk with a cubby-holed wall behind it. Settees and comfortable chairs were set about, some of them occupied by men engrossed in their daily papers.

When Michael walked up to the desk, a dark, young man appeared from a small side room and asked if he could be of help.

"I'd like a room."

"Staying long?" the clerk asked as he swung a large black ledger around for Michael to sign. At the question Michael's hand paused, and he glanced up at the clerk. Whatever else the clerk might have intended to say faded into silence. This was no man to question.

"Can I get some water? I need a bath and some food."

"There's a bath two doors down, and the Carter place across the street and down a ways is a good place to eat."

"Thanks." Michael took the key, put it into his pocket, and turned to walk out. As he stood outside, a tall man rose from a chair, lay his newspaper aside, and followed. He was just in time to see Michael enter the bathhouse. He walked to the restaurant and found a table where he could see the door. He was a patient man; he could wait.

Michael paid five dollars to have his water brought and his bath taken in private. He sank down into the hot water with a sigh of pleasure. His clothes hung over a nearby chair, but his holster and gun lay on the floor beside the tub. Within reach.

An hour later he came out of the bathhouse. For the first time in two years he was clean-shaven. It had occurred to him that he might not be so recognizable that way. Of course, the black patch didn't help, and the scar was capable of drawing an immense amount of attention as well. The scar combined with the limp, were identifying traits he would never be able to hide.

Now his appetite was demanding his full attention, so he strolled down the street, then crossed to the restaurant.

He found a table where his back would be against a solid wall. The man watching was convinced Michael was the person he'd been waiting for. He had to talk with him long enough to see if he was right, though. He took a great deal of pride in his ability to judge men. He'd been doing so for quite a while.

His keen judgment also told him Michael was a man who could be dangerous. He knew quite well the import of the gun that hung on his hip, just as he could tell that the gun had seen its use.

He stood up and walked slowly toward Michael's table, making sure there were no overt movements that might alarm him.

When he stopped beside the table, Michael looked up. Though he had seemed to be giving his full attention to the steak he was eating, in truth, he'd known almost from the moment he sat down that he was under scrutiny. He thought it might be just curiosity. Let the man make the first move. Michael was not surprised when he did. But he was surprised both by how the stranger looked and what he felt when he looked at him.

He was tall, six feet three or four, Michael surmised. Brawny, too. He must have weighed a good two hundred and fifty pounds. He was dressed in plain black. The most obvious thing to Michael's very experienced eyes was the fact that, in a time of law by the gun, this man didn't wear one.

"Evening," Michael said. He was wary, and not exactly in the mood for company.

"Evening." The man's voice had a quiet tone, not the kind of voice associated with a gunfighter. It puzzled Michael. It also got his interest in a way no attack could have.

"You looking for someone?" Michael inquired as he lay his fork and knife down.

"No. Well, ah ... yes, in a way I am."

"We've never met," Michael continued easily. "I don't think I'm the man you're looking for." If this man had any argument with Michael, now was the time to present it.

"No, we've never met. But I *do* think you're the man I'm looking for. If I'm not mistaken, you're Michael Cord."

Michael went still. If one man in this town knew him, maybe there were others that did, too.

"Mr. Cord, I don't mean to cause you any problem. I would just like to talk to you for a minute."

"Have a seat." Michael was uncertain. There seemed to be no animosity, but he'd looked into the eyes of men meaning to kill him and some of them had the eyes of innocent boys. Looks meant little, he had learned.

The man pulled the chair out and sat down opposite Michael.

"My name's Patrick Carrigan."

The name meant nothing to Michael, so he continued to wait. Patrick smiled and went on. "I live in Virginia City. In fact, I travel through most of Nevada pretty often. This is the first time I've been in need of help. One has to be a little careful who one asks for help today." His smile was warm, wide, and very Irish.

"You've never met me before. you tell me just how dangerous things are, then you ask me for help?" When Michael chuckled, Patrick grinned. "You'll pardon me if I make an obvious observation. You might be asking the wrong man to help you do whatever it is you need done."

"I think not. You see ... I may not know you personally, but I know of Michael Cord."

"I see," Michael said quietly. Of course he knew of Michael Cord. Hadn't they made sure Michael's name was branded. Gunfighter.

"No, I don't think you do."

"No?" Michael replied. "Let me tell you. You've run across something that you feel is unjust. Obviously whoever you're up against swings a lot of weight. So you think you'll hire a gun. Well, neither me nor my gun are for hire."

"I knew that before I sat down. There's a difference between a man who kills for pay and a man who's defending himself."

Now he had Michael's full attention. A man who understood this in the wildness of this territory was rare indeed.

"Just what is it you want from me?"

"First to ask you if you'd consider going on to Virginia City?"

Michael watched him carefully for a minute, but could read no subterfuge in his face. "Why should I go to Virginia City?"

"Virginia City is a big, boisterous town. With a little help a man could just vanish there . . . sort of melt into the city." He paused briefly then continued. "With a little help, a man could very effectively start a whole new life." He seemed to be implying he could provide that help.

"I see," Michael said again. "And you think that's what I want to do?"

"It was just a suggestion for any man who would like to shed his past. Sort of a favor in return for a favor, you might say.'

"You still haven't told me, what kind of favor you want?"

"I want you to find another man in this city who you think could be trusted. Then I want the both of you to travel with me to Virginia City."

Virginia City, Michael thought. That was just what he needed. To backtrack, even farther, to a place where the men searching for him might already be waiting. His first inclination was to say an immediate no. He didn't know why he didn't. He only responded, "That's all?"

"That's all."

"Doesn't make sense."

"Why?"

"You told me before that you've traveled all over this territory. Why do you find it so difficult to get from here to Virginia City?"

"I usually travel alone, and with few problems, but this time I'm carrying something very valuable. Valuable to me, and to my city. I feel there's safety in numbers. I'm also afraid my movements are being watched. What I'm carrying might be incentive to attack me once I'm out of town."

"Something valuable? Gold?"

"No."

"Silver?"

"Not exactly."

"Exactly *what?*"

For a minute Patrick was quiet, then, as if he had made a final decision, he replied, "I'm carrying a lot of money that's to be used to build a very important building. I don't want to be 'relieved' of it. With three of us they might reconsider. Besides, I know the way to Virginia City very well. With help, I could get the money there safely."

"I have to find another man."

"I could, but I want it to be someone *you* would trust."

"When do you want to leave?"

"Anytime you're ready."

"Can you pick out the people you think might be on your trail? I'd like to know what I'm going to be up against."

"Then you agree to do it?"

"I'll tell you what—You pick them out, give me a couple of days. If I can find someone, and if I think we can make it, then we'll go."

"Fair enough."

"Then you might as well join me for supper. After we've finished, we'll go look around. Maybe you can spot your suspicious characters. In the meantime, I'll be on the lookout for someone to travel with us."

Patrick agreed and ordered a meal the size of which made Michael laugh. As they both ate, Michael tried for more information about his newfound friend. But, at least for the moment, Patrick was as reticent as Michael. When they left the restaurant, neither knew much about the other except that deep inside the subtle beginnings of trust had begun.

Patrick was able to point out two men as he and Michael made their way to the different spots where crowds gathered. Both men were hardcases, but Michael had faced their kind before—all brawn and guns but very light on brains. Patrick told him there was one other man, but they couldn't seem to find him.

"Maybe we'll run across him tomorrow."

"Or," Patrick offered, "maybe he's trying to keep suspicion from him and just won't let himself be seen until we're on our way."

"Maybe. I don't think we have to worry about it. You, me, and one more, we can handle whatever they choose to throw at us."

"We still have to find the one other," Patrick reminded him.

"Well, we're not going to do it tonight, and I'm long past tired. I'm going back to the hotel to get some sleep. We have a couple of days. Tell me where you're staying, and I'll let you know when I run across someone."

"I'm in the same hotel you are. I've been sitting in that lobby every evening for a week hoping someone like you would come along. I'm in room 215. If you find anyone, let me know. Either way, I'd like to buy you dinner tomorrow night."

"I'd like that."

"Good. shall we walk back to the hotel?"

"I think I'll stop at the saloon first. I'm so tired it will be hard to sleep. One drink might help."

"I'll see you tomorrow night then."

"Yes. Tell me, where are you keeping this money? You leave it in your room, and it won't take long for someone to get at it. And if you carry it with you, you're asking for real trouble."

"Don't worry," Patrick laughed. "It's locked in the hotel safe."

"You think maybe our clerk is telling someone about your movements?"

"I never thought of that."

"We'll have to figure this out. If we take it out the day we leave, it's an open invitation for someone to follow. We might have to do a little maneuvering."

"Maybe I should take it out tonight and give it to you. No one knows we'll be leaving tgether, so it might confuse them."

Michael looked at him in shock. "You sure do beat all. I'm practically a stranger to you, and you want to trust me with . . . How much money do you have?"

"Twenty thousand dollars."

Michael whistled softly. "That's nearly a fortune. You so sure?"

"Yes, I'm sure."

"I don't understand you."

"You hear a lot of things about gunmen out here. Mostly that they're a pretty shabby lot. But your reputation is kind of different. I think I've put a bit of the story together myself. And I've come up with my own answers."

"Just what have you put together? Maybe I can tell you how wrong you are?" Michael laughed.

"Displaced soldier, on the wrong side of a war. Caught up in events against his will that made him reach for a gun. Making a couple of honorable mistakes and taking the responsibility. Running from the idea of killing another man no matter how justified it is." Patrick's voice grew softer. "Alone. Sometimes lonely . . . sometimes afraid. But a man who wears his own code of honor like a shield. Yes, I trust you, Michael Cord."

There was a long moment of silence as they continued to walk. It had stunned Michael that Patrick had come so close, touched the vulnerable spots so easily. Whoever and whatever Patrick was, he was an astute man. They stopped by the saloon door.

"You sure you don't want to join me for a drink?" Michael invited. He wanted to know more about the mysterious Patrick Carrigan.

"No, thanks. I've got a lot of paperwork and some reading to do. I'll see you tomorrow night."

Michael nodded and watched Patrick walk away. Then he entered the saloon. At the bar he had two drinks, then went back to the hotel.

He thought of what Patrick had said. Lose his identity. Be someone else, start a new life. Giving up all he was, all he'd known and loved, was not the easiest idea in the world to face. Although he had to admit, it was the smartest. Maybe, after a few years when others believed him lost completely, or even dead, he could make at least one trip to Fallen Oaks. Giving up the love and the sweet memories of his brother and sister forever was too painful to contemplate. He had to have hope, even if that was all he ever had.

He carried the bottle back to the hotel and drank more than half of it before he found a shallow and restless sleep.

Among the clouds of dreams Hannah walked freely. Beautiful Hannah, forbidden Hannah. He reached for her as a drowning man would reach for aid.

Still, whiskey and dreams did not stop the instincts long bred into him. His holster hung on the bedpost by his head, and a sudden loud noise in the street brought him upright, gun already in his hand.

He swore softly to himself as he stared down at the gun. This was the only true friend he had, yet he hated it. He knew, with resignation, that he must live by the gun until a bullet put an end to his life. Or . . . was Patrick right? Did he have a plan that would let Michael escape this brutal fate. He didn't know what Patrick had in mind, but he did know that Patrick trusted him completely and there was some kind of pride to be had in knowing he had a reputation like that.

He would help Patrick . . . and he would listen very closely to any ideas he had that would give him freedom. The idea came to him as he drifted back to sleep. Maybe Patrick recognized him because they were two of a kind. Maybe Patrick knew from firsthand experience. Maybe he had run, and found a way to live. Maybe Michael could find it too.

Chapter Two

Maxwell Starett had moved the tracks along at a methodical pace. Most of the time his mind was on the completion of his railroad line into San Francisco, but a small part of him remained with Michael.

Every night since Michael had gone, Maxwell's sleep had been disturbed. He worried. Lee Chu had been his constant companion and confidant. He was the only one who was there throughout the sleepless nights. He brought tea and they had talked often into the wee hours of the morning. Trace Cord had become like a son to both of them, and for the short time they had known Michael, they felt the same about him. It hurt them when Michael had gone.

The reasons Michael felt he had to go plus the fact that he had so casually pointed out the direction he had gone made Maxwell very uncomfortable.

Now San Francisco was an accomplished fact and the celebration had been uproarious. Champagne had flowed like water when the golden spike had been driven home.

But the men who had worked the long hours with Maxwell— the Cord brothers—were not there to celebrate what they had helped him build.

In his hotel room he dressed carefully. The first through run of the Starett Line was due to come in today. He was excited, for a lot of dignitaries were due to arrive to make the first run a momentous occasion.

Men who had doubted him, doubted his ability to make his dream come true, would be coming to offer him their hands in friendship. He smiled to himself. At least *some* of them would. Others would be trying to see if they could buy stock in his now-successful endeavor. None of them would know that he would never sell stock to anyone, especially those who he was certain at some later time would try their best to oust him and take over. No, he had divided his stock four ways. Fifty-one percent to him, since he didn't want to lose control, and the other forty-nine to be divided equally between Trace, Michael, and Allison Cord.

He stood before the mirror to make a last-minute inspection. He was a solid-looking man, his jaw square and hard. His skin was tanned and unlined, so it was very difficult to guess his age. His eyes were piercing blue and his hair crystal white. There was no excess fat on his body; he was a man clearly used to hard physical activity.

Satisfied, he left his hotel room and walked downstairs to be met by a crowd of enthusiastic employees.

"Great day, Mr. Starett!" one called out to him.

"Sure is, Tom. Bet there were times you weren't too sure we'd ever see it."

"Some," Tom agreed, laughing. "But it's here. Me and the boys were waiting for you so's we could go on over together. She ought to be coming in in about a half hour . . . if she's on time."

Maxwell's laugh echoed his. "She'll be on time. By tonight there won't be a sober man in town. You boys did a great job, Tom, and I'm proud to have worked with you. Did you tell the others about the bonus I'm paying?"

"Yes, sir. They're all pretty happy about that."

"Then let's get along. It's time to meet the first train of the Starett Line.'

There was a small crowd of men as they left the hotel lobby and walked the distance to the recently built train station. They joined the crowd that had been steadily gathering for the past few hours.

Maxwell took his watch from his vest pocket and snapped it

open. If the train were on time it should be sighted within minutes. He closed his watch and replaced it. As if in answer to his thoughts, a shrill whistle in the distance announced the imminent arrival of the train.

He could feel the excitement bubble in him, and it stirred even more when he could see the smoke from the stack. Then there was a shout, and loud cheers followed as the train pulled into view. Maxwell swallowed a heavy lump. If it hadn't been unseemly he actually could have wept, the pleasure was so intense.

When the train pulled into the station it was amid loud shouts, a billow of steam, and a long whistle from her engineer. When it came to a halt, passengers, as excited as the greeters, began to disembark.

Maxwell was so engrossed in the welcoming of the dignitaries that he did not notice the woman who stepped down on the platform from another car. She paused for a moment, looking in the direction of the crowd. She saw Maxwell, smiled a small half-smile, and picked up her satchel. She walked into the station and approached the ticket counter behind which an envious clerk waited. He would have preferred to be out on the platform with all the others. But someone had to retain their post, and he was the unlucky one.

He watched the woman approaching him and wondered why she would be in here when all the celebrating was going on outside. She was pretty . . . No, as she drew closer, he amended that to beautiful. Her hair, neatly styled atop her head, was a deep russet-wine color. The small feathered hat she wore complemented her oval face. Her eyes were the most brilliant green he'd ever seen, and were enhanced by the green traveling suit she wore. She stopped before the window and smiled at him, and he smiled back, unable to do anything else.

"Can I help you, miss?"

"Yes, if you please. I don't want to interrupt any of the celebration, but I've come to speak with Maxwell Starett. I'll arrange for my room at the hotel, then I'll be able to speak with him at a more convenient time."

"He's staying at the hotel, but I can go right on out and fetch him."

"No, no please. He and his men certainly deserve their celebration. We can talk later. Thank you.'
she picked up her small satchel and smiled at him again. "I have two trunks. I'll send someone from the hotel to pick them up.'
"Yes, ma'am. Do you have your receipts?"
She handed them to him.
"I'll take good care of the bags, and send them right over to the hotel."
"Thank you." She looked back once at the crowd outside, smiled, and left the station. The ticket clerk was left with the overpowering sense that she had some secret that seemed to please her a great deal.

It was well into early evening before Maxwell finally found himself free of his well-wishing friends and made his way back to the hotel slightly the worse for wear. One glass of champagne after another had been pressed on him. Too much champagne and too little food made him a bit unsteady.

But his euphoria remained with him as he finally got his key into the lock, entered his room, closed the door, and tossed the key on the dresser.

He knew he had to begin making some plans for the future, but at the moment he could not think of a challenge that intrigued him. Something would come to him, he knew that. He was not a man to rest on his laurels, or to sit around doing nothing.

For now he decided to get a little sleep. He knew that the night would be filled with parties. Besides that, he wanted to make sure his men got both their bonuses and his thanks.

He loosened his tie and removed his jacket and boots. Then he lay down on his bed and closed his eyes.

He'd had barely closed them and gotten comfortable when he heard the knock on his door. At first he was surprised, but then he concluded that one of his overenthusiastic men had decided he'd not celebrated enough.

"Go away!" he shouted, "I'll join you all later. I need to sleep off this champagne!"
The knock sounded again, just a bit more persistent.

"Go have some more champagne. I'll be along in an hour or so!"

Again the knock was a little stronger and more persistent. Maxwell was growing impatient. He rose from the bed with a sigh of exasperation. He shouldn't be angry. the celebration was an important release. He just needed some sleep. He walked to the door and pulled it open.

"Now come on, boys, I . . ." He stopped, stunned.

"Hello, Mr. Starett. It's good to see you again."

"Hannah!" Maxwell could hardly believe what he was seeing. "For God's sake, girl, what are you doing here?"

"I think we both know the answer to that. Are you going to invite me in, or must we . . . discuss our business in the hallway?"

"Ah . . . sorry." He stepped back. "Please come in."

Hannah walked past him, and he knew at once that this was not the young girl who had been left behind. She had changed in a way that was so far a mystery to him. He closed the door, then turned to face her again.

"He didn't come into town with you. Where is he?" Her voice was soft, but her eyes held him in a grip he found difficult to resist.

"I don't know," he replied honestly.

"Mr. Starett . . . please."

"Hannah, I really don't know where he is. Look, have you had dinner?"

"No."

"Then let's go downstairs and eat. I feel a distinct need to be very sober when I talk to you, and I'm not right now."

"All you need do is tell me where he is."

"No, I have to tell you a lot more than that."

"If you're thinking of sending me back on the next train, forget it. I've no intention of going until I find out what I want to know."

"Let's have our dinner and talk, Hannah. Maybe you'll change your mind. And besides," he smiled, "I want you to be friend enough to call me Maxwell."

"Do you believe I'll change my mind?"

"After seeing you, no. But I'd like to think I have a slim chance of changing it for you."

"Well . . ." she smiled a sweet, but very amused smile, "at least we can have dinner."

Maxwell put on his boots and jacket, retied his tie, and the two of them went downstairs. They found a table in the hotel's restaurant and ordered a meal that neither had much interest in. Finally Maxwell could prolong her questions no longer.

"I told you the truth. I don't know where Michael is. He left the line quite a while ago."

"Why? What made him leave? He had planned on finishing the job his brother had started."

"Inescapable circumstances—" he began.

"Stop it, Max. What does 'inescapable circumstances' mean? I know he was running from something, I felt it was . . ." She paused, as if she were seeking control of herself.

"Was *you?*" he added softly. "In a way it was."

"He had no reason to run from me."

"He had the best reason in the world. He cared about you. He didn't want you hurt."

"He thought me a child, incapable of understanding. That wasn't so. I understood. I understood and I loved him. We could have found a way. We could have run together."

"Don't you see, Hannah, that's the one thing he wouldn't . . . couldn't do. If you really understood him you would know that the last thing he would do would be to drag you from place to place. Never having a home. Never having a real life. Always looking back over your shoulder. Always waiting for the man who would kill him."

"Kill him!" Her voice broke, and her eyes grew wider. "Maxwell, please. Can't you at least tell me why someone would want to kill him? Don't you think I even have that right? Can't one of you consider how I feel about all this. Why must I be told to go home and hide my head under a pillow?"

"I suppose you're right," he said thoughtfully. "You are owed at least that. I'll tell you about Michael's past, but I want you to promise me that tomorrow you'll get back on that train and go home where you belong."

She contemplated his words for a while as she took a sip of her wine. Then she looked at him with a tentative smile of innocence.

"All right. If you tell me about Michael, I will take your advice. Tomorrow I'll go where I belong."

The residue of the champagne made Maxwell a little less wary, and her innocent look and sweet voice took him in completely. "It's a bargain," he said. He missed the satisfied look in her eyes as she lowered her lashes and waited.

Maxwell began with his first meeting with Michael and the revelation of his past as the two of them had continued to build their friendship once Trace had left the train. He revealed to her the hard bitterness that Michael carried with him. Tears formed in her eyes, but she held them back. They might warn him of her real intention.

". . . and so he did the only thing an honorable man could do. He kept you free of it all."

"You strong men and your honor!" Hannah said softly. "Do you ever think of a woman's honor at all? Do you ever think of what a woman needs and wants? Why must you always decide what's good for us? Your decisions are usually far off the mark. Women shouldn't be tied up in neat packages with ribbons and bows. Actually, we're as strong as you are and can make choice for our lives just as effectively . . . maybe better."

"Hannah, I'm sure Michael felt that what he did, he did for your own good."

"I suppose he did feel that way," she admitted.

"Right or wrong, it was because he cared."

"I know. It's just that I would have liked to have had the opportunity to at least tell him . . ." She paused, gave a slight shake of her head as if finishing the sentence was immaterial. "Max, Michael made a lot of friends while he was with the line, didn't he?"

"Yes, he did. In fact, there were a couple of them who might have gone with him if they'd had the opportunity."

"I should like to meet them," she said, hoping he would not notice her excitement. "At least to thank them and perhaps ask them a bit about Michael. After all, it seems I shall have only memories."

"I don't see why not. There's going to be a party tonight. I'd love to have you come as my very special guest. I'll introduce you to all the boys and you can talk to Jamie Bond and Joey Mason. I'd guess they were the closest to Michael."

"Thank you. I do appreciate all your help."

"I'm sorry I can't do more. Maybe it's best this way. Maybe Michael was right that he would only have brought you grief."

"So everyone has told me," Hannah murmured. At his quick look she smiled. "I'd be delighted to come."

He glanced at the plate of food she had barely touched. "Not hungry?"

"Not really. I guess I'm a little tired from the trip. Maybe I'll lie down for an hour or so. Shall I meet you in the lobby?"

"No, this town barely has the savagery scraped off it. It's not exactly safe for a woman as pretty as you to be alone. I'll come to your room."

They rose and went upstairs.

Hannah closed and locked the door behind her. While she was gone her trunks had been delivered. Instead of lying down as she had told Maxwell, she went to her trunks at once.

Their contents would have surprised Maxwell and made him nervous. They contained only two dresses. The balance of the clothes were rugged wear. Warm jackets, riding skirts, and boots. It was clear Hannah had never bargained on this trip being a social one. She already knew of the rough terrain she might be traveling through and had brought the kind of clothes necessary for it. She separated what she thought she could safely travel with and packed the balance back in one trunk, which she locked. She would leave it in the safekeeping of the hotel staff. If her adventure worked out, she would come back and pick it up. If it didn't . . . well, the pretty things inside would be of little use to her.

Satisfied, she set about making preparations for the balance of her plans. Tonight she had to look young, innocent, and give the impression of wanting to place herself in the care of a strong, resourceful man who, she hoped, would lead her to Michael. It was not a game of her choice, but it was the only hand she had to play, and she meant to play it to the best of her ability. She had come this far, and didn't mean to back away now.

She left her hair loose, the auburn waves falling well past her shoulders. It gave her the look she wanted. The dress she wore was sure to bring out the chivalry in any man. Demure white with tiny sprigs of turquoise flowers. The neckline, bordered with lace, was very decorous.

When she was satisfied that she could pass for everyone's younger sister, she picked up a white lace shawl and placed it around her shoulders.

She stood looking at herself with satisfaction and suddenly the mists of memory touched her and the smile died.

She remembered . . . a hard, firm man, with a touch as gentle as a whisper. She remembered . . . a kiss that ignited a fire that would never be extinguished as long as there was a breath in her body.

"Michael . . ." She breathed his name softly. She knew he had loved her as she had loved him. He would never have reached for her that one forbidden moment if he had not. This, and the wisp of memory, was what she had to believe in . . . it was all she had.

She had tried to forget, to push Michael out of her mind, but he would not go. So she had made her decision. She had to see him again. She had known Maxwell's final destination was San Francisco, and she had found out that the first train would be coming through the Roaring Fork. She had bought her ticket without telling anyone. In fact, knowing her family would do everything to prevent her going, she had left a note. She had waited until the moment came when no one was at home, then loaded her two small trunks in the back of a wagon. She drove into town, then hired a man to drive the wagon back.

Hearing that Michael had left the train had unnerved her . . . temporarily. Hannah was not a woman to back away from adversity. Surely he had to be somewhere near. After all, there weren't many places a man like Michael could go where he would not be noticed. Her naïveté was a blessing. If she had known the vastness of the places she intended to venture to, she might have become faint-hearted and returned home.

A knock on the door brought her back to the present abruptly. She opened the door and Maxwell smiled warmly at her. What a delightful child she was, he thought. *If I had a daughter I would choose her to be just like this.*

"Hannah, you look beautiful."

"Thank you, Max. I know this party is to celebrate your railroad's success. But . . . you and your employees are all men. I'm not—"

"Good heavens, child, no, you're not going to be the only female there. My men are also young and very interested in anything feminine. Trust me when I tell you there will most likely be quite a few other young ladies there."

"Good."

"Shall we go?"

Hannah nodded and they left the room. She locked the door carefully behind her. As the walked down the hall, Hannah took the opportunity to ask Maxwell some more questions.

"You said Michael had a couple of special friends among your men?"

"Yes. Brad Sinclair, Jamie Bond, Joey Mason, and Mac McCarthy. He got along with all the men, but with those four . . . well, I guess they got about as close to Michael as he'd let anyone get."

"Tell me about them."

"Let me see. Brad is the youngest of them, a few years younger than Michael. Kind of a shy kid, but the kind that always seems to be there when you need him. Jamie, he's a typical farm boy, came from Michael's hometown, same as Joey did. I still can't figure out how they got connected to the railroad. As far as Mac . . . I guess Mac was special to them all. Mac can find the humor in anything. He could keep all the men from getting too serious about anything. Sometimes he just kept them going. They were a good group."

Hannah kept Maxwell's words in mind, for if her plans worked out she would have to be dealing with those four men for some time.

When they walked into the large room that had been rented for the celebration, the party was in full swing. Hannah was introduced to man after man until she was overcome trying to remember names. But she kept four faces in mind and waited for the opportunity to get at least one of the three men alone.

It was very late in the evening before the chance arose. She found herself at the edge of the crowd with Brad beside her.

She searched her memory for what Maxwell had said about Brad: *He was shy, but he was loyal to a fault.*

"I've really been looking forward to meeting you, Brad."

"Me?" He stammered as he flushed in pleased embarrassment. "You're puttin' me on."

"No. I've heard a great deal about you. Maxwell said Michael considered you one of his closest friends."

"I'm sure pleased he felt that way. Michael was kind of special."

"How so?"

"I don't know. He wasn't rough-edged like the rest of the boys. Don't get me wrong, all of them are great. But Michael . . . he was educated and never acted better than the rest of us, and he was . . . well, it was like he belonged somewhere else."

"A paragon of virtue," Hannah teased.

"A what?"

"A perfect man."

"Oh, no, ma'am. He had a hell of a temper." Brad flushed a brighter red at his slip of profanity but went on doggedly. "And he could sure fight."

"He wasn't perfect then," she laughed. "But to you and his other three friends hew as. Brad . . . would you ride with me in the morning. I could rent a horse. I haven't ridden for a long time and I'd like to talk to you about something."

"I'd be real pleased."

"Do you think," she began slowly, as if it were an afterthought, "that you could invite Jamie, Joey, and Mac to come, too? What I have to talk to you about is very important and I need all the help I can get."

"Sure. I'll be there and I'll round up the other three. If you have something to say about Michael I'm sure there won't be any problem about them coming along."

"Thanks, Brad. How about around eleven?"

"That'll be fine."

Hannah saw Maxwell coming in their direction. She didn't want him involved in this particular conversation . . . not yet at least. She knew he'd feel she'd lied to him if he was aware of what she had planned. She hadn't *lied,* but trying to explain that to Maxwell at this moment might prove difficult.

"Max . . ." she laughed as he stopped beside her. "It's a lovely party."

"I'm glad you're enjoying yourself. It will be a fine farewell party for you, too. I'll be sorry to see you go home."

Brad looked at her in confusion, but he said nothing. If she wasn't going to say anything about their planned meeting the next day, he wasn't either.

"I think it's time for me to retire. I'm kind of tired."

"I'll take you back to your room."

"Thank you." Hannah started to follow Maxwell, then she paused and turned to look at Brad. "Thanks, Brad," she said quietly. He flushed and smiled.

When Hannah closed her door she was faced with the night and all the memories that Max, the other men, and the talk of Michael brought.

She was uncertain. Would Brad and the others listen to her? Would they understand if they did listen . . . and would they agree to her offer. Well, she'd hold the memories, and she'd pray for what tomorrow could bring.

Brad had very little trouble persuading the others to come along when he told them that Hannah wanted to talk to them about Michael. They felt compassion for Michael and the harsh circumstances that forced him away from any of life's pleasures and rewards. He followed a trail that they would like to turn him from if it was within their ability to do so.

For a while they rode in silence. Hannah wanted to put enough distance between them and town to make sure no word of their meeting could get to Maxwell or to any of his men.

Some miles from town Hannah found a thick stand of trees. Here was where she chose to stop.

Once they had secured their horses so they would not drift away, Hannah sat beneath a tree and the four men gathered near her. Jamie was the first to speak.

"Miss Hannah, Brad said you wanted to talk about Michael. Joey, Mac, and I wanted to go along with him, but he wouldn't hear to it."

"I don't suppose he would, Jamie," Hannah smiled. "He was that kind of man. He would protect everyone else at the price of himself . . . even me."

"Miss," Mac said, "it seems to me you don't agree to that."

"No, I don't. Michael has paid enough." There were tears in Hannah's eyes suddenly and she turned her face away. The men were silent, but she could feel their sympathy envelop her. After a minute she regained control and continued to speak. "I don't agree, because I love him. I love him enough to want to see him stop running. But to make him understand that, I have to find him."

"Maybe," Joey said quietly, "he can't stop just like that. Maybe he has reasons you don't know. Maybe it's best that he does what he thinks is best."

"If you believe that, Joey," Hannah met his eyes levelly, "then you need not take part in anything."

"I didn't say I wouldn't, I just—"

"He means," Mac said, "that maybe Michael has turned real gunfighter. That kind of man *can't* quit . . . not until someone stops him."

"No!" Hannah cried as she leapt to her feet. "No, Michael is not a killer. I know him. He's a man who cares too much for others and he doesn't deserve to be deserted. If we travel together we can find him, and when we do, we can stand with him. Then maybe he can stand, too . . . and stop running." She knelt back down on the ground and looked at the men pleadingly. "He deserves to have someone to stand beside him." Her voice became soft. "He deserves to find some love, and some peace, too."

"What is it you want us to do?" Joey asked.

"We need to find out from Max where Michael was going. Then, we must find him. I can't go alone and I know it. I would not last long out in the wilderness. But with you all beside me we could find him. I need your help."

The men exchanged glances. It meant days, weeks, maybe months of searching that might prove fruitless in the end.

"It will be long and hard," Mac said.

"I don't care." Hannah's voice was firm.

"It might not even be successful."

"It will." Her voice remained cool.

Again the men looked at each other. Then, one by one they answered.

"I'll go," Mac said firmly.

"I will, too," Joey said quickly. Hannah smiled and turned to face Jamie.

"Yeah," Jamie smiled, "I can't let you all go driftin' off by yourselves. First thing is, you'll get lost. Then I'll have to go find you. So I best go along to keep the rest of you out of trouble. There's only going to be one little problem."

"Problem!" Mac laughed. "You mean a problem outside of finding one man in a wilderness this size—and a man who doesn't want to be found at that?"

"I know what he means," Hannah replied. "Max."

"Yeah. He isn't going to be too happy. He's a civilized gentleman. The idea of one pretty girl and four men traipsin' off into the wild will upset him."

"Then we won't tell him," Hannah said softly.

"That'll hurt him bad," Jamie said. "He was kind of fond of Michael . . . and from the way he acts, he wants to protect you, Hannah. Max is the kind of man who stands behind those he cares for. He can't stop us if we want to go, but maybe we should trust him enough to tell him."

"I suppose you're right," Hannah admitted. "But I have no intention of being stopped."

"We said we'll go and that's an end to it," Joey said. "We'll listen to Max yell . . . but we'll go with you."

"When will we leave?" Hannah questioned.

"I suppose as soon as we can. I'll start things going. Get pack horses and everything we'll need. I guess in a day or two we can move out. Who's going to get the honor of tellin' Max?" Brad said. "I don't think I care for the job."

"I'll do it," Hannah said softly.

"No, ma'am," Jamie said. "I'm with you."

"I guess to do it together is best," Brad chuckled. "Me, I'm no hero, and Max is a tough gent."

"Then it's agreed." Hannah smiled for the first time. "Brad, when you have everything ready, let me know. I think the best time for us to tell Max is when we're ready to leave. One more thing . . . Do you really think he knows where Michael was heading?"

"No, Hannah, I don't," Brad said. "I don't think Michael knew himself. He's just drifting."

"We'll find him . . . We have to," Hannah whispered.

There was little more to be said. They walked to their horses and rode back in the same introspective silence they had ridden out in.

* * *

Maxwell did exactly as they had known he would do. At first he was stunned, then he went from protestations to anger. He forbade them to go and when that didn't work he pleaded, begged, thten raged in anger even he knew was futile. Finally, he could do or say no more. Still, they faced him, unmovable in their determination. In the end he respected their effort and loved them the more for it. Before they left he explained Michael's story in its entirety and Thomas Merrell's vow of vengeance to the boys, wanting them to know what might lie ahead.

He stood and watched the group ride away. His admiration for Hannah was unbounded. He knew the men who rode with her and knew that if there was any safety for her at all, these men would provide it.

But he also knew that the chances of finding a man like Michael when he didn't want to be found were very slim. In the back of his mind lingered the thought of another danger: the men who had also ridden in search of Michael Cord.

Maxwell held himself in control for a few days while Lee Chu watched with an inscrutable smile. Finally he knew Maxwell was at the end of his rope and he was afraid Maxwell might just go off after Hannah and the men. Lee Chu knew he was right, when he came in one evening and Maxwell was gathering some of things.

"You go after them, boss?" Lee Chu looked worried.

"You think I'm going on a wild-goose chase?"

"Maybe so. Maybe you need help."

"You talking about yourself?" Maxwell chuckled.

"No question," Lee Chu grinned amiably. "I go anyway." Maxwell began to protest, but Lee Chu shook his head. "You no argue, boss. Do no good, only make you red in face. I go with you."

"The hell you will."

"Lee Chu no stay here. You need fliend. I fliend," he grinned. "Beside, you not know how to make tea and no can sleep without tea. Before go, maybe think first."

"Think first? It's all I've been doing for the past few days."

"Maybe, send Mistah Tlace quick message. . . ."

"Telegram?"

"Telegram," Lee Chu nodded. "He come pletty quick, you see.

More people look, more chance somebody find. Mistah Tlace, he be plenty mad nobody tell.''

''Like I said, you're an old fox. Come on, let's send that 'quick message.' I'm sure you'll be able to fill in anything I miss.''

Lee Chu chuckled, but he did not refute Maxwell's words. They went to the telegraph office and stood for a long time composing the message to Trace.

Trace Cord

Michael forced to leave train. Stop. Gunfighters in pursuit. Stop. Desperately worried. Stop. Inclined to follow as quickly as I can. Stop. You'd better come. Stop. Firmly believe he needs all the help he can get. Stop. Hannah Marshall arrived here and left with Jamie, Joey, Brad, and Mac to find. Stop. I'm worried . . . No, scared as hell. Stop. How fast can you get here? Stop. Make it sooner than that. Stop.

Maxwell Starett

Chapter Three

Eatonton, Georgia

Fallen Oaks gleamed white and gold in the light of the setting sun. The tall white-pillared house nestled against the lush green lawns seemed to reflect a sense of peace. The green of the trees and the scent of magnolias added to the tranquil atmosphere.

Reid Anderson stood on the veranda and looked out over the vast rolling fields with a sense of pride. He had come to Fallen Oaks at Trace Cord's request after the war and promised to keep it safe until he returned from his sojourn with the railroad. That was Trace's only means to keep Fallen Oaks solvent.

With the money Trace had made sure was sent every month and a great deal of hard work, Reid had pulled Fallen Oaks back from the brink of disaster.

His own smaller place, bordering the Cord land, had fared just as well. For a time it had been difficult, but in the long run he had rescued both places.

That was small compared to what Trace had rescued. He had pulled Reid back from the devastation that had nearly put an end to his life.

When Reid had returned home he was shattered to find his home in ruins. That was tragic enough, but the blow that had really crushed him was to find that it was men from his own nearby decimated army that had killed his wife and son when they had tried to defend their home and what few possessions they had. They had tried to save what was left and in the process Reid had lost everything he had fought for. He had only the ruins of a house and two graves.

The war's destruction had turned him to the bottle and he had almost been lost in it. Trace had literally found Reid in the gutter. He would be grateful to the Cord family for as long as he lived. As far as he was concerned no sacrifice would be enough to repay the pride and sense of achievement they had given him.

He'd struggled from the day Allison and Trace had left, and at first it had been his hardest battle. But slowly his struggle had begun to lift Fallen Oaks. At first it was just him, Marsh, and Amanda planting the fields. But as time passed and money increased, he got more help, until there were many men to share the work. He had painted, repaired, and built furniture until his hands were calloused and hard.

Everyone bore scars from the brutal war. If Reid carried bitter memories of all it had taken from him, he had managed to put them in a dark place and lock them away.

Reid braced one broad shoulder against the carved pillar and scanned the horizon. She would be riding over the crest of those hills at any moment. He could never control the way his heart would race, or the fact that every sense came alive when he knew Allison would be approaching.

He remembered as if it were yesterday, the day that Trace, Jenny, and Allison had returned from Colorado. He'd known Allison most of his life, she had always been the mischievous friend from the next plantation. When Trace and Allison had left, she still seemed like a little girl . . . or he still had been so entangled in the memories of his lost wife and son that he hadn't noticed her. Hadn't noticed her! he laughed to himself. Now he knew everything about her. He knew the way her quick smile could grab his heart and squeeze the breath from him. He knew the way her laughter could make him happy and her tears could break him. He knew that being near her the rest of his life was his ultimate goal. And he knew that Allison really understood the grief that had pushed him. She understood, but she had not tolerated his self-pity. She had taken his hand and drew him out of the mire.

He thought of the day he had received the telegraph message that Trace, Jenny, and Allison would be home the next week. He'd been excited and nervous. He'd pushed the workers so that both Amanda and Marsh had to tell him that if he continued they all would collapse before the Cords got home.

He'd dressed carefully that morning to go to the station. He could hardly wait for them to see Fallen Oaks.

He had prepared every word he was going to say, practiced a speech of welcome until he knew it perfectly . . . and had promptly forgotten every word when Allison stepped down from the train to face him.

Trace and Allison were both amazed and very pleased with what Reid had done to Fallen Oaks. By the time they were settled back into their home and Jenny had been given a complete tour, Reid faced the fact that Fallen Oaks was no longer his. He had to go home.

Reluctantly, a few days later, when Allison and Jenny had the house under control and Reid had brought Trace up to date on the accounts, he prepared to leave.

They had a celebration dinner, and when it was over Allison walked to Reid's horse with him to say good-bye.

"God, I hate to leave here," Reid said as he looked at the moonlit beauty around him. "I guess I've considered Fallen Oaks home for a long time."

"Then you must go on considering it so, Reid," Allison said. "You live so close, I expect we shall see a great deal of each other."

He looked down into her blue eyes and smiled. "Allison . . . I want to say something. I love Fallen Oaks almost as much as you do. I've made it home for a long time. But . . . it didn't have the magic it's had since you came back."

"Reid, I . . ."

"No, let me finish before I run out of nerve." He inhaled deeply, then reached to take her hand. "Allison, I'd like to come to Fallen Oaks . . . often. But . . . but it would be to see you. I want you to consider thinking of me as more than a friend. I'm falling in love with you, Allison Cord, and I need to know how you feel about it."

"Well," Allison replied with a smile. "That was quite an elegant speech, Reid. Did you practice it?"

"Are you laughing at me?"

"No, you just sound so terribly serious."

"I *am* serious," he grinned. "And yes, I've been practicing what I would say for days. You have the darndest ability to make me tongue-tied and nervous."

"Oh, Reid, I've been the tomboy next door all our lives and you never noticed me before."

"Not the tomboy. But the *lady* is quite a different matter. You're beautiful, Allison, and I just can't get you out of my mind."

"So you think coming here often will help you do that?" she asked innocently.

"No! I don't want to get you out of . . ." He frowned. "There you go again." He reached out and took hold of her shoulders and drew her to him. "Don't play games with me, Allison. Not tonight, not about this. I need to know how you feel about me before I go crazy."

He would never forget the next few minutes until his dying day. Allison had looped her arms about him and moved so close he had to forcibly restrain himself.

"Then I'll tell you seriously, Reid Anderson. It's about time you've paid attention to me. I've practically been throwing myself at you from the minute we got home. Yes, I want you to come here as often as you can, and yes, it pleases me a great deal to know how you feel, because I feel the same. You're not hard to fall in love with, Reid."

He'd kissed her then, with a pent-up passion that threatened to explode into a conflagration. When he'd left a half hour later he was in a state of euphoria.

Now he stood, waiting for Allison to ride back from a visit to town and time spent with a few of her friends.

He watched the horizon, his hazel eyes glowing with expectation. His face was tanned, and his wide mouth was framed by a well-trimmed mustache. Every muscle in his six-foot frame was tense now. He brushed a nervous, long-fingered-hand through his thick, sandy-brown hair and drew a deep breath. He was always like this when Allison was away from him. The war had brutally taken his wife and son years before and he found separation from Allison very difficult to bear. He was afraid of losing her.

Then he saw her and jerked upright. She rode like the wind, her ebony hair catching the last rays of the sun. When she drew her horse to a stop he was beside it to lift her down and draw her into his arms for a long, lingering kiss.

"Mmm," he murmured. "You taste good. I thought you'd never get home."

"I've been thinking about you all day," Allison replied. "In fact, you're the reason I went over to talk to Ellen and Margaret."

"I'm the reason?"

"Yes," she smiled up at him, her blue eyes alight with laughter and teasing. "I had to find out if my two best friends would be my bridesmaids, didn't I?"

"Brides— Allison!" he said delightedly. "Then you're saying yes? You'll marry me?"

"Yes, I'm saying yes," Allison laughed. "You didn't really believe I was going to let you get away, did you?"

Reid caught her up in his arms and kissed her until his head swam and he was nearly lost. Allison was as responsive as he could have dreamed and he had to stop or he would have no longer been responsible for the outcome. He held her at arm's length and smiled.

"How soon?"

"Don't you think we ought to have an engagement first. Besides, we have to go and tell Trace and Jenny."

"Lord, I hope you don't believe in the traditional long engagement," Reid said as he put his arm about her waist and they walked into the house.

"I'm a very traditional lady." Allison tormented him with a soft laugh that belied her words. "But in this situation I think tradition could be bent a little if I have the right incentive.

"Give me the opportunity and I'll try to provide all the incentive you might need."

"Maybe I'll give you a small opportunity later. Right now I have to talk to Trace. There's a telegram from Maxwell. It might be important. Maybe, since it comes from California, the track might be all laid and Michael's coming home. I . . . I just can't see having a wedding without him.''

"That would be perfect. Trace is in the study. We've been waiting dinner for you.''

He kissed her once again, and they walked to the study. Even through the thick doors they could hear strong masculine laughter, accompanied by a woman's softer voice.

Allison knocked and opened the door. Jenny and Trace were standing in the center of the room, their arms around each other. Their happiness was too obvious to deny.

"Allison,'' Trace said. "It's about time you got back. We've been holding dinner. Besides, Reid is kind of out of control when you're not around.''

"I can see that you and Jenny missed me something awful,'' Allison said dryly. "You two wouldn't miss this house if it vanished around you.''

"Well, we have a real good reason to be happy,'' Trace said as he smiled down at Jenny.

"Something special going on?''

"Yes,'' Jenny said. Her cheeks were flushed as she pressed close to Trace. "Trace and I are going to have a child.''

"Oh!'' Allison shrieked. She rushed to Trace and Jenny, trying to embrace them both at the same time. "That is the most wonderful news! When will it be?''

"In about six and a half months,'' Jenny replied.

"I shall be an aunt,'' Allison marveled. "Can you believe it! Just think . . .''

"Of all the mischief you can teach her, Auntie Allison,'' Trace laughed. "How well I remember,'' he turned to smile at Jenny. "I suggest we keep the baby out of Allison's hands until she's at least sixteen.''

"Trace!''

"*She?*'' Jenny questioned with a laugh.

"I can see it now,'' Trace lamented. "If Allison has anything to say about it—*she,*'' he repeated firmly, "will be a handfull.''

"I don't see how you can say such a dreadful thing, Trace Cord? I'll teach her to be a model of decorum.''

"Shall I tell Reid about some 'model of decorum' activities

you've engaged in? Things like stripping down to bloomers and swimming down in the creek with the neighbor boys. Some decorum. You didn't sit for a week after that one."

"I will teach her to have fun," Allison laughed, "and I will also teach her that a 'lady' isn't just clothes and perfume. I'm going to have such fun and," she grinned at Trace, "there's not much you can do about it."

She turned to look at Reid, who hadn't taken his eyes from her. They smiled at each other. This was a time of promise for them as well.

"Reid and I have some exciting news for you both, too."

"You're going to get married," Trace chuckled.

"Trace!"

"Well, kitten, if anyone had seen you or Reid for the past few months and didn't recognize it, they'd have to be blind. Reid has been living in misery and now he's absolutely lit up. It's pretty obvious. The only question is when?"

"Maybe after you read the telegram I picked up while I was in town today. It's from California. It must be to tell us Michael is on his way home. Just think, Trace, we'll all be together for the first time in ages. I couldn't want anything more than to have all my family together for my wedding."

Allison reached into the pocket of her riding skirt, withdrew the telegram, and handed it to Trace. A feeling of excitement filled the room as Trace tore the envelope open and began to read.

Reid, Jenny, and Allison watched him impatiently. But their smikles faded when they saw him scowl and his brow furrow.

"Trace?" Allison's heart skipped a beat. Surely nothing had happened to Michael, she thought desperately. "Please," her voice was a whisper. "What is it?"

"You better read this," he handed the telegram to Allison while Reid read over her shoulder. But Jenny moved closer to Trace.

"What's wrong?"

"Maxwell thinks I should go and join him . . . to help find Michael."

"Find?"

"It seems Michael's on the run. He had some hard guns on

his trail that apparently mean to kill him. Jenny . . . Hannah
followed him with Jamie and Joey, and a couple of other men."

"Hannah! You mean . . ."

"That she's as lost right now as Michael. I can't just ignore this.
Hannah has good men with her, but damn it, it's dangerous."

"Trace, you needn't explain to me. Michael came when we
needed him, and Hannah, if she doesn't find Michael . . . or if
he's— You have to go. They need you."

"I hate to leave you at a time like this. But I know you'll be all
right. With Reid at the helm there should be no problems and
Marsh is a great foreman."

"What makes you think you're going, too?"

"Jenny, you can't . . ."

"Good heavens, Trace, I'm only about three months. I can
certainly travel by train, and if my memory isn't at fault, your
railroad crossed my land, so it wouldn't be too difficult to visit
my family while you go on to California. I'd like to see Pa, Buck,
and Emily. Don't you want to tell them we're having an addition
to the family?"

"Well," he was hesitant, "I suppose. You're sure it won't do
you any harm?"

"Of course it won't. I'm healthy as a horse and I'm strong.
Besides, I have no intention of losing your son."

"She's right, Trace," Allison agreed. "It won't be a hard trip
at all by train. We could take . . ."

"Who's talking *we*, kitten. You most certainly aren't going.
You're staying planted right here on Fallen Oaks. I don't need
to worry about two of you."

"Trace, that's unfair!"

"If I have to track Michael down, I can't leave you in California
alone. Besides," he smiled, "Reid would have my scalp. I don't
think he's about to let you go so easily."

Allison glanced from Trace to Reid, and a contemplative look
crossed her face. The men might not have been able to read what
was going on in her mind, but Jenny had no doubts about what
she was thinking. Allison gave no more arguments, but Jenny
knew the battle was far from over. Allison was just good at strategy.
She knew she would have much better results dealing with Reid
than with Trace. Reid was deeply in love with her and Jenny was

sure in the next few days that love was going to stand up to a rough test. She was also just as sure that Allison was going to win eventually.

Jenny smiled as Allison went to Reid and tucked her arm into his. "I suppose you're right, Trace."

Trace was pleased that the argument was over before it really got started. Reid was just as relieved to know that Allison wasn't going with them. But Jenny and Allison merely exchanged a look that had been understood by women since the beginning of time.

Dinner was quiet. Everyone was caught up in their thoughts. Reid had just begun to worry.

The next morning Trace went into town to get the tickets while Jenny packed their clothes. Allison helped her and when they were finished they sat on the veranda with their tea.

"I'm really happy for you, Allison. Reid is a good man. I'm sure he'll do everything to make you happy."

"I'm sure, too. Reid has always been a kind and gentle person. It's funny, but I've known him so long. He was," she shrugged, "always there. Then one day I realized how handsome and charming he was. But I knew he thought of me as a child. I danced at his wedding . . . and I was really jealous of the girl who got him. Then our worlds fell apart. I heard about how his wife and son were killed and I felt sorry for him. But he seemed to need a bottle more than a person. He's . . . he's not the same man. In a way he's even better."

"And he loves you completely."

"Yes." She turned to smile at Jenny. "It's wonderful, isn't it? I feel so . . . so special every time he looks at me."

"I'm sure he feels the same way. It's a feeling that shouldn't be taken advantage of, unless you're very careful and very sure."

"You know?"

"That he isn't as fortified against you as Trace is? That he'll try to make you happy no matter what you ask, yes I know. So . . ." Jenny smiled, "just how are you planning to get Reid to take you to California?"

Allison's smile was devilish. "I'm not sure yet. I have to reach into my bag of tricks and see what I can come up with."

"I'm beginning to feel real sorry for Reid. I have a feeling he's not going to know what happened to him until he's on a train. He'll probably be one step behind you his whole life."

"You think I'm wrong, Jen?"

"Men think different than women. They think they have to protect us like flowers. I cherish the way Trace feels . . . but it doesn't mean I always think he's right, or that I won't use my ways to convince him of what I want. You cherish the way Reid feels about you. But you need to do what you think is right, too. I have a feeling you know exactly what you're doing and that I'll see you on your way to California."

"I just need to know Michael is safe. If he needs us . . ."

"You're family."

"Yes . . . we're family."

"I don't think poor Reid has much of a chance. You have enough of the Cord charm to move a mountain. He'll see things your way. Besides, I think he knows a lot about family."

"I love him so much," Allison said softly.

"I know. Sometimes I love Trace so much it hurts. If we were separated I don't know what I'd do."

"I'll make Reid a good wife."

"I don't doubt that for a minute."

Both women suddenly stood up and watched Trace ride up to the porch. He dismounted, handed his reins to a young stable hand, and took the front steps two at a time.

"Well, I've got our tickets. We leave day after tomorrow. Can you be ready, Jen?"

"I'm almost packed now."

"Good." He turned to Allison. "You're not still angry at me are you, Allison? It's for your own good, you know. You need to start planning your wedding and getting your trousseau ready. Besides, we won't be gone as long as you think. Reid needs you here instead of clear across the country."

"No," Allison laughed. "I'm not angry at you, Trace. You can rest assured, Reid and I will be right where we belong."

"I'm glad you see it that way. I'd hate to go away with you angry."

"You just concentrate on finding Michael. Reid and I will take care of ourselves."

"I know how the neighbors would talk if I left you alone and unchaperoned here, especially since you're nearly engaged. So I've asked Mrs. Rineholt to come here to stay while I'm gone."

"Mrs. Rineholt!" Allison gasped. The last thing she had thought of was a third party being involved. "You can't mean that, Trace. Why she's so nosey, she'd ..." Allison grew indignant. "I won't have her! I won't! Mama never liked her. She never invited her here unless she couldn't get around it. Besides," Allison's voice was rising with her outrage, "where was she when we were struggling so hard, when I was alone? I didn't see her trotting her fat bottom over here. No, sir, she squatted over there like an old hen on a nest and just had a good old time gossipin' about everyone else."

"You can't have any gossip about yourself, Allison, and you'll need some company."

"But Mrs. Rinehold, of all the people in the world, Trace! Why ... I'd rather cozy up to a snake than share my house with that old witch." Jenny was trying not to laugh, Trace was looking a little put out and surprised, and Allison was reaching desperately for control of her temper. "I will not have that nosy, gossipy old woman watching every move I make!"

Trace looked so utterly helpless that Jenny almost laughed. "She's not as bad as all that," he protested.

"Then you take her with you! I'm not going to have her here. I warn you, Trace, if she comes I'm going to cause a big fuss. I'll just demand she leave, and *then* won't the gossips have a good time!"

"All right." Trace shrugged and extended his hands palm out as if to ward off an attack. "All right. I'll tell her tomorrow she doesn't need to come. But you'd better behave."

"Don't I always?"

"Allison, please," Trace chuckled and rolled his eyes heavenward.

"Well, I do," Allison grinned to acknowledge her lie.

"We'd better finish up packing," Jenny interrupted.

"Is Reid coming over tonight?" Trace questioned.

"Yes. And tomorrow night he wants us to go to his house for dinner," Allison said. "We'll take you to the station when it's time for you to go, so you won't have to leave the buggy in town."

"Good. Then I guess everything is settled."

"Yes," Allison answered in a voice uncharacteristically subdued. Trace stood with Jenny and watched Allison walk ahead of him into the house. Jenny looked up into his face to see a puzzled frown.

"Something wrong?"

"No," he replied. "It's just that Allison seems . . . just a little too accommodating. I learned many years ago that when Allison is agreeable she's after something."

"Oh, Trace, I don't think *you* have to worry about what Allison wants. I think she's just being cooperative about everything."

"Maybe . . . maybe. Well, I think we ought to go in and break all the news to Amanda and Marsh. Amanda had better know in advance she has Allison to cope with."

Jenny smiled, tucked her hand under Trace's arm, and they entered the house together.

Reid and Allison stood on the train platform and waved a final good-bye to the slowly receding train. Only when it was in miniature did Allison turn to Reid.

"Will you come back to the house for lunch, Reid?"

"I want to," he replied, "but I don't want to cause any problems."

"Now don't you start that or I shall surely scream. Reid, I'm not a child, and I won't let my life be controlled by people's whispers. Besides," her voice softened, "I want to be with you. We need to talk, to keep finding out more about each other."

Reid was so thoroughly caught that he could think of no argument against something he wanted even more than she did.

The trip was exciting for Jenny. It seemed she couldn't get enough of the view as they drew closer and closer to Colorado. Trace enjoyed seeing her so happy. He knew Jenny missed her family. That thought sparked an idea, and before they slept that night he presented it to her cautiously.

"Jenny, I'm sure Buck and your father have really missed you. They'd enjoy it if you could spend some time with them."

Jenny laughed softly and curled close to him. "Are you being overprotective again, Trace? Yes, I'd like to spend time with them. But I don't want to be away from you."

"Look, Jen, I'll tell you the truth. Much as I want you with me. I don't know what I will have to face in California. We might . . . no, we most likely will have to go out on the trail. You had the right idea. If you stay with your family, then I won't have any reason to worry. Besides, they should be able to share the news about the baby without worrying about you. With them I'll know you're in good hands and being well taken care of. I need to be sure of that if I'm going to be helpful in finding Michael."

"You can ease your mind. Staying with Pa will be fine. But I have some terms."

"Terms? What terms? Am I being blackmailed?"

"Just a little. I want you to ask Buck and Terrance to go with you. You see, I need to know you're being watched over, too."

"Have I told you that I love you, Mrs. Cord?"

"A few times."

"Too few. I need to say it every day."

"I'm happy, Trace. At one time I didn't think we'd have the chance to be this happy together."

"Fact is," he laughed, "there was a time when I thought you really were going to shoot me."

"Well, there *was* a time when I was going to do just that. You were the biggest problem in my life then and just too stubborn to step aside."

"If we're talking about that, I'll have to say, I hope, since you insist the baby is going to be a boy, that our son isn't going to inherit a good dose of his mother's stubbornness."

"And the same dose of his father's conceit," Jenny laughed.

"We ought to make a hell of a child."

"Maybe it will be a girl."

"Good God, can you see a girl that is a combination of us? She'd either be President of the country or the best damn bank robber in the business."

"I can't wait to tell Pa about his first grandchild. And it will be good to see our valley again."

Trace agreed.

"Will you stay there a day of two?"

"I don't think I'd better stay too long. One day might make a difference to Michael."

"I suppose. Max's telegram sounded as if he was really worried."

"He's gotten close to Michael. He treated me like a son. I guess Max is the kind of man to worry."

"Well, your wife is the kind of woman who worries, so remember that and keep in as much contact as you can."

"I will. I promise."

"The men who are after Michael, after all this time why don't they just give up?"

"They're paid by a man who doesn't know the meaning of giving up."

"That's terrible. How can one man hate that much?"

"I don't know. I wish there was a way to put an end to it."

"You'll find it, Trace. Somehow you and Maxwell will find a way."

"I just hope we find Michael before . . ."

"Don't . . . You'll find him. You will!"

Trace smiled and took her in his arms. Jenny's faith in him was always his greatest source of happiness. They made love, slowly, contentedly . . . and with a touch of the fear of separation.

The reunion in Bentonville was enthusiastic and filled with joy. Howard was the first to embrace and kiss Jenny. The tears in his eyes were tears of happiness. Then Buck caught Jenny up in his arms and hugged her tight.

Jenny realized, when she got a good look at her father and brother, just how contented they were. Howard looked younger than his close to fifty years, and even though there were strands of white in his auburn hair, there was warmth and vitality in the deep blue of his eyes. He was a tall man, who had passed on his height to both his children. Buck topped his father's six feet by two inches. He was broad-shouldered and his turquoise eyes matched his sister's both in color and sparkle. He also shared Jenny's gold hair and quick smile.

"Be careful, Buck," Jenny laughed, "or your nephew will be crushed."

"What? Nephew! That's wonderful. Jen, it's good to see you again. It feels like eternity!"

"A grandchild!" Howard exclaimed. He extended his hand to Trace, then hugged Jenny again. "Congratulations to the both of you. I hope you are as lucky as I've been."

Emily was excited, too, as she kissed Trace and Jenny and congratulated them.

When they went back to the ranch Jenny visited her mother's grave first. Then she and Trace rode through the valley to old familiar places, and for a few hours they renewed the passion they had first found there.

The next morning Trace and Jenny rode over to see Hannah's parents. The ride was two hours of scenic wonder. The small house the Grahams owned was nestled between two hills. The land rolled beyond it, lush and green. Here and there stands of tall trees stood, bending and swaying in the gentle breeze. Fields of buttercups and splashes of purple harebell and white yarrow brightened the verdant meadows. In the distance the silver thread of a sun-dappled river twined through the landscape.

They were overjoyed to hear that Hannah was safe. Jacob had a million questions, few of which could be answered as yet. He was a bear of a man, his chest massive and his arms powerful, a body that was used to hard work. His skin was as tanned as leather, making his hazel eyes seem lighter and brighter. His dark-brown hair was threaded at the temples with strands of silver.

In contrast Beatrice, his wife, seemed almost delicate, deceptively so. She was slender and her head came only to Jacob's shoulder, yet he'd be the first to claim her as the source of his strength. She had calm intelligence in her green eyes and her auburn hair was still lush and thick. Her smile gave her a shy look, but there were few in her family who didn't know her will was like iron.

At first Jacob insisted he would go search for Michael, too. "Hannah is my daughter. I have to know she's safe!"

"Mr. Marshall," Trace said cautiously. "I know how you feel. But you have to face the reality that we can travel faster and harder than you."

"You mean I'll slow you down."

"I'm afraid you would," Trace said truthfully. "I can only tell you that we'll do everything in our power to see that Hannah is safe."

Jacob looked from Trace to the others, then back to Trace. "All right," he said relutantly. Every quickly added their words of assurance.

Jacob had to be satisfied with their assurances that at the time of the telegram Hannah was all right and that she'd left on her search with four of the most capable men Maxwell knew.

"Hannah has frightened us to death," Beatrice said, "but she was always one to know what she wanted."

"She loves Michael," Jenny replied, "and he's like his brother. I must tell you, Mrs. Marshall, that I feel Hannah is a very lucky woman."

"I don't doubt it for a moment." Beatrice said quietly. "I can see how happy Trace has made you. It's only that it is Hannah's courage that frightens me. She will walk into a den of lions if she feels it necessary for one she loves."

"What a wonderful quality," Jenny murmured.

"Yes . . . but frightening for those who love her," Jacob reaffirmed quietly.

"You must have more faith in her. Hannah has a great gift: compassion. Maybe that was the quality that drew Michael to her in the first place. It's a rare and very valuable trait."

"Well, Trace," Beatrice said. "I hope you find your brother well and can put an end to these problems once and for all. It will be a happy day when you return with your brother and my daughter."

"And we'll return as fast as we can. I assure you that if I find Hannah in California I'll see that she's kept safe until she's home again. And Mrs. Marshall," Trace continued. "I've asked Jenny's brother and Terrance to go with me. Trust us that we'll do everything we can to put an end to this situation once and for all."

"Thank you."

"I think the sooner we leave, the better. If Buck and Terrance can be ready I'd like to go in the morning."

"Can't you at least stay to dinnertime," Jacob asked.

"I don't see why not," Trace agreed. "The ride back is pretty at night." If he had any other ideas Jenny's scrutiny couldn't interpret them.

They ate a leisurely dinner, and after Jenny insisted on helping with the dishes, she and Trace prepared to leave.

"I wish you both Godspeed," Jacob said.

Trace and Jenny were at the door when Mrs. Marshall spooke to him again . . . softly. "Trace. Bring my daughter home."

"I will," Trace replied just as quietly. Then he and Jenny left.

As they rode back toward the Graham ranch the land about them was bathed in moonlight. Trace drew his horse to a halt beneath the shadows of the trees. He dismounted and walked to Jenny's side.

"Trace?" she questioned.

"Let's walk for a bit. I haven't had a minute alone with you for the past two days. If I'm to leave tomorrow I don't want to spend the whole night in a crowd."

Jenny smiled and put her hands on his shoulders. Gently he lifted her down to stand beside him.

"You're upset tonight, Trace. Why?"

"Mostly it's just leaving you behind."

"And your promise to Mrs. Marshall to bring Hannah back safely?"

"That, too, I suppose."

"And Michael?" she added softly.

"Michael," he repeated. "Those men mean to kill him. Even if we find him, I'm still not sure how I can stop it."

Jenny turned to him and put her arms around him. She felt him tighten his embrace as if she were the only solidity he had.

"It will take one step at a time. First you must find him. Then I know you'll find a way."

He chuckled, then tipped her chin up to look into her eyes. "I love you . . . and I'll miss you very much." He bent his head to kiss her. "If I built a fire we could stay here for a while," he said huskily. "I've blankets on my saddle."

"Oh, yes," she whispered against his lips as he kissed her again.

They made a small camp and shared the evening and the star-studded night. It would be the last time for what might be weeks—or even months.

* * *

The next day Trace, Buck, and Terrance were packed and ready. The train was to leave before noon. Jenny, along with her father, Emily, and Hannah's parents came to see them off.

It was not exactly going to be the most comfortable ride. The only pullman cars were fully occupied, so the three men had to take general accommodations, which meant taking turns to stretch out on the hard benchlike seats.

Trace found sleep difficult that night anyway, so he found a seat near a window and let his thoughts run free. He knew Jenny would be safe and that Allison was in good hands. The mystery was Michael's whereabouts, and if he had already encountered the men who wanted his life. It frightened him that he might come a day, an hour, a minute too late.

It wasn't fair, he raged against fate. Michael was not a killing man. Trace remembered their childhood. They had grown nearly inseparable over the years.

Yes, he knew Michael, inside and out. But he also know a man could be forced into changes he really didn't want to make. Michael had been forced to kill, and that alone could destroy something within a man until he became like those who sought him.

Violence bred violence and it could be insidious, devouring the heart of a man until he could not stop.

The fear that Michael had turned that way made Trace break out into a sweat. Mentally he wished the time away, wished the train to move faster.

But neither the train nor the time complied with his wishes. The train chugged along at the same speed and the minutes ticked by at the same regulated pace. It was near morning before Trace squirmed into a reasonably comfortable position, and, using his jacket as a pillow, finally found a few minutes sleep.

Chapter Four

"Umm . . . umm . . . umm," Amanda clucked to herself as she lifted the bundle of clothes and started from the bedroom.

Behind her Allison was smiling at her reflection in the mirror as she brushed her hair.

"Stop fussing, Amanda," Allison said casually—casualness that belied the glow in her blue eyes.

"Chile, you can be downright wicked when you puts your mind to it. What yo got planned for dat boy? Yo got him runnin' in circles for the past few days."

"I don't know what you're talking about."

"You knows what Ih'm talkin' about right enough. Whatever you got in mind, you bettah forget it. I ain't goin' to let you act like no wicked town gal. I diapered you when you was a babe. I done tan yore hide then and I'll do it again. Why you drivin' dat boy wild anyhow?"

"Amanda . . ." Allison said warningly.

"An why you flirtin' wit dat Martin boy?"

"I was not flirting."

"You was doin' it on purpose, and I know why."

Allison turned around and frowned at Amanda, but it didn't intimidate her.

"What do you mean you know why?"

"You wants somethin' from dat boy. You already got him frothin' at the mouth. Keep on bein' a butterfly I suspects he be ready to do whatever yo wants jus so you be happy."

"So, Reid wants to make me happy. What's wrong with that? After all, we are going to be married . . . someday."

"Dere you go again. Yo're danglin' yourself in front of him like a ripe plum, then when he reaches, you jus' jump out of reach. You plain' some game and you better tell me what it is before you gets into somethin' you can't get out of. I ought to make Marsh have a long talk wit Mistah Reid."

"You and Marsh just mind your own business," Allison said defensively.

"I knowed it! I knowed it!"

Allison stood up and reached for the shawl lying across a nearby chair. She smiled as she draped it around her shoulders and walked across the room.

"You don't know anything," she stated as she opened the door.

"I knows dat dress is downright disgraceful," Amanda called after her. "It cut too low for a gal as grown as you is! Yore gonna give that boy ideas he shouldn't oughta have!" But the last words were said to a closed door. "That chile get somethin' in her head," Amanda muttered, "she jus' like those brothers of hers. She sets her mind and goes off and does what she pleases. Ain't no good gonna come. Her in a dress is gonna scandalize folks . . . an' her hair down like that, and smellin' from perfume!" She muttered, shaking her head as she continued to gather laundry. "Dat poor boy doan know he gots his hands full. He jus doan know . . ."

Allison walked down the wide stairway, crossed the foyer, and opened the huge double doors that led to the front veranda. From where she stood she could see down the long, tree-shaded lane that led to the house. She would see Reid when he approached.

Today was certainly the wrong time for her to be nervous. She had played her game and knew she was winning. But today was the day she had to convince Reid that it was *his* dearest wish to take her where she wanted to go.

Her destination was California. But it would probably be most acceptable to Reid to take her first to Colorado. He would have to believe she wanted to be with Jenny to wait for her brother's return.

She smiled to herself. Amanda was very astute. She'd always had a way of seeing through any kind of trickery. Allison promised herself that she would have to make it up to Amanda somehow, because she knew how upset Amanda was going to be when she found out exactly what Allison was planning. It made her wince to think of that explosion . . . but she didn't change her mind.

In the distance she could see Reid riding toward the house. She inhaled deeply, turned, and walked to the far end of the veranda, where she stood in a position assuring her back would be to him when he walked up the steps.

With calm concentration she mentally dredged up every moment of pain and fear the past had buried in her memory. She drew on every loss until the tears she wanted formed in her eyes.

Reid was confused. A week ago he'd had a grip on his life and everything in it. But for the past week, he seemed to be standing in quicksand. He knew he was off balance . . . and he knew the reason. Allison. However, he just couldn't put his finger on exactly what the problem was. Allison loved him. He knew it in his heart. He could taste it in her kiss and the feel of her in his arms. But on occasion she'd suddenly become like a wisp of smoke. It threw him off balance, gave him dreams he couldn't handle, and worse . . . it scared the hell out of him that Allison could fall *out* of love with him.

He would do just about anything to keep her happy and keep the smile on her face that had blossomed when they'd first found each other. But she never asked him for anything . . . nothing. Yet she seemed . . . discontented.

Well, he'd brought her a gift he hoped would please her.

He rode up to the house, dismounted, and started up the steps when he saw her standing at the far end of the veranda. Her back was to him and yet she had that same, groundshaking effect on him. Slowly he walked up to stand behind her.

"Allison?"

Her body tensed, but she didn't turn around to face him. Something was very wrong. He took her shoulders and turned her around to face him.

"Allison, what's wrong?"

"Why nothing, Reid, really. I'm fine. It's such a beautiful day, I thought I'd come out for some air."

But her eyes glimmered with tears, and Reid couldn't bear that.

"I know we were supposed to go riding this morning," Allison said in a subdued voice. She placed her hand against his chest and looked up at him with a tremulous look that melted any resistance he might have had. "But ... if you don't mind, I'd rather not." She turned from him and sighed as she looked out over the stand of mimosa trees some distance away. "I can't b ear how still it is. Maybe we could just take a walk under the trees."

"If you'd like," he agreed. At the moment he would agree to anything to see her smile reappear and the unhappy look disappear from her eyes. They walked across the green lawn toward the shade of the trees. Allison's goal at the moment was to get as far away from Amanda as she could. It would not take long for her to warn Reid, and then she could get a commitment from him. She knew, of course, that once he had committed himself, his own sense of honor wouldn't let him go back on his word, even if he wanted to.

"You've done such a wonderful job with Fallen Oaks, Reid. I'm so glad you didn't cut these trees for lumber. This was a favorite spot when I was a child. My brothers and I ..." Her voice broke and she turned her head from him.

So that was it, he thought. She missed her brothers and she was worried for them. It was not hard to understand. She must feel very lonely in this big house.

He assured her he understood how she felt. "I'll try to make it up to you," he added.

"Yes, I do miss them," she said softly, "and in a way you do make up for them being gone. You're so wonderfully good to me, Reid. I suppose I just want all the men I love to be together. You see, when they were gone all that time I was so scared. I promised myself I'd never again be here alone ... or be lonely like I was then. But here I am again, just worrying and waiting." She let her voice drop to a whisper. "I just can't bear it, worrying if they're all right. Outside of you, Reid, Michael and Trace are all I have. I ... I just can't think of planning my wedding until I know for sure." Her voice broke on what sounded to him like a nuffled sob.

"But if you don't plan now we'll have to put the wedding off until . . ."

"Until next year at least," she said with wistful sadness. "It's breakin' my heart, but you just wouldn't want a crying bride, would you?"

"I don't want you cryin' anytime, Allison, but I just don't know what to do about it." He was miserable. Waiting weeks to have Allison as his bride was hard enough, but waiting another year . . . He couldn't contemplate the thought.

"There must be a way, Reid, there just must be," Allison said. She held her breath, hoping Reid would take her lead.

He said the next words as a casual thought and knew almost at once he had put his foot into a sticky problem. "I suppose the best way would be to go and see for ourselves. But . . ." He stopped, amazed at his own words. He could draw a vivid picture of Trace and Michael's reaction!

Allison seized advantage before he could take the next breath. She spun toward him, her eyes alight and a brilliant smile on her face.

"Oh, I knew I could trust you to understand. I just knew if I trusted you, you would come up with the answer. You're so wonderful, Reid, and I'm so grateful!" She flung her arms around his neck and kissed him enthusiastically. Whatever protests he was about to make were drowned in the scent and the feel of her and the taste of her lips against his. When he finally did break the kiss off he looked down into her eyes. They were filled with warmth and love.

"Allison, I . . ."

"With you I don't need to be afraid. We can leave right away. Trace and Michael both trust you, and *I* trust you as well. It will be simple, and once I know they're safe we can plan our lives. I really don't want to wait to be your wife, Reid. I do love you so much and I am more than grateful."

She drew his head down to hers for a long, lingering kiss that tore his thoughts away from arguments . . . at least for the moment. He was sure he could bring her to her senses later, when they had more time to talk. For now she was warm and willing in his arms.

She gave him her love and her trust. That was of great import for Reid who had spent many lonely hours since the war.

Allison filled his days with sunlight and a new kind of ambition. She had become the center of his life, and he knew it would be a very bleak world without her.

Her mouth was soft and giving and slowly he became immersed in the heat of passion he had tried to control . . . until now.

Allison had not planned on the coiling heat that began to expand from somewhere deep inside her. She meant to break the kiss, but somehow her will got tangled with an emotion powerful enough to bend it beyond recall. She melted against him and took pleasure in the strength of the arms that held her. It had been a long time since she felt such a sense of protection and security.

Allison seemed to have the ability to reach into the heart and soul of him with a sweet caress. Slowly, tantalizingly, he explored her mouth, searching out its moist, heated center. With the kiss they seemed to become part of each other.

Allison's arms crept around him, holding him even nearer as she fervently returned his embrace, his kiss, her lips fusing with his, her tongue seeking his.

Reid wrapped the fingers of one hand in her thick ebony hair, reveling in the feel of its soft texture, while his other hand moved down, past the curve of her waist to her buttocks to pull her even tighter against him. She could feel the hardness of his passion pressed close against her.

His breath was like the sunny warmth around them, tasting faintly of tobacco and whiskey. The brush of his thick mustache against the corners of her mouth made her laugh softly. Then the laughter turned to a sound of passionate need.

When he released her lips she could only murmur his name as his mouth moved to the soft, scented flesh of the curve of her neck and shoulders . . . then down to where her breasts lay warm and full beneath his touch. She arched against him as she felt his lips burn over the smooth mounds that beckoned him so enticingly above the low-cut dress.

Her whole body felt as if it was on fire, and her flesh tingled as though it had been burnt . . . branded. An almost painful ache that was growing hotter and hotter threatened to consume Reid with its intensity and push him beyond any ability to stop.

The struggle was monumental, and Reid desperately drew on a very thin thread of reality. Before he did something he knew was against Allison's will, he had to stop his own slide into a passion that was nearly overwhelming him.

With a groan he put his hands on her shoulders and held her away from him.

For a moment they could only look at each other in total awe of the emotion that had come very close to exploding. Both were breathing heavily and trembling with unfulfilled need. They knew that this was only the promise of what they would one day share.

"God," he breathed. "Allison, I'm sorry. I didn't mean for that to happen."

"Sorry? I'm not sorry, Reid. I'm more than pleased to know how you feel about me, and I want you to know I feel the same. I suppose we nearly got carried away. But . . . I wasn't afraid," her voice was soft with her need to confirm their emotions, "and now I know I'll never be afraid of you."

"I'd kiss you again for that," he laughed shakily, "but I don't think I can handle that intensity twice. I think we'd better go back to the house."

"Yes. I must make plans. You will stay for dinner, won't you? I think it will take two of us to explain our plans to Amanda."

"Ah . . . about those plans, Allison. I . . . ah . . ."

"Don't worry, Reid, Amanda won't be too upset. We just have to make her understand how kind and generous you're being to me, taking me all that way when I could never do it alone." She tucked her arm in his and walked close beside him. "I've been so very miserable. You've not only given me some hope, but your strong character to lean on as well. I don't see how anyone would want to deny me my dearest wish, so if Amanda argues, we'll just have to make her understand that we have our minds set and we're going. When can we get the tickets? How soon do you think the next train will be leaving?"

Her chatter and the content of her words had firmly set him up as a fellow conspirator and he couldn't see a way out of it unless he dashed her hopes completely and put tears in her eyes again. He couldn't have stood that. So he shook his head and walked back to the house with her in silence. He was pretty sure how Amanda was going to take the news.

He might have been sure about what Amanda and Marsh would think, but he was definitely not prepared for their reaction and the predictions that went with it.

Amanda had served them a delicious stew for dinner and after he and Allison had eaten, they had gone to the front veranda to sit and enjoy the evening. Marsh carried out cool drinks and set one beside each of them. That was when Allison decided to break the news. Reid had been holding his breath and hoping secretly that Allison had thought better of her wild idea and changed her mind. But she hadn't; she had only timed everything as perfectly as a general planning war strategy.

"Marsh, tell Amanda I'm going to walk Reid to the front gate. In the meantime she can set out some traveling clothes and my trunk. Reid and I are going to join Trace and Jenny."

Marsh's forehead wrinkled in surprise and he cast a disbelieving look at Reid who was completely bereft of any words.

"Yo' all goin' to find your brothers?" Marsh asked, as if he doubted her words . . . or his hearing.

"Yes, we are."

"But, Mistah Trace . . ."

"It's not a problem, Marsh. We'll just join Trace and Jenny. Since Reid's foreman is quite capable of taking over, that won't be a problem, either. I don't want to sit home and worry, and I'm fortunate that Reid has been so kind as to promise to take me. So you see, you and Amanda have nothing to worry about."

"My, oh my," Marsh muttered to himself. "Amanda sho 'nuff gonna be put out about this. Not to mention what yore brothers are goin' to do."

Allison was sure of the same thing, but she was fortified with the promise she had entangled Reid in and she was more than certain he would stand beside her when a thundercloud named Amanda struck.

And strike she did, within minutes of Marsh's arrival in the kitchen and the delivery of Allison's words.

"Packin' up!" Amanda was aghast. "Traipsin' clear cross the

country! Dat girl got another think comin'." She wiped her hands on her apron and walked purposefully toward the veranda, where a very nervous Reid and a steeled Allison waited.

Allison was quick to attack. Playing chess with her brothers had taught her long ago that the best defense was a good offense. She stood up.

"Now, Amanda, I know this is short notice, but Reid and I just decided this afternoon. I'm sure you can . . ."

"Are you outta your mind? You can't do that!" Amanda protested firmly, her brown eyes blazing with indignant anger.

"And why can't I?" Allison asked innocently.

" 'Cause . . . it ain't seemly, a young, pretty girl like yourself travelin' unchaperoned."

"Who better to chaperone me than the man I'm going to marry?"

"Mistah Reid, yo gonna stand fo dis kind of thing?" She turned to Reid in an almost pleading way.

"To tell you the truth, Amanda," Reid smiled sheepishly, "if I don't *stand* for it, as you so aptly put it, I'm afraid I'm going to be *sitting* here . . . by myself. I think it's best I go along." He grinned at Allison. "Even if I think I've been taken advantage of."

Allison returned his smile joyously. Right or wrong, he was going to stand with her. At that moment she was proud that he was her man and that she'd had the good sense to say yes when he proposed.

"I love you, Reid Anderson," she said softly.

"I'm glad," he chuckled.

"Yore brothers gonna skin you alive. Trace, he's gonna put his foot down and you'll come home faster than you went."

"Put his foot down." Now Reid laughed aloud. "Like he did about Mrs. Rineholt coming here as a chaperone?"

Allison giggled in delight and Amanda shook her head. "You better hope both her brothers don't come for you with a gun instead of words."

"I'll just have to face that situation if it comes up."

Allison walked to Amanda and took her hands in her own. "Trust me, Amanda," she said gently. "I'll never shame my family, I promise. I just can't bear not to know if Michael and Trace are all right. It's unfair. Just because I'm a woman must I just sit and worry? I can't . . . and I'm prepared to take the consequences."

Amanda looked from Allison to Reid, who smiled. "You're as trapped as I am, Amanda. Might as well give up."

"I guess. Girl, you shore can twist things to suit yore own purposes. General Lee oughta had you, the South might have won the war then. It gonna be a war for both of yo when dose boys gets their hand on yo."

"You think," Reid said calmly, "that maybe we ought to get married before we go?" Now both Amanda and Allison turned to him in shock. He shrugged and grinned. "Just a thought."

"Well, you puts dat thought away where you puts any other thoughts. If she set on goin', she go, and I 'spects you to get her dere and back safe . . . perfectly safe."

"You're a hard woman, Amanda."

"I show you a hard woman if anything happens to dis babe of mine!"

"I don't doubt that for a minute," Reid laughed. "I guess I'd better get going if I'm to put some things together. Allison . . . didn't you say something about walking me to the gate?"

"Yes, I did." Allison joined Reid and they went down the steps arm in arm. Amanda still watched with an appraising and doubtful eye.

Marsh brought Reid's horse around and, taking the reins, he and Allison walked slowly, and in silence. Then Allison was the first to speak.

"Reid, did you mean what you said?"

"About what?"

"That you thought we ought to get married before we left."

"It wasn't a very noble thought, Allison."

"Oh?"

"I was thinking more about me than about you. I have a feeling this trip is going to test my nerves in a way a war never did."

"I would have, you know," she replied quietly.

They stopped by the gate and he turned to look at her. The moonlight washed over her, transforming her to an ivory goddess. He reached to touch her lightly.

"I'm grateful that you would. But I guess I wouldn't let you. You deserve so much more than a hasty wedding. One day we'll do it right. Until then," he whispered as he bent to kiss her, "I love you enough not to hurt you . . . and not to let you get hurt."

Allison moved into his arms. When their kiss ended he held her close to him for a few minutes, reluctant to let her go.

"I almost forgot something," he said as he stepped back from her. "I brought you something." He reached into his pocket and when he held his open palm out she could see the glimmer of gold in his palm. "It was my mother's, and I want you to have it."

She took the small gold heart-shaped locket with shaking hands. It gleamed in the moonlight. A scrolled "A" was elaborately engraved on the front.

"My father gave it to my mother the day they were married. It's all I have left. The 'A' is certainly appropriate." He took it from her hand and turned her around. When he draped the thin chain around her throat she pressed her hand against it, feeling *his* warmth against her flesh. Then she turned around and looked down at the locket, then up to Reid. This time the tears in her eyes were both happy and genuine.

"I shall cherish it forever, Reid," she whispered. "Oh, I do love you so much."

He took her in his arms gently, feeling her flow against him, entwine around him . . . feeling her complete surrender. He whispered her name as their lips blended.

Reid sighed. "It's going to be a long, long trip." He backed from her. "And if I don't leave now it could be a longer night. Good night, Allison. I'll see to the tickets tomorrow and ride out and let you know when we leave."

"Reid, you won't regret this. I know it's not the wisest thing to do, but . . . it's what I need to do. Can you understand that?"

"I'm counting on it."

"What?"

"It means that when you love, you love completely, and that's what I want from you. I want you to love me like that." His eyes held hers. Completely.

"Whatever I've done to deserve you, I'm certainly glad I did it," Allison smiled. "Good night, my love. Keep that in mind, will you?"

"I."

He kissed her lightly, mounted his horse, then bent to kiss her again. Then he rode away.

Against all Amanda's wishes and her mutterings, misgivings, and predictions of all kinds of dire repercussions, Reid and Allison left on the morning train three days later.

Michael stepped out onto the wood plank sidewalk. The streets were empty and the sun was just brimming the horizon. He had always been an early riser and now his sleep was lighter and more fitful than ever.

He was pretty sure Patrick wouldn't be awake yet, but he felt the need of a good hot cup of coffee. Across the street the proprietor of the restaurant was sweeping the sidewalk in front of his establishment.

As Michael approached the proprietor looked up and smiled. " 'Mornin'."

"Good morning. Any chance the restaurant is open for breakfast yet?"

"Wasn't, till a couple of minutes ago. Another fella came round. I think he was with you last night when you were here to eat. 'Pears like he's an early bird, too."

"Patrick," Michael smiled. "Then I guess I can get some coffee."

"Sure can."

"You have a good memory," the man looked at Michael quizzically, "if you remember Patrick and I were together last night."

"Well, sir," the man stopped speaking and rested his body lightly on his broom. "I won't lie to you. You ain't exactly the kind of person a man forgets. It ain't just the way you look, which is downright intimidating. It's the way you sort of . . . draw attention. That gun makes an impression, too. Ain't no question whether you know how to use it or not. There's something . . . and your friend is the same. He's a man you remember, too, whether you want to or not. And you . . . Man meets you, he ain't likely to forget it. I don't mean to give offense."

"No offense taken. I'll go join Patrick . . . if you'll supply the breakfast food and the coffee."

"My pleasure."

Michael walked inside the restaurant. His situation was even clearer now. He had to take Patrick up on his offer. He had to vanish. If he was so visible, even when he didn't want to be, there would be no trouble tracing him. He had to find an end to it, and fate seemed to have sent him Patrick to give him the opportunity . . .

An opportunity to die. The thought was so bitter it almost made him want to turn around and face the men following him and get it over with, once and for all. But he knew that instinct might make him a victor. He didn't run from fear, or lack of courage. He ran from success, because in this case success would mean death.

Patrick was seated at a table in the far corner of the restaurant, and even with the dim light inside and the morning sun behind Michael, Patrick recognized him at once. Few men walked with that same aura of strength and confidence.

"You're up early," Michael said as he slid into a chair opposite Patrick.

"Habit," Patrick answered. "Besides, morning is about the nicest time of day. It usually goes downhill from there."

Michael laughed.

"Think you'll have any luck finding someone to go to Virginia City with us?"

"I'm looking. Haven't run across many men I'd care to take a chance with."

"Maybe you'll have some luck today."

"Yeah, maybe." At the waiter's approach Michael turned his attention from Patrick and gave his order, the size of which made Patrick chuckle.

They had just started to eat when someone else walked into the restaurant. Michael glanced up quickly. Old habits were hard to break.

The man was obviously nearly destitute. His clothes were shabby, and his beard and hair were straggly. His stance indicated a man who had reached the end of his rope and was dangling on a thread.

Yet there was something about him that drew and held Michael's attention. Patrick turned his head to follow his gaze.

"He rode into town yesterday. Didn't have enough money to

find a room or care for his horse. I think he's agreed to a couple of days labor at the stable in return for his horse's care."

Michael said nothing. Someone who labored to see to the care of his horse could not be a careless man. Michael kept looking at him. A tug of something familiar made him slowly rise to his feet. Patrick watched, a little surprised, as Michael moved across the room.

"Zeb?" Michael questioned.

The man turned in Michael's direction. His face showed no recognition.

"Zebulon Parker?"

"Yeah." The man's voice was sluggish. He continued to look at Michael as he drew closer. Suddenly, when Michael was but a few feet away, recognition filled his face.

Patrick was aware of many things. The first was that the man's first reaction seemed to be one of shame. Then his shoulders straightened and he held Michael's eyes until Michael stopped near him.

"Lieutenant Cord." He extended his hand. "It's good to see you. I thought most of our company was wiped out in that last little set to. It's good to know somebody else made it besides me."

"It's been a while, Zeb. I'm glad to see you, too. How have you been doing?"

"Oh, managing, I guess. Thought I'd drift up to gold country. Maybe strike something."

"Come on over and join my friend and me for breakfast. Maybe we can talk over some old times."

"I ... ah ... don't think so. I was just about to ask the owner if I could work off breakfast. I'm not exactly flush at the minute."

Michael knew he couldn't offer this man charity. "I might need a good man for a job if you're interested. I don't know what the pay is yet. I'm just talking it over. But it will be a decent wage."

"What kind of work? I don't work outside the law."

"Neither do I."

"Sorry, I didn't mean that. I guess I'm a little touchy lately. Let's talk. I'll have breakfast after we decide if I'm working or not."

Michael led the way back to the table. "Patrick, this is a friend of mine, Zeb Parker. We fought at Bull Run together."

"Mr. Parker." Patrick stood and extended his hand.

"Lieutenant . . . I mean, Mr. Cord . . ."

"Michael."

"Michael . . . he said there might be an offer of work?"

Patrick was quick to pick up on Michael's intentions and just as quick to pick up on Zeb's pride. "There's work if you want it. Here, on the way, and in Virginia City. Sit down and I'll tell you about it."

Zeb sat.

"I'm on my way to Virginia City with a great deal of money," Patrick began. He continued to explain the rest of the situation. Zeb didn't interrupt. "So we need one more man to sort of balance some odds. After we get there I have work for you if you want to settle. It will include a small room and fifty dollars a month."

"Doing what?"

"Mostly carpentry to start. We have a building to erect. After that . . . well, what can you do well?"

"I'm a jack of all trades really. I can do just about anything."

"Good. Then I'm offering work."

"I'm obliged, and I'll take it gratefully."

"Getting from here to Virginia City might be a little chancy," Michael inserted.

"Seems worth it. To tell you both the truth, I haven't eaten for two days. If I'm going to die I guess it's better to do it on a full stomach."

"Then I guess your pay begins now. Let's have breakfast."

Zeb ordered his meal, and while they ate, they made plans to leave.

"If you could see to advance me some of my pay," Zeb said, "a set of clean clothes, a bath, and a shave would put me in better traveling condition."

"I agree," Michael chuckled. "Those clothes look like they're about to fall off."

"How's your first month's pay sound," Patrick said as he reached into his pocket for the money.

"You're pretty trusting. I could just take the money and leave."

"You could," Patrick eyed him levelly. "But you won't."

"You're so sure of me?"

"Maybe not, but I'm sure of Michael. If you're a friend of his,

I'm reasonably sure you can be trusted to turn me a good day's work and that you pretty much keep your word."

"I'll be ready to go when you are."

"I'll let you know our plans as soon as we get them made. I'd like it if nobody knew anything about this at all."

"Don't worry, no one will get word from me." Zeb turned to Michael and extended his hand. "Thanks. I'll repay this debt someday."

"You'll probably pay sooner than you think. This is not going to be an easy trip. Enjoy your bath."

Zeb chuckled. "I will. Thanks." He turned and left.

"Now," Michael smiled, "if we're as lucky in finding a way to get your money out of the hotel safe without word being spread, we might just stand a chance of getting to Virginia City in one piece."

"We'll think of a way," Patrick said quietly. "We have to."

Chapter Five

Michael finished his breakfast and left Patrick in the restaurant with his coffee. He walked slowly down the wood-planked sidewalk until he was just opposite the hotel. He stood leaning against a rough wood post that held up the roof of the emporium, and watched the hotel. There had to be a way to get that money from the safe so that word wouldn't spread.

He didn't expect to get much of a head start, but a few hours might mean the difference between making it work or not.

He knew the odds against them stood at three, possibly four, and if they pulled a surprise attack, which they most likely would, it put all the odds on their side. But they were still too vulnerable to suit him. He knew Zeb could handle a gun, but Patrick didn't seem too well acquainted with them.

His curiosity about Patrick grew. There was a huge blank, and it interested him.

The clerk in question caught Michael's attention as he crossed the street toward the hotel. He was a small man who walked with a clipped stride as if at one time or the other he had been in the military.

Michael had sniffed around a good deal since he'd been here, and he knew a lot about the clerk. The most important thing he'd found out was that he was a petty-minded little man who could be bought—no, *had been bought.*

Michael was exactly the kind of man to raise all the anger this kind of man held within him. It was as if Michael embodied all the things he would like to be and never could be.

Michael was pretty certain he would take a perverse kind of pleasure in watching him fight it out on the street against odds too great to beat.

There was no help to be had from this man. No, he had to find a way around him. Well, sitting in the comfortable seats in the hotel lobby might just get him some answers.

He crossed the street and entered the hotel just in time to witness a scene that made him smile to himself. He felt he was just in time to find his answers.

The young man behind the desk was obviously the one who had duty from late at night until early morning.

He would have thought little more of it, had he not walked into the center of an altercation. He could tell from the younger man's stance, and the look in his eyes, that he was annoyed and embarrassed. He was being taken to task for a minor rule infraction that should have been laughed away, and he could only mumble, "Yes, sir . . . yes, sir," to the lecture given by the smaller man who was obviously his boss.

Finally, chastised to the other man's satisfaction, the young man left and the small man took his place behind the desk. Michael smiled to himself. He'd found exactly what he wanted.

So it would not be too obvious that he was following the young clerk, Michael sat in the lobby for a while, reading a day-old newspaper.

When he was certain enough time had lapsed, he rose, lay the paper aside, and walked out of the lobby. He stood on the sidewalk for a minute, then went to find Patrick. Maybe he would have some information about the younger man. At the moment Michael didn't even know his name.

It took him a half hour to track Patrick down. He finally found him in the local mercantile store, buying some small articles. Michael drew Patrick aside as soon as his transaction was completed.

"Looks to me like you've found some answers to our dilemma," Patrick smiled.

"Maybe."

"So, what is it?"

"When I left the hotel this morning, there was a different man behind the desk."

"Yes, the night clerk. Jim Baxter. Nice kid."

"Yes, a nice kid. But I don't think he likes his boss too much."

"Oh?"

"I walked into a little set-to between them. I think our gossiping clerk is a bully."

"I take it that's good for us."

"Might just be. What time does he come on duty?"

"Oh . . . about eleven, I guess."

"Do you know where he lives?"

"At the edge of town in that white clapboard house. Has a wife, I think, and a little boy."

"Better and better. Patrick, I need some money."

"How much?"

"I won't know that until I talk to our young clerk. And I'll get the money after that talk."

"What are you up to, Michael?"

"I can tell you better once I've talked to him."

"All right, whatever you say. What do you want us to do now?"

Michael's grin was wicked. "You have two choices. You can go back to the hotel and take a nap or, you can go take our little banty rooster friend to lunch."

"Some choice. Considering my stomach, I'll take the nap."

"I figured you'd take that choice," Michael laughed. "Get some rest, Patrick. You're going to need it. As soon as I start things rolling, God knows when you're going to get any. We're going to be doing some heavy riding. I'll knock on your door when I'm ready to move."

"All right. Good luck . . . whatever your plans are."

"With any luck, tomorrow's daylight will find us a long way away from here. For now, I'm going visiting. See you later."

Patrick watched Michael walk away and was grateful again that he'd decided to approach him.

Michael took his time, as if he were just strolling around. He had no intention of using his horse since he didn't want to attract the wrong attention. On foot, no one would suspect he'd go far, or that he was doing anything more than looking around.

Slowly he made his way toward the white clapboard house. He kept a close watch to make sure no one was following him. His ruse had worked. They would stay close to the stables. With luck, they would be on their way long before word got out that they were gone.

He stopped in front of the small cottage, and for a minute he just stood looking at it. Before he could open the gate and go up the walk, the front door opened and a woman and a child of about five came out on the porch.

She was tying her bonnet and the child was impatiently waiting. They started down the front-porch steps before they saw him standing there.

"Good morning." He removed his hat and smiled. He didn't want them unduly alarmed.

"Can I help you?" Her voice was mellow and pleasant.

"Yes, ma'am. I'd like to speak to your husband if I may."

"He's just gotten home from work and he's rather tired. If you could come back later in the day perhaps."

It was obvious the young clerk had not come home in the best of moods and his wife was protecting him from any further annoyances.

"I'm sorry but it's really important that I talk to him now. I'm sure you will find it will be a mutually beneficial conversation." The woman was regarding him closely, but the child stared at his gun with a rapt expression. Then he looked up at Michael with a combination of curiosity and awe on his face.

"All right," the woman replied. "If you'll come in, please."

He followed her across the porch and into the house. It was immaculately kept, but even his inexperienced eye told him they had very little of substance.

"Wait here," she instructed, then went into a closed room. "Please, sit down," she said a few minutes later. "Jim will be with you shortly. If you'll excuse us, please, I have errands to run."

Michael nodded with a smile, but the child resisted.

"Ma, do we have to leave now? I want to ask . . ."

"You'll ask nothing, young man," she said firmly. "Come along."

Reluctantly the child left with his mother. Before Michael could sit down, the bedroom door opened and the young clerk came out.

"Jim Baxter?"

"Yes. I'm sorry . . . but do I know you?"

"No, you don't know me." Michael extended his hand. "My name is Michael Cord, and I have need of your help."

Jim took his hand in a firm grip. "Now I know. You were at the hotel this morning."

"Yes. That's part of what I want to talk to you about. I don't mean to be presumptuous, but please bear with me a while and I can explain."

"Go on."

"I'm afraid I overheard your little . . . ah . . . *argument* with Mr. Dunhill."

"One of many, I'm afraid. He's . . . he's a pompous ass."

"Why do you take it? Why don't you quit?"

"Mr. Cord, I have a wife and child to support. If I had alternatives I'd be on the stage tomorrow and back to Philadelphia, where my family and my wife's family lives. I made the mistake of thinking I could strike it rich out here. Well, I soon found out I'm not cut out to be a miner. So . . . it's take what you can get."

"Maybe . . . maybe not."

"I don't understand."

"I have a little proposition for you that might just get you on that stage and put a little money in your pocket as well."

"Maybe you'd better sit down and explain this to me. It sounds too good to be true."

"First let me ask what *does* the ticket to get home cost?"

"Probably cost at least a hundred apiece."

"Then six hundred ought to see you safely home."

"Lord, yes, with some to spare. I could go back to work in my father's bank. I . . . ." He looked at Michael suspiciously. "Just what is it I have to do?"

"You sit down," Michael chuckled. "We have a lot to talk about."

*   *   *

Michael left the Baxter house and went back to the hotel. As he passed the front desk he said a cheerful hello to Mr. Dunhill, who followed him up the steps with narrowed eyes. He was supposed to report to the men who paid him any attempt on the part of Patrick Carrigan or his friend to take the packet of money from the safe. He would get a nice reward if he did. But, so far, neither had many any effort to touch the money or to leave.

But they would, he thought greedily. They would. And they had no alternative but to go through him to get the money. He could be patient and wait.

It was nearing noon when Michael entered his room. He was quite pleased with himself. Let the watchers spend the afternoon watching . . . he was going to rest and get ready for the night, when they would be tired and not as alert as usual.

He removed his boots, hung his holster over the bedpost where it would be close, lay down on the bed, and closed his eyes.

Patrick was completely in the dark about what Michael planned to do, but since he had been so unsuccessful in finding a way out of his dilemma, he was quite prepared to follow his lead.

Michael knocked on Patrick's door around six and they crossed the street to the restaurant, where they enjoyed a long, leisurely supper and a couple of glasses of whiskey. Michael was certain that the men watching them must be getting very frustrated, and he was delighted.

"Now what?" Patrick asked.

"Now let's see if there's a little entertainment in this town."

"Entertainment?" Patrick said blankly.

"Sure . . . A good poker game maybe. I don't expect you have too much money on you at the moment."

"No. I . . . Michael, what in heaven's name are you talking about?"

"About the need for you to go to the hotel, get Mr. Greedy to give you six hundred dollars of your money . . . and casually drop the word that you'll be leaving in a couple of days."

"Six hundred dollars!"

"It's worth it to be able to get the rest while everyone else is off guard."

"And who are we playing poker with?"

"Oh, I think Zeb, you, and me are enough."

"I hope you understand all this, because I sure don't."

"You will, in time. Just trust me for a while. We're going to end up with about six hours head start, and in the meantime we're going to give a couple of people a new start on life. All we have to do is play it out . . . and hope to hell it works."

Patrick did as Michael requested, and both he and Zeb watched from inside the saloon. Minutes after Patrick's request for money and his innocent remark that he would be leaving in two days, a young boy dashed from the hotel . . . and there the clerk stood in the hotel doorway, a satisfied look on his face!

"Well, they've got the message. They've taken the bait. If there's no problem we'll meet around two behind the hotel. We'll go down the back stairs and be damn careful. Let's play poker for a couple of hours now. Then we can go back to the hotel."

"I don't know if I want to play poker with you," Patrick said grimly.

Michael chuckled, then bent closer to him and began to explain exactly what he had planned.

Around midnight they headed back to the hotel. For all intents and purposes they were on their way to bed.

Ten minutes after they entered their rooms, they extinguished their lights . . . and those watching them relaxed. There would be no problem tonight.

Michael had an inordinately good judgment of time. He had spent too many long, lonely hours not to be able to judge every second, minute, and hour that passed.

He rose from his bed a few minutes before two o'clock. He had never undressed, so he simply drew on his boots, buckled his gunbelt, and picked up his jacket, hat, and saddlebags.

He went to his door and cracked it open to look up and down the dimly lit hall. No one was in sight and the entire hotel was still. He left his room and closed the door quietly. He moved down the hall carefully, testing each step before he put his full weight on it.

When he reached Patrick's door he rapped as softly as he could. The door was opened so quickly that he knew Patrick had been waiting for him on the other side.

"Go down the back stairs. Zeb should be waiting. I'm going to get the money. I'll be out in about five minutes."

Patrick nodded. "Be careful," he warned Michael, then moved away on silent feet.

Michael made his way to the top of the steps and looked down. Satisfied that the lobby was empty, he continued down.

Jim Baxter was prepared. He'd already gotten the packet of money from the safe. Silently he handed it to Michael, who, in return, handed him six hundred dollars.

"You don't need to lie," Michael grinned. "All you need to do is not mention this until you're asked directly, which should be sometime late tomorrow. By that time we'll be out of reach, and you and your family can go home in peace."

"I'm grateful."

"No more than we are. Good-bye, Jim, and good luck in Philadelphia."

"Thanks." Jim watched Michael leave. Then he relaxed. He would never have to listen to Mr. Dunhill's derogatory remarks again. He would get his family away quickly. His wife, Tammy, was already packing. Home, he thought pleasantly. Home . . . and with money to spare. Wherever Michael Cord and his friends were going he wished them all the luck in the world.

Patrick, Zeb, and Michael were many miles away by the next afternoon when Mr. Dunhill opened the safe and discovered the money gone. He sent for Jim at once, who calmly told him that Patrick had taken his own money the night before and left, and, in addition, that he was quitting and going home.

Mr. Dunhill began to sweat. The men who'd asked him to tell them when Patrick left were not tolerant at all. In fact they were brutal . . . and he was in debt. Gambling . . . He began to tremble with fear and was in a bad state when he saw the stage leave with Jim and his family. There was no doubt that it was too late to follow Patrick . . . the start was too long. He was frightened, and the temptation to leave town himself was the only answer. Before he could be questioned he planned on doing just that.

Michael, Patrick, and Zeb rode straight through the noon hour and camped only when the sun went down and they were so tired they couldn't ride any farther. But they knew they were safe. Michael had ridden up a large hill from where he could see for miles. There was no sign of anyone following. He rode back to Zeb and Patrick with a broad smile.

"No sign of them. We're safe. There's no way they can catch up with us now."

"Thank God," Patrick said. "Michael, I'm grateful and to you, Zeb."

Michael simply nodded. "We'd better make camp. I'm so hungry I could eat my horse, . . . and we'd better roll in our blankets and sleep because we have to be on our way before dawn again. Just to make certain," he added when he saw the questions in their eyes. Neither of them said any more, but they did as Michael instructed. Before dawn the next day they were well on their way again.

They arrived in Virginia City, weary, dirty, and hungry. Six days of hard travel had taken its toll. They dismounted in front of the livery stable and saw to the care of their horses.

"I think we ought to get something to eat before I drop," Zeb said.

"Not till I get a bath and a shave," Michael replied. "I can't stand myself. I smell like a horse."

Patrick chuckled. "I'll take you both to my house and you can have a hot bath. Then, after I get mine, we'll see what we can do about food."

"Lead on," Michael said.

Patrick started down the street, and Michael and Zeb fell into step beside him.

Michael's face suddenly drew into a thoughtful frown. "Not that I'm against religion, Patrick . . . but you aren't planning on praying before we get cleaned up and fed, are you?"

"Praying?" Patrick's face was touched with amusement.

"Appears to me we're headed for the church."

"I am."

"Patrick . . ."

"I know. You're not against religion," Patrick chuckled, "and I'm sure glad you're not. I live right next to the church."

Michael stopped and Patrick followed suit to look at the surprised expressions on Zeb and Michael's faces.

"You guessed right. It's *Reverend* Patrick Carrigan. I'm the preacher hereabouts."

"Well, Ah'll be damned," Zeb said.

"Yeah," Michael grinned. "I guess I will, too. You in the mood to explain why you never told me this at the start?"

"I wasn't sure if you'd refuse if you knew. The money I'm carrying is for an addition to the church."

"Why would I refuse because of that?"

"Maybe because you wouldn't think it was important enough to change your plans. I had to offer you a way out of your . . . ah . . . situation. That was more of a cause. At least, until I knew you better, that was my feeling."

"Now you think different?"

"Yes," Patrick smiled, "now I think different."

"Ah'll just be damned," Zeb laughed. "Me responsible for helpin' build a church. Think it'll help me when the time comes, Preacher?"

"I wouldn't be a bit surprised," Patrick's laughter mixed with Zeb's, but his eyes never left Michael. "I wouldn't be surprised if it was very beneficial for the both of you."

Michael nodded and they continued on to Patrick's house, which turned out to be a two-story frame house. Neat and comfortable. Michael was the first to claim the cast-iron tub of hot water and soap, while Patrick and Zeb shared a drink of good Kentucky whiskey.

When all three had washed off the dust of the road and were fortified with a drink or two, they started out for the much-needed food.

It was close to twilight, and the boisterous night life of Virginia City was beginning. As they moved slowly down the wood plank sidewalk, Patrick spoke occasionally to one person or another. It soon became obvious that Patrick was more than well liked in the town and that his return was enthusiastically welcomed.

Patrick paused for a moment, and Michael's eyes followed his gaze. A tall young man was crossing the street. For some reason Michael began to sense that this was not just another passerby.

"Someone you know, Patrick?" he questioned quietly.

"Yes . . . yes, I know him . . . very well. I have a feeling you're going to know him pretty well, too."

"Oh?"

The next words were such a shock to Zeb that he made an audible sound as he swung around to look from Michael to Patrick.

"He's the man who's going to kill you."

"I see," Michael replied calmly. The words and Michael's reaction were a bit too much for Zeb to take calmly.

"Now just a gol-danged minute here," he sputtered in confusion. "What's going on? What reason would that stranger have to go gunning at Michael? Why, they don't even know each other."

"Well, let's go and get some food, something to drink, and we'll tell you a nice long story."

"Yeah. I think somebody had better. I ain't never heard a man talk about his dying so easy."

"Maybe it's not like you think," Michael chuckled. "Come on. This might just be the most interesting story you've ever heard in your life."

Micahel clapped his hand against Zeb's back and the three of them walked into the restaurant.

Patrick laughed and shook his head. "Three pieces of pie, Michael! I'm beginning to think you're a bottomless pit. I don't recall ever seeing a man eat as . . . hearty as you do."

Michael smiled, but it was a smile without humor. "I guess maybe it goes back to those days during the war in that prison camp. Sometimes you could go for days with just a crust of bread and some thin soup. I don't think my stomach has ever been full since then."

"I'm sorry."

"It's past. But it's just that . . . well, hunger is a thing you find hard to forget."

"Eat up. What is it they say about a condemned man?"

"Come on, you two," Zeb protested. "Now that we're scrubbed as clean as a newborn babe and stuffed with food, I have a story I need to hear."

"Fair enough," Michael agreed. "Why don't we just go over to the saloon?" He looked at Patrick. "I think there's someone you want to introduce me to."

"There is," Patrick nodded.

"This has gone far enough. I'm getting impatient."

"Then let's go," Patrick roared heartily. "I wouldn't want your impatience to grow any stronger."

Zeb started to walk with them, then paused.

"What's wrong?" Michael asked.

"Ah . . . you being a preacher," Zeb began as he turned to Patrick. "I mean . . . well, the saloon . . ."

"It's all right, Zeb," Patrick grinned. "A drink or two taken in moderation is not forbidden. Besides," he said innocently, "I find my better sinners there, so I guess that's where my work should take me. Don't you agree?"

"I guess so," Zeb replied . . . but he was far from convinced Patrick wasn't having a little fun at his expense. The twinkle in Michael's blue eyes shook his convictions even more. But he went along.

They found a table in a corner and made themselves comfortable.

As Michael sat down he glanced at the men who stood along the bar. The man Patrick had pointed out crossing the street was one of them. He stood with both elbows on the bar, nursing the drink in his hand as if he wanted to get drunk very, very slowly.

His attention was drawn back to Patrick who was explaining what he knew about Michael . . . and what their plans were.

Zeb whistled softly. "You think it's going to work?"

"I hope so," Patrick said.

"And he's going to go along with it?"

"I hope so," Michael repeated. "A man gets damn tired of being challenged by every smart kid who thinks he's fast enough to kill him and make a name for himself. There comes a time," his voice grew quiet, "when you have to stop it—stop *them* . . . or become one of them."

"You're not one of them, Michael Cord," Patrick said firmly. "If you were, you wouldn't be running. THat kind of man craves bloodletting and I think you've seen enough of that."

"So . . . when do we meet your friend? By the way, maybe you ought to tell me his name and a little bit about him."

"His name's Quinn Wayland. Wandered into town when he was a youngster of six or seven, delirious with fever. Couldn't remember his family or what had happened to him. Got plunked in the orphanage, so he has a few rough edges. He's got a reputation as hard and tough. Me, I think it's more lost and lonely. But he's a good friend . . . and a very bad enemy. That gun he's wearing is not a decoration, but I've only seen him use it once . . . and it was deadly. The whole town has been real rough on the kid."

"Sort of a diamond in the rough, you might say," Michael smiled.

"Sort of."

"How do you know he'll agree to go along with this plan of yours?" Zeb asked. "If he's good with a gun, he might just see if he could beat Michael."

"No, he won't," Patrick said quietly, "but I'm not free to tell you his reasons."

"I didn't ask," Michael replied with the same quietness. "A man's reasons should be his own unless he wants to tell them."

"I think," Patrick replied, "that you and he are alike in a great many ways."

"He has my sympathy if that's true," Micahel chuckled.

"So how do we present this little plan of yours to him?" Zeb questioned.

"I'm about to put that to the test," Patrick said as he set his glass down and slowly stood up, "I'll be right back." Michael and Zeb watched him walk slowly across the room to stand beside Quinn Wayland. "Evening, Quinn."

Quinn turned to look at the man who had intruded on his plans of obliteration by alcohol.

"Reverend. What are you doing here?"

"I'm with my friends. I'd like you to come over and meet them."

"I'm in no mood for people tonight, Rev. Some other time."

Patrick studied Quinn as he took another sip of his drink. He was a handsome man of about twenty-five years. His face was rough cut and shadowed, as if he did not find life very pleasant. He was tall and strongly built, with massive shoulders that tapered to a slim waist, hips, and then to long legs that supported his six-foot-two frame. His eyes were a deep slate gray and his hair was a thick auburn mane that curled against his collar.

"I thought you had this settled in your mind a long time ago, Quinn. You can't solve your problems with a bottle," he grinned. "It didn't work in biblical times and it doesn't work now."

"You preaching to me?"

"Me? Nope. Just practicing for when I do get ready to preach to you. When I do, you won't mistake it for anything else."

Quinn chuckled. Despite his penchant for being a loner, Patrick was the one man in the whole town he really liked.

"Come on, Rev . . ."

"You're going to drink here," Patrick shrugged, "so come over and do it at our table. What's the difference?"

It was so innocently said that even Quinn had to smile. And the smile created a vivid difference in him. It changed Quinn from a hard, cold man to a warm boy . . . but it faded as quickly as it came.

"I don't know. But everything tells me this is a whole lot more than you're saying. Okay, okay," he grinned at Patrick's even more innocent look. "I'll come." He picked up his drink and followed Patrick across the room.

Patrick sat down at the table and Quinn slid into the chair next to Michael. He looked at Michael with a puzzled frown.

"Don't I know you from somewhere?"

"Possible," Michael replied. "Where have you lived?"

"A few small towns on my way back from the war . . . until I found they were all the same as this one. So, here I am again. Born here . . . most likely die here."

"So you fought in the war?"

"Yep."

"Which side?" Michael questioned softly.

"At this stage of the game," Quinn replied just as controlled, "does it really matter anymore?"

"No . . . I suppose it doesn't."

"Michael, this is Quinn Wayland. Quinn, this is Michael Cord. He's a friend of mine. And this," he motioned toward Zeb, "is Zeb Parker."

Quinn started to extend his hand to Michael, paused as the light of recognition touched his eyes, then continued to shake first Michael's hand then Zeb's.

"Michael Cord," he said softly. "Well, well, well. I've heard a great deal about you."

"Don't count on everything you heard being the truth."

"If I did that I wouldn't be able to stand myself. Reputation can get to be a hell of a thing out here, can't it? Only thing I might really believe is that you're fast. Are you?"

"He's fast," Zeb said.

"Yes . . . he's real fast," Patrick added, "and that's the reason I brought you two together. I think you are actually the only man in Virginia City who could challenge Michael Cord and have it believed by anyone."

"Challenge?"

"Well . . . not actually."

"I hope not. I have enough problems of my own."

"Well, I didn't mean not actually, either."

"Just what is it you *do* mean?"

"What he means is . . ." Michael began. Then he paused.

"What I mean is," Patrick smiled a mirthless smile, "that you are the man chosen to . . . to be the one who kills Michael Cord."

This stunned Quinn into momentary silence as he looked from one man's face to the other.

"I don't think this is a joke," he said in an awed voice. "Rev . . . don't play games with me. I'm not going to kill anyone. Not even for you."

"This is no game, Quinn. We have to have a long talk. Michael needs your help . . . desperately."

"Why me?"

"Like I said . . ."

"I know, I know. You think I'm the only man that can do . . . whatever it is you have planned."

"That's right," Michael said. "You are."

Quinn studied Michael closely. Their eyes held for a long time, as if they were reaching into the depths of each other and seeing things no one else understood.

"All right. If I don't do anything else, at least I can listen. Suppose you explain what's going on."

Patrick nodded, folded his arms on the table, bent toward Quinn . . . and began to talk.

Chapter Six

Rena Brenden stood before her mirror, checking her hair and clothes for the tenth time in the past hour. She caught her lower lip in vexation. Would her parents never go to bed!

She had made what she felt was one of her finest performances when she claimed she was tired and meant to go to her room early. She had hoped that her parents would retire by ten, which was their usual way. But they sat in the front room and talked until Rena wanted to scream.

Quinn would think she wasn't coming! That really upset her. It was hard enough to convince him they were not doing anything wrong without making the problem worse by her not showing up.

Finally she heard their footsteps on the stairs. She blew out her candle and raced to her bed, drawing the covers up to her chin. She closed her eyes and in time steadied her breathing.

The door opened and a path of light found its way to her bed. After a few minutes the door closed again and Rena breathed a sigh of relief. No one would disturb her again until late in the morning.

Slowly and quietly she left the bed and picked up the shawl she had carefully lain on a chair near the door. She put it around her shoulders and reached for the doorknob.

When she opened the door it was just a crack, so that she could see down the hall. Her door to her parents' room was safely closed.

One tentative step at a time, she moved down the hall, hoping she would not encounter a squeaky board. At the top of the stairs she felt for the railing, because the area below her was completely dark. She groped her way down the stairs, then across the length of the back hall that led to the kitchen.

Once she was at the back door, urgency took over her caution. She opened the door and stepped out into the night, closing the door quietly behind her. Only then did she lift her skirts and run.

Quinn had never felt happier or more miserable in his life, and the opposing emotions were harder to handle than anything he had ever faced.

Quinn's life had been anything but easy. He couldn't remember anything before he was seven. Those years were a total blank. But the years that followed were easy to remember. They had been one day of misery following another.

He'd always been "that wild, Wayland boy," always been poor, and always been looked down on by the "better" citizens of Virginia City. Always "that boy from the orphanage."

He'd acquired an air of nonchalant arrogance to mask the bitterness and the pain of rejection, and he'd learned to use his gun well . . . very well, and that only served to annoy the townspeople even more.

Life in the orphanage had taught him to use his fists and his wits. Nothing special had ever existed in his life . . . until Rena.

Lord, he could remember every minute, every second, he'd spent with her, and the day that he met her was engraved in his heart.

As children their paths had never crossed very often. Rena was from a proper, well-to-do family and the side of town in which the orphanage was located was the wrong side. But it was Quinn's side. They went to the same one-room school until the eighth grade. Then Quinn quit and Rena hadn't seen much of him . . . but she'd heard a great deal.

Rena had been sent away to finishing school when she was fifteen. While Quinn made his reputation as a hard drinker, a hard fighter, and a problem ... still, few of the swiftly spread stories were true and the ones that were, were grossly exaggerated. But Quinn already hated the people of Virginia City too much to battle with them. He just let them talk. Being magnetically handsome didn't help matters much because "proper" girls cast their eyes longingly in his direction as often as the "improper" ones did. With some exceptions, he returned a few.

He expected life would go on its miserable path the same, day in and day out, until he acquired enough money to try to make a new future for himself. But jobs, were not easy for him to come by, either, so he generally had only enough money to exist on.

Then Rena came back from school and walked into his life like a dream.

It was a usual day. He'd been drunk the night before and had slept late. When he did get up the small cabin he'd built some distance from town was less than inviting and there was nothing to eat.

He'd gotten up in a miserable mood and it didn't lighten when he faced his hunger and the fact that he didn't have a dime in his pocket.

He washed and dressed and went out, to saddle his horse. Maybe if he rode into town he could scare up enough work to feed himself, he thought. His situation frightened him. He was distintegrating slowly and he couldn't seem to find a way—or a reason—to stop his downhill slide.

The road into town led past a stand of trees, on the other side of which was a meadow. Quinn had often hobbled the two horses he owned to graze there, since it adjoined his cabin. Now, as he rode by, he heard what sounded to him like someone singing.

He paused, then, unsure of his reason, he rode slowly off the road and into the trees. As he moved through them the sound grew more defined. It *was* someone singing. He stopped his horse just inside the shadows of the trees and looked out over the meadow.

Rena had been out riding, and had stopped when she reached the meadow, entranced by its beauty. Dismounting, she led her horse behind her until she stood in the center of the flower-strewn meadow.

The day was balmy and Rena had never felt better. There was

no doubt that she was completely happy and the discovery of this exceptionally beautiful place only lifted her mood higher.

In the center of the meadow a huge gray rock protruded from the ground. She tied her horse, gathered arms full of wild flowers, and climbed on the rock to enjoy a peaceful hour.

She began to hum to herself as she bound the flowers in a bouquet. Then softly she began to sing.

Quinn sat and watched her for a long time. In his entire life he didn't believe he'd ever seen anything or anyone so beautiful. Beauty was rare in his life, and for the short time that he could hold it, he intended to.

Mesmerized, he sat and watched her. She was delicate, like the flowers she touched. Her hair reminded him of a field of new wheat and seemed to gather the sunlight in its brilliant strands. He would have given anything to have seen the color of her eyes.

Suddenly he became aware of himself, and for the first time the pain pierced his shields.

What frightened his horse he never would know. Perhaps a small snake, or squirrel—or *something*. Whatever it was, his horse skittered sideways, rose on his hind legs, and dropped in a nervous little dance, taking Quinn from the shelter of the trees and out into the meadow.

There was no doubt Rena had seen him. She couldn't miss the fractious horse or its rider. She stood up on the rock and watched. It surprised him that she portrayed no sign of fear.

Quinn could only do two things. Ride over and speak to her, or turn and run. Cowardice had never been part of his makeup.

Besides, his mood was not one to tolerate snobbishness. When he stopped beside the rock, he had to look up at her. It really shattered his belligerence when she smiled.

"Hello. I'm sorry if I'm trespassing. It was just so beautiful here, I decided to stop a while."

He reached into his tangled thoughts for the right thing to say and came up with: "It's not my meadow." His voice sounded chilled and ugly even to him.

"I know you, don't I?"

"I doubt it."

"Of course I do. You're Quinn Wayland."

Here it comes, he thought. The superior look, the cold "I'm

better than you" look. He stiffened in preparation. But it didn't come.

"I'm Rena Brenden. You remember me, don't you? We went to Miss Tucker's school. I was two years behind you, but you . . ."

"I quit. Wasn't much use in me going. Besides, I had to work. Something I don't think you'd understand."

Rena was silent for a minute, then she held his eyes with hers and spoke softly. "Why are you angry at me, Quinn Wayland? Or are you just angry at everybody, even yourself?"

He was momentarily silent, unsure of why he'd felt the need to strike out at her. She was the only person in years that had in any way threatened his vulnerability.

Before he could respond again, Rena climbed down from the rock and walked over to stand beside him. Her eyes were the color of spring leaves. It jolted him again.

"I've got some food in my saddlebags," Rena said. "I'd planned on collecting a friend and having a picnic . . . but I wouldn't mind sharing it with you, if you'd care to join me."

"Do I look hungry?"

"Yep," she chuckled. "And I have two male cousins, and they are always hungry."

Her smile was unaffected and open, and to his surprise he found himself dismounting.

"And I'm sure a man your size has an appetite to match."

"Nobody ever warn you about picking up with strangers?" he said in a gruff, warning voice.

"Should I to be afraid of you? You're not exactly a stranger. If I'm not mistaken, you stole the ribbons off my braids in fourth grade."

"Probably." He found himself wanting to smile.

"Then, since we're not strangers, we can eat together," she teased him. "I have fried chicken . . . and a couple of biscuits."

He didn't mean to. If anyone saw them she'd be the one to pay the price . . . yet he found himself helping her spread the blanket.

He hobbled both horses, then sat with her and did more than justice to her supply of food. But it wasn't the food that held him, it was Rena.

He'd built barriers against the rich, but Rena destroyed them with a smile, a soft laugh, and eyes that trusted.

After a while he found himself opening himself to her, telling her of the terrors of a little boy with no past, and his lonely life in an orphanage. She listened with compassion clear in her eyes . . . and he loved her. As abruptly and completely as that. He loved her, and he knew he would never tell her so. She was a woman to be protected, and he'd be the one to protect her . . . even from himself.

They met, first by accident, then at random . . . then purposely. If the rest of his life was a void, when he was with Rena, all the empty corners were filled.

She was all that was bright and good in his world, and as he waited for her now, he vowed over and over again that he would leave her life. He knew her family wanted her to marry a rich man, just as he knew they would be scandalized and angry if they had any idea she was meeting him.

What was worse was the promise he had made to Reverend Carrigan and Michael Cord. He owed Michael Cord nothing, but he owed Patrick a great deal. Patrick was the one who had found him injured and delirious. He was the one who had found shelter for him, even though it was an orphanage.

He was also the only person, outside of Rena, Quinn had ever been able to talk to. Now the promise he'd made and one he intended to keep would cost him Rena. How could she be expected to understand when she had been the one to beg him to put his gun away.

The sensible part of his mind realized that for Rena's sake, it would be better if she left him. But the need deep inside tore him apart. He wanted to hold Rena forever . . . and he knew he couldn't.

Now he waited for her, scared she would come and just as scared she would't. He waited near the woods that bordered the cemetery, the only safe place they could meet, for, although Patrick didn't know their secret yet, Quinn was sure he would not betray them if he did.

The minutes ticked by and his thoughts tormented him. Her

parents had caught her . . . she had run into trouble on the way. It always scared him when she was by herself. The worst thought of all was that she had decided not to come at all. It might just be the last chance he would have to be with her.

The next evening would be the time he and Michael Cord would put on their show.

He paced impatiently . . . and time moved on and on.

Then he saw her. She was running toward him, across the churchyard. He held out his arms and wordlessly gathered her close to him.

He only said her name once against the softness of her hair and clung to her, gathering all the memories of the feel and the scent of her that he would have. Then he kissed her.

He felt the warmth filling him, the sense of belonging that only Rena could give. And she returned his kiss with a passion that made him tremble.

"I was afraid you wouldn't be here," she whispered as he crushed her to him.

"You know better than that. I would have waited all night if I had to." He held her a little away from him so he could see the moonlight reflect in her eyes. "This is what makes my days bearable. I couldn't go."

"Oh, Quinn, I love you so much."

"I know. It's like the light of a candle compared to the forest fire that I feel for you."

"Quinn, we have got to make some plans."

"Plans?" he repeated.

"We can't just continue to meet like this. Is this all you want? Am I just another one of your girls?"

"Now what's that supposed to mean?"

"I . . . I was in town today and . . ."

"And you've been listening to stories."

"No, Quinn, no. You know I don't believe their lies about you. But . . ."

"But?"

"I met Tricia James and she said . . . She was telling another girl that you and her . . . I can't stand to think of you with someone else. I guess I'm just horribly jealous."

"Well, don't be. It's a lie, Rena. I've never spent any time with

Tricia James. I've spoken to her, but she's not you. She swishes past me like she doesn't know me if we meet anywhere anyone can see us together. I guess she thinks telling her friends she's been with an 'outlaw' makes her life more exciting. As far as being jealous . . . Lord girl, there isn't another woman breathing that comes close to you. Now, what 'plans' were you talking about?"

"Us, Quinn. I want to be with you always. We're not wrong, we deserve a life together."

"Well, you're right about one thing. You do deserve better than this."

"I didn't mean it like that! Why do you let this town do that to you? You're as good or better than any man here."

"They'll never let it happen, Rena. You'd better understand it."

"Why? What have you ever really done?"

"What I did was have the bad luck to be from the wrong side of town. our kind and mine don't mix. They won't let it happen. I can't stand hurting you, Rena." He turned from her and inhaled raggedly.

But Rena came up behind him and put her arms around him, resting her cheek against his back. "I'm sorry, Quinn. I know you. I shouldn't have doubted you. It's just that I love you so much that I get scared. I . . . I don't want to lose you."

"Maybe that's what would be best for you in the long run."

"No, don't say that." He heard the tears in her voice and turned, taking her in his arms again.

"Listen, Rena. We have to think about your parents, too. You know how they'll feel. How are we going to get around the fact that they'd be hurt, too?"

She understood that never knowing his parents had caused terrible pain to Quinn. It was a fact that only made her love him more.

"I'm sorry," she said softly.

"For what?"

"For all the times you've been hurt, for all the needs you've never had fulfilled, for all the love you have stored up in you that you're afraid to give."

"Rena . . ." He said her name as a man would say a prayer. He knew their time together was limited. Before the sun set tomorrow he and Michael Cord would have played out their little charade. For all intents and purposes Michael would be dead . . . and so would whatever existed between him and Rena. He would set her free one way or the other. But that was tomorrow. Tonight was all he had left.

Their lips met, fused. In all the times they had met before, Rena had never surrendered to the magic as she did tonight. He could feel it in the way her body molded to his and the way her mouth parted to draw from him the blazing heat that filled him.

Quinn felt as if he would explode, disintegrate into a million fragments of light and color, he was so filled with Rena.

He wanted to celebrate the feeling by making love to her until they were both lost. He wanted to hold the dream, the dream of her lying with him, looking up at him with that shine of trust and laughter in his eyes.

He thought of her beneath him. He would be slow . . . slow and gentle and tender. Awakening her innocent, untutored body with care.

His hands moved down over her hips and he could almost feel the heat of her flesh.

His mind urged him to stop, that he was tormenting himself with a promise of things he could never have.

He realized that he was scared of loving Rena so much that the loss of her would cut his soul to ribbons.

He could bear no more of this exquisite pain. He held her away from him. Both were breathing raggedly. One more minute and his control would have been forever swept away. One more minute he would have carried her to the darkened shadows beneath the trees where the sweet-smelling grass was soft and still warm from the day's sun. The fantasy filled his mind and almost overwhelmed him.

He would have made love to her, and doing so would have destroyed her, because even if she didn't want to see that they could not possibly have a future, he could swear to it.

"Quinn?"

"It's time for me to take you back home."

"No, I don't want to go yet. Quinn, why . . ."

"Before I do," he insisted, ignoring as best he could her words and the look in her eyes. "I want to tell you something."

"Tell me you love me. Whatever else it is that upsets you so much is not important."

"I *do* love you. Maybe more than you'll ever understand. Rena . . . always remember that. No matter what happens, remember that I loved you and that love can't be touched by anything."

"I don't understand," she cried. Her voice broke on her fear. Somehow Quinn was letting go.

"Rena . . . don't make it any harder for me. I don't want to see you hurt and I can't promise to control myself if I hold you one more minute. It's . . . it's important to me for you to understand, to know in your heart that I'd never do anything to hurt you. Even if you hear whispers or stories, remember I do love you."

"You're frightening me. You sound so . . . final. As if you know we will never . . ." She choked back the last words and threw herself into his arms. "You're not going away, Quinn. I won't let you run from the dreadful people in this town. There are many good people here as well. We could have a life together. After a while everyone would see what I have always seen—that you are kind, and decent, and strong. Quinn, please, don't go away! I could not bear it!"

"No, I'm not going away. I . . . I guess I just can't put that much distance between us. But I need to know that you will remember how much I love you."

"How can I forget." She looked up at him, the tears glittering silver in the moonlight. "There is nothing or no one who could do or say anything to make me forget you."

"Ah, Rena," he murmured. The words he wanted to say were like a heavy weight in his chest. *Marry me, Rena,* he wanted to whsiper. *Come with me and stay with me. Let's build a life together that no one can touch.* But he couldn't. The love he had for her was too strong to bring her to his level. He couldn't see delicate, sweet Rena in his rough, cluttered, and not too clean cabin. He couldn't see her without the pretty clothes and jewelry and perfumes she was used to. He wouldn't do that to her.

He kissed her again, so deeply and hungrily that it made her legs weak and her heart begin to pound. She clung to him praying it was a promise. But Quinn, deep in his heart, felt it was a kiss of good-bye.

His head swam and his body burned with the desire for more.

He kissed her until he could hear the soft sound deep in her throat that told him they were both passing beyond barriers. Only then did he release her.

He took her hand and walked to his horse. He had to get her home safely before he did something that would prove he was exactly what the people of Virginia City thought he was.

He mounted first, then kicked his foot out of the stirrup and reached his hand down to her. She knew it was useless to try to change his mind now. They had met and fought this same battle before. Yet, when she looked up at him she had no real idea of how close to the edge he was.

He lifted her effortlessly to set her before him. As always, they would ride the outskirts of town so no one would see them, but eventually the path would lead to Rena's back door.

Once there he would not linger long, only until he saw her in her bedroom window. Then he would ride into the darkness.

Quinn rode slowly, allowing himself to live his dream, knowing it would be all he would ever have. Rena was unattainable, and he had finally faced that fact. Why in God's name couldn't he have wanted one of the girls from Sullivan's Saloon. One of them, he thought miserably, would be more appropriate.

When he arrived home he cared for his horse, then went inside his lonely cabin.

He laid his gun on the table to be oiled carefully . . . and later he would drink enough to forget the length of the days and nights that lay ahead of him.

He carefully prepared the bullet he would use, rendering it almost useless by removing most of the gunpowder. Patrick and his friends would have Michael prepared for the blow it would be . . . but it wouldn't kill.

Patrick would take care of the rest. It should prove a dramatic show for the townspeople. They'd chosen the exact time . . . as the sun was setting. In twilight people could be made to believe whatever they *thought* they were seeing was really there. And the excitement of spreading the news of the death of Michael Cord would keep them from asking too many questions.

Two of Patrick's best friends were the local undertaker and the doctor. Both of them and Patrick would see that the body was rapidly whisked away and that a quick funeral followed. Sheriff Horton, also a friend of Patrick's for many years, completed the maneuver. He would see the crowd dispersed before anyone could tell that the "dead" man was still very much alive.

Quinn wondered if Michael wasn't the lucky one. He could walk away from this. He could start a new life. Quinn couldn't stay, and he couldn't run. He might never be able to have her, but seeing Rena was the only pleasure he couldn't surrender.

He knew his reputation as a gunfighter would be permanent from now on.

"What the hell," he muttered. "It couldn't be any worse than it already is. Besides, it will give them something solid to pin on me for a change."

Once the gun was well oiled and polished, Quinn put it aside. Tomorrow would be time enough for it. He reached for the bottle. For tonight, oblivion was all he could hope for. He tipped the bottle up and drank deeply.

It was in the wee hours of the morning when he finally stumbled to his rumpled bed and gave way to the dreams, dreams in which Rena moved and he had the exquisite pleasure of holding her.

Rena rose early the next morning, and she wasn't sure why. She liked to lie abed and allow thoughts of Quinn to drift in her mind. Today she had a feeling of something portentous. It was like a heavy feeling in the air, and it made her restless.

When she went downstairs for breakfast, she found her father had just left for his office. He was a newspaper man of some stature in Nevada and he worked very hard for the influence and power he wielded. His paper was run honestly and always for the good of the town he loved. He abhorred violence and fought it editorially every chance he had. He worked well with Jacob Marley, the owner of the only other newspaper in town. Together their reach and influence wa a potent force. They had taken many years to make the right connections across the entire state, connections that included many other newspaper owners and other people of consequence.

Her mother, having a last cup of tea, was, to say the least, surprised at Rena's appearance.

"Well, good morning, dear. It's nice to have you share breakfast with me."

Rena smiled as she poured a cup of tea for herself and came to sit across the table from her mother.

There was a sparkle of warmth in Sphie Brenden's blue eyes. Rena knew her mother loved her dearly. She had lost three children before Rena and now Rena was her life.

"Did you sleep well?"

"Yes," Rena answered quickly, suddenly wondering if her mother had somehow found out that she had gone out.

"Rena, I have to discuss something with you."

Oh, dear, Rena thought miserably. *She does know.*

"Is something wrong?"

"No, of course not. I'm afraid I was the recipient of some gossip the other day and I wanted to ask you about it."

"Good heavens, Mother," Rena laughed shakily, "what would I know? I try never to be party to that kind of thing. People who gossip are mean and have no understanding in their hearts." She paused, knowing she had protested too strenuously. "What did you hear?"

"It's about that Wayland boy. He . . ."

"Mother, I wish you and everyone else would stop saying 'that Wayland boy,' as if he were some kind of disease. I knew Quinn in school and he's really a nice person."

"Goodness, Rena, I didn't mean it to sound like that." Her eyes widened in surprise.

Rena gulped back her words. "Well, you haven't told me what you've heard?" she asked with resignation.

"I was chatting with Reverend Carrigan. It seems he's very . . . rigid in his support. He seems to think that . . . I mean, Quinn's reputation is not all people say it is. I asked him why, in heaven's name, the boy didn't get a steady job and put those terrible guns away and stp getting into trouble."

"Maybe you—*we*—just don't understand him. He never had much, if any, family. Maybe he just needs someone to help him."

"You sound as if you know him."

"Not *him* so much—some of the people in town. They might

be scared of Quinn, so they muddy up the waters. Quinn doesn't have a chance, not really.''

"Quinn?"

"I told you." Her eyes evaded her mother's. "I knew him in school."

"Just in school?" Sophie said quietly.

"More rumors, Mother? What are you getting at?"

"I think . . . maybe you know Quinn Wayland better than you say."

Rena paused with her cup halfway to her lips. She wondered why her hand wasn't shaking, for she felt as if her whole body was. Her mother knew. There was no more doubt of that in her mind than about her next breath. She couldn't seem to find words. Their eyes held for a long, silent moment.

"Why have you never said anything?" Rena inquired, her voice subdued.

"I guess . . . maybe I was waiting for my daughter to trust me."

"Does Father . . ."

"No."

"You never told him? Why?"

"Because I felt I had to hear your reasons. I love you very much, Rena, and I think I know you. You are not a deceitful person, nor do you lie."

"Will you listen to me?"

"Of course I will. If you will listen, as well. Your father and I want what is best for you and what makes you happy."

"Maybe they are not the same things."

"It could be a very tragic mistake."

"I truly believe it would not."

"Then . . . tell me."

At first Rena was uncertain, then her courage returned. She was the only one who could convince her parents. She began to talk, became enthused . . . and her mother listened.

"Rena, we must tell your father," she said when Rena had finished. "It is not fair to deceive him. That is the one thing he would find hard to forgive. When he comes home tonight we must tell him."

"He'll forbid me to see Quinn. I know he will!" Rena cried.

"He will if he finds you've been lying to him. If you tell him the truth, he might just listen."

"I'm afraid."

"Of your own father, Rena!"

"Mother . . ."

"Maybe your father will talk to the boy, find out for himself what kind of a man he is. Samuel is not a monster. You cannot go on like this. It can only lead to a very serious mistake, one you both might regret."

"All right. I'll talk to him." Rena stood, nervously clasping her hands before her. Her mother reached out and lay her hand over Rena's.

"Rena . . . don't be afraid."

Rena smiled, but deep inside the fear gnawed at her. Her father was a strong-minded man; a man who had made his own success, who had worked hard, and fought hard for what he had. Rena knew he wanted her to marry, a man of affluence, a strong man who would stand well in the community and carry on his work. Rena wasn't very sure he would view Quinn that way at all.

It was the longest afternoon of her life. She worked, because her anxiety would not allow her to do otherwise. She had to stay busy or lose her mind.

She was approaching nervous exhaustion by the time six o'clock came along, and now it would only be minutes until her father walked through the door.

She insisted on helping with the evening meal and was setting the table when she heard his footsteps on the front porch.

For a minute her heart seemed to skip a beat and she could feel the perspiration on her palms and forehead. The only thing that gave her any courage at all keeping her mind on Quinn. This could be the chance they needed.

She left the dining room and walked to the foyer, where her father was removing his jacket. Her mother was already there.

"Terrible. It was probably the worst thing I have ever been a witness to. I thought this kind of thing was gone from Virginia City. It is an outrage."

"Father, what in heaven's name are you so upset about?"

Samuel turned to look at her and she saw that his face was grim and his lips a firm, and very disapproving, line.

"I've seen something I wish I'd never seen. Something this town should not put up with. No one can or will do anything about it. A fair fight they say. My God! It's uncivilized. Uncivilized! My editorial tomorrow will make my views of this ugly violence clear. We've got to put a stop to this kind of thing . . . and the people who do it!"

"What, Father? What?"

"A gunfight. A man died on the street today. Gunned down by another man, and nothing is going to be done about it."

"Who was killed?" Rena breathed, fearing something she couldn't name.

"A man named Michael Cord, they say. A fast gun, killed by a man who was faster."

"Who . . ." Rena began hoarsely, then had to lick her dry lips and begin again. "Who killed him?"

"That young renegade . . . Quinn Wayland."

The sound echoed in Rena's mind. Her face grew pale, her lips bloodless. Then she could only hear the faint echo of her mother's cry as Rena fell to the floor in blessed oblivion.

Chapter Seven

Hannah was sure that she had never been so exhausted in her life. They had stopped in so many towns large and small, tracing Michael's movements from the time he had left the train. Three times a man answering Michael's description had been seen . . . or had just left. Joey, Jamie, and the others were awed by Hannah's resistance and her determination. Awe was followed by a deep respect, and if they wanted to find Michael before, they wanted it more now—for Hannah's sake.

They sat around a campfire in companionable silence. The long days and nights hd unified them in a quiet, subtle way. They had become that rare thing . . . good friends.

Hannah had been quiet for some time and the men had exchanged cautious, anxious looks, but none of them wanted to bring up the subject of quitting.

"We'll be riding into Virginia City tomorrow," Jamie began.

"I know you're tired of the saddle, sleeping out, and Joey's lousy cooking. Maybe we ought to stop there and rest for a few days."

"I suppose. It's just so frustrating. It's like being on the trail of a ghost. He's always . . . just gone, or just been seen. Jamie, do you think we'll ever—"

"Yes, ma'am," Jamie interrupted firmly. "This is a real big place and that's the God's truth, but as far as towns and cities, it's kind of sparse. If we have to comb every one of them, we'll find him."

"Bless you all. You've been so generous with me. I know I'm not the fastest or strongest traveler."

"Hannah," Joey said, "I speak for all of us. We kind of thought you might give out a long way back. But you stuck in there. Kind of gives us a real idea about how you feel about Michael. You don't give up easy, I'll say that. You can count on us. We won't give up as long as you say Go."

Hannah swallowed the lump in her throat, smiled a misty smile, and reached out to place her hand over Joey's. "Thank you, Joey. I needed that reassurance. I'll keep going. I have to. I . . ."

"Yeah," Joey said quietly as he patted her hand. "I know."

"Maybe we all better get some sleep," Brad suggested.

Everyone agreed with that, and they unrolled their bedrolls. An hour later the men slept, but Hannah lay awake for a long time, looking up at a miraculous, star-studded sky. It was so clear and brilliant that she felt she could reach up and touch them.

"I wish you were here, Michael. I wish I could touch you, let you know. Oh, Michael, where are you?"

She was frightened, frightened that she wouldn't find him before something drastic had happened. She knew his gun drew challengers. She also knew that luck couldn't be his forever.

Suddenly she felt it, a sharp, heavy pain in her chest that made her jerk erect and press her hand to her suddenly pounding heart. A breathless feeling of utter desolation swept over her for a moment and she inhaled sharply. Then it was gone.

Slowly she lay back down, completely shaken. It was a long while before she slept.

Asleep at last, Hannah was still up first, and preparing coffee and breakfast. She smiled at Joey, who, caught by the scent of bacon, moved quickly to the fire.

" 'Morning. Want some coffee?"

"Sounds good to me," he grinned.

She handed him a tin cup of steaming coffee and he cupped his hands around it and sipped gratefully.

The others, brought awake by their growing stomachs, gathered. It didn't take the five long to eat and prepare to travel.

"How long until we reach Virginia City?" Hannah asked the question in general.

"Close to three . . . maybe four hours ride," Mac answered.

"Should be there near noon," Joey added.

"Might be nice to sleep in a soft bed for at least one night," Jamie chuckled, then became aware of Joey's dark scowl. He realized then that he'd implied Michael would not be found and they would only have one night to spend there. Hannah pretended to ignore the comment.

"Come. Let's get going," she said. She got to her feet and poured the rest of the coffee on the fire.

Minutes later they were riding away.

Sitting on a rise of land just above town, Hannah and her friends were silent. There wasn't one man who could not read Hannah's thoughts and didn't know she was praying.

"We might as well ride in," she said softly. "It doesn't do much good to just sit here thinking about it." She nudged her horse into motion and the others followed.

They rode slowly down the main street of town, aware that the atmosphere was strangely subdued.

"I seen the same kind of look during the war. Kind of shocked like," Joey said quietly. "Maybe someone real important died, like a mayor or something."

"Yeah," Jamie said. "Maybe we better stop and ask somebody."

They stopped in front of the Settlers Hotel, tied their horses, and went inside.

The clerk behind the desk looked up blankly at them.

"Not many visitors lately?" Joey inquired.

"Sir?"

"You seem kind of surprised to see someone coming in for a room."

"Oh, no, sir," the clerk smiled. "You're a stranger, so I don't suppose you've heard. I sort of expected a lot of folks to be out to the cemetery."

"I figured," Joey said. "Somebody important around here die?"

"Oh, it ain't like that. You see we had . . . sort of an event, you might say. A man . . . a friend of the Reverend's down to the church, got himself shot last night. Regular gunfight. I ain't never seen nothing like it in my life. The Reverend, he wouldn't let people get near him after it was over. Real upset he was. Him and the doctor they hauled him away. They're giving him a real nice funeral, too. Up there burying him right now." He stopped talking when he realized the men had become grimly quiet and the woman's face had gone so pale her green eyes seemed enormous.

"A gunfight. . . ." She breathed the words as if they were painful. "Who . . . who were the men involved?"

"One of our local boys. Bad kin. Been wild all his life. He's always one to find trouble. Fast, though. Boy was he fast. I wouldn't want to . . ."

"Please!" Hannah wanted to scream at him, but she controlled the urge. "Who was it? Who did he kill?"

"Some drifter. I'm not sure. He came into town with Reverend Carrigan, so I suppose they were friends. But he was a gunfighter. You could tell just by looking at him."

"You don't know his name." Hannah struggled for patience. "Do you know what he looked like?"

"Sure. Tall fella, black hair, bluest eyes you ever seen . . . except he wore a patch over one and he limped like maybe he . . . Miss?"

Hannah had released a kind of ragged moan and grasped the desk as if she were about to collapse. Joey and Jamie were quickly beside her to support her.

"Is she all right?" the clerk questioned.

"Get her a room!" Joey commanded. "And give me a key."

"Oh . . . sure, room twenty-seven. Here."

Joey grasped the key and they guided Hannah to the stairs.

Inside the room Hannah sagged to the bed as though she had no strength left. But she did not cry.

"Hannah . . ." Joe was unsure of any way to comfort her.

"You . . . you want us to go and . . ." Jamie began.

"No," Hannah said softly, "I'll go. I must see for myself. I won't believe it until I see for myself."

"You can't . . ."

"I can! I will!" She rose to her feet. None of the men tried to stop her. They could feel the old remembered pain of someone loved and lost. They followed.

At the bottom of the stairs Joey paused. Then he walked to the clerk. "Where's the funeral?"

"Out east, just beyond town, up on the hill."

"Thanks."

"Mister?"

"Yeah?"

"Was he . . . a friend?"

"Yes."

"I'm sorry."

"So am I," Joey said miserably. "So am I."

He rejoined the others, and in silence they went to their horses. None of them spoke as they rode. They would have given anything to wipe the misery from Hannah's eyes. All any of them could think was that they were one day too late . . . one day.

Patrick stood at the head of the closed coffin and recited the burial prayers. He was pleased that things had worked so well. All the people present were friends of his who had come because he had claimed Michael a friend.

He knew Michael was actually safely entrenched in a cabin a few miles from town that Patrick had built when he'd first come to Virginia City. Beneath him was a casket full of stones.

He'd given Michael a new lease on life, yet he knew the bitterness of what had been left behind him. He'd cautioned him to be careful, telling him that one day he would find a way for him to get word to his family. Right now he wasn't sure how he'd do that.

He'd been the one to have the rough headstone carved, and the name Michael Cord was clear for anyone who passed by to read.

Patrick was just about to finish the prayers when he saw five riders in the distance. When they stopped, dismounted, and walked toward him, some of his self-confidence slipped. He didn't know why exactly except for the girl's pale face, but he was certain these riders meant a problem.

They stood silently at the back of the crowd until he finished, then remained as the people began to drift away.

As they parted before her, Hannah could see the mounded grave and the stone above it. If it was at all possible, Patrick thought her face became even whiter. One of the men with her took her arm and they walked to the side of the grave.

Patrick stood and watched them for several minutes in silence, then he spoke gently.

"Can I be of help?"

Hannah raised her eyes to his, and it was a painful sight. He had not seen so much anguish in one so young before.

"You . . . you were his friend?" Hannah questioned.

"For a short while, yes. Did you know him?"

"Know him," Hannah repeated softly. She fell to her knees and rested her hand on the freshly mounded dirt. "I loved him."

Michael had told Patrick nothing about Hannah or the possibility of the presence of the group that faced him now. For a moment he was caught off balance . . . in fact, he was totally shocked. Hannah looked up at him again. "Can you tell me . . ."

"Do you think . . ."

"Yes," she said quickly. "I have to know."

"My dear, why don't you come home with me. This is no place to talk."

Jamie and Joey nodded and helped Hannah to her feet. Patrick's mind was churning as he walked to his carriage. He wasn't sure what to say.

They followed him back to his home, next to the church. He tried to make them comfortable, but he could feel the tension in the air.

He sat down close to Hannah and reached to take her hand in his. "What's your name, my dear?"

"Hannah . . . Hannah Marshall." Hannah quickly introduced the others who acknowledged Patrick with silence. They needed answers and they were patient . . . and protective of her.

"Well, Hannah, do you want to talk?"

"Yes." She looked at him hopefully. "You knew him. It's been so long. He wasn't a . . . a gunfighter! Michael was a gentle, kind man. He shouldn't have died like that," she sobbed.

"I'm sorry, child. I don't suppose that there is a reason or any kind of logic for this sort of thing. Violence is just . . . just an eruption.''

"But Michael was not a violent man. he *ran* from violence. That was why he was here.''

"Sometimes,'' Patrick said quietly, "violence just follows one.''

"Who killed him?''

"It wasn't murder,'' Patrick said quickly.

"Wasn't it?''

"Not by the standards out here. It was a fair gunfight. The sheriff has no reason to hold the man who shot him. He did nothing that was not . . . legal, even if it was deadly.''

Joey spoke for the first time. "If it was a fair gunfight, I'd like to meet the man who could draw faster than Michael Cord.''

"Maybe it really wasn't so *fair,*" Jamie said grimly.

"The man who . . . fought Michael wouldn't have fought any other way.''

"You sound like he was more your friend than Michael was,'' Brad said.

"No,'' Patrick replied. "But he's not all bad. And . . . Michael *was* my friend. That's why you found me where I was today. I was the only one here who could see that everything was cared for.''

"I'm sorry,'' Hannah said softly. "We didn't mean to take our sorrow out on you. I'm grateful for all you've done. But I must know.''

"His name is Quinn Wayland.''

"I want . . .'' Hannah sighed and buried her face in her hands. "I don't know what I want. I . . . I want Michael, alive and well. I . . .'' the sob tore from her, "want to love him. I just want to love him.'' She shook with the ragged gasps and Patrick knelt beside her, put his arms around her, and worried for the first time that he had made a very bad mistake.

Hannah struggled for control, and finally she moved from Patrick's embrace.

"I'm sorry. I didn't mean . . .''

"You have every right to cry,'' Joey said. "Reverend, you don't have any idea how she's tried to find Michael before something like this could happen.''

"I truly wish you had,'' Patrick said honestly. There was nothing he could do unless he talked to Michael first. He wondered if

Hannah Marshall was Michael's answer. Again he pondered the fact that he'd never mentioned her.

"What more can I say?" Patrick added. "If I could undo what has been done I would gladly do it."

Hannah managed a wavering smile. "I'm sure you would, Reverend. I think I'll go back to the hotel."

"Please . . ." Patrick insisted. "Won't you stay to share dinner with me tonight? I would like to hear more about . . . our friend."

"Why don't you, Hannah," Mac said quickly. "Me and the boys will go back to the hotel and get all our things settled."

"No, please," Patrick said, "I want you all to be my guests. Are you planning on going back home tomorrow?"

"It would probably be best," Brad said.

"Hannah, you ought to sell your horse here and take the train home," Joey added.

"Yeah, Hannah. We can pick up the rest of your belongings in San Francisco and send them along."

"That might be a good idea," Patrick agreed, even though he would much rather have taken Hannah to Michael. He could hardly stand the grief in her eyes.

"No. I'm not going home just yet. I . . . I want to stay here with him for a while."

"Hannah . . ." Patrick began.

"I know he's gone, Reverend Carrigan," Hannah said quietly, "but I just can't go away so soon. You see, Michael has been alone and lonely too long. I just . . . I just want to stay near him for a while. I have a feeling . . ."

"Of course," Patrick said. "And please, call me Patrick."

"Thank you, Patrick. I really am grateful that you have been so . . . considerate."

"I liked Michael . . . What are you going to do now?" He changed the subject, before he said more than he should.

"I'm going back to the cemetery now," Hannah added.

"I'll go with you," Joey said quickly.

"No, you return to the hotel. If we're going to join Patrick for dinner I'm sure you want to wash the trail dust off. I'll be fine."

Patrick could see that the young men were obviously more than reluctant to let her out of their sight. It seemed, whether Michael Cord knew it or not, he had some loyal friends.

"She'll be all right there, gentlemen. She needs a little time alone."

Hannah cast him a quick, grateful smile. Joey, Jamie, Brad, and Mac left, still hesitant and still protective of Hannah.

Hannah turned to Patrick. "How long did you know Michael?" Patrick could see she was anxious for any treasured memory he might be able to give her.

"Let me get you a cup of tea. Then we'll talk before you go the cemetery."

Hannah nodded. Patrick led her to the kitchen. He made the tea without talking. He observed Hannah closely and could see she was extremely tired. When he set the cup before her and found a seat across the table, he had decided to tell her everything he knew about Michael . . . except the truth surrounding his death. He intended to talk to Michael about that.

As they sipped their tea Patrick began to tell Hannah how he had met Michael and the experiences they had shared.

"How like Michael," Hannah smiled, "to take the time to do such a thing when he knew . . . Oh, Patrick, how lonely he must have been. And to die like that." Her voice trembled. "I can't bear it."

"You must. From the journey you have made and the difficulties you must have faced, I feel you are a very strong woman. Life is not fair, and we bear what we must."

"I know you are right. But if I had only arrived one day sooner. One day! I might have been able to do something to stop it!"

"Don't do that to yourself. We can't control what God gives us."

"I know," she said resignedly, then set her empty cup down. "If you don't mind, I want to leave now. I'll go back to the hotel after . . . after I leave the cemetery. What time do you want us to come for dinner?"

"I'm afraid I eat early. Around five or so."

"Are you sure we won't be an inconvenience?"

"Most assuredly not."

"Thank you. Then I'll be back later." Hannah rose.

"Hannah, I truly am sorry. You're a young woman. You must pick up the pieces of your life and begin again. I know it's hard, but maybe when you're back with your family it will be easier."

"You're very kind." Hannah turned to leave and Patrick followed her out onto the porch. He stood and watched her go to her horse and mount, then ride away.

Hannah stood by Michael's grave, the grief so heavy she found it difficult to breathe. The tears were hot, and they blurred her vision so that the name on the stone wavered. She sagged to her knees and wept with unrestrained misery.

For a long time she remained so, until the shadows of the nearby trees lengthened. It was nearing sundown. Still, the knot of grief within her had not loosened. She began to wonder if it ever would.

Reluctantly she returned to the hotel, bathed, and changed her clothes. Just as she finished dressing she heard the rap on her door.

The four men stood before her, anxious eyes regarding her. She tried to smile, but it didn't fool any of them.

Though the food was excellent, the dinner was subdued. Patrick repeated the story for the men, of how he and Michael had crossed paths.

"He has a friend here in town, Zeb Parker. He's working for me . . . adding some rooms onto the church. You might want to talk with him. He and Michael rode together for a short while." he didn't go on to tell them that he had made all haste to Zeb to make sure he was prepared. Zeb had been less than happy about the situation.

"Why the hell didn't he warn us?" he wanted to know. "He could have told us so we'd be ready."

"Maybe he had no idea she was coming. Maybe that was the past he was afraid to drag into his life."

"I suppose. But I sure as hell hate to look into her eyes and pretend he's dead. She must be hurting real bad."

"She is. I guess Michael would think it was better to be a little hurt now than a lot of hurt later."

"Maybe. But I don't think it's a *little* hurt, from what you say," Zeb said.

"I meant the hurt of leaving her behind, not this. I just don't believe he has any idea she's anywhere near here."

"Maybe I should go tell him."

"No, I think it best if I tell him. He's coming to my house after midnight, I'll tell him then."

"Fine with me. I don't relish the idea of telling either one of them. I think I'll just lay low and stay out of everyone's way."

"They're going to want to talk to you eventually. It's no secret you were with him when he rode into town."

"I guess so," Zeb replied miserably.

Patrick had left him like that, sure that Zeb would stand firm no matter how much he disliked the situation.

Now he could only soothe Hannah and her friends as best he could and explain everything to Michael when he came that night.

He knew that Michael had to stay put until the men who sought him came and went. If he were spotted anywhere, all the effort to decieve them would have been for nothing.

But he saw the look in Hannah's eyes and he knew Zeb would not only be found, he would be asked a million questions. He hoped Zeb was up to it.

"H-how long do you all plan on staying?"

"I'm not sure, Patrick. I'm too confused and tired to even think of traveling. I suppose we'll be here for a few days."

"Family is a healing thing at a time like this."

"Yes, I know. But it will be so terrible to have to tell Trace and Allison and all the rest of the family, and the people who love him that Michael is . . . gone. He was hut so terribly in the war, and suffered so much. It's just unfair that it should be this way."

"If it's any consolation, Hannah, I know that Quinn regrets what happened, as well. It was just a sudden . . . rather explosive thing. Tempers led to disaster."

"That's funny, too, Patrick, because Michael wasn't like that. He didn't have a hot, uncontrollable temper. He always seemed in control."

"Maybe time and the way he was forced to live changed him."

"I don't want to believe that."

"There are no answers, Hannah."

"I know. But I have to see him, this Quinn Wayland. I have to talk to him."

"What do you expect to find?"

"I don't know."

"I wish you'd reconsider. Maybe after a good night's sleep you'll see that it can't make a difference."

Patrick could see that Hannah's four friends agreed with him. They were anxious now to get Hannah back where she was surrounded by security and love.

It was past eight o'clock before they left, and Patrick dimmed the lights and unlocked the side door. He wanted to be prepared when Michael came. Hannah had insisted on helping clean up the dishes, so Patrick had little to do but wait.

He sat in a rocking chair and picked up the book that had always supported him in his hours of need. His Bible. By the light of the dimmed lamp he began to read.

Once back at the hotel, Hannah put an end to being hovered over by insisting she was tired and wanted to get some sleep.

"Then I guess I'll go down and look around for a while," Joey said. "Any of you care to join me?"

The three others agreed and Hannah breathed a sigh of relief when they closed the door behind them. She loved all of the men dearly, but tonight of all nights, she needed to be alone.

She lay across the bed, her arms across her eyes, and allowed her mind to swirl with memories. After a long while she fell into a deep sleep of utter exhaustion.

She had no idea of what it was that wakened her. She had turned the lamp as low as she could and the room was cast in the shadows. She reached out and extinguished the lamp completely. In the darkened room the moonlight outside made everything seem as if it were bathed in the glow of pale light. She rose and went to stand by the window, drawing the curtain aside to look out.

A huge white moon hung low in the sky just behind the church steeple. She felt the heavy weight in her heart and the need to find some release for it. Maybe the church was her answer. She could at least try. Maybe afterward she could talk to Patrick again. He seemed so kind and understanding.

The streets below her were deserted. Picking up a shawl, she put it around her shoulders as she left the room.

* * *

Micahel paced the small cabin floor like a cated lion. Being confined like this reminded him of the prison camp in which he had spent the last two years of the war.

It was still hard for him to believe that as far as the world was concerned, he was dead. It was an eerie feeling, as if he had no ties to anything . . . was drifting in a void. It scared him to death.

He fought the things that were slowly strangling him. His brother and sister, Fallen Oaks, Maxwell, and the other friends he had known. But the deepest, darkest, most threatening shadow he held away. It was not one he could face and master. Hannah . . . He almost said her name aloud. But he knew he didn't dare. The ghost of her loving presence was just waiting for entry, waiting for that weak moment he couldn't afford. Her memory could push him to the brink of despair.

He took out his pocket watch and checked the time. A quarter to twelve. He could leave now, ride the shadows of the woods and rocks until he got to the back of the house. Then, he could slip in to see Patrick.

He knew the men who pursued him could not be too far behind. Once they had come and been given conclusive evidence that indeed Michael Cord was dead, and once they had gone to carry the word to the senator, he would be free. Free. He laughed bitterly. He would never be free again. In return for life, he had given up . . . everything that made it worthwhile.

He went outside, carrying his saddle, blanket, and bridle. He saddled his horse, mounted, and rode toward Patrick's house.

The house was dark except for one window where a very dim light shone. He put his horse in the stable, careful to close the door and look around, then crossed the clearing to Patrick's door. He rapped softly. The door was opened quickly. Patrick had been waiting for him because he didn't want Michael outside any longer than necessary.

"Michael . . . come in. Quickly."

Michael slipped inside and closed the door behind him. "Well, Patrick, my friend. It looks like we pulled it off so far. Now all we have to do is wait and convince my hounds that I'm dead."

"I'm afraid we have a few additional problems, Michael."

"What? Did we slip up somewhere? Does somebody know the truth? Quinn, did he . . ."

"No, no. Wait a minute. No one knows you are alive. Quinn didn't lose his nerve. It's just . . . well, you have some mourners at your grave that none of us counted on."

"Mourners, me?" Michael laughed dryly. "Nobody in this territory cares if I'm alive or dead."

"No, no one in *this* territory. But how about four friends, Joey Mason, Jamie Bond, Mac McCarthy, Brad Sinclair, and . . . one very special friend."

Michael's face had gone grim, but when Patrick added the last name it turned a deathly pale.

"Hannah Marshall."

"Oh, God," Michael groaned. He felt as if someone had struck him a nearly mortal blow. Hannah . . . Hannah was close enough for him to reach . . . to touch . . . to hold. It almost undid him completely.

"Patrick?"

"No one has told her anything."

"How is she?" he asked softly. "How does she look?"

"She's grieving for you. She's blaming herself for being one day too late to try to stop you. She spent hours at the cemetery today, and her eyes were red from weeping. She's suffering, too, Michael. But she's a beautiful woman." Patrick added the next sentence to see the depth of Michael's love. "One who need not stay alone for long if the right man came along."

If anything, Michael's face grew paler and deep grooves of strain appeared around his clenched mouth. He loved her, Patrick knew it, but could he convince Michael to reveal himself to the woman who had traveled so far to save him?

"As much as she seems to love you, she seems to be trustworthy. Why don't you tell her you're alive and how you feel?"

"I can't do that to her. My life will always be one of chance, of running. I don't want that for Hannah. She deserves much more than me."

"You don't give her any choices at all, do you?"

"I can't afford to," Michael said, half in anger.

"Or you're afraid to."

"Maybe. Maybe I'm afraid that if we were forced to run, one

day she'd look at me and feel regret. Maybe I'd watch her love die slow, and I don't think I could take that. If she thinks I'm dead . . . Maybe it's better that we just leave it as it is."

"And she'll go home."

"Yes." Michael's fist clenched.

"Marry, have a home and children . . . someone else's children."

"Stop it, Patrick."

"You can't think about it, yet you condemn her to it? Can you just walk away like that?"

"Don't you think you're a little unfair?"

"To whom, you or Hannah?"

"I've done it *for* her, please believe that. Don't think I wouldn't rather have it different. But it would be standing her up in the line of fire. I love her too much to do that. I'd rather see her live."

"I'm sorry for both of you, Michael. I wish things could be different for you."

"When is she leaving?"

"You want to see . . ."

"Just from a distance. It will have to be enough."

Patrick knew all the arguments were not getting him anywhere, and he also knew he could not break Michael's confidence in him by revealing the truth himself. Within, he prayed that providence would take a hand in matters.

"Are you hungry?"

"No. I think it best I go. If your light is burning all night someone might think there is a problem and come to help. I've caused you enough problems." He walked to the door and put his hand on the knob, then turned to face Patrick again. "You know where I'll be. I'll stay put. Send word when they've come. Maybe this will all be over soon."

"All right. I'll let you know."

Michael started to turn the knob, when he realized that someone on the outside was already turning it. He stepped back in shock.

Hannah had gone to the church, looking for some solace for her misery. She had knelt to pray, but even after an hour the hollow feelings, the feeling of desperate loneliness persisted.

She rose to leave the church. When she stepped outside and

walked down the steps, she noticed one light still burning in Patrick's small home. If he was up, maybe he wouldn't mind talking to her for a while. She knew she would never be able to sleep.

She crossed the yard on silent feet and walked up the three steps to Patrick's back door. It was then she heard the voices.

One was a voice her heart would never forget. She froze in shock. It was impossible! Yet as the voice continued she knew without doubt it was Michael.

The second voice was also undoubtedly Patrick's. The two men seemed to be arguing. She pressed her ear to the door and heard the last words . . . heard Michael say he loved her too much to bring her hurt. But the words that echoed in her mind were the only ones she wanted to hear. He loved her.

She put her hand on the doorknob and could feel the resistance of another hand on the other side. It was just as quickly released and she turned the knob to push the door open.

She knew what she expected to see, but both Michael and Patrick were unprepared for the sight of Hannah standing in the doorway.

For a minute the three simply stood and looked at each other. Both men were still too shaken to find words.

A painful relief flooded Hannah. Michael was not dead. She understood the ruse almost at once. She'd found a very alive Michael, and her heart sang with the joy of it. She stepped inside and closed the door. Then she smiled.

"Don't you think it's time one of you explained what's going on? You see, I have no intention of leaving here until you do."

"Hannah." Michael brathed her name and the urge to gather her into his arms made him sweat to control it. "You are the stubbornest female."

"Thank God for that. But you," she laughed softly, "haven't seen what stubbornness is . . . yet."

Chapter Eight

Michael tried to reach for words, but nothing logical would come into his mind. At the moment it was too full of Hannah. No matter how he had always held her in his heart, her beauty now seemed so much more ethereal and poignantly heart-rending.

"Hannah . . . you've got to listen to reason about this."

"Yes, my dear," Patrick added. "Letting one person in this town have any suspicion about the trick we've just pulled off and you just might *be* filling that grave out there."

"Are those horrid men that close on your trail?"

"Think about it, Hannah. If you and the boys could trace me, just how hard a job do you think it's going to be for them?"

"Of course," she concurred softly.

"Then you've got to use your head. Gather the boys in the morning and go back to your family."

"Do you really believe I would go? And just like that? I find you and you bluntly tell me to go away. Oh, no, Michael Cord. We have to talk, and I don't think it's safe to do so here."

"Now wait a minute . . ." Michael began.

"She might be right, Michael," Patrick cautioned. He could see that Hannah meant what she said. "Someone could come here at any time. There's still a few hours until dawn. Maybe you ought to talk this out once and for all."

"Where! In that little cabin?" Michael was already shaking with the thought of him and Hannah alone, all the rest of the night . . . in that small cabin . . . deep in the woods. The thought of it was enough to rattle his reserve.

"It's the safest place I know. No one has ever been there except you."

"Michael, you can't believe I'm just going to walk away? I've been trying to find you for so long. You owe me more than that."

"I owe you your life, too, and it wouldn't be worth much if those hardcases following me ever found out you meant a thing to me."

"Do I?" Hannah questioned quietly.

Michael didn't answer, but Patrick smiled to himself. A man, or a group of men, couldn't stop Michael Cord. But this girl with the wide green eyes and warm smile had just done it. He had a feeling Michael was meeting an opponent whose fighting rules Michael just didn't understand.

"Hannah, be reasonable."

"I think I'm very reasonable. Whatever you're going to do, I think I have the right to know about it. You can't go on endangering Patrick, either. These men could be a threat to him, as well. Maybe there needs to be more than one person mourning at your grave when they do come."

"She might have a point there."

"Patrick, don't encourage this!"

"Michael, please." Hannah reached out a hand toward him. "I only want to help. The men with me will be recognized easily by them. If they . . . and I . . . and everyone mourn your death, how can they not believe?"

"Hannah, you don't know these people."

"You thought you were safe before I came. I found out what had happened, simply because I couldn't give up easily. Are they the kind to give up without all the proof we can provide?"

This silenced Michael. She had all the arguments on her side. But he was scared for her. He was also scared that if he let her stay, that time could change everything and he wouldn't be able to let her go at all.

Right now his future didn't look like much, and to ask a woman like Hannah to share exile with him was too painful a thought.

"It isn't just them! Not just this little game! It's . . . it's more. It's so much more."

"You still think I'm that little girl you rescued so long ago. Well, I'm not. You'd best understand, Michael Cord. I'm not going anywhere. So you may as well get it through your head. The best thing we can do is to talk, and then make plans."

Michael scowled darkly, but if he thought his anger was going to intimidate Hannah, he was wrong. For several quiet minutes he paced the floor.

"You're going to play this game out, aren't you?" He finally spoke as he paused before her.

"Yes, I am."

"All right," he said calmly. Neither Patrick nor Hannah were taken in by his sudden quietness. Michael wasn't one to give up that easily. "So we talk."

"Then we'd best get out of here. It's not safe for Patrick."

"I have a closed carriage," Patrick offered. "Hannah, you can use it. That way if someone sees it coming or going, they'll think it's me. Michael, it might be best if you tie your horse to the back of the carriage and ride inside. This time of night if anyone saw the carriage they'd never recognize who's inside. They'll just think someone came to fetch me for some emergency. It happens all the time."

Michael nodded. Hannah sensed he was seething inside, but this time she did not mean to let him walk away from her. She might never see him again.

Patrick blew out the lamp and midnight darkness filled the small house. Hannah could feel Michael close beside her. When Patrick opened the back door all was stillness outside except for night sounds.

"The carriage and horse are in the stable. Be careful with Nell. She's an old lady and a trot is pretty much to ask of her."

"We'll return it before morning," Michael said. Patrick didn't answer. He wasn't too sure of that.

"Just have Hannah come back in the carriage. That way there will be no questions asked. It will just be *me* returning home. In fact, Hannah, you could use my carriage while you're here if you'd like. Michael, you should stay here."

"I don't think it will be necessary after tonight, and it might look . . . unusual."

"I suppose you're right," Patrick conceded. "I know you're not going to stay put, and it's better to be careful. I guess using your own horse is advisable."

"*I* should have stayed put tonight," Michael replied.

Carefully Hannah and Michael slipped out. Patrick watched as they disappeared into the shed. A short while later the carriage left and Patrick closed the door. He smiled. He knew Michael was more than a little off balance at the newest course of events, but if it gave him a chance at some happiness in his life it would be worth the uneasiness.

They rode in complete silence, and the small, enclosed carriage was dark enough that she could not see Michael's face. But she could feel the tension in him. He was sitting too close for her not to.

Michael moved the carriage expertly between the trees, keeping away from the road, although it was hardly likely that many of the citizens of Virginia City were traveling the road after midnight.

They traveled what seemed an interminable time to Hannah, and when the cabin suddenly appeared, it startled her. She realized that if no one knew where it was, it was unlikely anyone would ever find it.

It was an exceptionally small structure, and as soon as she stood inside and Michael lighted a lamp, she could feel the confinement. To Michael, it must be like a prison, she thought. He had carefully covered the only two windows, making it even worse.

When Michael turned from the lamp to look at her, she could hardly read his thoughts. He was doing his best to close himself off from her. She returned his look with all the courage she could muster. This was going to be the most difficult challenge of her life, because she knew Michael was going to use every weapon at his disposal to drive her away.

But, as she looked around her, she knew that if he succeeded in driving her out, this was all he would have left, and she couldn't let him face it alone. The only thread of real courage she had was the memory of the words he had spoken to Patrick. He loved her. That was the rock she had to cling to as she faced him.

After the gunfight, Quinn had gone off and gotten completely and totally drunk. He remained drunk all the next day. He awoke near midnight, the following night, feeling as if he had lost weeks instead of thirty-six hours. He felt foggy and disoriented. Then the destruction of his life returned with a vengeance.

He wondered if Rena had come to the churchyard the night before, if she had waited while he hid in his oblivion . . . and, more important, he wondered, if she'd come again.

He went to the churchyard, and knew he would wait until dawn if he had to. As he arrived he saw Patrick's carriage leave. He remained in the shadows. He didn't need Patrick's good advice now.

If Rena did come, he knew he only had to hurt her more. Some part of him knew this would be the best thing for her, but a deeper part hungered for her, for a moment's peace, like a starving man.

The time ticked slowly by . . . and he knew she wasn't going to come. He knew he had done what needed done. But losing her had torn away a part of him that would never be replaced.

There was no doubt word would spread. The men who sought Michael would come. But once they had realized they had come for nothing it would all be over. He would be left alone to go on with the same aimless life. At the moment he didn't care anymore.

Reluctantly he left the churchyard.

Rena lay very still. She prayed silently that if her mother thought she was asleep, she would leave her alone. She had to see Quinn, she had to.

This nightmare couldn't be true. There was an explanation. Surely he could explain it to her.

But her mother continued to sit by her bed, her knitting in her lap. If she tried to go to Quinn, her father would stop her and maybe cause Quinn more problems.

Sophie knew Rena was not asleep, just as she knew Rena meant to go to Quinn. But she wasn't going to let her daughter throw away her life. Before, it had been different. Quinn's reputation was based on nothing but the fact that he was a loner, an oprhan, and wild as a man without a family man might be. Before, it might have worked. Rena might have changed his life. But now, the whole town had watched him kill a man, and even Rena's love couldn't change that. This time, she would stop what she knew Rena intended to do, no matter what it took.

Quinn sat at a table with his back to the wall, methodically lowering the contents of the bottle before him. The table was in a semishadowed corner and no one had the courage to bother him. He was left completely alone and that's the way he wanted it. He wanted to lose himself and chew his own thoughts over in his mind. He didn't even realize when Mac and Joey came in and found a table a short distance away. They, too, recognized a man who wanted to be alone.

But somehow tonight, the whiskey didn't offer the escape for Quinn it always had before. Every nerve he had, every sense he had, seemed to be acutely alert.

That was why when the three strangers walked into the saloon he knew who and what they were with an amazing clarity.

So, Patrick's timing *had* been just about perfect. One more day and they couldn't have pulled it off.

Quinn motioned to the bartender, who happened to be one of his few friends. When he came, he brought another bottle with him and was surprised to find Quinn's first bottle still half full.

"You want something, Quinn?"

"Yeah. Those three newcomers at the bar," he motioned, and the bartender turned to look.

"Gunfighters," he said quickly. "Rough-looking bunch."

"Yeah, well, they might be looking for me."

"What makes you think so?"

"Just a hunch. I'm in no condition to handle them, so how about keeping 'em off me for tonight."

"Sure," he nodded, "I'll take care of it."

"I owe you."

"Don't worry about it." He set the full bottle on the table and walked back to the bar. "Can I help you, gents?"

"We're lookin' for a man," Jonas said shortly. He was tired of the saddle and the search.

"Word has it he's been in Virginia City," Logan added.

"Who is he?" the bartender asked.

"Man named Michael Cord. Tall fella, dark hair. Has a limp and wears a patch over one eye," Hammond added.

"Sure, he was here. But there ain't no sense in lookin' any further. The man you're looking for is dead."

The three men exchanged quick glances of total surprise and disbelief.

"Dead? How did that come about? You sure?" Jonas questioned quickly.

"Sure as I'm breathin'. I watched him fall. Killed right out here on the street. His grave is up on the hill outside of town. You can go have a look-see yourself."

"Damn!" Jonas said angrily. "Old man ain't gonna like this. Besides, I was lookin' to drawn on him." He licked his dry lips and ordered a drink. When the bartender had filled three glasses, he drank swiftly and set his glass down.

"Who's the fast gun that got him? I'd kinda like to talk to him."

The bartender knew then that Quinn had been right. These men were killers. "Sorry, but he ain't around. In fact, he ain't been to town since the fight. For all I know, he might have ridden on."

Some instinct in Jonas made him look closely at the bartender. There was a lie here and he just wasn't sure of the purpose of it. Why would he be protecting a stranger?

"Was he someone just passing through."

"Well . . . sort of," the bartender began to sweat under Jonas's narrow eyed scrutiny.

"Man must have had a name," Jonas said softly.

"Sure . . . sure he had a name."

"Like to share it with us, friend?" Jonas's smile never reached his eyes, and the bartender saw the threat.

"Name's Quinn Wayland."

"He must have been pretty fast. I hear Michael Cord was real handy with a gun," Logan said.

"Yeah . . . he was fast."

"Give us another drink, and bartender . . ."

"Yes?"

"If this Quinn Wayland should come in, I'd be real obliged if you'd point him out. We'll be around for a couple of days. Or if he should show up and we ain't here," Jonas grinned a cold grin, "you tell him Hammond Gordan, Logan King, and Jonas Holt are looking for him. It's real important business."

"Sure . . . I'll tell him."

The three ordered a bottle of whiskey and went to a table. When the bartender turned to look for Quinn, he was gone. He returned his attention to the new arrivals, who were in deep conversation at the table. He had no doubts they were very deadly.

"I told you we should have skipped those last two mining towns," Logan complained. "They were too small to hide someone like him."

"We had to check out every place," Jonas said. "It might have slowed us down a bit, but we couldn't take the chance on passing over."

"Well, we were so damn careful not to miss a town, that we missed killing him," Hammond grumbled.

"Not much we can do about it now," Jonas said, "except check every little detail out. If we're going to report to the old man, we'd better have all the answers."

The two agreed reluctantly. None of them were very happy about the situation. A few tables away Mac and Joey quietly regarded each other as they tossed down their drinks and rose to leave.

Quinn rode hard. He'd thought of going to Patrick first, then changed his mind. Michael needed to be told and he was the only one right now who could get word to him, to make sure he didn't move around. He couldn't be seen now, by anyone, or the consequences would be terrible.

The whole thing would be over when the three gunfighters were satisfied about Michael's death and left town. But the next few days were going to be touchy, because he didn't want to draw a gun on any of the three, either. They looked deadly.

He was surprised when he neared Michael's cabin to find Patrick's carriage outside. There was no light showing from the cabin, but Quinn knew this didn't mean much, for Michael kept the windows well covered.

Since Patrick was already there, he could at least, be sure both men were awake. He dismounted and tied his horse. Then he went to the door and knocked lightly.

"All right, Hannah," Michael said. "You wanted to talk. So let's get things cleared up once and for all. You have little-girl dreams, no matter how grown you are. But they aren't reality. They never can be, and the sooner you accept that, the happier you're going to be. You can't change things. All you can do is cause more problems."

"Michael, you're being unfair to me."

"I'm being more fair than you can possibly imagine."

"I . . . I wish you would stop believing that I'll accept whatever you say without question."

Michael was momentarily silenced. He had never been called a liar to his face before. But, he began to reason with himself, he'd accepted a lot of other labels, so he might as well accept being called a liar, too.

"Accept whatever you want. Just be smart. Get on the first train home and forget you ever met me."

"I couldn't do that before, and I can't do it now. Michael, sometime, someplace, you've got to stop running and start living again."

"The day I stop running, I have to face three rabid animals. I either kill them . . . or they kill me. It's better I stay dead."

"Do you know how many people you're hurting?"

"That's better than slowly turning into a killer. There's not a fast gun o ut here that won't look me up. Just to see if they're a little faster than I am. One day, one of them will do the job right. Let it go, Hannah."

"I can't," she cried softly.

Michael had kept as much distance between them as the small shack would allow. He could handle anything else, but not the need or the control to fight the desire that licked like fire through him. He'd held Hannah once, touched the pure sweetness of her love, and he knew if he touched her again it might just be beyond his control to let her go. He turned from the tears in her eyes, and from her soft promise of the gift of herself he knew was there. His back to her, he spoke as coldly and brutally as he could.

"Go away, Hannah. I don't want you here. I don't *need* you here. You're an interference I can't afford, and all you can cause is trouble. Why don't you just leave me alone."

There was silence, and he found he could not turn around and look into her eyes again. Hannah was a dream that had been his only solace for much too long. He waited to hear the door close.

He heard her move and steeled himself for the final sound of her leaving. He expected it . . . but he didn't expect what happened next.

Hannah had watched him for several minutes. The tears had blurred her eyes and she felt his hurt more than her own. Then slowly she moved toward him. She felt his body stiffen as she put her arms about him and rested her head against the hard muscle of his back. She spoke softly, and each word pierced Michael's defenses.

"Michael, I love you. I have always loved you and I won't let you live this kind of life alone. I can't bear to know you can't reach out to anyone. I can't bear to think of you lonely . . . or sick and having no one. I know that you had no reason to lie to Patrick, Michael . . . and I was standing outside his door when you told him that you loved me. You can't force me away or pretend to hate me away. I love you and I won't let you give up everything, I just won't."

She could feel his body tremble as he fought for control.

Michael found the months of enforced loneliness were taking its toll. His body raged with need. To hold her once more, to feel her gentleness and soft warmth, to taste one last time what was forbidden him.

"God . . . Hannah." He reached for anger. It was the last defense he had. He turned so quickly, Hannah was unprepared. When he grasped her shoulders and gave her a rough shake she gasped.

"Stop it, Hannah! Do you really believe I'm going to drag you along with me! Well, forget it. You're just being a stupid, spoiled little girl, demanding your own way. Go back home. I don't intend for you to be part of my life . . . now . . . or ever."

Hannah gazed up at him. Then she reached up to rest a hand against his cheek. "All right, I'll go."

He breathed a sigh of relief . . . a few seconds too soon.

"If," she continued, "you can look at me and swear by all you love, that you don't love me. That, at this minute you don't want me as much as I want you. Tell me," she added firmly, "the honest truth."

Barriers Michael had thought forged from steel began to melt like heated butter. He wanted to say the words, but her eyes held his, and her intimate proximity was playing havoc with his senses.

Hannah read more in his silence than any words could have told her. She gave a soft, confident laugh, moved into his arms, and drew his head down to hers.

When their lips met, Michael's last defenses were shattered to unredeemable pieces. His arms came around her, crushing her to him while his mouth fused with hers, grasping all the dreamed-of pleasure he'd thought lost forever.

Hannah felt as if she could not draw a breath. Michael's arms were like iron about her, lifting her from the ground. But she didn't care. She had won! And it was all she thought it would be. She could feel him drawing all the stored-up passion from her. His mouth was hard against hers, parting her willing lips to respond fully to the heat that now engulfed them both.

Michael could feel her softness melt against him, filling the dark corners of his heart until he felt as if he would explode.

Only when neither could breathe at all, when they were dizzy with the overwhelming fire, did they stop to gasp and look at each other.

"Michael . . . ?"

"I don't understand you. You're like no other woman I've ever met before. You have everything to lose and yet you give everything. Hannah, you won't even listen to what's good for you."

"*You're* good for me."

"This has got to be a dream. I've wanted it too long. You are the stubbornest . . . most beautiful woman and I do love you. I can't deny it. But . . ."

"No . . . there are no buts. I'm here to stay. You and I will wait for the 'problem' to go. Once they've seen your grave and heard us mourn, they'll go away. Then," she smiled hopefully up at him, "you can change your name and we can be married. Oh, Michael, I'll go with you wherever you want. Just don't think that you're ever going without me again."

"I'm not sure that I could let you go now even if I wanted to." Michael laughed, but his eyes were serious. "You are something else, woman. No wonder I couldn't forget you. I always remembered how you felt in my arms, the way you tasted. The way you looked at me as if I were everything."

"Memory," Hannah said softly, "is not enough anymore . . . and you *are* everything."

"Hannah," he whispered. His lips touched hers again. Gently this time, warming her, coaxing her, until her mouth parted and she sighed softly.

It grew, this long-denied desire, into an engulfing thing that closed their minds to everything but each other. Michael was immersing himself completely, surrendering all the past loneliness in the magic of Hannah's passionate response.

It was why Michael, long accustomed to being cautious and alert, did not hear the muffled sound of a horse's approach. In fact, neither was aware of anything but each other . . . until the door was flung open.

"Michael, I . . ." Quinn froze in the doorway. It was difficult to believe what he was seeing, and when he did finally digest it, was off guard and uncertain. This was one thing he hadn't expected.

"It's all right, Quinn. Come on in and close the door. I've got some explaining to do."

His eyes still on Hannah, Quinn closed the door behind him.

When all the explanation had been taken care of Quinn was both satisfied and a wee bit jealous. Of course Michael had a lot of problems yet to face, but he had Hannah . . . and his friends. It was a whole lot more than Quinn had, or most likely would *ever* have.

"Quinn," Hannah said, "I'm so grateful for what you have done for Michael. I'll never forget it. I'm sure it was a sacrifice for you."

"Don't worry about it, Hannah. If Michael can just keep hidden for as long as it takes to get these men satisfied and out of town, everything should be all right. Maybe then you two can find a nice quiet place and settle down. Find a little happiness of you can."

"No matter what happens, Quinn, Hannah and I will never forget what you've done."

"Yeah, well," Quinn grinned, "it was a return favor for the Reverend more than anything else. I'd do just about anything for that man."

"He's sure been a big help to me, too," Michael admitted.

"I'm going back to town and keep an eye on those fast guns. You'd better lay low and quiet. It wouldn't do my reputation much good if the ghost of Michael Cord was seen walkin' around, now would it?" Quinn said.

"You're right. I'll stay put. I'm only worried about Hannah. Word has probably gotten around that she was at the cemetery. I don't think I want them asking her any questions."

"Don't you think I can be convincing?" Hannah asked with annoyance.

"Sure," Michael chuckled. "I'm just afraid you'll set that stubborn mind of yours and do something like challenge all three of them."

"Don't be funny," Hannah said in warning.

"Who's being funny?"

"Michael!"

"You stay away from them, Hannah. Seriously, they're the kind of man you don't know anything about. I don't want them to even look at you." Michael turned his attention to Quinn. "Stay close to her, Quinn."

"I will."

"I have enough protection," Hannah replied. "There's Joey, Jamie, Brad, and Mac. They rode with me. You don't think I came by train, do you?"

"Rode? Hannah, you came overland!" Michael looked at her with a combination of shock and amused disbelief.

"I was perfectly safe. Besides, Virginia City was never the destination. We had to search a lot of towns until we found you."

Both men looked at her with expressions that made her laugh.

"I'm going to kill those four," Michael grumbled.

"Don't even think that, Michael Cord! If they hadn't agreed to come along, I'd have come alone. You owe them some thanks, and I expect you to trat them the way they deserve."

Again Michael and Quinn exchanged glances, then Michael chuckled and spoke with a gentleness in his voice. "Ever see anything like her, Quinn? This is one lady who doesn't back away from anything." He looked at Hannah with a warmth that made her feel as if she were melting. "I'm sure glad you're on my side, Hannah love."

"So am I," she returned his smile.

"Well, look, I'd better get back to town," Quinn said. "If they really want to look me up, I'd better be around to answer questions."

"Quinn," Michael said warningly. "Don't give them any problems, or any reaseon to come after you. They're hard noses. They'd sas soon kill as eat."

"Don't worry, I've had all of that I want. I'll answer their questions, confirm your quick exit from this world, and keep out of their way. They won't have one rason to buck me."

"Good. I think you'd better ride along with Hannah. At least as far as Patrick's. I don't want her out alone."

"I thought Patrick was here when I first rode up. Sure, I'll see she gets back safe." He looked from Michael to Hannah, and smiled. "I'll wait outside."

He left so quickly that Michael chuckled. Even Hannah had to laugh. She walked to Michael and felt the comfort of his arms around her again. "Now, *that* is a gentleman," she said firmly.

"You read my mind. God," he said softly, "I hate to let you go."

"Michael, why can't I stay here with you?"

"Because you'll be missed, and, besides, this," he gestured about him, "is no place for you. It's only a matter of days, Hannah . . . just days. It's hard for me to believe. I thought this was only to be a dream. You don't know how often I've held you like this. I thought it was all I would ever have."

"You see," she smiled up at him. "I told you you should have taken me with you. We've wasted so much precious time."

"If I had known what a stubborn little tiger you were, I might have."

"You thought I was such a child," she murmured as she pressed close to him.

"Well, I'm sure not under that illusion anymore," he answered as he tightened his arms around her. He could hear her soft laugh before he kissed her.

The kiss was lingering and so gentle that it stirred Hannah to the depths. It was not a hurried, violent thing anymore, but a sensual touch, as if he wanted to memorize everything about her. He brushed her forehead, her cheeks, and both closed eyes, savoring the feel of her in his arms.

Then he held her away from him. "Hannah, you'd better go now. It would take a man a hell of a lot stronger than me to stand any more of this."

"Michael, if I were careful, I could come back . . ." she began.

"No! You're jeopardizing your life and our future. Now that I've found it, I can't afford to lose it again. If this works, it will take an army to get me away from you again. But, for now, we just have to wait." He sighed deeply. "You can't possibly imagine how badly I want to keep you here with me. But I'm not going to spoil the chance of having you for the rest of my life. So be understanding. Go, before I lose the ability to let you."

Hannah knew he was right. She stood on the edge of control herself. She nodded reluctantly. He kissed her again, then put an arm around her and walked to the door with her.

Outside he watched her get into the carriage and drive away with Quinn following. When he reentered the cabin it seemed smaller and lonelier than ever. But he had an additional shield now . . . Hannah.

Patrick had waited anxiously for Hannah to return, hoping he had not made a bad problem worse by forcing Michael and Hannah together. He just wished she would come back and tell him that all was well. It seemed like the hours passed so slowly.

It had to be nearing dawn before he heard the carriage. He blew out his lamp and stepped outside. He wasn't surprised to see the carriage, but he *was* surprised to see a rider behind it. Had Michael been foolish enough to come back with her!

But after a few minutes, when the carriage stopped before the stable, he could see the rider was Quinn Wayland.

"Now how in the name of heaven did this come about?" he said half aloud. Then he smiled and looked heavenward. "Sorry, I shouldn't have asked."

Both Hannah and Quinn were smiling as they walked toward him, so he was assured things had been settled, at least between the three involved.

"Hannah?" he said as she came closer.

"It's all right, Patrick. Thank you for worrying about us. Michael and I . . . I hope we've resolved our problems."

"Don't count your chickens before they get hatched, Hannah," Quinn cautioned. "We still have a few days to spend outfoxing that bunch. They're not dumb, so don't sell them short."

"Bunch? What 'bunch' are you talking about?" Patrick questioned quickly.

"Oh, Reverend . . . I forgot, you don't know. That gang Michael has been outrunnin', well, they're here, in Virginia City. Rode in tonight. Our timing couldn't have been more perfect."

"Thank God," Patrick said.

"Amen," Quinn laughed. "I was just telling Hannah . . . all the way here, I might add . . . that we have to be more careful for the next few days than we've ever been, about anything."

"He's right, dear," Patrick added. "We'll have to be very, very careful. I'm sure, as Quinn said, these men are not only not dumb, they're heartless. You make one slip and they'll catch it."

"I'll be careful. Don't worry, they'll be convinced. I'm going to be the grievingest woman that group has ever seen."

"Well, for now you'd better get back to your hotel. We don't want your friends to raise an alarm and draw attention to the fact that you're gone."

"Heavens no!"

"I'll walk you back to the hotel," Quinn said.

"I'll be all right, quinn, really."

"I'll walk you back," he repeated with a firmness that brought an end to any further argument from her. "Besides, if something was to happen to you right now, I don't see how anyone could face Michael."

"It's nearing dawn," Patrick said. "You two be very careful. You're not exactly supposed to be friendly."

"You're right," Quinn agreed. "Come on, Hannah, let's get a move on."

Hannah stood on tiptoe and kissed Patrick's cheek. "Michael and I will never be able to repay you for this."

"You might," he grinned.

"How? Anything you want."

"How about you two getting married in my church and letting me officiate? I'm an incurable romantic and I love to see a love story work out."

"I'm sure I can speak for Michael and tell you we'd both be more than honored."

"Good night . . . or rather good morning. The sky is kind of gray out there."

"Good night, Patrick."

Quinn and Hannah left, keeping to any shadowed area they could find. Before Quinn left Hannah outside the hotel, she had gotten a full description of the gunfighters from him. She knew somehow she had to see them face-to-face . . . and she was beginning to get an idea about just how to do it.

Quinn continued on to his own place. If he'd been pleased with himself an hour before, opening the door to his cabin brought him down at once.

He knew he had to learn to accept what he would have for the rest of his life, but after seeing Michael and Hannah, he found it very hard to face the grim reality of days that would be devoid of Rena.

So, three people found the coming day a difficult one to face!

Quinn knew there would be a sameness about all the days from this minute on. The future looked very long . . . and very bleak.

For Rena the misery was just as intense. She knew that the next day her parents were going to begin to be more cautious. Now that her mother knew about her and Quinn . . . and knew that Quinn had been involved in the gunfight, she would face the barrier of their disapproval and their guard. She wondered if she would ever have the opportunity to try to meet Quinn again . . . or if he would be there if she did.

For Hannah the sleepless night was one of the happiest she

had had in a long time. She had not only found Michael, but now the truth she had hoped for had become reality, a wonderful reality.

Tomorrow she would make sure she was seen going to Michael's grave. She worried she wouldn't be convincing enough. She had to make sure they saw the depth of grief. Then she would wait and pray that they believed.

She would count every hour, every minute, every second until they were gone, and she and Michael could be together.

Chapter Nine

Logan, Jonas, and Hammond were definitely not early risers and they had kept a very late hour the night before, in the hopes that Quinn would come into the saloon.

It was past eleven when the three walked into the restaurant.

Patrick and Hannah had kept a watchful eye for their movements, knowing they would eventually go to the cemetery to see Michael's grave for themselves.

Hannah now stood with Joey and Jamie across the street from the restaurant while Patrick, Brad, and Mac observed from other places. With no way of knowing that Michael was still alive and what Hannah's plan really was, the four men meant to accompany her to the cemetery for one final good-bye. They didn't like this, either, but they would stick by her to the bitter end and see that she got back to her family safely.

Hannah and Patrick would have been even more tense if they had known that Michael was observing as well. The church steeple made a fine observation point. Its latticework sides made it easy for him to look out over the cemetery. He had been too afraid that the three men would be able to somehow get past Hannah's determination to stay in the cabin while she faced them. So he had come to the church in the wee hours of the morning.

It angered him to be a helpless onlooker. Yet, he had a great deal to look forward to now, and he didn't want to kill another man. He couldn't do it and then just go on with his life. It would haunt him forever. Too many eyes haunted him now.

Hannah could feel the tension in the air. Joey and Jamie had voiced strenuous objections to what she was doing, but she had overcome them by standing firm and making it clear she intended to do it with or without their support.

Hannah had gone to the store early in the morning and purchased a rough black cotton dress, a wide-brimmed hat, and a long flowing veil which made her face seem vague beneath it. She had laughed to herself when she put it on and looked in the mirror. She truly looked like a grieving widow. Joey and Jamie had said nothing, but she could read the effect she had in their eyes. It made her promise herself she would tell them the truth as soon as possible. They were both stricken with her sorrow.

"Hannah, ain't it enough you had to suffer through this once? Why do you have to go back to his grave?" Joey said. "You know darn well it ain't necessary to talk to those three men. There's nothing nobody can do now."

"I need to do it, Joey." Hannah said gently, knowing she could not tell them the truth just yet, but appreciating their consideration and sympathy nonetheless. "I know as well as you that someone will be checking out the grave just to see if it's true. I have to see them for myself."

"Joey's right, Hannah," Jamie argued. "It's not going to make a bit of difference and none of us want to tangle with them."

"Jamie, you and Joey have been more than kind. You've been more like brothers to me. If the two of you don't want to go up there with me, you don't have to."

This was unthinkable to both men, whose pride and loyalty would never let them consider any other move.

"Hannah, that's not fair," Joey said. "You know darn well Jamie and I wouldn't let you go up there alone. We were Michael's friends."

To this Jamie nodded. Hannah smiled; she had not underestimated either of them.

"Then I think it's time we go."

Neither man would say another word; glumly they followed Hannah.

Now they walked close to her as she made her way to the cemetery, knowing that almost every eye in town was on her.

Just before they reached the cemetery gates, Joey bent close to her.

"They started this way."

"How do you know?"

"I just took a quick peek."

Hannah didn't look behind her. Instead she continued through the gate and slowly toward the grave.

Above her Michael had to smile. He'd have to compliment her . . . and remember in the future that she was a consummate actress.

"Hannah, love," he laughed softly to himself. "I damn well think you're enjoying yourself." Then the smile faded when he saw the three men who were behind them.

Hannah reached the gravesite. Even from Michael's lofty position he could hear her mournful cry as she sagged to her knees beside the grave. She began to sob wildly, and if Michael was stricken with amusement, Joey and Jamie were even more stricken.

Both men knew she had felt grief, but neither of them expected these hysterics. They were miserable and helpless.

Hannah was quite aware that the three men she was performing for were coming close. She pressed her handkerchief to her eyes with one hand and bent to lay her hand on the mounded dirt.

"Oh, Michael, Michael! Don't leave me like this! I can't go on without you!" Her sobs and cries grew.

Joey and Jamie's misery intensified and Michael was struggling not to laugh out loud.

When the three reached the grave Michael watched Hannah struggle to her feet. Her expression was forlorn and helpless when she looked up at the gunfighters questioningly.

"Are you friends of Michael's?" she sobbed as she turned to them. "If you are, then I'm very grateful that you came. It's so terrible that he was gunned down in the prime of life!" She continued her lamentations while the three new arrivals watched, and the two friends stood gazing at Hannah in something close to awe.

Hannah continued. "I don't know what I shall do. We were to be married. Ohhhh," Hannah moaned and dropped to her knees again. "What will I do?"

Joey had taken all he could stand. He bent to take hold of Hannah's heaving shoulders. "Come on, Hannah, you can't carry on like this. It would be better if you came back to the hotel and rested . . ."

"No, I can't. I can't sleep. I keep dreaming of Michael . . . dying here, alone . . . without love or friends. Ohhh," she cried out again.

It took both Joey and Jamie to lift a weeping Hannah up from the grave. She sagged in their arms. The three continued to watch from across the grave, as Joey and Jamie tried their best to get Hannah away from it.

Michael, by this time, was leaning against the wall, fighting his laughter.

"Come on, Hannah," Jamie urged, "you'll make yourself sick. You got to stop crying."

Hannah seemed to be struggling with all her might. Slowly she straightened her shoulders. "I," she said in a deadened voice, "may never stop crying again." She pressed one hand to her breasts and the other she raised to press its back to her forehead. "I will never marry because," her voice lowered in deep sadness, "I shall never love again."

This nearly broke Michael, who had to turn his back on the scene below before he betrayed himself completely.

Hannah finally, although she had really warmed to her perfomance, allowed Joey and Jamie to lead her away. Her sobs echoed behind her.

"Damn fool woman," Hammond snarled. "Friends!" he laughed. "I'd like to have caught up with that . . . friend."

"Looks like we did," Jonas said as he motioned toward the headstone.

"I can't believe our luck. One damn day," Logan said.

"That Quinn Wayland gent, what are we going to do about him?" Hammond questioned.

"We don't have no quarrel with him," Jonas replied. "But I'd sure like to ask him a couple of questions."

"Yeah . . . like what was his fight with Cord all about," Logan said thoughtfully. "Seems like more than just luck to me."

"Well, let's look him up," Hammond grinned.

Michael watched the three walk away, hoping the ruse had worked and the game was finally over.

Joey and Jamie walked beside Hannah, whose head was bent so that they could not see her face. Neither man had expected her to fall apart like this and both were left without words. It was impossible to see the look of satisfaction on her face.

They refused to leave Hannah until they reached her hotel door.

"Please . . . come in." Her voice was soft.

Jamie gulped back his resistance. He found it very hard to cope with her in this state. Joey was no more enthusiastic, but neither had the heart to leave her alone with her overwhelming grief.

They were in for another shock. When Hannah closed the door she took off the hat and veil and tossed them on the bed. She stretched out her arms and spun around, laughing softly.

"We did it! We convinced them, I know we did. It was the icing on the cake."

"You mean . . ." Joey began. He was still puzzled.

"That was just for them?" Jamie said. "You mean . . ."

"I mean that it was needed," Hannah replied happily, "and I wanted to get a look at them," her smile faded a little, "so I will never forget them again and what they did to Michael. I think," her smile reappeared, "that I gave a performance that would make any actress green with envy."

"I . . . that was . . ." Joey began. "Hannah! You put us through all that and it was just because of those . . ." He was without words.

"Oh, Jamie, Joey, don't be angry with me. There was no time to explain *everything* to you."

"Everything?" Joey said suspiciously.

"I just wanted your reactions to be perfect, and they were. I'm sorry . . . I really am. But you'll forgive me when you know the truth."

"Things get odder and odder every time you open your mouth. Hannah, why don't you tell us just what's going on?"

"I will, gladly. Patrick is explaining to Brad and Mac right now. So I think it's time to tell you." She looked up at them, her eyes aglow with excitement. "Michael's not dead."

Whatever they expected, this announcement wasn't it. They stood silently, not quite able to accept the full import of what she had just said.

"I don't . . ." Joey began, the idea just began to register. He began to smile. "Hannah?"

"It's a ruse. The grave is empty, or rather it's full of rocks. Patrick and a couple of his friends worked it out. And it worked! It worked! Michael is alive and well, but as far as those three are concerned, he's dead and buried. Now, until they leave, we all have to play our parts."

Now both men were grinning broadly.

"I can't believe it. What about that Quinn Wayland?" Joey asked. "The whole town seems to be down on him."

"I suppose they are, but we should all be grateful to him. Who knows, somehow before this is over there might be a way we can help him."

"I don't think so, Hannah," Jamie said. "A reputatino is built like that. Unless you say it was a joke and show that Michael is still alive, no one is going to be able to help him."

"I still want to talk to him again. I *have* to thank him . . . I *have* to do that much at least. None of this is fair to Quinn. Michael owes him his life, and I owe him more . . . so much more."

"You better wait until that group is gone. If one of them suspects a game is being played here, there's going to be hell to pay," Joey cautioned.

"I'm not going to jeopardize Michael's safety now. If and when I talk to Quinn, I'll make sure he's alone. If we're lucky, in a day or two the three of them will move on. Then . . . Michael can be in peace for a while."

Joey and Jamie were happy for Hannah and Michael, and both ignored the twinge of insecurity. They were afraid that she was being optimistic about the fact of the gunslingers leaving. They were more than worried about Quinn Wayland . . . and knew that one small breach could lead to another.

Michael could not move from his hiding place until night fell, and even after that he knew he had to be more careful than ever.

Still, he wouldn't have missed Hannah's performance for anything in the world.

On the ride back to the cabin he enjoyed it over and over again in his mind. There was no doubt about it, Hannah Marshall was a unique woman. She had as much or more courage than any man he'd ever known.

"And she's a damn sight prettier," he chuckled. Memory tugged with delicious fingers. "And softer . . . and sweeter, and more than a man like me has a right to. But I'll be damned if I'll ever give her up now . . . for anything or anyone."

Even the cabin had lost its ghosts, and felt less empty and lonely. He knew it wasn't wise for her to come . . . he knew the last thing she should do was come . . . But God, he wished she were here.

"Oh, well, Michael, my friend," he murmured to himself, "count your blessings. One of these days she will be here. You've lived on dreams a long time, you can stand it a little bit longer."

He went to the bed and sat down to remove his boots, then he lay back and folded his hands behind his head.

Again he drew on the remarkable vision of Hannah, garbed in black, wailing and weeping and putting on a show that would have entertained royalty.

Michael couldn't let his thoughts untangle themselves. It amazed him that he could remember every second with Hannah, every argument, as well. It didn't cease to amaze him that she had actually convinced Jamie, Joey, Brad, and Mac to bring her all this distance. Of course, at the moment, he could believe Hannah could convince the angels to leave heaven, and he wondered who really brought whom. He wasn't sure his four friends had much of a chance to do anything else. For the first time in an eternity Michael allowed himself to dream. It was a new and exciting thing. He kept the one thought at bay . . . What if it failed?

He heard the sound from outside and was on his feet, gun in hand, in seconds. He blew out the one small candle he'd allowed himself, moved to a place behind the door, and waited.

When the door opened he remained still until her voice broke the silence. "Michael?"

He pushed the door shut and she gasped as she was caught up in strong arms.

She was startled only for a minute, but the deep chuckle and the awakening of her senses told her who it was. Her arms were around his neck and her lips found his.

It was several minutes later that he let her feet touch the floor, released her, and went to light the candle.

"Hannah," he smiled. "Who brought you out here, Quinn?"

"Nobody."

"Nobody!"

"I remembered the way myself."

"Do you realize how dangerous it is! I swear I'm going to strangle those boys."

"They don't know, either. They think I'm safely tucked in bed."

"What am I going to do with you?" He held out his hands in a supplicant gesture, and looked heavenward as if seeking divine intervention.

Hannah only laughed and came to him to stand on tiptoe and kiss him lightly. "Count your blessings," she said teasingly.

"I've been doing that for the past couple of days. I enjoyed that little scene at the cemetery today."

"You were there!"

"Up in the church steeple. Even Patrick didn't know I was coming."

"That was a dreadful chance to take."

"Look who's talking about taking chances! I think you've taken quite a few lately, and that little performance was one of them."

"I was rather good, wasn't I?" she said archly.

"A little cocky, aren't you?"

"No . . . just convinced."

"You don't think you overdid it a bit when you threw yourself across my . . . grave?"

"No. I think I was excellent. You just don't appreciate good acting when you see it."

"Oh, I do, I do," Michael laughed. "Sarah Bernhardt herself would have been forced to applaud. If no one believed I was dead, they would have after that."

"I'm glad you acknowledge my superior talent. It," she said nonchalantly, "is only one of my fine qualities."

"So I'm beginning to find out. I don't really know what to expect next from you."

"Kind of makes life exciting, doesn't it?" she asked smoothly.

"Hannah," he shook his head and laughed, "life with you is certainly never going to be dull."

"I will keep you on your toes!" She laughed with him, enjoying his laughter and knowing it had been a long time since he had found a reason to laugh. He looked so much younger when he did.

"If you don't kill me with worry."

"When you get clever enough to catch me permanently you won't have to worry."

"Why do I doubt that?"

"Now, Michael," Hannah walked to him and slid her arms around his waist and looked up at him with such innocence that he had to grin. He had to remember that when Hannah seemed her most innocent, she was actually her most devilish. "Why would you doubt me for a minute?"

"Because, my sweet little angle, I don't put anything past you. It seems to me you're a lady who knows exactly what she wants and won't let any fences stand between her and it."

"I can't afford to. What I wanted," she added softly, "was going to walk out of my life. Because of some misplaced sense of honor, I suppose. I just had to convince you that you were wrong."

"Well I've, as you said, become more clever since then. I intend to catch you, and *very* permanently."

"It's about time, Michael Cord. I had a feeling I was going to have to chase you forever. Across the country is long enough. It's time to give up graciously and admit I was right all along."

"What I did, I did for your good, Hannah," he said seriously. "I never thought of this scheme then or things would have been different."

"You wouldn't have left me?"

"Wild horses couldn't have dragged me away. You don't believe leaving you was easy, do you? It had to be one of the hardest things I've ever done. And don't believe I haven't wanted you, and lived with your memory every day and night. There were times . . ." He paused. He didn't want Hannah to be part of the black side of his life.

"Don't do that to me."

"What?"

"Shut me out. I'm not a delicate little girl and I wish you'd stop putting me on a pedestal. I want to know . . . everything. I want to be part of all of you, not just what's easy and good. The only way to rid yourself of the bad memories is to drag them out, share them, then throw them away."

"It's going to take me a while to learn that this is not a game for you."

"No, Michael . . . this is our beginning."

He looked down into her eyes and felt the truth of what she said. There would be no more running, no more loneliness . . . no more dreaming of Hannah. She was here, in his arms, and was offering him all he'd hoped of.

He'd never wanted anything as much as he wanted her. And right now. But he was well aware of the circumstances. They were not exactly in the ideal place.

Hannah was aware of it, too. She reached up and held his face between her hands. "Michael . . . nothing else matters. It's us . . . just us."

The candle flame flickered in a gentle breeze and bounced eerie shadows across the ceiling. For a log moment he simply held her, gazing down at her as if he wanted to etch her into his heart. He breathed her name softly, then gathered her closer to him. Their mouths touched, tasted, and then blended.

Hannah was stirred so deeply by the infinite tenderness she felt that it brought tears to her eyes.

Both had dreamed of this too long and too often to want to hurry it in any way.

Michael began to slowly undress her with fingers that trembled. She felt her heart begint o pound as his hands lightly touched her.

She closed her eyes and shivered with expectancy. Michael moved to stand behind her, and brushed her hair aside to kiss the nape of her neck. His arms came around her, his hands caressing her. She rested back against him and surrendered to the pleasure.

But she wanted so much more. She turned in his arms and

began to unbutton his shirt. He didn't help; he was too caught in her.

Hannah gasped as her fingers traced the scars of his wounds. Her eyes rose to his, brimmed with tears.

"You must have suffered so terribly."

"It no longer matters, Hannah. Whatever pain I have ever felt is gone now. You've made the world right."

She moved into his arms, pressing herself intimately into his hard body and raised her lips for his kiss. She felt the mounting warmth of belonging . . . of a sense of rightness as she surrendered herself completely.

He released her lips reluctantly, and with one arm around her waist, he put the other under her knees and lifted her against him. She clung to him, pressing her lips gently against his flesh. Then she closed her eyes and felt him place her gently on the cot that suddenly seemed as welcome as the softest bed. Her arms linked about his neck she whispered his name softly, as she felt the length of him hot against her.

Hannah felt as though she had been tossed into a current he could not fight. Her body raged with a fire she would never again be able to extinguish.

His effect on her was so vital, so overpowering, that she could feel the fevered pounding of her blood. His hot mouth found the rapid pulse at the base of her throat and he heard her soft moan of pleasure.

He teased her with gentle hands and torturing lips until she was twisting and turning beneath him, her world filled with nothing but him and a virulent pulsing need.

His lips skimmed down her body, nipping, then caressing, her flesh with his tongue until she wanted to scream out in ecstatic torment.

Everything, every thought and every breath, was Michael. He filled her world. Gently he caressed her thighs, separating her legs. His lips, gentle and seeking, stroked her flesh, until he found the pulsing center of her sensual being. He was fierce and possessive, and when she felt she could bear no more, when her body was ablaze, when the white-hot need was like an unquenchable flame along every nerve, she could hear from a great distance her own voice pleading for release.

She heard his incoherent words of love, whispered in passion beyond the power of reason. Only then did he press himself deep within her, taking away her soft cry of pain with his lips. Then he was part of her, his hard maleness stroking within her, driving to the depths over and over again, endlessly, demandingly, lifting her higher and higher.

It was a nearly violent, explosive release that soared them to the ecstasy of fulfillment.

Michael raised himself on one elbow and looked down into Hannah's eyes. With a genlte hand he brushed strands of hair from her damp forehead, then bent to kiss her forehead and cheeks.

"Hannah," he murmured. "I love you."

It was so gently whispered that Hannah couldn't be certain her ears heard it, but her heart heard the beat of his and savored his gentle touch.

When their eyes met Hannah knew that this was where she would want to spend the rest of her life . . . in Michael's arms.

"Now," she said, with a touch of laughter in her voice, "are you sorry I came?"

"If you hadn't, I would have missed the only perfect thing in my life. Have I told you how beautiful you are?"

"I'll never get tired of hearing you say it."

Michael rolled on his back and Hannah nestled against him, her fingers lightly stroking his chest.

"Can you really imagine it?" he said. "For once in more years than I care to remember, I can really make plans. It's so wonderful that it staggers me."

"You'll have to change your name," Hannah said quietly. Michael didn't see the look of mischievous humor in her eyes. "And your occupation."

"Absolutely. I just don't have one idea of who or what I can be."

"I have a few ideas."

"Oh? Like what?"

"Well . . . you have to admit I did a pretty good job of tracing you across the country."

Michael looked puzzled. "Yeah, but I don't . . ."

"Just listen," Hannah was trying to hide her smile against his chest, "you know that the Pinkertons make a lot of money."

Her train of thought really escaped him now. "Hannah . . . what's the Pinkertons got to do with us?"

"I thought we might open an agency of our own," she continued. "You could change your name to . . . Let me see . . . what about Marshall? I can see it now: Marshall Detective Agency, Mr. Hannah Marshall, President. Doesn't it sound intriguing?"

Michael was silent for a moment, completely without words as a very terrible picture formed before his eyes. He gave a low, guttural sound and was rewarded by a muffled giggle. He tightened his arm about her until he heard her gasp. She tried to wriggle free, but he held her and slowly turned to look at her.

"*Mr.* Hannah Marshall, is it?" He scowled.

"Now . . . it's only a thought." Her laughter bubbled. "There's no need for violence." He continued to look fierce as his other arm came around her.

"Don't you think we ought to get dressed? I really must go. I . . . Michael!" She yelped as he crushed her against him, then squealed as he pulled her across him. "Don't you dare!" But her warning fell on deaf ears as he raised a hand to smack the enticing derriere that was exposed. She wriggled helplessly, caught between laughter and the uncertainty that he might achieve what he threatened. Michael's hand fell, not with force . . . but with a caress.

"But," she looked at him in all innocence, "you were the one looking for suggestions. I was merely trying to be what a good wife should be. A partner."

"You know, I never realized how much like my sister Allison you are. There's enough devil in you to share with three women. Allison spent more time getting her rump swatted by our parents than Trace and I put together."

"I take it that means you don't care for my idea."

"I'll try to think of something better," he said, his voice fighting amusement.

"Michael," Hannah said seriously, "what are we really going to do? We . . . we can't go home, can we?"

He knew Hannah would do what he wanted, go with him wherever he wanted to go, but it pained him to know that because of him she would have to give up everything. The sacrifice she was willing to make had him a little awed.

"We can't even begin to make any kind of plans. Not until we know for certain that our little trick worked. A couple of days of nosing around ought to be enough to see our three friends on their way. Then we can resume our lives."

"Michael, don't you think you could tell me now why you've had to go through all this? Max told me only as much as I could force from him. I'd like to know everything, and only you can tell me."

"I suppose nobody has more right to the truth than you do." He turned so that Hannah lay on her side facing him and he could watch her face in the flickering candlelight. Then, with no hesitatino in his voice, he told her the story.

"What a vindictive man he is! And a senator! How can he condone this kind of thing?"

"He's drunk on his own power, and he lost his only son. The combination was too much for him. He just wanted to see me dead."

"Then, as far as he and the world are concerned, you are."

"Yes. Thanks to Patrick."

"I know how hard it must be not to let your family know . . ."

"In a couple of months Patrick is going to make a trip. He's going to look up Trace and Allison and tell them what happened. One day . . . we'll go home."

"Michael, I'm glad I'm here. I wouldn't want to be anywhere else in the world." She said the words quietly but firmly. "I love you."

He was shaken by the depth of his feelings for her. He reached out and tangled his hand in her hair, drawing her to him. "There are rewards in heavens," he murmured with a soft laugh. Their lips met then and all else was forgotten.

Michael sat on the edge of the cot and watched Hannah dress. His brow was creased in worry.

"You can't go on riding back and forth at night, Hannah. It's just not safe. I don't want you in these woods alone . . . and I don't want you to rouse the suspicions of those men.''

"I've no intention of riding alone.''

"Oh?''

"From now on I'll confide in Patrick, Quinn, or one of the boys . . . but I won't give up the chance to be with you.''

"You can't come here again,'' he said firmly. He stood and walked to her. "One mistake and the whole game is over. I'll have to face the three of them, and they don't play fair. Hannh, no matter what they are, I don't want another man's life on my conscience.''

"I know,'' she reached up to rest a hand against his cheek, "it's just so hard. I . . .''

"I know.''

He held her and kissed her and reluctantly let her go. He hated the thought that she would have to ride to town alone. When he finally blew out the candle he opened the door and walked outside with her.

She bent to kiss him after she had mounted her horse. Then she was gone, merging with the dark shadow of the trees. He felt her absence at once. He expelled a rgged breath and returned to a cabin that seemed even smaller and emptier than it had before. The next few days, Michael was certain, were going to be the longest he had ever spent . . . and the nights even worse, because, if he could find a way to get to Patrick, he was going to make certain Hannah never took this dangerous trip again.

Hannah rode slowly. The terrain was unfamiliar and the darkness made it difficult to be certain of her path. She would never admit to anyone that she was scared silly, and she pushed the fear aside in favor of the memory of the short hours she had just spent with Michael.

She knew he refused the idea of her coming again . . . just as she refused the idea of staying away. She couldn't stay away. Not now, not when she and Michael had finally found each other. She just couldn't have him alone and lonely, no matter how much he argued. She, too, felt the next few days were going to be the longest she had ever spent.

Quinn had found sleep impossible, and, worse, drinking didn't ease his situation at all. He felt like a blind man lost in a desert.

He didn't want to go to what he laughingly called home. He didn't want to talk to anyone, and he wished he could just block out the ugly parts of his life. But there was no way to do that, since whiskey had, for the first time, failed him.

It was nearing three in the morning when the saloonkeeper finally made it clear he wasn't going to stay open one more minute.

Quinn walked toward the stable, which was located a short distance away from Patrick's house, in a morose silence. There was no one on the street and he walked slowly, not caring about time. Somewhere in his mind he was aware of movement a few seconds before it really registered that someone was leading a horse into the stable and that someone looked like a woman . . . and a very familiar woman at that.

He broke into a trot, sensing the only reason Hannah Marshall could be out this late. It was dangerous.

He slipped inside the stable noiselessly and could hear movement as she unsaddled and cared for her own horse. At least she was smart enough not to awaken anyone.

He moved on silent feet down the long row of stalls until he neared the one in which Hannah stood. She was still completely unaware of his presence. She soothed her horse with softly whispered words to keep him calm.

Finished with his care, she turned to leave the stall and gasped in sudden fear as a large, broad-shouldered form loomed before her.

Hannah had never been as scared as she was now. She felt her mouth go dry, and her whole body began to shake.

"Hannah, what the hell are you doing out here this time of the morning?" His voice was gruff with tense anger, but she could have wept with relief when she recognized it. She held on to the edge of the doorframe for a minute, because she wasn't sure her trembling legs were going to support her.

"Oh, Quinn . . . you scared me out of a year's growth."

"You *should* be scared. What if I was someone else—one of Michael's old friends maybe? Where have you been?"

"To see Michael," she answered quickly. "Don't be angry, I had to."

Quinn was silent for a moment. He had accurately interpreted her feelings and sympathized with her.

"Yeah . . . I guess you did. Well, come on, at least let me take you back to the hotel."

"We shouldn't be seen together."

"The town's dead. Nobody will see us."

They left the stable and crossed the street. Although it was obvious that no one was awake, still they moved as rapidly as they could. Outside the hotel he took a moment to caution her not to repeat her actions.

"Hannah, for God's sake. You could have led them to Michael. Next time let someone know."

"I will. I'm going to see him again, Quinn. No matter what anyone says."

"Your friends are going to be tied up in knots."

"I won't tell them if you don't," she smiled.

"Hannah," he said in exasperation, "you'd better go inside."

"Good night, Quinn . . . and thanks."

Hannah went inside and Quinn turned back toward the stable, neither aware that a curtain had been drawn back in a window above them. After a few minutes it fell back into place.

Chapter Ten

Jonas hadn't been able to sleep. A finely honed instinct for trouble was bred in him too long and now he felt an uncomoftable nagging at the back of his mind. Something just wasn't right.

He, and the two men who traveled with him, had remained in the saloon late, looking for Quinn Wayland, but he'd never made an appearance . . . or no one would point him out. The last thought was one that had just occurred to him, followed by another question: Was Quinn Wayland staying out of their way on purpose? *Something just wasn't right.*

Now he stood at the window, looking down on the street. He watched as two shadowy forms left the stable and walked toward the hotel. He couldn't make out their features until they came closer. Then the clouds that had shadowed the moon separated and he could finally see them. The man was someone he didn't recognize, but the woman was the one he had seen at the cemetery . . . and she was completely different now. The black dress and veil were gone, and she was certainly no longer weeping.

It surprised him that a woman who was grieving a few hours before over her lost love would be out riding with another man late at night. Again the nagging instinct nudged him. This wouldn't be appropriate behavior.

Hannah, the men at the cemetery had called her. Well, Hannah was going to bear some research, as well as the man who was with her.

He looked at the man carefully, putting his face deep in his memory. Jonas Holt forgot nothing and no one. Tomorrow he'd find out who he was and what he was doing with Michael Cord's "grieving love" in the wee hours of the morning.

Jonas was dressing at daybreak. He left the hotel and stood on the boardwalk, watching the town awaken. Slowly it stirred and began to move around him. He watched the people and faces, but the man he had seen with Hannah didn't appear.

It took very little time to find out Hannah's last name and the names of the men with her. She didn't fit a mold. Hannah Marshall looked like a lady, yet she traveled with four men . . . alone . . . met another man late at night, and she grieved as if she were dying at another's grave. She was an enigma he meant to solve.

She was also a damn beautiful woman, and if she chose to share her favors so esaily, he wouldn't mind being a recipient.

He continued to watch and, after a while, he was joined by Hammond and Logan.

"We moving on today, Jonas?" Hammond asked. "All you need to do now is wire the senator that old Michael Cord's been brought to ground."

"No. Not yet."

"Why not? This town's gettin' on my nerves."

"Well, you can just settle back and forget leavin' for today. I have something I've got to look into," Jonas replied in a cold, clipped voice that no one cared to dispute. He walked away.

"What the hell's bitten him?" Logan said with a dark scowl.

"Beats me," Hammond grinned. "Why don't you ask him?"

"Me! Hell, no. When he's in that kind of mood I'd just as well keep my distance."

"*Something's* botherin' him, that's for sure. He said something about lookin' into something, so we may as well leave him be. I'm gonna get myself something to eat."

"Yeah, that's a good idea."

The two men walked slowly down the boardwalk to the restaurant.

Jonas walked down the street slowly, watching each face. At the end of the street he crossed over and started down the other side. Still, no one appeared who even resembled the man he'd seen the night before. But Jonas was a patient man ... He'd keep looking.

He crossed the street again and stood in front of the hotel. An hour passed ... and still he stood.

Then he was rewarded for his patience. The man he'd seen with Hannah Marshall the night before came right into town. Jonas watched him ride down the street and walk into the general store. He crossed the street and entered the store a few minutes after Quinn.

Inside it was still dim, though the morning sun was already lifting the shadows.

Quinn stood at the counter. "Make it two pounds of coffee, Hank, and a pound of sugar. I'll need a slab of bacon, and some eggs, too."

"You plan on a siege?" Hank asked with amusement. "This is your second huge order in a week."

Quinn *did* plan on a kind of siege. He planned on getting what supplies he needed and staying out of town for the next few days, or at least until Patrick sent him word that the gunfighters were gone.

"I'm just a big eater," Quinn replied.

Jonas walked slowly around the store, as if he were examining the merchandise. But he listened. He wanted to hear a name, but he had no success.

Quinn paid for his supplies.

"Box 'em up, Hank," he said, "I have one more stop to make, then I'll drop by and pick them up."

"Ain't seen much of you last couple of days."

"I've been busy."

Quinn didn't need Hank's conversation. He'd become aware of the close scrutiny of the man behind him and he'd also become aware of where he'd seen him before. He was one of the ones looking for Michael.

"See you later." He walked to the door and left, never turning to face the gunfighter at all. He was certain that he didn't know who he was yet, but equally certain that a question or two put to

Hank would soon have him knowing. If he hadn't run out of food he would have stayed in his cabin until Patrick had told him it was safe. Now he only prayed he hadn't upset the apple cart. From now on he fully intended to stay out of circulation.

But the questions were already being asked.

"Can I help you, sir?" Hank questioned with a smile.

"Yeah, I'll take a box of those forty-five's."

The clerk lifted the small box of shells and set them on the counter as he quoted the price. Jonas reached into his pocket and slowly counted out the coins.

"Say, I think I know that fella that just left. Name's Tom Ryan, isn't it?"

"The man that just left? No, sir. Name's Quinn Wayland. You must have him mixed up with someone else."

"Yeah, I guess I must have. Thanks."

"My pleasure," the clerk smiled.

Jonas left the store in time to see Quinn ride away. It was too late to try to follow him. By the time he got his horse saddled Quinn would have been logn gone.

Then his mmemory shifted again. Quinn had said he had one more stop to make. That meant he wasn't leaving town. Why then, did he ride out? The question drew Jonas's suspicious nature to a sharper edge. He rode out because he was running from something! The puzzle grew hazier. A gunfighter never ran from much. If Quinn Wayland was that fast . . . and if he wasn't afraid of something, then why act so nervous?

Jonas crossed the street to the hotel with a plan in mind. Inside he climbed the steps to the third floor—the top floor. At the end of the hall, on both sides, were windows. He walked to the one that faced the direction Quinn had taken.

Since the hotel was the tallest building in town, he had an unobstructed view for some distance. Quinn Wayland was nowhere in sight, but that was nearly an impossibility if he was leaving town . . . which confirmed Jonas's thoughts. He hadn't left at all. The next questino was, where had he gone?

Going back downstairs again he went outside and stood thoughtfully examining the street. From where he stood, and from the direction Quinn had taken, there weren't too many places Quinn could stop.

Determined to solve the puzzle, he went back to his room, dragged a chair to the window, and settled himself in to watch the street. An hour later he was rewarded for his patience.

He sat back in his chair, a frown touching his face. Why had Quinn Wayland decided to visit the local preacher? Either he was a repentant sinner or there was a whole lot more to this little game than Jonas knew. He walked to his bed and lay down. Folding his arms behind his head, he concentrated on all the threads he had so far, trying to draw them into one. He came up with several possible answers, but there was one answer he meant to have . . . and he meant to have it tonight.

Quinn had been shaken when he found himself in the general store with Jonas Holt. He knew he'd made a mistake and he intended to put as much distance between him and town as soon as he could. But he felt he had to warn Patrick first. Patrick, the doctor, the sheriff, and the local mortician were the only ones who knew the truth and they had to be prepared. He rode past the church, circled around, and wound up at the back of Patrick's small stable. He tied his horse out of sight and went to the back porch. His knock was answered by a more than surprised Patrick . . . who became thoughtful at Quinn's explanation.

"I'll go and pick up your supplies later. You get out of town as fast as you can and stay put. Let's hope the only reason he's interested in you is to test your gun. If that's so, he should give up in a couple of days when it looks like you're not going to show up."

"I hope so. I was close enough to look into his eyes. That man is a real killer and I don't think he'd stop at anything or anyone who got in his way. That includes you."

"We've got to see this out. When they can't find you, they'll eventually give up. Once they leave we can all breathe a sigh of relief."

"I sure hope it's soon."

"So do I . . . and so do a few other people."

"I think you ought to get to Hannah. Tell her not to go to

Michael tonight. Those men are like hawks, and since she's made herself so visible, they'll be watching her . . . and most likely her friends as well. They better all lay low."

"I'll join her for supper tonight." Patrick finally smiled. "Maybe if the boys know what's happened, the five of us will be able to pin Hannah down."

"Knowing her, as I'm beginning to," Quinn grinned, "it's probably going to take all five of you."

"She's a determined young lady, and a pretty strong one, too. Not too many women would have done what she has. Michael must consider himself a pretty lucky man. Despite what he's lost, he's gained Hannah . . . and that is a good balance."

"I'm glad it's all working out . . . at least for them," Quinn said, then made it obvious by his expression that he regretted the second of insight he'd given Patrick.

"Quinn?"

"I have to go. The longer I stay here, the more dangerous it becomes. I can see how Michael feels. I wouldn't want to face down any of those three men."

Patrick knew there was a wealth of words left unsaid, but he could also see Quinn had no intention of saying them. He followed Quinn as he walked toward the door. When he closed it behind him, Patrick made himself a promise to see what he could do to help make Quinn's life better. He owed him that much.

Hannah felt more in control when she woke up. A few days! After all the time she had spent wondering and worrying, in a few days it would all be over. She and Michael would be together and the running would be done.

She yawned and stretched in delicious relaxation. The night before had been like a dream, a dream she could still not quite believe.

But she meant to see him again. No matter what his arguments were. She was certain her performance at the cemetery left no question in the minds of the men who had plagued Michael. Soon they would be free.

A knock brought her back from her meditations. She rose, slipped into a robe, and went to open the door.

"Good morning, Hannah," Jamie smiled. "We were waiting to go to breakfast, but it started to look like you were going to sleep all day."

"I'll be glad to join you. It will only take me a little while."

"Okay. We'll be downstairs in the dining room. Oh, by the way, Patrick sent around this note." He handed the folded paper to Hannah.

She unfolded it and read quickly, hoping nothing had gone wrong with their plans.

Hannah,

I hope you and the boys will join me for dinner tonight. I know it's premature, but I think we should celebrate. I'll meet you at the restaurant around seven.

Patrick

Hannah knew the dinner could go on for hours and she wanted to go to Michael.

"Can you go over to see Patrick while I dress?"

"Sure."

"He wants to have dinner with us tonight. Sort of a celebratino, he said."

"Sounds good to me."

"If it's all right with the rest, tell him we'll meet him."

"Okay. See you at breakfast."

Hannah closed the door and leaned against it thoughtfully. Premature celebration didn't seem right for Patrick. But as much as he had done for both her and Michael, she could hardly refuse. She brushed the uncomfortable thoughts aside and went to dress.

The day seemed long for everyone. But eventually the sun began to set. Hannah and her friends left the hotel at a quarter to seven and walked toward the restaurant.

They found Patrick there already, and if he was a little tense, none of his guests were aware of it. Neither were they aware that he did everything in his power to make the dinner a long drawn-out affair.

Michael paced the confines of his cabin and Quinn, too, felt the bite of nervous strain.

But Jonas and his men were involved in a plan that had at first shocked both Hammond and Logan.

"Dig up a grave!" a gray-faced Logan questioned.

"You have to be crazy," Hammond added. Fear of doing such a bizarre thing made him nervous.

"No, I'm not crazy. If what I think is going on, is actually going on, we're in for a surprise. Or at least *you* are. Me, I think I've got this thing figured out."

"I don't understand a damn thing you've said for the past hour. And I ain't going out there at night and dig up no grave."

"Scared?" Jonas chuckled mirthlessly.

"No, I ain't scared. It just ain't right. Nobody ought to be digging up a man who's been dead a couple of days. It ain't right."

"Well, that's what we're going to do," Jonas's eyes had grown as cold as his words. Neither of the men with him chose to argue. But Hammond gathered nerve.

"Jonas, what the hell has gotten into you the past couple of days? We had a job to do and it's done. Even if it was done by someone else, it's done. Why can't you just let go? Cord is dead. That ought to satisfy the senator . . . and it ought to satisfy you. You been all-fired strange since the day we got here. It's time to go back, collect the rest of our money, and put this behind us."

"Any other time I'd agree with you. But this time is different."

"I don't see how."

"I don't like to be had . . . and I think that's what we've been. There isn't a man alive can make a fool out of Jonas Holt and get away with it."

"Now it's sure I don't understand. How the hell do you figure we been had?"

"I don't believe Cord's dead."

The two men looked at him in stunned disbelief.

"Now that's the craziest idea I ever heard. The whole town seen him die. He was buried by the preacher."

"Doesn't that bother you a little?"

"What?"

"A gunfighter dies, the local understaker just plants him and gets paid a couple of dollars by the city. This man dies and the local preacher takes the time and expense to bury him, buy a nice big stone so the whole world can see and a whole group of friends go cryin' at his grave. Sounds like playacting.''

"Maybe," Hammond half agreed. "Maybe not."

"Then figure this out. The man who shot him makes himself real scarce. Ever see a gunfighter do that?''

"Well, no, but . . .''

"No buts. There's something real wrong here. And I intend to have the answers I want. If they've been making fools of us, don't you think someone ought to pay for it?''

Both men were half convinced Jonas had a point but still wary of the unwelcome job of digging up the grave of a man who'd been dead for a couple of days.

"It's past dark and the cemetery is far enough away that nobody will hear us.''

"What about the preacher?" Hammond questioned.

"If he's home, Hammond, you hold a gun on him. Once we've finished digging, it won't matter. Then . . . we'll ask him real nice just where Michael Cord and Quinn Wayland are.''

There were no arguments left and a still nervous and reluctant pair followed Jonas, out the hotel by the back door. He had already put three shovels he had stolen from the cellar of the hotel in the dark alley outside. He cautioned both men to be quiet. "It's not far. We'll walk. Cut across the street and come to the cemetery by the woods. Hammond, you go check on the preacher. If he's there, bring him out. If he's not, come back and help us dig. The faster we do it the better.''

There were no more questions after that. It was firm in both men's minds. They were more scared of facing Jonas than they were at the prospect of digging up the grave of Michael Cord.

In less than half an hour Hammond was moving slowly up the back steps of Patrick's house. It took him very little time to find out that Patrick wasn't there. He joined the others in the cemetery. They dug without speaking.

When the shovel scraped across the rough pine of the casket it felt as if it was grating along their nerves. But grimly they continued their gruesome task.

Then the lid of the casket was pried loose and the three men could only gaze down at the pile orf stones that had compensated for the weight of a man.

"I'll be damned," Hammond half whispered.

"You sure as hell figured this one right. They must be laughing in our face," Logan said angrily.

"Let them laugh," Jonas smiled his cold, narrow-eyed smile, "we'll have the last one."

"What are you gonna do, Jonas?" Hammond asked.

"Me?" Jonas said softly. "I'm going to compliment a lady on a great piece of playacting. Then, we're going to have her send our regards to the soon-to-really-be-dead Michael Cord."

"What about the others?"

"The preacher has a little debt to pay, too. I don't like to be treated like a fool. It's going to be time to pin down Quinn Wayland, too. His part of this is going to cost him a whole lot more than he thought it would."

"Should we fill in the grave?"

"Yes," Jonas chuckled. "We don't want to tip our hand until we're ready. This ought to prove interesting . . . real interesting."

When they left the cemetery the grave gave the appearance that it had never been touched.

The dinner had been very good and Patrick had turned on all his Irish charm to keep Hannah's mind from how late it was. He'd just finished telling an amusing story, and everyone had shared in the laughter.

Still, impatience stirred in Hannah. She was about to do something to put an end to the prolonged meal when her attention was drawn to a pretty woman who stood in the doorway of the dining room. She looked around, as if searching for someone.

"Who is that, Patrick?" Hannah inquired.

Patrick followed her gaze.

"Rena Brenden. She's a nice girl. I wonder what she's doing here?"

"Looks like she's looking for someone."

Rena was approached by the waiter. They could see them converse and the waiter point in their direction. Rena looked toward them. Then she walked in their direction.

The men rose as Rena approached the table. It was Patrick who spoke first. He was under the immediate impression she had come in search of him.

"Rena, my dear. How nice to see you again. How are your parents?"

"Fine, Reverend . . ."

Patrick noticed that she was pale and her eyes looked as if she had been crying. "Can I be of help to you, Rena?"

"I . . ." She looked at Hannah. "You are Hannah Marshall, aren't you?"

"Yes, I am."

"I've come to talk to you if I may."

"Of course. Please, join us."

"No. I . . . I need to talk to you privately if you don't mind."

"Of course," Hannah replied, but she was just as puzzled as Patrick and the others.

"We'll wait for you outside, Hannah," Patrick said. "I want to make sure you are safely in for the night before I go home."

"You don't need to worry," Hannah laughed. "I'm sure I can find my way back to the hotel myself."

"We'll wait," Patrick said firmly. He and the others moved away. Hannah had a momentary sense that something was out of sorts, but she returned her attention to Rena.

"Won't you sit down?"

"Thank you," Rena replied. She sat opposite Hannah and clenched her trembling hands on the table before her. "It's very kind of you. I'm sorry to have interrupted your dinner."

"Don't worry. We were finished eating anyway. Actually," she bent toward Rena with a conspiratorial smile on her face, "I was looking for a good excuse to leave."

"There is something I have to say to you. I have done nothing but think about it for days, until I feel I can't stand it any longer."

"What is it?"

"I . . . I heard about . . . about your being at the cemetery. I know you must be suffering terribly. I've come to say I'm sorry and to try and make you understand . . ."

"Understand what?"

"This had to have been a terrible mistake! Quinn is not a killer! He's not a gunfighter. He's a gentle man . . ." Rena's eyes had filled with tears, and as she dug into her reticule for her handkerchief, Hannah studied her face.

There was no doubt in Hannah's mind that Quinn meant a lot to this woman. It surprised her that he had never said anything about her to anyone, especially Patrick, who had arranged everything.

"I'm sure he's not," Hannah said softly.

Rena paused to look at her in surprise. There was no hatred here, no vindictive quest for revenge.

"You love him very much?"

"Yes," Rena replied in a voice broken with misery. "Oh, this is all so terrible. I must make you understand. Quinn is . . ."

"You don't need to explain. I know this must be very hard for you."

"It is worse for Quinn. It's not fair! It just isn't fair!"

"I agree with you. It isn't. Tell me . . . does Quinn know you are here?"

"No. I have had enough trouble getting to see you. I don't know where Quinn is. He . . . he won't come to see me." Rena looked as if she were ready to cry again, and Hannah could not let her go on.

"Please, Rena . . . there is something I have to tell you. Maybe it will ease your pain a bit."

Rena looked at her with puzzled eyes. This was certainly not the reaction she expected to get from Hannah. Quinn had killed the man she loved and Rena didn't understand her reaction at all.

"Something to tell me?"

Hannah was grateful that the crowd of diners had diminished. Only a couple of tables besides theirs had any customers at them. She bent as close to Rena as she could and watched her face turn from despair, to stunned amazement . . . then to something very close to anger.

"So you see . . . Quinn is guilty of nothing."

"Nothing," Rena repeated. "Except destroying any chance we had at happiness and letting people, who always wanted to think the worst of him, really believe he . . . You say he is guilty of nothing?"

"Looking at it from that standpoint I can see what you mean.

But I don't see why you just can't go to him. Tell him you know and that you understand.''

"It's not so simple." Rena went on to explain the situation between her and Quinn. "You see, my family . . . everyone, would never understand?"

"Does that really matter?" Hannah said gently.

"What?"

"I said, does it really matter?"

"I don't know what you mean."

"Is it important that the town approves . . . or that your parents approve? Or is it more important that you and Quinn are together? I can't give you advice on what to do, but I know what *I* would do. If Quinn is the kin of man you say he is, and from our short acquaintance, I think he is, I would simply go with him, marry him, and stand by him no matter what anyone said."

"I wish that could be so. My biggest barrier is Quinn!"

"You said he loved you."

"Yes. He is the one who says he won't hurt me by loving me. He thinks he's not good enough."

"Then you have to take matters into your own hands. Even if it scares you to death."

"I just don't know how."

"I do believe," Hannah smiled and her eyes sparkled with her own particular brand of wickedness, "that you are being forced to compromise Quinn . . . and hope his own sense of honor won't let him walk away from it."

Rena's cheeks grew pink, and for a minute she looked totally shocked. Then the idea began to register in her mind.

"Oh, dear," she said softly as it brought mental pictures.

"What do you think he is likely to do if you simply show up in the middle of the night and make it clear you have no intention of going home."

"He'd be furious."

"Does that scare you?"

"No. But he's liable to drag me right back home."

Hannah smiled. "Then from there on it will be up to you. You just have to convince him of three things: first that you know about his involvement in Patrick's little game. Second, that you love him no matter what. And third, that you have no intention of letting anyone, including him, put up any more barriers. You are a beautiful woman, Rena. I don't think I have to say much more."

"You have so much more courage than I do."

"Ridiculous! I have no more courage than any other woman. Men like Quinn and Michael have this ironbound sense of honor, and sometimes a woman just has to find a way around it or it can make them as obstinate as a Missouri mule."

"I'm glad I met you, Hannah Marshall."

"I hope it all works out and you're as lucky as I am. If I were you," Hannah laughed as she rose, "I wouldn't mention a thing to Patrick. He might just feel it's his moral duty to stop you."

Rena rose to stand beside her. "Thank you."

"You're welcome. Now I'd better go out and let my guards walk me home. You'd think I was made out of spun sugar the way they treat me." She put a comforting hand on Rena's arm. "Stand by what you think is right and best for you and Quinn. Don't let anyone else rule your life or you might just miss a lot of happiness."

Rena smiled as she and Hannah walked to the door of the restaurant. Outside they were met by Patrick and the men who fashioned themselves Hannah's protectors.

Rena said good night and walked back to her carriage. She needed a few minutes to think and forumlate her plans.

They all walked slowly back to the hotel. Hannah knew the men were purposely slow.

"Was there something special that Rena wanted to talk to you about?" Patrick questioned. "I didn't know that you knew each other."

"I didn't know her until tonight. But I've found we have a great deal in common."

"Really?"

"She . . . she was just being sympathetic. It was nice of her to try and console me."

Patrick wasn't sure there wasn't a lot more to this meeting, but he was just as sure that Hannah wasn't going to tell him one more thing.

He left them at the front door of the hotel but cautioning all four men to see Hannah didn't leave the hotel room. They were determined to comply with Patrick's wishes.

At her door she turned to say good night.

"Hannah," Jamie said with a warning smile, "I know you're not going to take to this idea much. But it sure would upset me and the boys if you was to decide to take a midnight stroll."

"Why, Jamie, the idea never crossed my mind. But thanks to all of you for worrying about me. I'll be as good as I can be," she promised with wide, innocent eyes. Of course she wasn't stating just how good that was. She was also quite sure that none of the four believed her for a minute.

"Well, just to make sure nobody bothers you, we're going to take turns sittin' on that chair at the end of the hall. For your protection."

"You're very thoughtful," Hannah said dryly. "Good night, gentlemen." She opened her door and went inside.

Joey and Jamie exchanged looks. "She ain't too happy with us," Jamie stated.

"If it keeps her from getting into trouble, then it's worth it," Joey said.

"Who gets first watch?" Brad spoke quietly, hoping his voice didn't carry inside.

"You first, Brad, I'll spell you in a couple of hours, then I'll wake up Jamie," Joey said. "I sure hope this is over soon. Hannah can be cold as ice when she's mad."

Chapter Eleven

Hannah was frustrated. She knew quite well she would never be able to slip out again the way she had done before. She might have fooled her friends once, but it was unlikely she could do so again . . . at least, not the same way. She sat on the edge of her bed for a minute, trying to figure a way out of her dilemma.

It was past midnight now and she knew Michael would not expect her; still, she hated just giving up and spending the night alone in a bed that had become decidedly empty.

She waited . . . and waited, until she could bear it no longer. Then she rose, went to the door, cracked it open, and looked out. From an uncomfortable chair, tipped back to rest against the wall, Brad grinned sheepishly at her and waved.

"Night, Hannah . . . sleep well."

Hannah could do no less than smile. She found it difficult to be angry with someone who had become so dear to her. She closed the door and leaned back against it. There was nothing she could do about it. Her friends were going to protect her if it killed them . . . or her.

Half angry and half amused, she finally gave up. She took off her clothes and put on a nightgown. Then she put out her lamp and climbed into bed.

For a long time she couldn't sleep. She relived the long hours she had searched for Michael . . . and the wonderful but short hours they had shared.

Knowing that time could solve all their problems did not make the waiting any easier. She thought of Quinn and Rena. She had seen in Rena's eyes the fact that she truly loved Quinn.

In her heart she felt that if Rena could only gather her courage and face the disapproval of her family and the town, Quinn could prove his worth in time.

It would not be easy and Hannah felt Rena might, as she had, get the most resistance from Quinn himself. She smiled to herself. How much alike Quinn and Michael really were—bound by some unwritten code that made them so abominably stubborn where women were concerned.

She rolled over and hugged her pillow to her, knowing the same flaw was one of the things that had drawn her to Michael in the first place. The pillow was small consolation for what she wanted, but it and her dreams were all she had . . . at least for tonight.

Quinn paced the confines of his house, unable to control the pent-up energy that threatened to explode.

He tried to make plans, but a jumble of confused thoughts was all he got. He would leave Virginia City . . . but wherever he went Rena wouldn't be there. At least if he remained here, miserable or not, he would see her. He would know how her life was . . . maybe even find a way to make sure no one could hurt her.

He thought of the days and nights that lay ahead and he wasn't sure he would be able to handle them.

He left the cabin and saddled his horse. He knew he should stay away from town, but he needed something to ease his misery. Deep in his mind was the thought that Patrick would be angry. But it was matched by another. Let the trouble come. He would use a bottle and his gun until one of them killed him.

He ignored the obvious tares of the townspeople, tied his horse in front of the saloon, and went inside. At the bar he smiled at the bartender.

"Give me a bottle, Jake."

"Quinn . . ." Jake began. He was one of the few in town who harbored any kind of sympathy for Quinn.

"Not tonight, Jake," Quinn said softly. "Just a bottle."

"Look, Quinn, I'm not telling you not to have a drink. I'm just trying to give you a warning. Don't get drunk. Those fellas . . . those gunfighters . . . they're on the prod and looking for you. Seems, so they say, they have a couple of questions to ask you. You got no quarrel with that bunch, do you?"

"Nope, and I don't intend to put my tail between my legs and run. So give me the bottle. If they want to talk to me . . . well, I'm here."

Jake handed him the bottle and shook his head helplessly as Quinn took it and moved to a table in the corner farthest from the door.

Quinn sat down and poured a drink . . . but he didn't drink it. He merely sat looking at it for a long whle. It wasn't the answer and he knew it. But it *was* a promise of a few hours of oblivion. He reached for the glass slowly and was just raising it to his lips when the swinging doors were pushed open and Logan King walked in.

For a long second the glass remained motionless, then Quinn tossed the liquor down and set it aside.

Logan looked around the room, and his eyes paused at Quinn for a long moment. Then he let the doors swing shut behind him and walked to the bar.

Quinn was pretty sure the bartender would not reveal who he was, so he decided to remain quiet and just watch and listen.

There were only a few men in the slaoon. Five of them were playing cards at one table and paying little attention to what was going on around them. Two were at the opposite end of the bar engrossed in conversatno. Another three sat at a table several feet from Quinn. A piano player was talking to one of the girls, who leaned against the piano while he absently moved his hands over the keys, and two other girls in their briliant dresses were standing near the cardplayers, intent on their game. Their purpose was to judge who the night's winners were, so they could choose the evening's company wisely.

Logan ordered a drink and, to Quinn's relief, turned his back and began to sip it. Through the mirror over the bar Quinn could watch his face and he seemed to be engrossed in his own thoughts.

Quinn hoped Logan would have a drink or two, then leave, and for a while it looked as if it would happen that way. Then the swinging doors opened again.

Of all the people Quinn thought. Why did it have to be one of the men in town who felt he had a particular grudge against him? Winslow Baker had been a student in school with Quinn. A spoiled, antagonistic boy, who was dominated by his mother, had grown into a sly, vindictive man. And Quinn had been his target, although Winslow had failed to harm him in any tangible way.

Winslow's smile was malicious. Quinn closed his eyes for a minute, knowing what was coming and the futility of trying to do anything about it.

Winslow stopped a foot or two from Logan and ordered a drink. He took the glass in his hand and turned his back to the bar. He raised it in a silent salute to Quinn, who remained still. Then he turned to Logan.

"I hear you're lookin' for a fella."

Logan turned his head toward him, but did not answer

"I also heard it was Quinn Wayland you was lookin' for. The man who was ast enough to gun down Michael Cord."

"You know him? He a friend of yours?"

"Hardly a friend of mine, but I know him . . . yes, I know him. In fact . . . he's right here."

Logan stiffened and his hand momentarily froze. Then his eyes returned to Winslow. "Here?" He turned around to survey the room, and he didn't need to be told who the lone man at the corner table was.

If he was tense Quinn showed no sign of it as Logan moved from the bar and walked slowly toward him.

" 'Evening." Logan watched Quinn's eyes as he spoke.

" 'Evening" was Quinn's curt reply.

"Your name Quinn Wayland?"

"It is."

"You been pretty scarce hereabouts lately."

"No more than usual. I don't spend a lot of time in town."

"Mind if I sit?"

"Yeah, I mind. I have plans on drinking alone."

Logan's face grew hard and the smile that touched his lips was frigid. "Real hard case, are you?"

"No . . . just choosy about who I drink with."

"I hear tell you're pretty fast with that gun."

"Passable."

"I also hear tell you was the one that put Michael Cord up there on the hill. That takes a pretty fast gun."

"You come over here to tell me that? Being fast is no great accomplishment."

"Maybe not, maybe not. But it sets me to wondering about how fast you *really* are." His voice softened to a deadly calm, and Quinn knew he was not going to be able to bluff his way out of a confrontatino.

A boiling anger made him see red for a minute. He'd been pushed all his life, and he was getting tired of it. But anger never made for a steady mind or a steady head, and he needed both now. So he smiled, poured another drink slowly, and watched Logan's face as he drank it.

"I don't suppose wondering is going to do anybody any harm."

"Could be I plan on doin' more than wondering."

"What you plan is your business. Just don't include me. You see," Quinn smiled, "I don't give a damn how fast you are. I'm not interested in proving anything to anybody. So I killed Michael Cord. He and I had a disagreement. That's got nothing to do with you. Now, why don't you go and enjoy your drink and leave me alone to enjoy mine."

Quinn knew it wasn't wise to appear weak in front of Logan, but the last thing he wanted was to seem as if he could be persuaded to go for his gun. He watched Logan's eyes. It was always the eyes that reflected the movement first.

Logan backed up a step or two and his eyes became as cold and deadly as a reptile's. His hand, hanging loose at his side, twitched nervously.

"Don't be a damn fool," Quinn said quietly.

"You're a coward. You want to stand up like a man or don't you have the nerve to face someone who just might be faster than you?"

Quinn didn't move, and that alone took a lot of control. Men had called him a lot of things, mostly behind his back, but never a coward. He could feel every nerve inside him coil into a tight knot.

"You're making a mistake," he tried to caution Logan. But Logan was past caution.

"Come on, coward boy," Logan taunted. "What'd you do, shoot Cord in the back?"

There was no way he was going to get past Logan and Quinn knew it. Slowly he rose.

He began to realize he was scared. This man thought he'd killed Michael, that he was faster than Michael. The truth was, he would never know. He and Michael had never really drawn against each other . . . only Logan didn't know that, and Quinn couldn't tell him.

The entire room was so still, Quinn could hear his own heart thudding furiously.

Seconds ticked by . . . and the two men locked their gazes, each waiting for the blink of an eye or the twitch of a finger.

And the moment came. Both men drew so quick that it happened within the blink of an eye. At the same moment Logan felt himself lifted from his feet and slammed backward, Quinn felt a piercing pain in his side. He looked down in shock, both that he was still alive and that he was bleeding. He felt no pain . . . Logan lay still on the floor.

He couldn't talk. He pressed his hand to his side and looked around him at the stunned men. A minute later the sheriff, Bill Horton, came in.

"It was a fair fight," Quinn rasped, worried that he was looking at serious trouble.

"He's right, Sheriff," one of the cardplayers said quickly. "The guy pushed him into it."

The others agreed, to Quinn's relief.

"Quinn, you better go on over to the doc's. I'll take care of this."

"I'll take care of myself," Quinn said. He put his gun in the holster and started toward the door.

"I said you better go see Doc."

"I'm all right. I'ts only a scratch. I . . . I didn't want . . ."

"I know," Bill said, "so go on home if you're all right. I'll take care of this. Go on home, Quinn."

"Yeah," Quinn muttered. In his mind he could read everyone's eyes, imagining their condemnation. He imagined every pair of eyes as Rena's . . . every pair making him understand that this would be the final blow. If he hadn't destroyed Rena's love before, he had now. Without another word he left the saloon and started home.

Rena had thought all day about what Hannah had said to her. Did it matter what anyone said as long as she knew she loved Quinn and he loved her? No. Did she have the courage to do what Hannah had suggested? Yes, she did. The only question that presented itself was . . . how?

She paced the floor, considering alternatives. There seemed to be only one. She must have drawn her mother's attention with her pacing because the light rap on her door interrupted her thoughts.

When the door opened, Rena smiled at her mother, but the response was not so spontaneous.

"Mother?"

"You didn't come down for dinner, Rena."

"I wasn't hungry. I had some thinking to do."

"About Quinn Wayland?"

"Yes," Rena said honestly.

"And you've come to a decision?"

"I'm sorry, Mother. I don't know if you or Father will ever understand. I know what you want for me . . . but I have to do what I feel is best for me."

"Rena, the man has . . ."

"I know what you think he's done."

"Think! Rena, there is a grave to testify to his actions."

"Things are not always what they seem to be. You should not judge Quinn by what other people say. Mother, you don't know him."

"Your father will forbid you ever talking to him again. You know that."

"Then . . . I will have to find whatever way I can." Her chin lifted proudly. "I love Quinn and I am not ashamed to say it. You don't know or understand him. If you did know all the truth you would feel differently.''

"You love him because you are young and have a romantic notions. You were always one to care for stray animals and injured creatures. But don't be blind, Rena. This is not a fairy tale. You just might not live happily ever after.''

"I shall just have to take my chances on that. Quinn will prove himself to all of you one day. But he does not have to prove himself to *me*. I love him as he is.''

Samuel appeared in the doorway to hear his daughter's last words. "Maybe I can change your mind, Rena,'' he said quietly. The look on his face was less one of satisfaction than of sympathy and distress. "Word has just been brought to me. There has been a man shot in the saloon. A man named Logan King . . . he was shot by Quinn Wayland. It seems this man has gone on a killing rampage.''

Rena was momentarily stricken. Then the name of the man Quinn had shot stirred her memory. He was one of the gunfighters who had been looking for Michael Cord.

"I'm going to go see Quinn,'' she said determinedly. "I want to hear the story from him and not from an onlooker who *thinks* he knew what was behind what he saw.''

"I must give you credit, Rena,'' her father replied, "for your loyalty. You don't give up easily.''

"I almost did once. I regretted it then, I won't regret any decisions I make now.''

"Are you sure?''

"Father, you once told me a good newspaper man always dug to the heart of his story and found the *real* truth before he printed anything. You don't know that real truth, yet you condemn Quinn and you want me to do the same. Well, I won't do it, because I know so much more than you or anyone else does.''

Samuel looked at his daughter with a gleam of respect in his eyes. "I don't want you hurt, Rena.''

"I know,'' Rena smiled weakly, "but give me credit for being my father's daughter . . . and let me show you that Quinn is not what you think he is.''

"You . . . you aren't going to go see him?'' Sophie gasped.

"Yes, Mother, I am.'' She looked directly at her father as she spoke. He filled the doorway and she knew she could not pass him if he chose not to let her. "I don't want to sneak off anymore," Rena said quietly. "I would rather you let me go."

Samuel's gaze held hers for a long, breathless moment. Then he moved aside. "Have our carriage harnessed. I'm going with you."

Rena felt a surge of love for him that brought tears to her eyes and a smile to her face.

"Thank you," she whispered.

"Don't thank me yet, Rena. I haven't changed my mind about him. It's just the newspaper man in me. I like to get to the bottom of the story . . . and I like the truth."

Rena nodded. She knew she could not expect her parents to understand. There was no way to make them see without telling them all the truth and she couldn't do that yet. But she could go to Quinn . . . and she meant to stay with him no matter who put up an argument . . . even Quinn.

Quinn had discovered, as he rode toward home, that he was bleeding more heavily than he had thought. He was dizzy when he slid down from his horse. Knowing the horse would graze contentedly after a long ride, Quinn struggled to remove bridle and saddle, letting them fall to the ground with the idea that he could put them away tomorrow.

He staggered up to the door, fighting the blackness that threatened to claim him. Gratefully he fell across his bed and surrendered to oblivion.

He did not hear the carriage approach, nor did he hear anyone enter the house. Rena and her father were surprised to see his equipment lying outside. They were both shocked to find the door standing half open. It was Rena who saw the trace of a bloody handprint on the door.

With a cry of alarm she had pushed the door fully open and went inside quickly. Her father lit a lamp, and only then did she see Quinn's inert from across the bed . . . and the red stain that was slowly seeping into the blankets. She ran to his side and knelt by the bed, reaching a shaking hand to brush the tangle of his hair from his sweaty brow.

"Quinn . . ."

Samuel could hear the pain in her voice.

"Let me help, Rena," he said firmly. He rolled Quinn on his side and examined him. "He's been shot, but I don't think it's fatal. He does need a doctor, though. Right now I'll do what I can, then you stay with him and I'll go fetch Doctor Simpson."

Rena raised her eyes, welling with tears, to her father. "He won't die?"

"No, he won't die. He's as strong as a bull. Can you find me something to clean this wound with and something to bind him up? I think he'll be as good as new in no time."

Rena looked around her, but could find nothing, so she bent to lift the hem of her dress and removed one of her petticoats. This she tore into several pieces which she handed to her father.

"Heat up some water," Samuel ordered.

Rena moved swiftly to light the fire in the small stove and find a basin.

She watched as her father cleansed the wound. To her it looked terrible, but her father kept assuring her it was not.

Quinn was bandaged and made comfortable, then Samuel left Rena with him while he went to find the doctor.

"Just be sure he remains quiet. I will be back as fast as I can."

"Father . . ." Rena's voice stopped Samuel as he was on his way to the door. He paused and turned to look at her. She rose and walked to him. "I'm grateful for what you've done. Once you really know Quinn . . ."

"Rena . . . because I don't want to see a man die like a lonely animal does not mean I understand or accept any reason he might give to kill another. I've done what I can for him . . . and I will get the doctor. But after he is cared for, you must tell him you cannot see him again. You're coming home with me."

"No, I'm here . . . and here I will stay."

"We'll see. Maybe he will understand even if you don't."

"Again you don't understand, Father. Even Quinn can't drive me away. I love him and I know he loves me. I intend to stay until you all come to your senses."

Samuel stared at his daughter, amazed at the fiery defiance combined with courage in her eyes.

"We'll see," he said.

"Yes . . . we will see."

Samuel closed the door, realizing there was a battle to fight . . . and not sure he could win. He wondered if he could make Quinn Wayland see how wrong this was and force Rena out of his life.

Quinn struggled up from the depths, sure that he was dreaming. The scent of perfume and the feel of a gentle hand touching him had to be a dream.

He opened his eyes and the misty shapes before him slowly began to solidify. He blinked. This could not be believed. It must be only his wishful thinking. He closed his eyes and opened them again, sure that Rena would vanish in the meantime. When she didn't, he spoke her name.

"Rena . . . how did . . . what are you doing here?"

"I heard . . ."

"That I killed another man."

"Don't waste your time any longer on that little farce," she smiled. "I know too much to swallow any more fairy tales."

"I don't know what you're talking about."

"No? How about the fact that Michael Cord is not dead?"

"Rena . . ."

"Hannah told me," she said softly.

"Oh." There was no more point in saying more.

"I'll bet your parents are pretty satisfied with the stories about the new victim to Quinn Wayland's gun."

"My father has gone for the doctor. Before he left me here with you, he took care of you."

Quinn could only look at her, unable to understand what had transpired.

"Quinn, maybe if we had approached my parents at the beginning, none of this would have happened. I don't know. I only know the battle is over for now."

"Suppose you start at the beginning. I don't understand any of this."

"Before I do that, you tell *me* what happened."

"Rena, I didn't start this. I had no choice except to defend myself." He went on to tell the whole story.

"He's one of the men who were looking for Michael?"

"Yes. He thought I was fast. Hell, I almost wasn't fast enough for him and I'm real sure Michael is faster. I wouldn't want to face those other two. I got out of this with a lot of luck, and just by the skin of my teeth."

"I have to talk to Michael."

"No, Rena. They think he's dead. Let it lie for a while yet. Trust me. I'll be smart enough to stay out of their way in the future."

"Quinn . . . they won't let you! You've killed one of them. They just might come after you!"

He reached out and took hold of Rena's shoulders, drawing her closer. "Don't lose your nerve. You're a lot tougher than that."

"I'm afraid! Oh, Quinn . . . we have a chance. We just can't throw it away."

"And would you have me grab my chance at the expense of other lives?"

"Yes!"

"Rena," he laughed, "you and I both know better than that. We'd never be able to look at each other, much less be happy. If we ever did have a chance, I don't want to do anything to end it. Please, Rena." His voice grew gentle. "Understand. I want you to look at me and know that I'm not a betrayer of friends or any of the other things this town has labeled me."

"Interesting speech, young man." Samuel's voice came from the doorway. Dr. Simpson appeared behind Samuel, and Quinn knew from the look in his eyes that he had told Samuel nothing.

"Mr. Brenden," Quinn said. "I'm sorry about this. You'd better take Rena home."

"Quinn!" Rena said sharply.

"He's right, Rena," Samuel said. "Come on, you can't stay here."

"Oh, but you're wrong, Father," Rena said quietly. "You're both wrong." She could see the glow of respect in John Simpson's eyes. "I belong here, and here is where I intend to stay. I wish you and Mother felt differently. But I can't let that stop me. I intend to stay with Quinn . . . from now on."

"Rena!" her father said angrily. "You come with me. Now!"

"No." Quinn was stunned to silence. "I love you. But I love Quinn . . . and I intend to remain."

"If you don't come with me now . . ."

"The threat is useless. I'm staying with Quinn. Good night, Father."

Samuel was furious. He slammed the door and the cabin was suddenly silent.

"Damn it, Rena," Quinn said miserably. "You'll ruin your life. Go home with your father. Forget about me. Go home. Go back to the life you know."

Rena spun to face him. "And you don't have the strength to fight me. I'm staying. Doctor Simpson, look after your patient while I make something to eat. I believe I'll start cleaning this place first thing tomorrow."

The doctor looked as if he wanted to laugh, but he said nothing. He was proud of Rena Brenden, and he felt Samuel Brenden and Quinn Wayland had both just met their match.

Jonas was so furious that his lips were white. Hammond had just brought him news of what had happened to Logan.

"What did that damn fool have in mind! He's stirred up trouble we didn't need and only made everything harder for us!"

"He was drinkin', Jonas. You know how he was. When he found out Wayland was in the saloon he just had to try and prove he was faster."

"So now he's dead and he proved nothing. Do you think he said anything about us knowing Cord's alive?"

"No . . . someone would have said something. Hell, the whole town would be buzzing if anyone knew that," Hammond assured him.

"We got to bring him out in the open," Jonas said thoughtfully.

"Now how we going to do that? We go around saying he's still alive and the people will think we're crazy. The sheriff sure ain't going to let us dig up no grave to prove it, and who's going to believe what we say when the sheriff, the doctor, the undertaker, and that preacher say different? I'd say we have to make him mad enough to want to come out of hiding," Hammond suggested.

"Yeah, there has to be a weak spot somewhere, but what . . ." He paused, then smiled. "Could be his soft spot is that girl we saw doing all the crying at his grave. Hannah Marshall, she sure must have had a good time making fools of us. Maybe it's time we paid her a little visit."

Hammond returned Jonas's smile. Hammond sported a boy's face, and the heart of a monster. Women who had been lured by the first had often become victims of the second. Jonas knew quite well he would enjoy himself immensely if he were given the opportunity to try to force Hannah to lead them to Michael.

"I don't want her hurt . . . not just yet. We'll save that for when we get rid of him. For now we'll just rough her up a bit and scare the hell out of her. That ought to bring him running."

"Yeah." Hammond licked his dry lips. Hannah Marshall was a beautiful woman. He planned on having a good time. "How we gonna get to her? She always has those saddle tramps hanging around."

"I'll think of a way. Right now there's nothing we can do. Tomorrow, we'll take care of Hannah Marshall."

Hannah rose early the next morning and joined her four sheepish friends for breakfast.

"If it will satisfy you," she smiled sweetly as she spoke, "I intend to do some shopping this afternoon. Then I will go on over to the church to talk to Patrick and Zeb, who are busy working on the church addition. It's broad daylight, so no one will bother me, and I promise on my honor that I have no plans of leading those men to Michael."

"Hannah . . ." Brad began lamely.

"I know . . ." Her voice gentled and the teasing was gone from her eyes. "You're doing this for me, and I am grateful that you care so much. I don't mean to be such a problem. I won't try to see Michael today. That is a promise."

"Today," Jamie grinned. "I don't suppose that promise will hold until . . ."

"Until midnight at least," Hannah smiled back at him. "After midnight it's every man for imself."

"That's a bargain," Joey said. "I know I can trust your word."

"Thanks, Joey. Now can I go shopping in peace? I'll be having lunch with Patrick if any of you decide to check up on me."

"That won't be necessary," Jamie said, holding her gaze with his. "Michael's life is in the balance . . . and we have your word. That should be good enough. We'll see you *before* midnight, though," he smiled. "Just to keep you from sleepwalking."

Hannah laughed and stood up. The four men watched her leave.

"Joey . . . ?" Brad said.

"She gave her word, Brad. She'll keep it," he chuckled. "But after midnight we'd better be on our toes. That lady is clever enough to handle the four of us."

Hannah did shop until noon. Then she leisurely walked toward Patrick's small house. Patrick had been such a pillar of strength for her that she went to see him as often as she could just to talk. He had a way of putting her world in order and easing her mind.

She shared a quiet lunch with him, allowing him to pull her mind from her dilemma. They were laughing when someone knocked on the door. They exchanged glances of uncertainty, then Patrick went to the door to find a young boy with a note for him. He read it quickly, then turned to Hannah.

"Hannah, I have an emergency. It seems there has been an accident on the Old Plank Road and they need me."

"Well, I'll just clean up these dishes and go back to the hotel." Hannah laughed. "I promised the boys I would be on my best behavior today, so I better make an appearance before they begin to wonder."

"You don't need to clean up here. I can . . ."

"Patrick, there's practically nothing to do and it won't take me but a minute. Go on . . . take care of your emergency." Hannah could see he was reluctant to leave her alone. She had no way of knowing he was fighting a strange, instinctive feeling that something portentous hung over them.

When he was gone Hannah began washing the dishes, which took her only a few minutes. Standing with her hands in the sudsy water, she suddenly became aware of the sound of footsteps on the porch.

She smiled to herself. Obviously Patrick had had second thoughts about leaving her alone and had come back, possibly to

get her to go along with him. She went to the door and opened
it.

"Patrick, this is . . ." She froze when she looked not only into
the cold smiles of the two men who faced her, but into the barrel
of the guns they had pointed at her!

Chapter Twelve

Hannah's eyes had widened and her face had gone pale. A tight knot formed deep in the pit of her stomach. She had no doubts in her mind about what she might be facing. After the first wave of shock passed, she tried to restore her control. Though she was more scared than she'd ever admit, she tried to retain a calm demeanor.

"I'm sorry, gentlemen, Reverend Carrigan is not here. If you want to talk to him, I'm sure he'll be glad to see you first thing in the morning."

"Cute little baggage, isn't she?" Jonas said to Hammond. "Don't play any more of your games with us, little lady."

"Games? I don't know what—"

"And don't say you don't know what we're talking about. Playing dumb isn't going to work anymore."

"And thinkin' we're going to fall for any tricks anymore is sure off the mark," Hammond sneered.

"What do you want?" Hannah's voice was chilled.

"We want you to take a little stroll with us," Jonas said.

"I'm not . . ."

"Don't give old Hammond here a reason to get rough with you," Jonas said. "Now you just come along."

"What do you want with me?" Hannah tried to hide her fear.

"Well . . . we're going to have you carry a little message for us." Jonas's voice hardened. "To our very old friend . . . Michael Cord."

Hannah gasped softly and took a step back. "Michael is dead."

"Funny about that," Jonas said quietly. "Me and the boys was considerin' how we never really got to say good-bye to our old friend. Yep . . . we got to really worryin' about that. So one night we take us a trip to that cemetery out there, and we did us a little diggin'. It kind of surprised us, and," he put his free hand against his chest and smiled, "kind of hurt us, not to be let in on you and the preacher's little secret."

Hannah's heart began to pound, and a black fear uncoiled deep inside her. They knew! They knew Michael wasn't dead!

They read her stunned silence as easily as she read the ugly viciousness emanating from them.

Jonas smiled again and motioned with his gun. "You coming, or do we have to drag you?"

"What do you want with me?"

"I told you. We want to have a little talk with you. We have a message for you to carry to your friend."

Hannah shook her head negatively, her fear too vibrant for her to speak.

"If you're considerin' screamin'," Hammond said viciously, "I'll have to lay this gun alongside your head, and I don't think you'd like that." He motioned toward the porch where the setting sun was casting the last shadows as it settled beyond the horizon. Cautiously Hannah moved between them, leaving the door open behind her. But with a smile of acknowledgment Jonas reached out and pulled the door closed.

It surprised Hannah when, walking on either side of her, Jonas and Hammond headed for Patrick's small barn. It was dark inside, with only pale shafts of the dying day reflecting through the small spaces between the wood planking. It gave only enough light that she could make out the two silent men.

She had never been so frightened in her life. Her mouth felt dry, she could barely swallow, and her hands were clenched. Drops of perspiration formed on her brow. She felt extremely helpless.

Patrick had stored the hay for his two horses in one corner of the barn. Hannah was forced to walk there. She turned to face them.

"If you very brave men are planning on killing me, then get on with it. I'm tired of your games."

"I got to give you credit," Jonas chuckled softly. "You got a hell of a lot of nerve. But we don't intend to kill you. Never was one for killin' ladies . . . especially pretty ladies."

Hannah swallowed heavily as she considered his words. She watched Jonas move aside to lean against a wood beam as if he were going to participate in a relaxed conversation. Then her eyes flew to Hammond and a muffled cry involuntarily came from her.

Hammond smiled and moved slowly toward her while he unbuckled his gunbelt and dropped it aside.

She didn't intend to give up without a battle. She backed up a step, watching him. He stopped a foot or so from her. Hannah could hear her ragged breathing.

With a soft laugh he reached out to touch her cheek. She slapped his hand away. .He reached again, this time with a lightning-fast hand, and she felt the solidness of his open-handed blow as it made her stumble backward and she could taste the blood in her mouth.

She tried a sudden dash past him only to be caught by a solid, muscled arm and thrown back on the pile of hay. Before she could scramble to her feet, he fell upon her with just enough calculated force to knock the breath from her.

She gasped for air and tried to flail out with both fists, but he caught them as easily as if she were a child.

He straddled her and held her arms over her head with one hand. With the other he slowly and deliberately slapped her, one cheek then the other until her head spun and she could hear her own moaning cry.

When her fighting began to weaken, he stopped the stinging blows. She was half conscious and sobbing brokenly.

He still straddled her and she could look up from what seemed a great distance to the black form that hovered over her.

"You tell Michael Cord this is only one little lesson," he said brutally. "You tell him to stop hiding behind your skirts."

Now Hannah knew their purpose. They did not mean to kill

her, they meant to get to Michael! With all the energy she had, she spat at him and could hear his angry curse. She expected him to hit her again. She did not expect what he actually did, which was to catch his hand in the front of her dress and rip it away. She battled weakly and could hear the rending of her clothes until she felt the cool night air against her skin.

With ease that made her despair she could feel his hard hands brutally fondling her, leaving bruised flesh where he touched.

"Hammond, that's enough." Jonas's voice came from a distance.

"Let me have her. Let me take her now. That'll bring him around."

"I said, that's enough!"

Hannah was shaking like a leaf, knowing the extent Hammond would go if Jonas could not get him to stop. He was still roughly running his hands over her, and his weight left her unable to move.

"Jonas . . ."

"Damn it, I said get off her!"

Reluctantly Hammond ceased his rough handling, but he raised his hand and struck her one final blow that dropped her into unconsciousness.

When Hammond stood up, Hannah lay still on the hay, her torn clothes scattered about her. They stood together and looked down at her inert form.

"You should have let me take her. She might convince him this ain't enough to fight over," Hammond said.

"You don't know Michael Cord," Jonas said. "This is enough. You've handled his woman, you've broken her pride, and you've left your mark. If that doesn't work . . . we'll finish the job later."

"Want me to dump her back in the house?"

"No, leave her right here. C'mon, let's go." Jonas turned and walked out. But Hamond knelt by Hannah. He ran his hand over her and bent close to brush his lips over hers and inhale the soft scent she wore.

"I hope he don't listen. I'd like a chance at you again. Maybe . . . maybe I'll have my chance after I kill your man. Then I'll have you, sweet thing."

Reluctantly he rose and looked down on her, putting the memory of her pale, lush body into his mind and promising himself the next time he would assuage the need that burned in him. After a long moment he turned and left.

Less than an hour's ride had brought Patrick to the place where the "accident" was to have occurred. There was no sign of anyone at all and Patrick, quick to realize what must have happened, raced back to his house quickly.

He felt a tug of fear when he found the house empty. He tried to think, but his thoughts stumbled over hope. Hannah had gone back to the hotel . . . Hannah had gone back to the hotel.

He covered the distance between his house and the hotel in minutes. But Hannah was not in her room. Worse yet, none of the boys were there, either. It took him the better part of an hour to find them, and their look of shock and distress when he told them of Hannah's disappearance only made Patrick's fear worse.

"Cover the town. Look for her! She's got to be somewhere."

Without questions the men separated, but Hannah was nowhere in town . . . and neither were Hammond Gordon or Jonas Holt.

"I'm going back to my house," Patrick said. "Continue the search. As soon as I get my horse I'll come back. We'll go on searching until we find her."

"We better find her and find her fast, Patrick," Brad said. "I don't think I want to go to Michael and tell him that those men are taking any of this out on Hannah. Maybe they're frustrated because they can't get to him anymore. There won't be any holding him down . . . not if they've laid a hand on her."

Patrick agreed.

"But if we don't tell him that Hannah's missing and if she comes up . . . I mean, if something . . . hell, Michael will never forgive us for that, either," Jamie said.

"We'll give ourselves a little more time. One of you check Quinn Wayland's place and one of you go to Rena Brenden's house. We could be fired up over nothing," Patrick ordered hopefully.

"You really believe that?" Joey questioned.

"I don't know. I'm afraid to believe anything else. Why would they pick on Hannah now? They have no reason."

"That kind don't need much of a reason for anything. They're the kind of men that do as they please and don't care who they hurt. They might have used up a bottle and decided to take a little of their meanness out on Hannah, since they can't get to Michael,'' Jamie replied.

"Jamie . . we've got to have hope. Go on searching. I'll go back home and get my horse. We'll cover the whole territory if we have to.''

"Yeah . . . yeah, let's get going. We're wasting too much time,'' Joey said. "I'll go out to Quinn's place. Jamie, you take Rena Brenden's house. Brad, check every place in town, and Mac, why don't you go with Patrick. We'll meet you in an hour in front of the church. If we haven't found her we'll go on an all-out hunt for those two hard cases.''

There was no discussion about the matter. The men split up. With grim faces they set about their quest.

Mac and Patrick went back to his house. But a few steps away from the door Patrick stopped.

"What's the matter?'' Mac questioned in a whisper.

"I closed my door. I *know* I closed my door. It's standing wide open now.''

Mac and Patrick exchanged glances. Then Mac eased his gun out of his holster and the two made their way quietly up the porch steps.

No sound greeted them from within. Slowly Patrick pushed the door open and the sight that greeted them brought a cry of mingled pain and fury from them both.

Michael found he had no appetite, didn't have a taste for the bottle of whiskey that sat on the table, and could not calm his nerves enough to stop pacing the small cabin.

He needed sleep and he couldn't find one logical reason why he couldn't just lie down on the bed and find some relief. It was as if some force was trying to stir all his senses at one time and leaving him in a state of profound confusion.

Time. He knew time was all that he needed now. But he thought of all the time t hat had already been spent and could never be reclaimed. That thought could make him coldly angry if Hannah's face did not waver between him and the anger. Hannah . . . who had given light and hope. She seemed to be the only source of whatever promise remained for the rest of his life.

It would be only them. Michael and Hannah. He wasn't so much worried about himself. He was used to being alone, to not being able to reach out. But Hannah had led a different kind of life and he knew what she was giving up for him.

He walked to his cot and lay down, and the scent of her came to him. He made himself promises. He would make Hannah happy. He would take her someplace where they could begin a life together, and he would work every day to make that life as full as he could. If love were enough, he knew he had enough to content her, for he loved her to the depth of his soul.

He covered his eyes and tried to sleep. The sun had just set and hte cabin was growing shadowed. But he didn't care to get up and light the lamp.

He allowed memories to fill him. She had come to him when there was no one, and she had filled him with warmth, and pleasure, and happiness. He sighed, letting the scent stir the memories until he was content and enfolded in them. Slowly his mind reached out for Hannah—beautiful, soft, loving Hannah.

Suddenly it struck him. Fiercely! Like a wound from a bullet. The pain of it was so hard and so deep that he sat bolt upright, gasping for air.

He couldn't breathe for a moment, and the shock of it stunned him into immobility. Then a heavy blackness seemed to crash over him. Michael had fought the darkest of emotions, but nothing like this had ever claimed him before . . . and he had never tasted fear, but the fear he felt now was overwhelming.

He rose from the bed and staggered halfway across the room, coming up against the table and grasping it for support.

He fought to try to understand what was happening to him, but he couldn't.

As suddenly as it had struck it faded, and he felt . . . empty . . . hollow, as if he were suspended in a dark part of oblivion. The emptiness was worse than anything else. It was beyond belief and beyond control. He went to the door and flung it open, hoping the night air would make him feel better. It didn't.

He made his way to his horse. Later he would never remember how he got it saddled or even how he got mounted.

Some instinct drove him forward, an instinct he did not understand. He simply rode . . . until he realized he was headed toward Patrick's . . . and that was when the real fear took hold.

Hannah had regained consciousness and was instantly immersed in a sea of pain. For a minute she was afraid to move. She could feel the chilling air on her skin and knew she was naked.

She did not know what had been done to her, but her body ached and her head throbbed. She could feel her swollen lips and was aware that she was tasting dried blood when she tried to lick them.

She moaned softly as she rolled first to her side, then to her stomach. It was a struggle to get to her hands and knees.

She fought to gain control of her thoughts. They had done this to her because they knew Michael was alive. But she didn't want Michael to face these men. If they used her this way, she knew they would not fight fair with Michael. She also knew if Michael found out what they had done to her he would be so enraged he would not worry about being careful. This . . . could mean his death.

Desperately gathering her thoughts, she got to her feet. Her nakedness frightened her, yet somehow she knew she had not been violated. She couldn't guess why . . . unless frightening her was all they had in mind. But Hannah was getting over her fear . . . she was getting angry.

She bent to pick up her clothes. They were in pretty poor condition, but she dressed as best she could. Patrick would understand. He would know why she couldn't let Michael see her this way. It would be at least two days before he would expect word. Two days for them to decide what to do about the situation. She needed to look at herself, to see if two days would be enough to camouflage what had been done to her.

Once she had struggled into the tattered remnants of her clothes she found it difficult to move.

Her head was pounding and her vision was not very good. Things seemed to be dividing into two. To compound the problem she was becoming nauseated, and the world around her seemed to be tilting precariously.

"Oh, Lord, give me strength," she whispered softly.

She staggered from one support to another until she reached the door of the barn, but the distance from there to Patrick's door seemed to her to be as wide as the ocean.

She pushed herself away from the barn door and was halfway across the yard before she stumbled to her knees. Grimly she got to her feet again. She made it to the steps this way before her legs buckled beneath her.

She climbed the steps on hands and knees and crawled to the door. Then she used the doorknob to pull herself erect again. She put her weight against the door and turned the knob at the same time and let the swing of the door carry her inside. She clung to it until she could get enough strength to get to a chair, which she sagged into gratefully.

But the numbness was beginning to wear off and shock was taking its place. She felt it rise up in her and could not fight the sobs that began to wrack her body. She shook with them. They emanated from her cracked lips like the ragged cry of a bereft chid.

It was at that moment that Patrick and Mac entered the house. With the path of moonlight behind them they could see Hannah clearly, and the sight filled them both with shock so deep that for a minute they could only stare. Then Patrick rushed to Hannah's side.

"Aw, damn, Hannah," Mac muttered as he knelt beside her. He reached out a hand and touched her hair.

"Hannah . . . child," Patrick said gently.

Neither man knew quite how to handle the situation at the moment. Hannah seemed so fragile . . . so broken.

It took all of Hannah's concentration to gather herself and try to stop crying, but finally she inhaled a deep breath and became still.

"Hannah . . . I'm so sorry," Patrick said miserably. "I never should have been tricked like that. I should have known better. I'm so sorry, child. I'll get the doctor . . ."

"You . . . you must promise . . ." Hannah said, her voice muffled because of the cut on her lip. "Michael . . ."

"I'll go get him," Mac offered quickly.

"No! No . . . please. He . . . he mustn't see me like this."

"Hannah, you're distraught," Patrick said. "You can't keep this from him."

"Patrick . . . they know . . ."

"Know . . . what, Hannah—what?"

"They know Michael is alive."

"How? They can't know!"

"They were suspicious. I don't know why, but they were. They dug up the grave. They know. Don't you see, they did this just to make him so angry that he would come up against both of them. He'll be killed. Patrick. He must not see me like this!"

"Hannah, I don't know how we can do that," Mac said. "He'll be askin' questions, mostly about you. It's hard enough on him to stay penned up like that and not bein' able to see you, but lying to him . . ."

"Mac . . ." Hannah sobbed. "I can't see him die. Not for this. I can't see him die."

"All right, Hannah, all right. We'll get you some help and we'll discuss this later when you've been cared for and more comfortable. You're just too distraught to handle this now. Mac, why don't you go on down and bring the doctor here."

"Sure, I'll be right back." Mac reached out and touched Hannah's hair again, his eyes reflecting the combination of sympathy and the anger he was trying to control. "Take it easy, Hannah. We won't do anything you don't want us to do. You know you can trust us. I'll get the doctor. You let us take care of you now. We'll talk about Michael and what we have to do about this later."

"Thank you, Mac. I knew you'd understand."

"I do. Rest easy. I'll be back in no time."

She nodded and Mac rose and left the room.

"Hannah, child," Patrick said. "Can I help you . . . make you more comfortable?"

"I . . . I can't move, Patrick. I get too dizzy if I try to stand up. Do you have a mirror?"

"No," Patrick lied. He didn't want Hannah to look at her battered face.

Her lip was cut and her chin had dried blood on it. A huge bruise on her left cheek was already a deep black-and-purple color. There was another wine-colored bruise on her right cheek and the flesh around her eyes was already darkening. Her hair had cushioned the blow, but there was a crust of blood on her hairline that revealed the jagged cut. Her clothes were tattered, and through the rents in the fabric red-and-black bruises were already beginning to form.

"Hannah . . . did they . . . Did anyone . . . ?"

"No, Patrick. I don't believe their attack was as much to violate me as it was to show their brutality to Michael . . . to make him so furious he can't think."

"Thank God. If they had . . . well, I don't think Michael would allow any words of reason after that."

Hannah put her hand over Patrick's, which had been resting on her shoulder. "Thank you, Patrick," she said gently.

"I only hope I can look Michael in the eye and tell him a lie that will convince him."

"It's a lie we have to . . ." Hannah paused at the sound of footsteps on the porch, and before Patrick could move, the door swung open and Michael filled it.

Patrick could not think of a word to say and Hannah simply closed her eyes.

Michael may have expected a lot of things but not Hannah's presence or her condition. He had no question anymore about the sudden violent thing that had filled him . . . drawn him here. He knew.

Bitter guilt assailed him first, followed by the blackest wave of fury he'd ever known. He held it in control as he walked across the room to Hannah and knelt before her. He had brought Hannah to this. In their blind desire to get to him, they had trampled the only thing of beauty there was in his life.

He cupped her face gently in his hands and only then could she lift her eyes to meet his. What she saw there brought tears to her eyes.

"Hannah," Michael said gently, "what have I done to you?"

"No . . . Michael," her voice was pleading.

With gentle fingers he brushed the bruises on her cheeks and touched her lip.

Michael looked up at Patrick and could see the truth in his eyes. "They know, don't they?"

"Yes, they do. Don't ask me how. They told Hannah they'd

been suspicious and dug up the grave. I never thought it would come to this, Michael. I hoped . . ."

"That hope doesn't really amount to much, does it . . . not anymore." He returned his gaze to Hannah. "Have you sent for a doctor?"

"Yes, Mac's gone for him."

"Hannah . . ." Michael's gaze pierced her, as if he could read her thoughts. "They didn't . . ."

"No, Michael. Don't you see! This was done to reach you. You can't . . ."

"I'm tired of running and hiding." Michael's voice was firm. "I'm tired of letting someone else fight my battles for me. This is as much as my fault as it is theirs. I knew what kind of men they were." He caught her hands in his and lifted them to his lips. "God, I'm sorry."

Patrick could feel his own eyes mist and he saw Hannah's tears. Both knew that Michael was saying a kind of farewell. But Hannah was not about to let that happen.

She rose unsteadily to her feet and Michael rose with her. But her body had taken all the punishment it could.

"I won't let you do this! Michael, for the sake of all we mean to each other, please, don't let them . . ."

"And after being a coward and running again do I let them think that it's all right to attack the people I love? That I'll stand by and let this happen? Hannah . . . how long could our love exist like that?"

"Forever! Michael, I want you alive!" The room was beginning to spin again and a wave of nausea cut her words short. She began to weave on her feet and reached out a hand toward Michael before the blackness claimed her. He caught her up in his arms as she fell.

"Bring her to the spare room," Patrick said quickly. "I have a feeling she must have taken a pretty hard blow to the head."

Michael knew without any more words needing to be spoken that such a thing could be extremely dangerous. He had seen a man once who had taken a fall from a horse, claimed he was fine, and had suddenly died a few hours later.

That memory sent a streak of real terror through him. Gently he carried Hannah and followed Patrick to his bedroom, where he laid her on the bed. Then he turned to Patrick. "Get me some water and clean cloths and one of your night shirts."

Patrick did as he was asked. The look in Michael's eyes was not one to tangle with.

"Leave us alone for a while," Michael said when Patrick brought the required articles. Though he spoke the words quietly and calmly, Patrick could feel the wave of violence that was flowing like a raging river just below the surface. He left the room and closed the door behind him.

Michael set the basin of water on a chair near the bed, then, sitting on the edge of the bed, he moistened a piece of cloth and gently wiped the blood, tears, and dirt from Hannah's face.

This done, he began to remove her clothes. Their tattered condition only stoked the fury that was being contained by a sheer act of will.

The bruises on her arms, wrists, and body made him curse under his breath. Still, he carefully and very gently bathed her and dressed her in Patrick's nightshirt. Then he drew the covers up over her.

Finished, he dropped the cloth into the basin and set it aside. Then he returned to sit on the edge of the bed and take one of Hannah's hands in his.

He had been through a lot in his lifetime. The wounds he had suffered had been a painful nightmare and the prison had been hell. But nothing had ever hurt him as much as this did. It brought a hard lump to his throat and tears to his eyes.

Hannah moaned softly, then spoke his name. "Michael."

"I'm here, Hannah love, I'm here."

Slowly her eyes fluttered open. Vaguely, like a form shrouded in mist, she could see Michael bent above her.

With only one lamp lit in the room, and positioned on a table some distance away, it was as if their corner of the room was set apart from the rest of the world. Hannah wished it could really be true, that they could be apart from the ugliness that swirled about them.

"I feel . . . What happened?"

"What happened is you took more punishment than you thought. You collapsed. But you'll be all right." He said the words, hoping he was right.

Everything flooded back into Hannah's memory at once. She clutched his hand and felt the warmth and the strength of it enclosing hers. But her worry and fear was not for herself. She had one ray of hope. She had to keep Michael with her.

"Michael . . . don't go . . . don't leave me."

"You know I won't leave you. I'll be right here. You just need to have the doctor look you over and make sure you're all right."

"But I'm feeling better already."

"Don't even give a thought of getting out of that bed. This is one time you're going to do as you're told."

"I'm afraid," she whispered.

"Don't be. Something like this will never happen again, that I promise you."

"And that promise is what is making me afraid. Michael . . . I can't bear to hear that sound in your voice."

Michael bent over her and brushed her mouth lightly with his. "Hannah," he said softly, "I love you. You're every breath I take. You're the good, clean part of my life. You talk of what you can't bear. How do you expect me to bear this? To let them reach out and hurt the one thing that is precious to me. It's beyond what any man could stand."

"I love you, too, Michael, and if you die I just can't go on. Promise me . . ."

"No, Hannah. No promises. I'm tired of running and I know if I don't stand here, this kind of thing can, and most likely, will happen again. It has to stop here."

Hannah breathed a muffled sob. She knew she could no longer stop Michael, just as she knew the odds were against him. Jonas and Hammond were only two, but how many would they hire to help gun Michael down?

She wept softly and Michael gathered her into his arms and held her. No words were going to change what had to be done, but he needed this moment to hold Hannah close.

She clung to him, frightened that it would be the last time she would be able to do so.

When the door opened again, Patrick was accompanied by the doctor. Michael laid Hannah back against the pillows and rose from the bed.

"Michael!" Hannah clung to his hand.

"I'll be outside, Hannah. Let the doctor examine you. I'll be right here."

Reluctantly Hannah released his hand. He stood over the bed and looked down at her as if searing her into his mind. Then, wordlessly, he bent, kissed her lightly, and left the room with Patrick.

As they walked downstairs both were quiet. Michael, his mind set on what he had to do, had no words left and Patrick, searching for words to stop him, knew he couldn't find even one that would prevent what he knew was coming.

"Michael . . ."

"Don't, Patrick. I don't want to hear what you have to say. Our little game failed. And for God's sake, don't tell me to turn the other cheek. If it had been me, I could have tried. But not Hannah. That is too much."

Patrick grew silent. He wasn't sure he wouldn't feel the same way.

"The three of them are going to pay for every second of pain and fear she endured, and nothing outside of killing me is going to stop it."

"And if they kill you, that will be worse for her than anything they could do."

Mac had been caring for the doctor's horse and carriage, and he stepped inside the house in time to hear the last part of Patrick and Michael's conversation.

"Mac . . ." Michael said. "It's been a long time." He extended his hand to Mac, who grasped it in a firm grip.

"I'm sorry it had to be this way. I take it you're going after them."

"All three of them. I'll dig them out wherever they are."

"Michael . . . there's only two of them. It seems one of them was in the saloon and prodding Quinn Wayland pretty hard. They went for their guns and Quinn took him."

"It isn't enough Hannah has to take the brunt of this, I have an innocent man doing my fighting for me. This has got to stop here and now."

"I'll stand with you."

"No. This has always been my fight. It's time I put an end to it."

"I wouldn't be surprised you find them over at the saloon . . . drinkin' . . ."

"Celebrating," Michael said angrily. "This is the kind of thing that breed would celebrate."

Patrick and Mac both felt helpless, and were still without words when the doctor came downstairs.

"Doc?" Michael questioned quickly.

"She'll be all right. You just have to keep her in bed for at least twelve hours. She'll be sore for a while, but I expect the bruises will fade soon. Who in God's name did this to her? It's monstrous."

"Don't worry," Michael said grimly. "They're going to pay for it."

"The men who were after you?"

"Yes. They found out the truth. It was their way to me."

"Barbarians!"

"You're right," Michael said. "Can I see her now?"

"Of course. I gave her something to make her sleep."

"Thanks, Doc. I owe you," Michael said. Then he turned and went upstairs.

The three men exchanged glances. There was very little left to be said.

Chapter Thirteen

Mac left Patrick's house and went on a quick search for his three companions. He found them, one at a time, in assorted places, and when he had them gathered together he explained quickly what had happened.

They were enraged at the news of Hannah's treatment and wanted to go out and hunt down the perpetrators at once.

"We ought to string them up," Brad said angrily.

"That's too good for 'em," Jamie claimed. "There's a lot of worse ways to make 'em suffer."

"I can think of a few," Joey added.

"Well, we're not doin' nothing just yet," Mac said.

"Nothing! Mac, what the hell you talking about? We can't just sit here!" Brad was incensed at Mac's attitude.

"Brad . . . much as I'd like to, we can't. This is Michael's fight, and he wouldn't be too keen on us takin' the pleasure away from him getting those two."

"Two against one," Jamie said coldly. "I guess that's the only way they know."

"Sure as hell they'll hire help," Joey muttered.

"Well," Mac smiled, "that's what we're going to be here for. Just to look over their shoulders and make sure nothing gets out of hand."

"That's more like it," Brad grinned.

"I think we'd better do something else, too," Mac said. "I think we'd better send Max a telegram. He's probably worried sick."

"Yeah, you're right," Brad concurred. "Max will be purple by now. If we don't get to him pretty soon we sure won't be able to talk him out of stringing us up when . . . *if* we get back," Jamie concluded.

"I dno't think we'll be going back for a while. Maybe, if we send Max a telegram, he'll come here," Joey said.

"Wouldn't be surprised," Mac agreed.

"Mac . . . you think Michael is goin' after those two tonight?"

"Depends on how Hannah is, but it wouldn't surprise me none if he did."

"And we can't send that telegram till morning."

"So," Mac said softly, "I guess, for tonight, we'd better see if we can run acros them and be there in case Michael finds them."

"Sounds like a good idea to me," Jamie agreed.

"Maybe we'd better split up," Joey added.

"Another good idea," Jamie said.

"Everyone is right." Mac rose to his feet. "Joey, you and Brad start at the far end of town and work your way in. Me and Jamie will start at the north side. We find 'em, one of us stays put and the other goes for the rest."

They all nodded their agreement. Whether Michael wanted it or not, his four friends intended to give him all the support they could. As they started to walk away, Mac laughed softly.

"What's funny?" Jamie quesitoned.

"There ain't nobody in this town besides us that don't believe Michael Cord is dead. It sure is going to be a shock when they see a very angry ghost walkin' the streets. Going to scare some righteousness into them, or scare the hell out of them. One way or the other."

Jamie laughed at the picture Mac's words drew. It was going to be interesting to watch the reactions. "I wonder what Michael is going to say about what we're doing."

"Right now," Mac said, "he's so fired up mad, I don't think he'll notice what *anyone* is doing. He's just looking for them and not caring much about anything else. Later . . ."

"Later?"

"He'll be mad as all hell," Mac laughed. "Probably threaten to knock our ears off . . . just before he shakes our hand."

"Mac . . . you think it could all end here?" Jamie asked.

"Not unless someone gets to the senator, and that just ain't likely. None of us run in his circles. He ain't the forgivin' kind. He's a hard, ugly, lonely old man and he ain't going to be happy or give up until Michael's dead."

"That sure is carrying hate a long way."

"Kid was his only son and he don't have nothing else to do with his money. The only trouble is, he just won't hear the truth. The men he ought to get are the ones who prodded his son into coming up against Michael in the first place. But the old fool is blinded by hate, and you can't talk sense into a man that feels that way."

"So even if Michael escapes from this one, it won't matter. He'll still be running."

"I guess so. I don't see a way out . . . unless someone puts a stop to the senator. And I don't know anyone who has that kind of push."

"God," Jamie muttered. "That's a hell of a life."

"Yeah. I was hopin' Hannah might make a difference, that maybe the two of them could beat the game. Now . . . I don't know."

"Well, we can hope. Maybe Hannah *will* make the difference. We'll just have to be as much help as we can . . . and hope for the best."

They continued their hunt in silence, the thoughts of each man on Hannah and Michael.

When the four friends came together again it was with puzzled faces. In the entire town, as far as they could see, there was no sign of Jonas Holt or Hammond Gordan. It was as if the ground had swallowed them up.

"I don't believe this," Joey claimed.

"They wanted to make Michael sweat. Now they'll lay low, hoping to stretch his nerves and make him a little less careful," Mac said. "But they have to be somewhere."

"Yeah," Jamie said quietly, "and knowing Michael, he could find a needle in a haystack. He'll run 'em to ground."

"And," Joey said, "maybe be alone when he finds 'em."

"I think," Mac finally said, "we'd better get back to Patrick's house and see if we can convince him to let us help him."

"What would you say our chances were of that?" Joey asked.

"About as much," Mac said with resignation, "as a snowball has in hell."

The three followed Mac as he started toward Patrick's house.

Michael opened the door to the bedroom only after he had stood outside for a few minutes gathering his composure. He could not go to Hannah with the rage so out of control within him. He knew she would read it in his face, and the fear for him would only make matters worse.

He would retain his calm exterior until the sleeping powder the doctor had given her took its lulling effect, if it killed him.

He opened the door as quietly as he could, actually hoping she was asleep already. Closing the door softly behind him, he walked to the bed. Her eyes were closed and he had that moment to look at her without shielding his emotions.

It was the most difficult thing he had ever done, to contain the black fury that boiled up, almost uncontrolled inside him. he had never *wanted* to kill before . . . and now he wanted to so badly, it nearly took his breath away. He struggled with it until he leashed it . . . holding it until the time came when he would make the kind of weapon of it those men would understand.

Hannah's eyes fluttered open, took a few minutes to focus, then held Michael's. She reached for his hand. "Michael."

He took her hand in his and sat down on the bed beside her. Gently he kissed her fingers. "How do you feel?"

"Sore, tired . . . awfully sleepy."

"Good. Sleep is good for you."

"Michael . . . please."

"What, Hannah?"

"You have to promise me you won't do anything foolish."

"That's not a hard promise. I won't do anything foolish." Not for a mintue did Michael think killing the men who had done this to Hannah as foolish. He considered it a cleansing of an evil from the world.

"Oh, Michael, I love you so much," she sighed raggedly, fighting the sleep. "Please," she said softly, "hold me."

Gently he bent to lift her in his arms, resting her on his lap, her head against his shoulder. She felt an unbelievable security with the feel of his arms around her. He rocked her lightly.

"We'll go away," she whispered, her breath warm against his throat. "We'll go someplace far where they'll never find us. I just want to be with you . . . to love you."

"I know, Hannah, I know," he soothed. He knew her battle against the sleeping powder would soon be lost.

"Michael?" Her voice grew softer.

"What, love?"

"Do you think I could already be carrying your child?"

The question stunned him for a moment. He refused to see the barrier that even in her drowsy state she was raising against his desire to carry out his vengeance.

"I suppose you could," he admitted honestly.

Her next words were just as overwhelming.

"I hope so . . . I really hope so." her words were becoming slurred, but not to the point that they did not reach their mark. He only hoped it was the drug talking.

"Hannah, you don't mean that, not now anyway."

"Yes, I do," she insisted. "He'd be so beautiful . . . like you." Now Michael had to laugh. The medicine had sure broken Hannah's reserve. "You'll be such a good father."

"What if we have a girl?"

"No," she said firmly. "It will be a boy first. Then we'll have a girl."

"Somehow, love," he chuckled, "I don't doubt it."

"Well," she sighed as she began to drift into real sleep, "if I'm not . . . I'll have to do something about it." Her last words faded.

"Hannah?" Silence. "Hannah?"

Michael sat for a long moment, holding her close to him and realizing all that she could have brought to his life. How close he had come to having everything . . . and how quickly it was being snatched away. It was hard to let go of Hannah's softness when he knew it might be the last time he would hold her.

He stood, lifting her in his arms, then turned and gently laid her on the bed. He bent over her and kissed her lightly and the faint taste of blood that lingered on his lips brought reality crashing around him.

Only now he had a hold on the rage. He would use it and not let it use him. Finally he stood and looked down at her. Her skin was bruised and her lips were still slightly swollen. He knew the evidence of force was on her body. Drawing the sheet over her, he turned and left the room.

Only Patrick remained downstairs. "She's asleep?" he questioned.

"Yes. How long do you think she'll stay that way?"

"Doctor Simpson says at least three or four hours."

"That's good."

"Michael, what are you going to do?"

"The less questions you ask, Patrick, the less you'll have to answer for Hannah when she wakes up. I want you to make sure she stays here. No matter what you hear, make her stay here. I don't want her in this kind of danger again."

"This is the one thing she came to stop."

"What do you want me to do?" Michael said, his anger surfacing despite his effort to control it. "Quinn faced a man who was after me . . . and killed him. That's a life on *my* conscience. I left Hannah unguarded, and she paid for it. That's on *my* conscience, too. I can't back away now. Who knows which of my friends they'll hit next. It might be Hannah again, and next time they won't let her off so easy."

"Easy?"

"This could have been worse, and they know I know it. This was a threat. Next time . . . next time they'll hurt her bad enough . . ." He couldn't go on. Patrick knew what he was saying.

"You need help."

"That's the last thing I need," Michael said calmly. "Trust me that I can handle this alone. I know better than anyone else the breed of man I'm facing."

"You have friends!"

"Friends I don't want dead." Michael started toward the door. "Take care of Hannah," he added quietly, and before Patrick could answer, the door was already closing behind him. Patrick sank down into a chair and prayed as he had never prayed before.

It was less than an hour later when he heard footsteps on the porch. He was rising from his chair when the door opened and Brad, Jamie, Mac, and Joey came in.

"Is Michael upstairs with Hannah?" Mac qustioned. He paused to study Patrick's face. "Patrick?"

"He's not here. He left an hour ago. He's gone to find those two men."

"And you let him go!" Brad said sharply.

"Brad!" Mac cautioned. "You know Michael. Patrick couldn't have stopped him if he wanted to. How's Hannah?"

"The doctor gave her something to make her sleep."

"Well, that's one good thing."

"Good thing," Patrick repeated. "What in heaven's name is good about any part of this situation?"

"The only good thing I know," Brad smiled, "is that we took this town apart and those two men aren't here. Michael will be back when he can't find them and maybe we can change hte odds and make him listen to reason."

There was a deep silence and Patrick kept his eyes on Mac. "You don't quite believe that."

"I hope it."

"But you don't believe it?"

The other three watched Mac closely. "No, I guess I don't."

"You think Michael might know where they are?"

"I think . . . I think he knows them and maybe he's in their minds enough to figure where they'd hole up. If it's so, he'll dig 'em out . . . and he'll finish it."

They exchanged looks, but none of them had any more to say.

Michael sat his horse deep in the shadows of the trees. Both horse and man were immobile. He was searching mentally, using experience and knowledge in place of physical energy. He knew these men and all those like them. He knew how they thought. He also knew they were hoping he'd react with anger only so that they could catch him at a time when he'd become frenzied by his fury.

He also knew they would not want to face him alone. They would get help. It was a matter of time. They would not expect him yet, thinking he was stunned by what they had done to Hannah.

He had to get to them . . . catch them when they didn't expect him, and he knew not only how . . . he knew where.

Hammond sat on a blanket, his saddle propped behind him to support him. A cigarette hung limply from his mouth and he was concentrating on checking the gun he had cradled in his hand. He'd cleaned it carefully and loaded it. He wanted to make sure, when he got the chance, that Michael Cord was really dead.

Jonas had warned him over and over to be careful, and he was. When the time came he would be prepared to handle Cord.

He laughed maliciously to himself. No matter what Jonas said, once he'd gotten Cord he intended to go back and pay his lady another visit. He could remember clearly how sweet and soft she had been . . . and how helpless to stop him. He could still feel her body beneath him.

It wouldn't be long. He imagined that cord was involved in a frantic search. By the time another day was past his anger would make him careless.

He wondered if Jonas had gotten any information or noticed any excitement near the town. He'd been scouting around for over an hour.

He reached behind him, in his saddlebag, and retrieved a half-full bottle of whiskey, uncorked it, and tipped it up to take a deep drink. His hand froze when the sharp click of a gun hammer sounded close to his ear. Before he could move he could feel the cool steel barrel touch his cheek. The soft voice that accompanied it made him begin to sweat.

"I'd advise you not to make any sudden moves, my friend. It's time you and I had a little talk."

"Cord." The name hissed through Hammond's clenched teeth.

"Very smart." The voice was soft . . . and deadly. "Too bad you weren't so smart a few hours ago. It might have saved you a lot of grief, friend. You see, I think you've made a real, real bad mistake."

The soft voice, coming from the emptiness behind him,

shrouded in darkness, could be enough to shake Hammond, but knowing who it was and how dangerous Michael Cord was, was truly terrifying.

"I . . . I don't know what you're talking about," he said, but the gun pressed harder and a soft and cold laugh followed. "Hell, I've been right here all night. You got the wrong man."

"Where's your courage? The courage you had when you beat a helpless woman. That was a message for me, if I'm not mistaken. Well, I'm here to answer your invitation."

"Look," Hammond licked lips suddenly gone dry, and he knew his hands were shaking. "This . . . ain't right. You got the drop on me."

"My, my," Michael's voice was taunting, "we want to play by rules, do we. All right. Suppose you stand up, real slow."

Hammond wasn't sure his legs were going to hold him as he obediently moved slowly to climb to his feet.

"Drop the gun on the ground and move a couple of steps away."

Hammond did as he was told, desperately seeking any way he could find out of his dilemma. He could hear movement behind him. He did not have the nerve to even think of turning around, but Michael ordered him to do so.

Hammond didn't want to. He wanted to run, to find a place to hide. His stomach churned in fear. This was not supposed to be happening. Jonas had sworn that Cord would be dead in a matter of hours. Now . . . he was here. Unsteadily, Hammond turned to face his aggressor, and he wished he hadn't. He'd dealt out death before, but now he was looking it in the eye. It sent real terror through him.

Michael stood before him, a smile on his face so cold and so brutal it was like shards of glass. The gun he wore slung low on his hip looked so intimidating that Hammond's breath caught deep in his chest. He realized his heart was pounding furiously.

Michael made no move to go for his gun, but watched Hammond for several minutes. Then he took a step or two that brought him within a foot of Hammond.

"What are you going to do?" Hammond whispered hoarsely.

"First I'm going to give you a taste of your own medicine . . . then I'm going to kill you," Michael answered evenly. Then he laughed the same cold laugh. "Of course, I'll give you a chance to draw."

"I ain't drawing against you!"

"Not when you're alone," Michael chided.

"No way. I ain't going to do it."

"No?" Michael questioned gently. He lashed out suddenly with a fist that cracked against Hammond's cheekbone so viciously that it lifted him from his feet and sent him sprawling. Hammond climbed to his feet only to feel the force of Michael's blow driving him to the ground. For the next twenty mintues Michael slowly and methodically beat him until he was bloody and sobbing, rocking on his hands and knees and refusing to get up again. Only then did Michael back away.

"You have two minutes to get that gun holstered. If you don't, I'm going to take my time and kill you real slow."

Hammond crawled toward the gun, the newly cleaned, carefully loaded gun meant to kill the man who stood waiting. He reached out an unsteady hand to lift it slowly and drop it in his holster. Then he got to his feet and faced Michael.

"You never should have touched her," Michael said stonily. "You hurt someone who never should have known a minute's pain. Now tell me . . . where's your friend?"

"He . . . he was out lookin' . . ."

"For me?"

"No, just . . . keepin' a lookout for what you was doin'."

"Which one of you was it?"

"Huh?"

"You can hear . . . and you can understand me clear. Which one of you was it?"

"It was Jonas's idea! I swear, it was Jonas's idea."

"But it was you that laid hands on her?"

"I swear to God . . ."

"Don't swear to something you don't believe in," Michael snarled. "Mercy isn't your strong point. It's time to quit talking. You have a chance. It might be better to take it."

Michael's hand hung close to the gun. He became still and his gaze pierced Hammond like a sword. There was no mercy here, either.

The night seemed to grow still and only Hammond's breathing

broke the silence. His hand twitched. He could take Cord . . . he could take Cord. He kept running the words through his mind. Michael seemed to stand relaxed . . . calm . . . waiting.

In a blur of movement two hands reached, two guns barked. One man died. Michael turned and walked away.

If Michael expected release from the black thing that gripped him, he was disappointed. Instead of freeing him, what he had just done had sickened him. He could feel his hands shake.

It was time to find Jonas . . . before he lost the edge that made it possible to do what he had to do. He was reasonably sure Jonas was searching out and buying what help he thought he might need, and that it was unlikely he would return to the camp where he'd left Hammond until sometime the next day. That was too long for him to remain still. If he remained still and waited, the shadows would catch up with him and he might not be that split second faster than Jonas.

Maybe he could get Mac or one of the others to find out if Jonas was in town. He didn't want to lose the element of surprise.

It was that quiet time of night, when the moon was nearing the horizon and the stars had blinked out but the sun had not risen, when Michael rode up to Patrick's back door.

It did not surprise him when he entered to find Patrick still awake and his four friends seated around the table. He closed the door before he spoke.

"How's Hannah?"

"She's started stirring, but she's not up yet. I suppose," Patrick continued, "she'll be awake soon. She's been fighting that sleeping powder all the way. Michael . . . ?"

"Did you find them?" Mac finished what Patrick had hesitated to say.

"I need a little help, Mac."

"You have whatever you want."

"I have to find Jonas Holt. He could be in town. He isn't at his camp and I don't think Hammond was expecting him. I need you to ride into town and find out if he's there."

"Michael, don't do this," Patrick said. "It won't help. It will only make things worse."

Michael couldn't deny that he felt worse, but he had surrendered all thought but one: what they had done to Hannah. He smiled a bitter smile, but his words were aimed at Mac.

"Just find out where he is."

"Michael, we've checked every place in town a man can be. Jonas Holt isn't here. I don't know where he is, but he's not in town."

"You wouldn't lie to me, Mac?" Michael asked softly.

"No . . . I'd stand with you." He gestured around him. "All of us would. But we've been searching. He just isn't around."

"He has to be somewhere. That kind of a killer doesn't run."

"You've holed him up. He'll stay away from you until he's ready."

"You mean until he's gathered up some friends."

"I guess that's what I mean. He's not going to be found until he wants to be found."

"So I have to wait him out."

"Michael, sit down and have something to eat . . . some coffee," Patrick urged.

"Thanks, Patrick. I'm not hungry."

"But you're exhausted. That's pretty dangerous for you, considering what you plan to do," Mac said. "Why don't you get a little rest and let me and the boys do your looking for you?"

"Maybe you're right," Michael inhaled a deep ragged breath and Patrick could see, fro his quick glance toward the stairs, just where Michael's mind was.

"Why don't you go up and see her," Patrick said softly.

"I don't want to wake her."

"You don't have to wake her to see her. You need some peace and quiet. Why don't you rest."

"Maybe . . . for a couple of hours," Michael agreed.

"Soon as day breaks we'll look the town over," Mac said. "If he's here we'll find him. Just remember, he's the one who's outnumbered now. It could be he lit out for parts unknown. Maybe . . ."

"Mac . . . he's somewhere. Believe me, he won't run. One way or the other I have to face him."

"I'm not going to argue that, just . . . you need to get hold of yourself. What happened . . . ?"

"Don't ask what you know the answer to, Mac."
Patrick closed his eyes for a moment.

Hannah seemed to be floating upward in a dark tunnel with only a light at the top. Her first feeling was that her head ached, followed by the fact that every muscle in her body felt as if it had been strained beyond endurance.

It took some time for her to really remember what had happened and where she was. She realized the doctor must have given her something to force her to sleep. She had a vague memory of Michael being here with her, holding her, talking to her, but she couldn't bring any spoken words to mind. She fought to tear aside the veil of confusion, and when she did, fear took its place. She sat upright, trying to ignore the pounding in her head and the stiffness in her body.

"Michael," she murmured. Knowing for certain he had been here . . . had held her . . . and when she slept he had gone. Gone to . . . ? The thought was brutal.

While she had slept Michael might have been meeting his death, or dealing out death himself. She forced herself erect. She had to know where he was and what had happened. She tried to take a step toward the door and felt a wave of weakness so fierce she grasped the bedpost and clung to it for a minute until the weakness passed.

She looked about her for something to put on, but her clothes were gone and there was no sign of a robe. She stood uncertain for a moment and then she decided, modesty be damned, she had to know where Michael was.

At that moment the door opened and Michael stood framed in the doorway, surprise stopping him for a moment as he came face-to-face with Hannah.

"What the . . . what are you doing up?" he demanded with a worried frown.

"I'm all right, Michael, really. Just a bit of a headache and a little stiff. I . . ."

She didn't get a chance to finish her last thoughts before he crossed the distance between them in a few long strides and swept her up into his arms.

He meant to deposit her on the bed, but the feel of her in his arms was so warm and welcome that he held her for a moment. Hannah put her arms about his neck and bent to kiss his cheek, then his neck and on to any place her lips could find.

"Oh, Michael, I'm glad you're here. I'm glad you stayed. When I woke up I was so scared. I didn't know if you'd gone . . . or if you'd come back in one piece."

At the moment Michael didn't want to tell her where he'd been or what had happened. Now she felt warm and safe in his arms, and he needed that warmth and love badly. There was too much left to do.

To take her attention away from any other questions, he chose to change the subject quickly. "You fell asleep on me," he laughed.

"It's that darn doctor. I think he must have slipped me something."

"He needed to, Hannah. You needed sleep to heal that bump on your head." He moved to the bed, but still didn't put her down. "But we had a real interesting conversation before you drifted off."

Hannah lifted her head and looked at him suspiciously, one brow lifted in question. "Conversation?"

"Yeah." His half smile suggested the conversation was not one she would have taken part in hd she been in control of all her faculties. "You asked me, very sweetly, if I thought you might be carrying my child yet."

He watched her mouth drop and her eyes go wide. Best of all, he watched her blush down to the open neck of Patrick's nightshirt. "I didn't!"

"Oh, that's not the best part. You even promised me it would be a boy. We could have a girl next time, you said. Then, just before you went out, you said something like . . . if you weren't carrying a child now, you'd have to do something about it."

He watched the pink of her cheeks grow a shade deeper. "Michael, you're laughing at me. I didn't say that. You're just making it up."

"I swear, Hannah, those were your exact words, and I'm not laughing at you. Nothing in the world could have made me love you more than I did at that moment. I don't know about your dreams, love," he said gently, "but you sure touched on mine."

He could see the melting look appear in her eyes and he turned his head to touch her lips with his. A soft, muffled sound made him realize her mouth must be tender. He pulled away, fighting a need almost too strong to stop. He let her legs drop slowly and drew her into his arms.

"I'm sorry. I didn't mean to hurt you."

"It wasn't pain . . . it was pleasure," she murmured as she drew his head to hers. The kiss was lingering and gentle.

"Michael . . . why can't you just go back to the hotel and get me some clothes? I don't care about the rest of my things. We could leave now. We could go . . ."

"No, Hannah," he said softly. "We can't."

"I don't understand. They . . ."

"They won't let it end here. In truth, you and I both know they won't ever let it end. This is the time and the day I have to stop running."

She looked at him intently and he did not back away from the depth of her gaze. He watched her face grow pale. "You . . . you didn't stay here last night, did you?"

"No."

"You went after them."

"I found one of them. The one who did this to you."

"You killed him," she whispered.

"Not until I let him taste a bit of what he so easily handed you," Michael said grimly.

"And you're going after the other one."

"For some reason he's vanished. But I don't believe for a minute he's gone. I'll find him."

"Will this ever end?" Hannah said miserably.

"No, I don't think so. The man who wants me has an arm that can stretch around the world. He'll never give up. I can't ask you to share that, Hannah. What I want is only a dream that's out of my reach. If you stand with me you can only get hurt. I won't . . ."

"You won't let me," Hannah smiled grimly. "Michael Cord, I have traveled half the country to find you. I've heard all your arguments, but I also heard you say you love me . . . that you need me. Do you believe I can walk away from you? I will stay here, be here for as long as you stay. I will go with you where you go. I will be with you, and unless you agree to go with me . . . I will not agree to go anywhere, anytime. I hope that's real clear because I don't aim to have to say it again.''

"You can't . . .''

"Who do you think is going to stop me?''

"What if I said I don't want you here?''

"I'd call you a liar,'' she smiled. "I have a good memory for whispered words, too. That lie won't hold water.''

"Then your memory needs a push. What happened to you can happen again!''

"Not if I stay very close to you.'' She tightened her arms about his waist. "And I intend to stay very close to you . . . day and night.''

"Hannah, how can I shake some sense into you?''

"The only misjudgment I ever made was the day I let you ride away from my home. And that's a mistake I never intend to make again. Michael,'' she said sweetly, "go and get me some clothes.''

Michael expelled a breath half of anger and the other half of disbelief. "I ought to make you stay in that nightshirt until you get some sense.''

"Go ahead,'' she said seductively. "I don't mind, as long as you stay with me.''

Her bruised face and tangled hair, coupled with a body sheathed only in a nightshirt several sizes too large for her . . . and added to her cool and absolute stubbornness, left Michael with no other alternative but to laugh.

"Hannah Marshall, if by some miracle we do get out of this, and we do have any children, they ought to be the damnedest ones the world has ever seen.''

She recognized his surrender and laughed as she hugged him fiercely and felt his arms enfold her and hold her . . . knowing he would never willingly let her go again.

"I thought you'd be asleep when I came up here.''

"Disappointed?''

"No,'' he laughed. "You feel pretty good. I wish at least one of us was in a condition to do something about it.''

"If you thought I was asleep, why . . .''

"I thought I might find a little rest myself.''

"Then, I suggest you do that,'' she replied. "There's plenty of room on that big bed for both of us and I'd like to be with you a while longer before the world gets in the way again."

Michael thought the idea intriguing. He took off his boots and lay down. Hannah climbed into the bed beside him and curled against him.

"I could learn to make this a habit," Hannah said. "I'm so comfortable I could purr."

"If that world you mention *wasn't* in the way," Michael admitted, "I could get pretty used to it, too."

"Then let's forget everything. The door is closed and the world is outside. Let's leave it there for a while."

Michael agreed silently, drew her close to him, and after a while, he drifted into sleep. Hannah lay still. For now Michael was hers and hers alone.

Chapter Fourteen

Washington, D.C.
Senator Thomas Merrell sat behind a large mahogany desk and clamped his unlit cigar between strong white teeth. He was a large man, square of shoulder, yet his body had slowly been deteriorating because of too much drink and fast night life.

He was a clever man, expert at his job. But since the death of his son, Scott, his life and wealth had been dedicated to finding the man who had killed him. It didn't matter to him if he had to search the balance of his life, he could not let Michael Cord live.

He had watched several men fall before Cord's gun and now he had three of the best, and fastest, gunmen he could find on his trail.

Thomas's deep brown eyes narrowed and gleamed with hate at just the thought of Michael Cord living while his son was buried in the family plot. He ran his fingers through thick salt-and-pepper hair in frustration. It had been months since he had heard from Jonas Holt. Surely they had caught up with Cord by now, he thought.

He hoped every day for the word to come. Every morning when he woke up, his first thought was that this would be the day that he would be notified. Every night he went to sleep with the same dream.

He ate, slept, and drank his dream. It kept him going. He was used to doing as he pleased and having what he wanted. He was worth millions of dollars. Some of it had been inherited but a great deal of it had come from knowing where to find the secrets that led to making money and how to use those secrets. His methods had not always been the best, but they had been effective and successful.

He rose from behind his desk and crossed the thick, wine-colored carpet to gaze out the window.

"Weeks," he muttered. "Months." He inhaled a deep breath. "Why does it take so long to find and eliminate one man? You'd think he had nine lives."

As if in answer to his questino, a light rap sounded on his door.

"Come in," he called. It was long after the hour that his secretary usually left, so Thomas was a bit surprised when he stuck his head around the door.

"Sir . . ."

"Well, Oliver, what is it? I thought you would be on your way home by now."

"No, sir. I . . . ah . . . have to talk to you."

"What is it? Something wrong?"

"Well . . . ah . . . yes, sir. I'm afraid something is."

"Well, come on, man. Tell me what it is."

The young man came in hesitantly, as if he were a bit frightened. In fact, he was.

"So what has gone wrong?"

"I'm afraid I've run across something that should have been brought to your attention some time ago."

"What is it?"

Oliver handed Thomas an envlope with a hand that was trembling. Thomas took it.

"A telegraph message," he scowled at Oliver, "and two weeks old. For God's sake, Oliver!" He continued to unfold the message. Then he read, and his face grew darker and grimmer with each word. "How did this get . . . lost?" he asked coldly.

"I don't really know, sir. It seems it got moved with the files. Was it of great importance, sir? I'm so sorry."

"Important . . . yes, it was important. Never mind. Go on home."

"But, sir . . ."

"Oliver! Go on home. This is something I can take care of. Don't worry about it."

"Yes, sir."

Oliver left, reluctantly, and more than a little worried about the future of his position. When he was gone Thoams again studied the telegram.

Senator Thomas Merrell:

Things have not gone according to plan. Stop. Hammond and Logan dead. Stop. our friend is still alive and well in Virginia City. Stop. If you want this job finished send more money. Stop. I intend to play out this little game. Stop. He's tried a real tricky move but it won't do much good. Stop. Two can play the game and I'll end up putting the prize in your lap. Stop.

Jonas

Thomas crushed the telegram into a ball, squeezing it in his fist as if he were squeezing the life from Michael Cord himself.

"The man is like a curse," he muttered. "It seems if you want a job done right, you'd best see to it yourself."

He turned, left his office, and walked down the now-darkened corridors of the office building. He'd been mistaken about Cord's abilities. But he would not make the same mistake twice. This time he would not put it in the hands of others, others who seemed to be extremely incompetent. From tonight on, he would handle this job himself.

He had an unlimited supply of men who would do anything for money. He'd always used force as discreetly as possible, but he did use it when he felt the ends justified the means. This was one of those times.

The wealth he controlled made it possible to buy and sell both the life and the death of any man he chose. He'd done it before, and he planned on doing it now.

When he arrived at his spacious . . . *empty* mansion, he ordered his valet to pack some clothes.

"Will it be an extensive trip, sir?"

"I hope not. But I'm not sure of the length of time. Have my railroad private car made ready and find out when the next train leaves for Virginia City. Make the arrangements to have my car linked up.''

''Yes, sir.'' The valet knew from past experience to obey without question. Thomas Merrell did many things that appeared strange to those about him. But those same people had learned it was best not to see, hear, or speak of what went on in the senator's mansion, or in the senator's life.

By nine the next morning Thomas was comfortably settled in his private car, on his way to Virginia City.

He would be making only one stop along the way to pick up a man he knew could be as dangerous as Jonas. This time there would be no waiting and watching. This time he meant to be in on the kill.

The man who would accompany him was a man like Jonas Holt, a cold man who would do what he wanted without question. The price Thomas paid assured him of that.

As the scenery rushed past him, Thomas Merrell could see ony one thing—Michael Cord lying dead in a pool of blood. Dead by a gun . . . the way Scott had died.

Maxwell Starett paced the floor like a caged tiger. Lee Chu watched with his usual impassive face. He was quite used to Maxwell's methods of releasing pent-up tension.

''I'm going to do something to speed up my own damn train system,'' he muttered. ''How long does it take to get here from Georgia anyway?''

''Tlace say they stopping at Jenny's home so that she can remain with her family while he comes here. He also want to bling Jenny's blother, Buck, and Hannah's blother, Terrance. They have not had enough time to arrive.''

''I swear, I wish I had your patience, Lee Chu.''

''I am *imp*patient,'' Lee Chu admitted, ''but roaring like a wounded lion does not change matters . . . it only makes you tired.''

Maxwell laughed. ''I don't doubt you are right.''

''All your worry does not make tlain run faster.''

''Well, it makes me feel better.''

Maxwell paused at the sound of a knock on the door. He exchanged a quick glance of surprise with Lee Chu, then went to the door to open it.

"I've a message for you, Mr. Starett. It came by wire an hour ago."

"Thanks." Maxwell accepted the wire, closed the door, and tore the letter open. He read quickly and Lee chu watched his face as he did. To Lee Chu, Maxwell's face was as easy to read as a map.

"It's from Mac," Maxwell said. "He says they're in Virginia City and have found Michael but that there are a lot of problems and they need help."

"Better we go pletty quik then."

"We can't, Lee Chu. Trace is on his way. We'll just have to sit tight until he gets here. The wire says so far everyone is fine . . . but I don't quite trust that 'so far.' It sounds pretty ominous to me. Like it's a temporary situatino. You know, if they found Michael, surely the men who were looking for him did, too. Lee Chu, there's a big explosion brewing and I'm helpless to do anything right now but wait. I'm going down and get a drink."

Maxwell left the room and Lee Chu did not try to stop him. There was a time when some form of release was necessary and this was one of them.

Two days, two long, restless days and sleepless nights, and Maxwell was reaching the end of his rope.

"Lee Chu, if they don't come in on this afternoon's train I'm going on ahead and you wait for them and bring them along. I've got to get out there and find out what the hell is going on. Mac wouldn't send for help if he really didn't need it."

"You are right. Maybe today will bling tlain that carries friends."

"We can hope. But if not, I leave on the afternoon train tomorrow."

Lee Chu nodded. He knew that Maxwell would not be able to tolerate the waiting any longer than that.

Maxwell and Lee Chu ate a late dinner that night, disregarding the stares of the curious. They could not understand the immaculate, well-known, and very affluent Maxwell Starett . . . and the small Chinese man who shared dinner with him in a restaurant that most likely would have forbade Lee Chu's entry under any other circumstances.

The situation amused Maxwell and seemed not to reach Lee Chu at all.

"You have everything I need packed, Lee Chu?"

"Yes. All is ready."

"I'll let you know as soon as I get there and apprise you of the situation."

Lee Chu stretched his mouth into a thin smile. "No need," he replied calmly.

"You have the patience to wait until I get back?"

"Even my estimable patience does not extend so far."

"You're not thinking of . . ."

"Have gone long gone past thinking. Have decided already. I will go with you."

"But Trace and the others!"

"Will have no problem reading the message we will leave behind. Confucius say, 'It is no good to think twice about a decision, when once is enough.' " Lee Chu said bluntly.

Maxwell chuckled. "And I quote a philosopher, too: 'The only way to be absolutely safe is never to try anything for the first time.' "

One of Lee Chu's eyebrows raised slightly and he seemed prepared to launch into a philosophical debate, something Maxwell already knew he couldn't handle.

"All right, Lee Chu, all right. I surrender. If you want to go, you go. I'll leave a message at my hotel. They'll see Trace gets it as soon as he arrives."

Lee Chu nodded and Maxwell grinned, wondering if Lee Chu was not just a little disappointed that Maxwell did not take up the challenge.

They walked slowly back to the hotel together. Lee Chu went upstairs to check on the last of the preparations while Maxwell decided to go into the bar, have a drink, and read the evening paper.

He found a comfortable seat, ordered a whiskey, and sent for the paper. Both were delivered to him within minutes.

He sipped the whiskey, lit a thin cigar, and sat back to read leisurely. A few minutes after he opened the front page, he sat suddenly erect and withdrew the cigar from his mouth to mutter an exclamation of pleasant surprise. The article that brought the gleam of interest to his eyes might have surprised anyone who knew of his present problems, for they seemed totally disconnected.

> President Ulysses Grant will be honored by the mayor and the citizens at St. Louis on his tour of the Midwest. He will spend several days in St. Louis to discuss some legislative ideas. The next stop on the President's tour will be Springfield and Chicago. He will go on to Philadelphia, and then return to Washington. He is . . .

Maxwell continued to read, and as he did, the idea swelled within him. When he completed the article, he stopped reading to develop an idea that had just presented itself.

It was an hour later, when his plan had solidified in his mind, that he dank down his whiskey, rose, and went upstairs to bed.

The next morning Lee Chu was the one who was surprised, for Maxwell seemed to have developed more patience overnight than he'd exhibited for the past fifty years.

"You seem to have had pleasant dleams last night," Lee Chu said as Maxwell drank his morning coffee.

"Do I?"

"When you become calm it is only because you have found an answer of some kind. Did your ancestors speak to you during your sleep?"

"No, actually the newspaper spoke to me before I went to bed."

"And would you like to share the wisdom this newspaper imparted to your already greatly endowed mind?"

"I would be delighted. I've just found out that a very dear friend of mine is traveling this way. He won't be in San Francisco, but he'll be close enough for me to reach within a week or so . . . and I intend to do just that."

Lee Chu looked at Maxwell in somber disbelief. "You go to visit one fliend while another's life depends on you? I do not understand."

"I go to visit one friend," Maxwell answered with a soft chuckle, *"because* another's life depends . . . or *could* depend on me. I think I've run across someone who can help . . . I mean *really* help. Not with a gun, or with any other kind of weapon. But with power, Lee Chu, power that can move mountains. I'm going to hand him my mountain and pray to God he can move it."

"The fliend must be very powerful to have an arm that will reach that far. I have heard the man who is behind Mistah Michael's ploblem is a senator. That will take a lot of power."

"My friend, a man I fought, ate, slept, and drank beside through four long years of war, has been made President of these United States," Maxwell laughed softly. "How's that for power?"

"So we are not going to Virginia City?"

"Not right away. Now I'm going to St. Louis, but first I'm going to wait for Trace's train. It's best that we inform them of all we know as fast as we can and send them on their way."

"And we go in the opposite direction. They will be surprised."

"It's a chance, Lee Chu . . ."

"Of course. You are a man who knows both the dangers and rewards of taking chances." Lee Chu finally smiled. "Neither of us want to call on all our ancient philosophers to rush into our discussion again."

"No, Lee Chu, I know when I'm outnumbered. It's been a long time for us," Maxwell smiled up at Lee Chu, "and I hope it will be a lot longer, and for all our friends, too. You pray to your ancestors and I'll pray to mine . . . and we'll both pray for the same thing."

"Yes," Lee Chu said softly as he nodded his head. "Yes, that is wise."

"And I think it wise that we get down to the station and wait for that train."

His transportation taken care of, Maxwell and Lee Chu planned on waiting at the station to see if Trace and the others would arrive on the next train. Neither of them really wanted to leave anything but a cold message behind.

The time seemed to tick by with almost unbearable slowness.

But finally the shrill sound of the train whistle could be heard in the distance.

Neither Maxwell nor Lee Chu said a word, their concentration on the train whose smoke they could now see, since they'd gone out onto the platform at the sound of the whistle.

Now the rapid chuff, chuff of the train and the sound of metal on metal could be heard and the huge black engine hove into view. The screech of brakes and hiss of steam brought the train to a halt.

Lee Chu and Maxwell watched both ends of the train, unsure of which door to expect their friends to exit . . . or even if they would exit.

"Max!"

Maxwell grinned and took the few steps toward Trace Cord to accept his outstretched hand.

"Trace! God, boy, it's good to see you again."

"It's good to see you too, Max. I only wish it was under different circumstances."

"I see you showed up with half the family," Maxwell said, as he saw the two young men who had just stepped out of the train car. "Terrance, Buck . . ." He extended his hand to both men.

"Mr. Starett." Buck shook Maxwell's hand.

"Nice to see you again, Mr. Starett," Terrance added as he, too, shook Maxwell's hand.

"I thought we'd need some help," Trace said.

"If he hadn't put up a fight, and if Jenny hadn't been too pregnant to travel, she would have been here, too." Buck laughed.

"Pregnant!" Maxwell laughed as he clapped Trace on the back so hard that Trace was almost knocked from his feet. "That's the best news I've had in weeks."

Trace turned to the smiling Lee Chu and extended his hand. There was a great deal of respect obvious in Trace's attitude, and sincere pleasure registered in the eyes of the small Chinese man.

"Lee Chu!" Trace smiled. "You old fox, it's good to see you again."

"Mistah Tlace," Lee Chu smiled broadly, "you are a pleasure for these old eyes to see again. And I rejoice in your happiness for the coming child. May he be a warmth for your old age. Still,

I sorrow for the reasons that made your trip necessary. It must be difficult to leave your wife at this time."

"Let's get back to the hotel," Maxwell said. "I have a train to catch later today and I have a lot of explaining to do before I go."

"Train . . . late?" Trace questioned, "I don't understand. Where are we going? I thought . . ."

"There's too much to explain out here. Let's go back to my hotel. I'll tell you everything. Then, I think we all have some more traveling to do. Where's your baggage?"

"I'll get it," Buck said.

Terrance went with Buck to pick up their few bags, while Lee Chu, Maxwell, and Trace stood waiting.

"Since we're here at the station, I'll see that you get three tickets to Virginia City."

"Virginia City? We just passed through Virginia City, a couple of days back. Why would we want to backtrack?"

"I'm sorry. When I sent for you, I didn't know exactly what to tell you. Michael is in Virginia City."

"Good lord! We could have gotten there . . ."

"Well, it's too late to worry about that," Maxwell answered. He motioned to Buck and Terrance to follow them when he saw them approaching, and the five men headed back to the hotel.

After putting their baggage in the room that had been Maxwell's they all went down to the bar to get a drink and let Maxwell explain.

"So that's how it is, Trace. Mac, Joey, Brad, and Jamie went with Hannah because they were scared for her. And I can say I was just as certain she would have found a way to go alone if they hadn't. No one knew where Michael was. Then, I got the telegram from Mac. You know Mac, he never would have asked for help if he hadn't really been shaken up."

"It's like Trace says," Buck spoke quietly. "We could have been in Virginia City by now."

"I know, and I'm sorry. But there is a morning train."

"You said you're going this afternoon." Trace was puzzled.

"Lee Chu and I have a harebrained idea and we have to give

it a try. It's a long story and too complicated to explain. If it works, you'll know. If it doesn't . . . well, I'll join you in Virginia City as soon as I can."

Any other man might have been asked a million questions, but this was Maxwell Starett, and Trace and the others not only trusted him completely, but would never question his motives for doing anything he thought was right.

"All right. We'll be on that morning train. It just gets to me that we've wasted all this time and all those miles. I hope we're not too late to help Michael. Max . . . you saw those men. What are they like? What are their names?"

"I remember their eyes, Trace. Gunfighters, hard men. One told me his name was Jonas Holt . . . as if it was a name I should have known. I guess he's got some reputation, all right. I've heard the name later. He's killed a dozen men or more."

"And there's three of them," Buck said softly.

"Yeah . . . hell of a place for Hannah," Terrance added. There was a moment's silence as each man thought of the courageous young woman who had willingly walked into the danger.

"Well, Lee Chu and I have to get a move on. I don't want to miss that train."

"Max, will you show up in Virginia City soon?" Trace asked.

"Yeah. As quick as I can. In the meantime, find Michael, Trace. As far as he knows he's alone out there and when he left here he was in no mood to fight. Killing men is setting on him pretty hard."

"I know. Michael doesn't have a killer's mind. I wish you'd known him before the war. It seems when the war came, it took the world right out of his hand and it's never been given back."

"Well, I guess that's why we all care so much. We just have to prove to him that all of us want to help as much as we can. He'll know that we've put forth every effort possible."

There was a silent amen to that by everyone present. Then Maxwell again extended his hand to each of the men.

"Good luck."

"Same to you, Max," Trace added. "Whatever you're up to, I hope it works."

When Maxwell and Lee Chu had gone, the friends sat in silence for a while. Then Trace spoke.

"It's not going to do us any good to just sit around here and think. It's been driving us crazy and we've got to keep our heads. Buck, why don't you go over, check the time for our train. Terrance, you get a few more rooms. I'm going over to the telegraph and let Jenny know what's going on. She can tell your parents and assure them everything will be all right."

"Good idea, Trace," Buck agreed. "I know how I'd feel if it was Emily."

"See you boys in a while. Then we'd better go get something to eat. No drinkin' and no late night. We don't want to miss that morning train."

The next day the three were at the station long before the train was due. They sat quietly on the bench outside the station door and waited.

Each man was deeply involved in his own thoughts. Michael had touched lives in a way he could hardly know. He and Trace had shared a happy childhood. Trace alone knew the brutality Michael had encountered during the four long years of the war. Still, he had come back to help Trace at a time when he was desperately needed, only to walk out of his life searching for a way to keep from dealing out death again.

The ride toward Virginia City was a long and dusty one. They stopped in a number of towns, long enough to eat and stretch their legs. They slept on the hard, benchlike seats of the train and their clothes showed the signs of the dust and soot from the engine that found its way into the cars.

Maxwell and Lee Chu knew their trip was going to be a difficult one. The faulty timing of the trains taught Maxwell a lot of lessons about the structure of his own rail lines.

Lee Chu chuckled at Maxwell's mutterings. "It is so much easier to learn of the difficulties of a ploject when one makes personal contact, rather than from a desk. Is that not so, Maxwell?"

"Very funny," Maxwell chuckled. "I'm going to make it a special project to have faster times, well-padded seats, and some way to carry some good Kentucky whiskey. I miss my private car."

"One would get the impression that you are a somewhat spoiled man," Lee Chu mused humorously. "At least parts of your anatomy."

Maxwell grinned but refused to answer.

They had several overnight stops that irritated Maxwell, then caught the earliest trains that could take them the longest distance in a day.

Time . . . time was their nemesis. They had to get to St. Louis while Grant was still there. Otherwise they would have to trail him all the way to Washington.

The first stop was in Nevada, and Maxwell and Lee Chu left the train in a state of near exhaustion. They had less than six hours sleep on beds that would have been complimented had they been called uncomfortable. Dawn found them again on the train crossing Colorado.

Things began to look familiar to them and brought them memories both good and bad. Colorado was where Jenny and her family had very nearly brought the Starett Railroad to a stop . . . it was also both where Jenny and Trace had met and fell in love, and where Michael had entered their lives.

They were grateful when they began to move across southern Kansas. It meant that Missouri was on the next border. Of course he had to get across Missouri, but St. Louis was coming closer and closer with every minute.

When Maxwell and Lee Chu stepped down onto the train platform they were so stiff they could barely move.

Maxwell knew he wasn't going to even attempt to see his old friend in this condition. But he had to find out if he'd arrived in time. They walked the distance into town, and it only took them minutes to realize that he had, for the entire town had an air of celebration about it.

Red, white, and blue bunting hung from every structure and crisscrossed the streets. The entire town seemed ablaze with lights, and as they walked down the streets, they could sense the excitement.

"He has to be here . . . he has to." Maxwell stopped the first man on the street. "What's going on?"

"The President of the United States, sir, is honoring our great city."

"Thank God," Maxwell breathed softly. "He's here, in town now?"

"Yes, sir. The Charles Hotel. But you can't get close to it. Got it surrounded. Can't be too cautious."

"You're right. Thank you," Maxwell replied. The man smiled and walked away, and Lee Chu and Maxwell continued on. "He's here, Lee Chu. We made it."

"Yes. Now we must clean off the dirt of tlavel and find a way to reach him."

"I'll bet there's not a hotel room to be had."

"I would surmise not."

"Well, I have some friends here. I'll find us some rooms. Don't worry, Lee Chu, I'll see him if I have to start another war to do it. Come on."

If Lee Chu had any doubts at all, they were soon put aside. Maxwell was right. The Starett name was not unknown, and he did have friends. Friends that soon found a room where he and Lee Chu could have a hot bath and change their clothes.

President U.S. Grant, veteran of the Civil War, was not really prepared or equipped to be President of the United States. He knew neither the theory nor the pratice of politics and he had begun to regard his office more as a reward for past service than a solemn public trust.

The dark-haired, dark-eyed, bullish, two-fisted drinker was suddenly immersed in the world of politics, and he wasn't quite sure he liked it. He was also surrounded by those cold, emotionless men whose job it was to protect him from the fawners and favor-seekers who plagued him daily . . . sometimes hourly.

He'd just concluded a meeting with a group of such men, and as he and his entourage returned to his suite, he would have given anything to share a bottle and a memory or two with a friend who wanted nothing but conversatino. The new presidency weighed heavily on his shoulders already.

Once back in his suite he poured himself a drink and walked to the window to look down on the street.

"Mr. President . . ." A strong, young voice from close behind him cut into his thoughts. He turned to look at the man who stood near him. A young man . . . tall, strong, and devoted.

"What is the problem, Mr. Wright?"

"It's best you don't stand at the open window, Mr. President. A pistol or a rifle could do a fine job from the street."

"I know it's your job to protect me, but by damn, I think I felt freer when we were fighting the war and there were thousands of guns there."

"You weren't President then, sir, and you weren't my responsibility."

Grant sighed and moved from the window. "Pour yourself a drink, Mr. Wright."

"No, sir, I'm sorry. I'm on duty and I need a clear head."

"Of course . . . of course." *Hell*, Grant thought, I *wish I* were *in the camp again.* At least I could share a drink or two with a friend. He tried to think of the last time he'd sat and had a companionable conversation that wasn't weighted with politics.

His secretary came in with a sheaf of papers that made Grant mentally groan.

"Stewart, don't you have anything better to do tonight than make work for me?"

"Sorry, Mr. President," Stewart grinned. He was well used to Grant's irritability. "But if I save these until tomorrow they'll never get done. We're on the way by nine tomorrow."

"All right, all right. Bring them in."

"Oh, by the way, sir. I checked your appointments and saw you had nothing scheduled for tonight, so I took the liberty of telling the gentleman in the bar downstairs that you could not meet him. Rather pushy gentleman."

"Oh," Grant replied, hardly listening.

"Yes, sir. Downright demanded he get to see you. Said it was a matter of life and death. But they all say that. Had the strangest man with him. A foreigner . . . Chinese, I believe."

Grant's head came up from his contemplation of the papers spread before him. "A Chinese? His name, man, what was his name?"

"The Chinese, sir? I . . . I don't know. I never asked."

"Hell, no! Not the Chinese, the other. The one who wanted to see me?"

"Ah . . . I believe he said it was . . . Starett. Yes, that was it, Maxwell Starett."

"And you told him . . ."

"That you were much too busy," Stewart said with smug confidence. "Besides, sir, he had no appointment. Do you realize how far behind schedule this will put you. Why, I . . ."

"Stewart," Grant said calmly.

"Yes, sir," Stewart replied. He wasn't too sure he liked the look he saw in Grant's eyes, and when Grant next spoke, he knew his instincts were right.

"Get your bottom off that chair, and get down to that bar and find Maxwell Starett and his friend and bring them up here at once. At once! Do you understand me? And you'd better pray they are not gone or you'll be spending half the night hunting them down!"

"Yes . . . yes, sir." Stewart rose from his chair much more rapidly than he had sat down in it. He'd never seen Grant angry, and it startled him into rapid decisive movement.

Grant grinned to himself as the door closed behind Stewart. He took a deep swallow of the whiskey and lit a cigar. He would have an hour or so to share time with a man with whom he had shared so much more on the battlefield.

When the door opened, Maxwell and Lee Chu walked in, followed by Stewart, who looked defiantly uncertain.

"You can leave us for a while, Stewart."

"But, sir . . ."

"Two hours, Stewart . . . then we'll get back to business. I promise."

"Yes, sir." Stewart cast Lee Chu and Maxwell a look when he left that spoke volumes. He did not know who this man was, but he intended to remember his face. He had to be someone very important. He closed the door softly behind him.

Grant chuckled deeply. Maxwell smiled. Then he extended his hand. "Mr. President."

This brought a deep, rumbling laugh from Grant, who took Maxwell's hand in a firm grip. "Not to you, Max . . . not to you."

Chapter Fifteen

Bentonville, Colorado

"It's from Trace, Pa," Jenny Cord said, as she took the telegram from her pocket and handed it to Howard Graham. "He, Buck, and Terrance have just joined Maxwell in San Francisco. It seems Hannah has gone to Virginia City. Word came from Mac and the others that Michael's there."

"This must be terribly hard on Hannah," Howard said.

Jenny smiled at her father. "I have a feeling Hannah can handle herself pretty well. But I do suppose her family is very worried. I think I'll go over and see her parents. Let them know she's well."

"Good idea. Want me to go along?"

"No, I can manage," Jenny smiled. "I'm pregnant, Pa, I'm not an invalid. Im as strong as a horse."

"Only in your mind. The rest of you, my dear," he came to Jenny and put his arm about her shoulder, "is my sweet, wonderful daughter, and the future mother of my grandchild. So *I* will harness the wagon, and *I* will drive you over to the Marshall's."

"All right, you win. You were tough as a father and I have a feeling you're going to be an even tougher grandfather."

Howard smiled at his daughter, his love for her reflecting in his eyes.

"Jenny girl," Howard said gently. "We've come through so

many things, haven't we? Some good, some bad. Now we have so much to look forward to."

"And I want my family—all my family and all Trace's family, too—to share this baby. Michael did so much for us. I only hope Trace finds him and brings him back here. This child needs every member of the family, and that includes uncles."

"Well, I'll fetch the wagons and we can get going. We could stop by and see Will and Joanne on the way. They're always asking if we've had any word from you and Trace. Will is a bit torn. His heart is here with Joanne and Georgina, but his thoughts are on Trace and Michael."

"I know. I guess Will is the kind of man who would feel a touch of guilt, thinking he should be a support to everyone."

"Well you have to admit," Howard replied, "he's certainly has been the answer to Joanne and Georgina."

"Absolutely. Joanne has never been happier, and Georgina dotes on him as if he were her real father."

"And he's sure made that little farm bloom."

"Oh, yes. It's surprising what three years of devoted, loving attention will do." Jenny laughed. "I met Georgina at the church the other night. She's over twelve now. In fact, in two months she'll be thirteen. That's so hard to believe. She's growing into a lovely young lady."

"Why does that amuse you?" Howard asked.

"Because Will is beginning to growl like an overprotective father. By the time she's sixteen he's going to have every young man in the state scared to death they'll step out of line."

"He can try," Howard chuckled. "*I* did, and look how it turned out."

"Satisfied, Pa?"

"With you and Trace? I couldn't be happier. Now, I guess we'd best be on our way."

"I'm ready, I know how upset the Marshalls must be. They haven't heard from Hannah since she left. They will be overjoyed to at least know she got to Michael safe and sound."

"I see that Trace wants you to write to his sister Allison to let her know all is well."

"Yes. I'll do that after I talk to the Marshalls."

"Fine. And I'll see to that wagon."

When Howard left, Jenny paused a moment to look around her. This was the house in which she was born. This was the lush green land over which she had roamed so freely as a child. She knew every inch of it, every green valley and rugged hill.

She stepped out onto the porch that ran the entire length of the house and stood, caught in the magic of remembering.

Her mother rested beneath the huge trees a short distance away. She'd knelt by the grave so often and conversed with her.

Some distance away the river rippled and it, too, brought memories. She had first met Trace on the banks of that river. So many things had filled her life while she lived in this valley. Memories swirled about her, memories not only of childhood, but of the sometimes chaotic, sometimes magical days when she had first met Trace. It had been a confrontation that had set sparks flying across the valley she'd called home, when Trace Cord, foreman for Maxwell Starett and his railroad, had come to lay their rails across her land. Theirs had been a fiery connection, and she had learned that love could conquer all. She knew of love, so she was one of the few who had understood when Hannah had followed Michael.

From Trace she'd heard Michael's story, and she had prayed for the two to find each other. Now . . . maybe it could be.

She was brought out of her reverie by her father's voice. He had told her the wagon was ready to go.

She laughed at her own clumsiness and her father's caution as she climbed up on the wagon seat.

As they neared Will and Joanne's farm, evidence of their past, complimentary words could be seen in the well-repaired fences and neat, well-cultivated fields.

They were still some distance from the house when they saw a lone rider approaching the dirt road from across an open field. For a moment they pulled the wagon to a halt and sat in awed admiration of the rider.

The horse approached the fence at a breakneck speed, and Jenny gasped as it took the fence in a graceful leap.

When the horse skittered to a halt by the wagon, Georgina Carter smiled at them casually, as if nothing untoward had occurred.

From a shy child, Georgina was evolving into a young woman

who would one day be a beauty. her ebony hair was braided in a ropelike fashion that hung down her back, her face was flushed and her blue eyes sparkled with fun.

"Georgina," Jenny laughed, "if Will sees you take a fence like that, you might not sit down for a week."

"I know." Georgina laughed the delighted laugh of a thirteen-year-old who had no cares and was surrounded by love. "I trust you not to tell him."

"Would it stop you if I threatened to?" Howard chuckled.

"No," she giggled, "but it sure would make Will mad, and I don't want to do that."

"All right, we'll keep your secret," Jenny said. "But please be careful."

"Will taught me to ride and he knows I'm almost as good as he is. But I promise to be *very* careful . . . and do it right if I have to do it," she added with contagious mirth. It was obvious to both Jenny and Howard that Georgina was a completely happy girl.

"Are Will and Joanne at home?" Howard asked.

"Yes. They were when I left."

"We have to get along, Georgina,' Howard said. "We need to talk to them for a bit then go on over to the Marshalls' house."

"Has something interesting happened?"

"Yes," Jenny replied. "We've heard from Trace. It seems he's found Michael."

"Oh, wonderful! That will make my mother and Will happy. Do you mind if I race on ahead? I'd really like to tell them."

"Sure," Howard said. "Go on."

Georgina expertly kicked the horse into motion, and soon she was again flying toward home. Jenny had to laugh.

"So much for her promising to be careful."

Howard chuckled, nodded, and slapped the reins against the horse's rump to get them on their way again.

Fifteen minutes later they were being met by Will and Joanne, who stood on the front porch and watched their approach.

Will seemed to have grown younger in the three years he'd been married to Joanne. The hard work of rejuvenating her run-down farm, the love he had shared with Joanne, and the joy Georgina had filled his life with, had wiped the cobwebs of past memories away.

He was a tall, long-legged, a sturdily built man, with warm brown eyes, sandy hair, and a quick even smile.

Joanne, too, had flourished under Will's tender and devoted care. Now she smiled often. Her blue eyes were filled with the love for a husband who had righted her topsy-turvy life a few years before and rescued her from a nearly tragic mistake.

"Hello, Jenny . . . Howard," Will said. "Step down and come in for a spell."

"Yes," Joanne agreed. "There's hot coffee on the stove."

"I wish we could, but we just stopped by to tell you the news," Howard said. "We got a telegram from Trace. It seems he's found Michael."

"Oh, that's wonderful! Now maybe this will all be over and Michael can find some peace," Joanne said.

None of the other three quite believed it was going to be that easy. But Joanne's world was a happy one and her desire to have everyone she knew be just as happy was something none of them wanted to destroy, so they kept silent.

"Want me to ride over with you?" Will asked, "I could saddle up real quick. Maybe," his eyes glittered with fun, "I could race Georgina. With a bit of a head start and no fences to jump, I'd be able to beat her."

His hazel eyes glowed with affection for Georgina . . . a girl as close to his own daughter as was humanly possible to get. He'd adopted her when he and Joanne were married and they had soon become very attached to each other. Will's six-foot frame still dwarfed Georgina, but he recognized her speedy growth frmo the child of eight he had first met.

"Will!" Georgina said in humorous shock. Her dark-blue eyes sparkled with their shared fun. She was turning into a young lady and Will represented the father she sometimes had trouble remembering. She always admired Will's firm but gentle control. With his calm, easy way he'd remolded her life. Large, steady hands had taught her to ride. A quick, warm smile and a slow, drawling voice had always seemed to ease any problem. First for her mother, and then for her.

"I couldn't miss you, pet," Will chuckled. "I was up in the barn and you can see the south field real easy from there."

"You're not mad?"

"I think I've run out of mad," he laughed. "Now, all I have left is worry . . . and trust."

Georgina's eyes glowed with love, and she and Will exchanged a look that made Joanne's heart sing.

"We've got to get going, Pa," Jenny urged.

"Yes. Come along if you want, Will."

"Georgina and I will catch up with you."

"Fine." Again the wagon was put into motion.

The trip to the Marshalls was scenic. The day was pleasantly warm and made better by Georgina's laughing conversation and Will's solid company. They were greeted warmly, especially by Emily, who'd been as worried as anyone else and had truly wanted to go with Buck.

The atmosphere turned even brighter when Jenny told them of the message that had come from Trace.

"That's such wonderful news," Emily said. "I wish I could have been with Buck and the others when they found them."

"I know," Jenny said. "I tried to argue Trace into letting me go, but maybe he was right. We had no idea of what they were going to run into, and they did not need to have to worry about us as well."

"Then my daughter is fine," Beatrice said in relief. "We have been so worried."

"I've been frightened to death, to be exact," Jacob added. "If I'd had an idea where to find her, I'd have done so."

"Well, she's all right and with people you can trust implicitly. Besides, Trace and Michael are with her now, so you can rest assured she will be fine."

"Jenny . . ." Jacob said. "We had no real idea about how Hannah truly felt about Michael. But . . ."

"But what?"

"But if Michael felt the same, why did he go and leave her like that? Can it be that he didn't feel the same and didn't want to hurt her?"

"No, Mr. Marshall," Jenny said soothingly. "Michael loved Hannah. That was the real reason behind his leaving." She went on to explain that Michael felt he was leaving to protect Hannah.

"So . . . those men are turning him into a lost soul."

It was obvious Georgina was absorbing every ounce of what was being said. Will could watch her mind spinning. But the last sentence caught her always vivid imagination.

"What's a lost soul? Michael isn't lost."

"No, he isn't lost, not like you think." Will, as always, tried to answer her honestly. "Do you remember the day I found you crying by the creek? You felt kind of lost then, didn't you? But you knew your way home. It was just . . . your spirit was sort of lost."

"Oh," Georgina answered, and had it been anyone else, Will might have laughed. But he knew quite well that she grasped his meaning.

"Poor Michael," she murmured.

"I suppose that's why he fought loving Hannah so hard," Jenny said.

"Obviously," Emily smiled, "he did not know my sister well."

"No, I guess he didn't," Jenny laughed.

"Hannah was a quiet, gentle, and sweet child," Beatrice said. "Always one to come dragging home every hurt critter she could find and nurse them back to health."

"I suppose," Jenny said thoughtfully, "she recognized Michael was wounded in a way no one could see, and she wanted to heal the hurt."

"Don't you think I ought to go . . ." Jacob began.

"No, Mr. Marshall," Jenny said. "There are enough people already on their way. They'll bring Hannah home . . . and Michael, too, I pray. I think it best we all remain here and not cause any more confusion."

"I guess you're right. But waiting is sure going to be hard."

"Why don't you take me into town, Mr. Marshall," Jenny said. She realized her father was looking at her with complete understanding. She wanted to take the Marshalls' mind off their problems. "I think it best I wire Allison instead of wasting all the time it would take a letter to get there."

"Good idea, Jen," Howard said. "And I shall sit here and enjoy a piece of that fine-smelling pie I see cooling on the windowsill."

"You're quite welcome to as much of it as you'd care to have," Beatrice laughed.

"Hey," Jacob chuckled. "Don't say that. That's my favorite pie."

"Then get to town and hurry back." Howard's eyes twinkled.

"I can't make any promises about how much will be left. And take good care of my little girl."

Jacob and Jenny left and Howard sat at the table to enjoy a thick piece of blueberry pie and Beatrice and Emily's bright conversation.

"It is really wonderful news that my sister has found Michael. But do you think it's going to make a lot of difference?" Emily asked Howard. "I mean, Michael knew his problems were right behind him. He left Hannah to make sure she wouldn't get hurt. What do you think he'll do when she shows up?"

"I don't know, Emily," Howard replied. "I honestly don't know. I *do* know that Hannah and Michael deserve to be able to find some happiness. I just hope Trace and the others can help him find a way out of this. If they can . . ."

"And if they can't?"

"I don't think Michael is a killer at heart. I'm afraid that if this continues, something inside him will break. He might become the kind of man the senator is already labeling him as."

"That would destroy his and Hannah's life completely."

"Yes. I don't doubt that it would."

"What a terrible thing."

"You mean Michael and Hannah?"

"No, I mean the senator. His life must be an empty shell. How can one man be so cold and hard?"

"Emily," Beatrice said. "When a man loses a child, something within him breaks as well. I guess he can become a better, stronger man and learn to love and live again, or he can turn bitter and vindictive. From what Trace said before, his son was a spoiled, wild boy. Maybe what the senator is really feeling is a bit of guilt."

"Guilt?" Emily questioned.

"Yes. He knows that whatever he hoped to make of his son, he failed. He knows that mnoey and power was his son's ruination, as much as it was the father's greatest love. He had to put the blame somewhere, or face the realization that it was actually *he* who killed his son and not a bullet from Michael Cord's gun."

Howard looked at Beatrice with a touch of admiration. She was a quiet, well-organized woman, who had obviously raised her children with great care. Now he also realized she was a very observant and a very intelligent one as well. Beatrice smiled. "Chil-

dren are not always easy to handle, and most of the time no one
has the right answers. I feel sorry for the senator's son as well.
He died before he had a chance to discover the truth."

"Or," Howard said gently, "maybe it was the truth that killed
him."

"Maybe. But we shall never know. Now, all our thoughts and
prayers must be with Hannah and Michael, and our trust must
be with Trace, Buck, Terrance, and the others. Let's hope it's
over soon."

"Amen, Beatrice," Howard replied fervently. "Amen."

The ride from Jacob's ranch to town was one of beauty, and for
some time they rode in silence, just absorbing the tranquility
around them.

"I wonder how Trace hopes to help his brother solve his problems," Jacob said.

"I don't know," Jenny replied honestly. "If the senator had
attacked the Cord family in the open, at least a day in court could
end it all one way or the other. But like this, no blame can be
laid at his feet. He can proclaim innocence in the whole matter."

"Then he doesn't want justice, he wants vengeance."

"Yes. If . . . if one of those men is able to kill Michael, then, in
the senator's heart, he will consider it justice."

"And if they fail . . ."

"He'll send others," Jenny said resignedly. "No one knows how
to stop him. He has tremendous power, wealth and, I might add,
influence."

"Maybe, deep inside, I can understand how the senator feels
after losing his son. But this terrible relentless pursuit, this need
to see a man die, it's . . . it's . . ."

"Insane," Jacob said quietly.

"Yes. He can no longer be rational. He's possessed with this
thing. A normal person would have given up when one man after
another he sent had been killed."

"He has little conscience, it seems. I wonder how many men
he is willing to sacrifice before he gives up."

"I don't think he'll *ever* give up, any more than I think a man's life means anything to him. He'll sacrifice as many as it takes. How . . . how can Michael go on when he knows it's endless?"

"He must be very strong. I think maybe my daughter must be a very good judge of men."

"She must be a great consolation to Michael, but, if he's anything like his brother I'll bet he's fighting her like crazy. I didn't know Michael very long, but he and Trace seem so much alike. Is Hannah determined?"

Jacob chuckled. "If it comes to a contest of wills, Michael will soon find out he's up against a solid wall. *Determined* is a very mild way to describe Hannah. Even as a little girl she was as stubborn as a mule, and when she set out to do something, she had a way of getting it done, come hell or high water."

"Good. I have a feeling that is just what he might need. Trace never said a word, but I know how his heart must have been breaking when he thought of how lonely Michael must be."

"There just has to be a way to put an end to this."

"I don't see how, unless someone can reach the senator and put his vendetta out of commission."

"Boy, that would have to be someone pretty powerful."

"Absolutely, and none of us know anybody like that. I just hope Trace and Michael can find some answers."

Jacob drew the team to a halt. "If you don't mind, I want to stop at the mercantile. I'll do that while you run over and send your telegram. You wait there for me, I'll be along in a few minutes," he added as he helped Jenny down from the wagon.

Jenny walked down the planked sidewalk until she reached the telegraph office. Inside, she worded the message, paid the cost, then left the office. She meant to stay there until Jacob arrived.

She stood, her attention drawn to the still-remarkable sight of a train arrival. Several people disembarked, but her attention was riveted on two. She couldn't quite believe her eyes.

She went down the two steps from the walk and crossed the street quickly. She smiled as she grew closer to the couple who stood deep in conversation.

"Well, my, my. Allison Cord! What are you doing here?" Jenny's smile was knowing and amused.

Allison spun around, startled to hear the familiar voice when she knew she wasn't expected. Then she laughed in delight and closed the distance between them to embrace Jenny enthusiastically.

"Jenny! It's good to see you. You were pretty sure I wouldn't be too far behind."

"After being married to your brother, I had no doubt of it. I've just sent you a telegram and suddenly here you are." She looked at Reid with amusement in her eyes. "Trace is going to be very curious as to how this came about."

Reid flushed, but with a grin. "If Trace knows his sister as well as I think he does, he'll have no doubts at all. I have no more control over this than a spoon of butter in the hot sun."

"Somehow I don't doubt that a bit," Jenny replied. "But, Allison, this is not going to make Trace very happy."

"Oh, Jenny, you understand, don't you? I . . . I just needed to be as close as I could, to be near if Michael should need help. I have as much right to that as Trace does."

"Of course you do," Jenny soothed. "I'm sorry, I didn't mean for it to sound like that. I only meant he'll be a little upset at you coming all this distance."

"Yes. Sometimes he still thinks I'm a child."

"Anyway, you must come home with me. You're both probably tired and hungry."

"I'm famished," Reid admitted.

"And a good bath would help my condition a lot," Allison added.

At that moment Jenny saw Jacob approaching. He smiled at Allison. "Allison Cord. What a surprise. I don't need to ask what brought you here. It's sure nice to see your pretty face again."

"Thank you, Mr. Marshall," Allison replied warmly. "This is Reid Anderson, my fiancé. We've only just arrived and found a piece of luck with Jenny being right here."

Jacob extended his hand to Reid, who grasped it in a firm handshake. "Pleased to meet you, Mr. Marshall."

"Reid, nice to meet you. It is a funny piece of luck, isn't it, you arriving and Jenny being here to meet you. Maybe it's a good sign that luck has turned your way."

"Our way," Jenny added softly.

"Oh, I hope so," Allison added.

"Come along. Let's get on out to my place. It's a long trip, and I know you two must be ready to rest up, eat a bit, and get settled."

Reid and Allison exchanged a quick glance, but Allison gave a quick negative shake of her head and Reid remained silent.

"Thank you. I was just telling Jenny I'd give anything for a good hot bath."

"Well then, let's get going."

The four of them started toward the wagon. Jenny was quiet, but she hadn't missed the subtle message that had passed between Reid and Allison.

Quinn had reached the point of total exasperation. He had cajoled, he had pleaded, he had begged adamantly, and he had even resorted to anger. But Rena would not budge. Instead, she smiled with infuriating calmness, knowing at this point he could do little more than resort to verbal pressure.

"Rena, your parents will be disgraced," he said miserably.

"Why, what are they doing?" she asked innocently.

"You know what I mean."

"I have no idea what you're talking about. My parents are highly respected. As for me, I'm responsible for what I think is right. And I think this is right. What I feel for you could only be called disgraceful by the old spinsters who live up on the hill. I'll bet a lot of other women in this town would love to share a bit of my . . . disgrace."

"You're impossible, damn it! I'm not going to let you ruin your life."

Rena sat on the edge of the bed and took Quinn's hand in hers. Her eyes had been dancing with amusement, but now they turned serious.

"You listen to me, Quinn Wayland. I love you. If all the goodie-goodies in this town think that's wrong, well, that's a difficulty they'll have to handle themselves. I love you, and I intend to stay here with you and see to your care until you can get out of that bed. After that," she smiled again, "I want you to start seeing to *my* care."

Quinn looked at her for several minutes in silence. Then he

reached out and slid his fingers into her hair, drawing her to him for a long, leisurely kiss.

"I don't know when I'm going to begin to believe this. Right now it's too much like a miracle to accept. Rena . . . it's not too late. Go home."

"When you're strong enough," she murmured softly as she bent to kiss him again, "you can get out of that bed and throw me out. Of course, I intend for you to be so used to me by then, you won't want to."

Quinn closed his eyes and groaned softly. His body was playing havoc with his sense of logic. She was here, warm and giving, and the whole house seemed brighter.

Rena began making matters even harder for him. She promptly set about cleaning everything in sight. He lay, incapable of doing anything more, and watched her as she moved around. She hummed to herself, and he was shaken with the idea that she was actually happy.

His deep gray eyes watched every move she made, watched the sunlight through the window glaze her hair into gold. Occasionally she would glance his way, her green eyes would lock with his, and he'd again feel that molten feeling, as if every bone in his body had turned to hot lava.

It took him two days to actually start moving around. He felt stiff and sore, but he knew he was healing well. He also knew that whatever stories were going around, it was much too late to stop them now.

He couldn't pin Rena down. She eluded him and his ideas and worries with casual ease. But there were too many things for them to talk about for him to let her get away with it much longer.

She cooked them a supper. Its tastiness did not surprise him. In fact, nothing she did seemed to surprise him much anymore.

"Rena . . what are you going to do about your parents? I know how much you love them."

"I'm going to go on loving them and hope they come to their senses, like I did."

"Like *you* did?"

"We met in secret, Quinn, and that was the only thing we did wrong. We were afraid, and we shouldn't have been. We have a right to love each other and be together. One day, I hope my parents will see that. But no matter what, I'm not denying that I love you." She reached across the table and placed her hand over his. "And I'm home, Quinn . . . I don't intend to ever leave again."

Quinn found it difficult to swallow the thick constriction in his throat, and his heart seemed to be determined to skip a beat or so every other second.

He rose from the table, walked around it, and drew Rena up to her feet and into his arms. Teir lips met, first in a soft, feather-light touch, then in passion that grew in intensity so quickly that neither could control it.

In their complete awareness of each other it seemed as if everything came to a breathless halt. They looked deeply in each other's eyes for a moment of suspended time.

The second kiss had lost all its hesitancy and they blazed with raw, hungering need.

Quinn tasted her responding mouth with his again and again. One hand caught in her thick hair while the other stroked the roundness of her buttocks and thighs, molding her to his lean frame. He wanted to press her to him until his body knew every line and curve of hers.

A flame of brilliant pleasure swept Rena away, and she was lost in the intensity of this wildfire.

They were in the universe alone, it seemed, and both were filled with the joy of sharing their own private world. They were free, free of all the restriction and the fears.

Rena slid her arms around his waist and heard his swift intake of breath.

"Oh . . ." She tried to move back from him. "I've hurt you."

"God, no," he laughed. "You'll hurt me a lot worse if you move away."

Rena laughed seductively. "Maybe it would be better on your poor, wounded body if you were back in bed."

"Maybe, but it would be awfully lonely."

"Then you need company. I don't want to neglect you."

They laughed together as they moved toward the bed. Rena's sudden lack of inhibitions with him was intoxicating. When she gave herself, it seemed she gave so completely there was little room for any kind of reserve.

They undressed with teasing laughter, gentle touches, and many kisses. And before long they were together on the bed.

Making love with Rena was heady enough to make Quinn's senses feel as if he had touched a hot fire. She was unique in so many ways, but in this she surpassed any woman he had ever known. She filled him as he filled her and they loved to perfection. It left Quinn feeling as if he'd just reached out and touched the stars. This, he felt, was as close to heaven as he would ever get.

They lay together quietly, not needing to talk. It was a rare moment of absolute contentment that would have been impossible to describe in words.

He could not get his fill of looking at her, touching her, watching the way light and shadow fell across her skin. The way her hair reflected the glow. In fact, everything about her was always inviting . . . always new.

For a moment the depth and the reality of what she had done brought the sting of tears to his eyes.

Rena, too, was caught in the afterglow of this longed-for time. She wanted to wrap Quinn in her arms and hold him forever. She had tasted a love so deep that it had pierced her soul with a ray of brilliant light. She would never be the same, and she didn't want to be.

Taking Quinn within her, she had made him part of her, and to do that she had given a part of herself to him. From now on it would take the two of them to make one whole person.

"Rena?" Quinn said softly.

"What?"

"If it would make you happy . . . if you wanted, I could go to your father. Try to explain. Maybe I could get him to understand."

"No, Quinn. Don't you see? I won't have you bring yourself down ever again. We need to give them time to understand that everything they think is wrong. In time, they will begin to know that . . . when you and I build this place into something fine . . . and maybe present them with a grandchild—"

"Hey! Whoa! Wait a minute! Aren't you putting the cart before the horse? I don't have one dime to rub against another and I sure can't afford to have any kids."

"Not now," Rena said calmly, "but you're not going to be in this position long."

"I'm not?" he grinned.

"No, you're not."

"With you beside me," Quinn laughed, "I must just end up being mayor if I'm not careful."

"Nope," she laughed. "I wouldn't give the people of this town that much satisfaction to think they had the power to vote for you. No, I think you ought to be the biggest rancher in the state."

"Grand plans. Lady, when you dream, you sure dream big."

"And that, my love," Rena said gently, "is just what I want to teach you to do. Dream again."

"Dream *again,*" Quinn chuckled. "Rena, I never had a dream in my life, except you . . . and maybe knowing who my parents were and where I came from."

"I can never give you that, Quinn. I wish I could. But I will be here . . . always. And, if we have chilren, we'll make sure we give them all the things you've missed. Maybe somehow that will help make up for your loss."

"Do you know, at this moment it's hard for me to remember any loss."

"Good," She rose on one elbow and bent to kiss him.

"Rena?"

"Uh huh."

"Things . . . things seemed to happen all of a sudden. I always thought you were just a bit scared of your parents before. What changed things?"

"I guess I *was* a little timid before. Two things changed me. Suddenly knowing I could lose you . . . and Hannah Marshall."

"Hannah Marshall?"

Rena went on to explain what Hannah had told her. "And when I saw that it all had to begin . . . or *end* here, I realized I couldn't let go."

"Well, I guess it *does* begin here."

They spent the night in their warm cocoon of happiness.

The train came to a rattling, gasping halt at the station in Virginia City. There were few people around to see Senator Thomas Merrell and three other men step down onto the platform. They found transportation and gave their destination as the Grand Hotel.

Chapter Sixteen

Michael had a well-ingrained, instinctive habit of coming awake quickly. There was never that moment of disorientation. He'd had too many bad experiences not to learn that his life depended on his alertness.

His first realization was that Hannah was no longer in the bed beside him. He sat up abruptly and swung his legs over the edge of the bed. He was stiff, and the old wound on his hip throbbed.

A crisp breeze from a sun-bright new day stirred the curtains at the window. He wondered what time it was. Seconds before, he had wondered how long he had slept, and how sound. At any other time, Hannah would never have been able to leave the bed without him knowing it.

"I must be getting old," he muttered as he rose to his feet. He felt badly in need of a bath and a shave.

When he opened the bedroom door and stepped out into the hall he could hear voices and laughter from below.

He descended the steps and walked into the kitchen, where he found Hannah holding court around the table. It was obvious she had shared a late breakfast with Patrick, Mac, Brad, Jamie, and Joey.

Michael smiled, but when he saw the bruise on her cheek, the small scar where her lip was cut, and the rough red marks on her chin and cheeks, the old rage gripped him. He fought for control and Hannah realized it.

"Good morning, Michael." Hannah smiled, rose from her seat, and came to kiss his cheek. "Are you hungry?"

"I'm having a contest."

"A . . . what?" She was puzzled.

"A contest. Between my stomach, my luxury-loving body that's desperately in need of clean clothes and a bath, and," he grinned wickedly, "other inviting ideas."

"Michael!" She felt herself blushing and heard the soft laughter behind her.

"Come, sit down and eat," Patrick said. "There's hot water on the stove and you can use my razor."

Michael sat down opposite Mac. "You've been out today?"

"Yes."

"And?"

"Nothing," Mac said. "We checked his hotel room and he's gone. Wherever Jonas Holt is holed up, it's not in town. We checked this town closely as it can be checked. He's not here. That kind . . . that kind that runs in packs, maybe he's not so courageous when he's alone."

"Don't count on it, Mac. Jonas is not a coward. I don't think he's afraid to face me. I just think he feels a little . . . bigger, safer if he has his cronies around him. That kind, as you so aptly put it, needs an audience to make him look important."

"Then where has he gone?"

"Waiting for word from the big boss, I suppose. Did you check to see if he sent out any telegrams?"

"No," Mac said with a frown, "but I sure will."

"Michael," Joey said, "what are you planning on doing?"

"Waiting him out," Michael replied calmly.

"You could take Hannah and go," Patrick smiled.

"Where?"

"California maybe. I hear the ocean is a pretty thing to see."

"Now, Patrick . . ." Michael chided with a grin. "You and I both know better than that, don't we? Hannah was right. It's time to stop running. We'll go see the ocean some other time, when there's no shadows behind me. If it can't be that way . . . then it will be no way at all."

"Then you're just going to stay here, in Patrick's house?" Jamie said.

"Nope. I think I'll get cleaned up and take Hannah into town and buy her a pretty new dress." He turned to smile at her. "Just in case she needs one for a special occasion one of these days."

Hannah returned his smile, her eyes warming. She had a heady feeling, as if she were melting inside.

"Are you by any chance asking me to marry you, Michael Cord?"

"The thought has crossed my mind a time or two lately."

"I have witnesses, you understand," she laughed softly. "I'm not going to let you get away."

"I told you, I'm not running from anything anymore. That means the bad . . . and the good. It's going to be hard on you, Hannah."

"I've been worrying about you for a long time, Michael. I don't think *that* could be any harder. Only now . . . now I'll have something to hold, something to hang on to. It will make the hard times a bit easier."

"This is the best news I've heard since we met," Patrick said enthusiastically. "Maybe Jonas has really gone back to wherever he came from. Maybe his courage did fade and he felt the possible loss might not be worth it."

"Maybe," Michael agreed.

Patrick thought he saw something fleeting in his eyes that looked a bit like the old fear. There was something here he wasn't sure of.

Michael finished his food and stood up. "I'll take advantage of that razor and hot water now, if you don't mind."

"Sure," Patrick said quickly. "I'll get it for you."

"So, you're going into town," Joey chuckled.

"I know what he's thinking." Mac laughed also.

"The townspeople are in for a whale of a shock," Patrick agreed. "It ought to bring a bunch of them into the church."

"Scare the devil right out of 'em," Michael agreed, his eyes sparkling.

"Come on, Michael," Patrick said. "I'll help you carry this water up."

"Fine."

"I'll take care of these dishes and be ready whenever you are," Hannah said.

Inside the room, Patrick faced Michael and set the bucket of water down.

"All right, Michael. What's on your mind?"

"What?"

"Don't play innocent with me. This business of you and Hannah."

"Business? You mean asking Hannah to marry me?"

"You have more on your mind than that."

Michael couldn't escape Patrick's piercing gaze.

"All right, I do. Hannah said something that's been on my mind ever since."

"What?"

"She . . . she asked me if I thought she could be carrying my child."

"And there's a chance of that?" Patrick asked. There was no accusation in his voice, nor condemnation in his eyes.

"Yes. And that's something that has to be taken care of. Let's face the fact that this thing is not going to be over until I'm . . . Anyway, I don't want Hannah hurt any more than she has to be. This way . . . she's my wife. Patrick . . . I don't want my child to be illegitimate. If I do have a son I want to give him my name, so he and Hannah will both know how much I loved them." He sighed deeply. "She'll be my wife for what hours I can steal, and she'll have my family's protection and love. I'd like my child to be raised in the same loving family I was."

"Michael . . . maybe . . ."

"I've lived on maybe's too long. I won't run. So it has to end here. I just want you to see that my family knows about Hannah and me. You'll see to it, won't you?"

"I'll do whatever you want."

"Thanks, Patrick, and . . . let's not be talking about this while Hannah's around."

"All right."

"It wouldn't make it any easier for her. At least we can live part of our dream for a while, and I'll know, just in case, that she'll get the best of everything."

"The best of everything would be you."

"Don't worry, I intend to grab every bit of it I can, for as long as I can."

"Lord, I pray there's some way out of this."

"Miracles are hard to come by, and I don't think Jonas Holt has ever heard of them."

"I still pray." Patrick smiled. "I've gotten a few responses that might surprise you."

"You do that. Now, go down and keep Hannah and the boys company before they think we're cooking something up."

Patrick nodded and left the room. For a few minutes, Michael stood in the silence. It did no good to think of anything past today. As he told Patrick, he meant to grab every second of happiness he could and leave Hannah everything good to remember.

After a while he set about shaving and bathing.

Hannah had never felt happier. She chatted with Mac, Brad, Jamie, and Joey while she finished the dishes. They decided to take another quick search of the town just in case.

Only when Hannah was temporarily alone did she gather the thoughts that had been spiraling out of control. It was when she had that quiet moment to hink, that the truth struck her like a physical blow. Slowly she sat down at the table, reality turning her legs weak.

She was still sitting there when Patrick came into the room. He needed only to take one look to know she already knew what was happening and why.

"Hannah . . . don't say anything. Enjoy these days and let Michael enjoy them, too. Maybe things will be better than you can believe now. You have to have some faith."

"Faith brought me here," Hannah stated proudly, "and it will keep me beside Michael for what time we have. He'll never know that I know his reasons. But . . . oh, Patrick, I love him so much, this makes me love him even more."

Michael was whistling softly as he came back downstairs. He smiled at Hannah, who returned the smile, feeling her heart squeezed with a sharp new pain. He was wonderful! She loved him so much, she ached with it . . . and she was terrified to know that at any time she could lose him.

"Well, love, are you ready?" Michael asked.

"Anytime you are," Hannah responded.

"Let's see to that dress. A nice stroll through town ought to prove interesting."

"Like a circus," Patrick laughed. "You'll have to tell me all about it, I'm afraid I won't be there to watch. Zeb will be here soon, and he and I have a lot of work to get finished."

"Then let's go." Michael offered Hannah his arm, and she smiled up at him as she tucked her hand under it and they left Patrick's house together.

To say they startled the entire town would have been an understatement. Faces that had warm smiles turned pale and the smiles faded. One woman even fainted an the blacksmith dropped his hammer on the anvil with a sharp clang.

Hank, the storekeeper, could hardly keep his eyes from Michael. They were wide with shock. When Hannah and Michael came in, he was severely shaken and blurted out the words before he thought.

"You . . . you're dead! I saw it! I saw it!"

"Well, I hate to disappoint you, but I'm very much alive. We have a few purchases to make."

"Oh . . . sure . . . sure," Hank said, almost tripping and sprawling on his face as he tried to come around the counter to help them. His hands shook so badly, Michael wondered if he'd be able to gather any of the things they pointed out.

When they finished at the store, they crossed the street to the dressmaker, Alice Prosser, who did her best to smile while Hannah tried to explain what she wanted. But she, too, could not keep her eyes from Michael, who only smiled pleasantly.

But his smile faded when she proclaimed that she could not possibly have the dress made in less than a week.

"A week," Michael frowned. "That won't do. We need a dress right away."

"Right away!" She was aghast. "That is impossible."

"If I told you that Reverend Carrigan was going to marry the lady and me the day after tomorrow, would it make a difference?"

"Married." Her face softened. "I can't make you a dress in less than a week, but I have something I made for the dance in two weeks that might be altered by tomorrow."

"May we see it?"

"Of course. Wait here, I'll bring it right out."

When she left the room, Hannah smiled at Michael. "Michael Cord, I shall have to keep both eyes on you, or keep you very busy. You're a real charmer."

Michael chuckled and drew her to him for a quick kiss. "Just keep your eyes on me," he said softly. "Keep all your concentration on me."

Alice returned with the dress over her arm. "I'm sure I shall have to take it in a bit, but if you like I can make the alterations in time." She held the dress up for Hannah to see.

"You do magnificent work," Hannah breathed softly as she reached out to touch the dress. It was a shimmering pale-green silk, soft to the touch and beautiful to behold.

Michael watched Hannah's eyes light with pleasure, and he decided to buy the dress no matter the cost. But there was no way he would wait the days to have a dress made. Anything could happen in that time.

"That color will only make your green eyes more beautiful," Michael said softly. "I can hardly wait to see you in it."

Alice looked from Michael to Hannah with a small smile on her face, feeling the warmth that flowed between them and her own satisfied feeling. She had never felt more pleased with anything she had made. She knew she would end up going to the celebration in last year's gown, but it didn't matter. The creation would be this beautiful, blushing girl's wedding dress, and that was enough to make her feel happy about selling it.

"How much do you want for it?"

"Ah . . . oh . . . twenty-five dollars."

"Hardly," Michael said with a wry frown. She paused, unsure of his meaning. Did he think the gown was not worth it? "That dress is worth a hundred dollars if it's worth a dime," Michael continued. Now she knew he meant to overlook any extravagance.

"But if you had asked me for every dime I had on me, it would have been well worth it. A hundred it will be."

"If you want to come into the back room with me and try the dress on, I can adjust it. If it's not too complicated an alteration I can have it ready for you the day after tomorrow."

"You go ahead, Hannah, I have an errand to take care of. I'll meet you back here in . . . say, an hour?"

"An hour will be quite adequate," Alice said. She was aware of sudden tension in Hannah, and the look she gave Michael seemed as if she were suddenly afraid of something.

"It's all right, Hannah," Michael said softly. "It's just that. A short errand. No . . . no problems and I'll be back safe and sound in an hour. I promise."

Yes, the seamstress thought, there was something very mysterious going on here. She watched as Michael took Hannah's hand and drew her to him to kiss her lightly, and she watched Hannah's gaze worriedly follow him as he walked out.

"Miss . . . Miss?"

"What? Oh, I'm sorry, I was just . . . Let's try it on."

Hannah accompanied her to the back room where she stood before a full-length mirror in silence while Alice pinned the seams in carefully.

She knew Hannah was not seeing her own reflection in the mirror, but, from the haunted look in her eyes, something that was obviously wrestling this happy moment from her grasp.

"He is a very handsome man."

"Who? Oh, yes," Hannah smiled for the first time. "Yes, he is. Very handsome."

"I think you are a very luck lady."

"I think I am more stubborn than lucky," Hannah laughed softly.

The seamstress would have given anything to know all the juicy details of what was brewing here, but it soon became obvious that Hannah was not going to offer any more enlightenment on the subject.

When they left the back room and stepped into the shop, it was only minutes before Michael's arrival. The relief on Hannah's face when he came in only enhanced Alice's curiosity. But Michael was ready to leave.

"I hope the both of you have a lifetime of happiness."

"Thank you," Hannah said. "And I'm grateful for your sacrifice."

Alice watched Hannah and Michael leave and was confused. They loved each other, it was obvious. Yet there was an aura of sadness about them and a touch of mystery that stimulated her imagination.

Michael and Hannah returned to Patrick's house, walking slowly. Hannah sensed that Michael was very alert. He seemed to be concentrating on her, but she knew he missed nothing that was going on around them. If just this made her tense, she wondered how he had been able to bear similar strain for all these years.

She tucked her hand in his arm and pressed it close to him, and when he smiled down at her, she knew he understood exactly what she was feeling.

When they walked up the steps to Patrick's door, they could hear laughter from inside.

"Sounds like Mac and the boys are back," Michael chuckled as he reached to open the door. There was another burst of laughter as they entered Patrick's kitchen.

"Michael, Hannah, . . ." Patrick said. "It seems your 'resurrection' has caused quite a stir in town."

"Watching you two was kind of like watching a real circus," Joey laughed. "People were so downright shocked some of 'em just couldn't stop starin'. Old man Peterson fell off the sidewalk and Tom Pritcherd must have dug his spurs into his horse 'cause it took off with him."

"I wonder if he's still running," Mac joined in.

"I wouldn't doubt it for a minute," Jamie added.

"I've never seen such a thing in my life," Brad said. "This was worth the whole danged trip."

"I'm sure sorry I missed seeing it firsthand," Zeb said. "It sure must have been something."

"So, Michael?" Patrick questioned. "Did you two enjoy yourselves? And did you accomplish what you went after?"

"Yes to both quetsions."

"Then," Mac's eyes grew gentle as he looked at Hannah, "I guess we're going to have a wedding. When will it be."

"Day after tomorrow, if the dress is finished. I'd like to ride over and ask Rena to be my maid of honor," Hannah replied.

"And I guess after all he's done, if Quinn can get to his feet, he should be the best man," Michael said.

"Another good idea," Patrick said. "Maybe you and Hannah ought to take a ride out and see how those two are doing. I spoke to Rena's father yesterday and he won't even discuss the matter. He thinks Quinn is wrong for her, but she won't leave him. It's grown into a complicated affair."

"Is that why you want us to go there, Patrick," Michael asked. "Or are you just trying to keep us in a safe place?"

"A little of both, I'll admit. But what harm would it do if you remained out of circulation for a while?"

"None, I suppose. Besides, the day after tomorrow has suddenly become very special, and I think I'd like to be around to celebrate it." He turned to Hannah. "Shall we ride out and see them?"

"Yes."

Michael laughed softly in understanding, and there was no one in the room who did not understand Hannah's reasons . . . and her anxiety. She wanted Michael as far away from town as he could get, and she didn't really care what the reasons for it were.

"Then I guess we'd better go now," Michael said. Hannah smiled. He knew what she felt, and he was considering this, along with the fact that they might have very little time left together.

There was a heavy silence in the room when they left, each man wishing he could find a way out of this dilemma.

"So, Mac," Patrick said, "I have a feeling you have a little more to tell us."

"Yeah. Old Jonas sent a telegram. I don't know to whom for sure, but I'd guess the senator and be pretty close to right. Jonas is near . . . real near."

Again the same silence filled the room and each shared the same thoughts . . . the same fears.

When Michael and Hannah arrived at Quinn's house they were greeted warmly. Although they had not known how Quinn had lived before, they were now welcomed to a house that had suddenly become a home.

Quinn seemed to be getting around pretty well, and neither Michael nor Hannah had to ask any questions about their intentions. It was obvious Rena was there to stay, and just as obvious that Quinn worshipped the ground on which she stood.

It was Rena who opened the door when they knocked, and she wore a wide smile when she saw who her visitors were. Only Rena knew the depth of her gratitude to Hannah.

"Good heavens, Hannah! What happened?" Rena and Quinn were shocked at her battered face.

"Jonas Holt and friend," Michael said grimly.

There was no need to say more, and both knew Hannah didn't want to talk about it.

"Come in, please." Rena stepped aside, then closed the door behind them. Quinn rose from a seat at the table and walked to Michael, his hand extended.

"Michael, it's good to see you again. Rena, this is Michael Cord." Rena smiled and warmly told Michael he was welcome. "Hannah, you look as if you're happy about something," Quinn continued. "Should I guess?"

"I don't think it would take a genius to guess," Hannah laughed. "As a matter of fact, Michael and I have come to ask you a question. We're going to get married by Patrick the day after tomorrow. Will you be my maid of honor, Rena?"

"Oh, Hannah, I'd be delighted."

"And," Michael inserted, "Quinn, I need a best man and I can't think of anyone I'd rather have than you."

"I'd sure be proud to do it, Michael," Quinn said.

"Why don't you both stay and join us for supper," Rena asked the happy couple. "I think we all have a lot to talk about."

"Well, whatever's cooking smells good," Michael laughed. "And I'm as hungry as a bear."

"I have a feeling that's your perpetual state." Hannah's laughter joined his. "We'd love to stay." It fit her plans very well. This would be one evening she would not have to worry about Michael's safety.

A rapport blossomed between the four. Because of the fragility of their relationships and the present danger in all their lives, they seemed to have found two unique things: a strong, vital, and enduring love, and a bond of friendship that was forged of the steel of adversity and would be impossible to break.

The supper was eaten amid compliments to a pleased Rena and relaxed laughter. Hannah had never seen Michael so at ease. For the first time she caught a glimpse of the happy-go-lucky boy beneath the surface. It made her realize there were so many facets she still didn't know about him. The thought of new daily, discoveries excited her.

Rena and Quinn both protested when Michael said they had to leave.

"It's still early," Quinn said.

"I'm afraid it's Patrick we have to consider. Hannah and I have his buggy. He might need it at anytime. I hate to keep it tied up too long."

"I suppose you're right," Rena agreed reluctantly.

"So, you want us to be at the church day after tomorrow," Quinn said. "What time?"

Michael looked at Hannah thoughtfully. "Whatever time Hannah thinks. I'm not well versed on this kind of thing."

"What about three in the afternoon. That way Rena an help me get dressed. I know I'll be all thumbs."

"Three it is," Quinn stated. "We'll be there."

"Good night, you two," Hannah said, "and thank you so much."

"You don't need to thank us," Quinn laughed. "One day soon you might be asked to return the favor."

"*Might?*" Rena grinned as she looked up at Quinn. "Are you having second thoughts, Quinn Wayland?"

"Me? No! Good Lord, I was only considering the fact that you might."

"You'll have a long wait for that," Rena laughed.

"We sure are going to shake this town up," Quinn siad. "First, Michael Cord comes back from the dead, then Rena Brenden marries me. It may never be the same again."

"Seems like the town needed a few changes anyway. Might do them a world of good. So, good night, and we'll see you at the church." Michael shook quinn's hand again and kissed Rena's cheek. Then Rena and Quinn stood in the lighted doorway and watched until the buggy vanished in the night.

Quinn was quiet for several minutes after they closed the door. "What are you thinking, Quinn?"

"Oh, I guess about how my life has changed." He came to her and put his arms around her. "A few days ago I had nothing. Tonight, I think I have the whole world right here. For the first time in my life I've begun to think there's not only tomorrow, but it might be a better tomorrow than I've ever dreamed of."

Rena's eyes filled with tears even though she smiled. She meant to find a way to give Quinn all the tomorrows it would take to make up for the empty yesterdays. She drew his head down to hers for a deep heartfelt kiss.

Michael and Hannah rode along for some time in a contented silence.

"Michael?" Hannah finally spoke. "I think Rena and Quinn are going to see an end to their problems one day soon, and I think we're very fortunate to have two such wonderful friends."

"I agree. Not many men would do what Quinn has done."

"And not many women would have the courage to do what Rena is doing."

"You should understand that," Michael laughed. "If I ever met a woman with courage that matches yours, I sure don't remember her."

"I'm so lucky," Hannah murmured as she moved closer to Michael.

"Lucky?"

"Lucky," she repeated, "I wouldn't trade a minute with you, wherever we are and with whatever we had to face, for anything in the world."

Michael drew the horse to a halt and tied the reins carefully. Then he turned to Hannah. "If I've never told you how whole you make my life, let me tell you now. You're everything good I ever hope to have. I love you, Hannah Marshall. Never forget that no matter what else happens in our lives, remember I love you."

He kissed her then, a deep, bittersweet kiss, and Hannah clung to him, praying that this was truly their beginning.

* * *

Samuel Brenden locked the front door of the newspaper office and checked its security. Then he walked to the edge of the sidewalk and took a few minutes, as he almost always did, to look over the town he loved.

Although he felt he ran the best paper in town, he did not run the only one. Together with Jacob Marley, they had fought to make their town what it was. And both had gained a great deal of stature throughout the country by acquiring a chain of friends who owned papers across the country.

He was pleased with the bustle of early-evening activity. The town was growing by leaps and bounds, and he was proud not only to be a part of it, but a vibrant instrument in its growth.

He consulted his pocket watch, then turned and started slowly toward home. He'd always enjoyed his walk home before, but now his mind was tangled in thoughts of Rena.

Rena, the child he loved more than his own life. He knew it was obstinate pride that kept them separate. But he could not accept the fact that the lovely woman he had raised so carefully had given her heart and her life to a man to whom life meant so little.

Yet he longed to see her again, to hear her laughter fill his house. Her memory was a ghost that lingered in every corner of his home.

He paused for a minute, wanting to drop every other thought and get his wife and go to Quinn Wayland's . . . hovel and take his daughter by force if necessary. But he remembered the look in Rena's eyes and, knowing her as well as he did, he was sure that even if he could force her to come home, she would only fly to Quinn's arms again at the first opportunity. No, she had to learn a lesson he knew would be bitter and hard. But he would be there when Rena did find out what a cold and heartless no-good she was involved with. He would be there when she was repentant and needed to come home.

"Mr. Brenden!" Samuel continued to walk, deep in his thoughts. "Mr. Brenden!" The man called a second time, and only then did it register that he was being hailed. Samuel turned to see Tab Carter rushing toward him.

Tab had long ago become an excellent source of hometown news, and Samuel had depended on him quite often.

Now he paused at Samuel's side, gasping for breath, his face flushed with enthusiasm and his eyes dancing with excitement.

"I tried to get to the newspaper office before you left, Samuel, but I was jut a few minutes too late."

"What's got you in such a flurry, Tab?" Samuel chuckled. "Has the nation gone to war?"

"No, sir. But it sure is almost as exciting."

"What is?" Samuel questioned patiently.

"That business about Quinn Wayland."

"There is nothing Quinn Wayland could do that would be of any interest to me or my paper."

"I think you'd better reconsider that. The news has got the whole town buzzing and in a state of shock."

"Good Lord, man, the news is several days old already. Quinn Wayland killed two men. So why is the whole town buzzing?"

" 'Cause Michael Cord ain't dead," Tab said firmly, and watched disbelief and shock finally register on Samuel's face.

"Not dead? Have you been drinking?"

"Nope. Not a sip. It seems there's a long story to go with this, and only Reverend Carrigan and Sheriff Horton know the real goings-on. But Quinn didn't kill nobody. It seems it was all kind of set up."

"How do you know this is true?"

"Because Michael Cord and that young lady friend of his took a walk this afternoon right through town. I can say it caused quite a stir. A whole lot of folks is still sure they been seeing ghosts. Yes, sir, pretty as you please he just comes into town and goes shoppin', don't you know? Seems he and the young lady are going to get hitched right here in Reverend Carrigan's church."

Samuel's face had grown pale as he listened to Tab's chatter. When he could finally break away, he headed for the sheriff's office.

His heart felt like lead. He had to know if he'd just made a terrible mistake. A mistake that might have cost him his daughter.

Chapter Seventeen

Sheriff Bill Horton was just preparing to go home for the evening himself when the door burst open and a very upset Samuel Brenden came in.

He could tell with one look at Samuel's face that he was extremely upset about something.

"Samuel, something wrong?"

"I'd say there is, Bill," Samuel replied, half in anger and half in desperation. "What's going on here? I've heard a rather surprising piece of news. Now the whole town is buzzing with it."

"News, what news?"

"It seems the man you swore was dead is very much alive . . . " He paused, and when Bill didn't respond he knew what he had heard had been the truth. He sighed and sagged into a chair. "It's true then. Michael Cord was never killed here."

"No, Samuel, he wasn't. Maybe you better listen before you get any more upset. There was a real good reason for what we did."

"I'd like to hear it, because you have no idea what this little farce might have cost me."

"We did it to try and save a man's life, to give him back a life."

"I think you'd better explain more than that."

"All right, providing you keep quiet and listen until I'm finished. This story isn't like anything you've ever heard before. You see, Patrick thought . . ."

"Reverend Carrigan?"

"Yes, he . . ."

"This was his idea?"

"Every step of it."

The sheriff explained the entire plan from start to finish. Samuel sat in silence, realizing the horrible truth. He'd judged and condemned Quinn Wayland the same way everyone else in the town had done.

He regretted few things in his life, but this was an exception. The worst of it was that he didn't quite know how to rebuild the bridge he had burned.

When Bill finished the story, he began to wonder why Samuel was so shaken by an event that had no bearing on his life.

"What is it, Samuel? I don't understand why you're so upset about all this. None of it had anything to do with you."

"I'm afraid it had more to do with me than you know."

"I don't see how."

"This . . . this Wayland boy. I think maybe he's been misjudged by a lot of folks in this town."

"Like you?" Bill asked quietly.

"Yes, like me. Only I think I have a better reason than most. You see, Rena . . . my daughter, it seems she and Quinn had been seeing each other. She never believed in his guilt. I did. I'm afraid I said some things that I now regret."

As if he were dragging the words from the depths of him, Samuel tried to explain what had happened. Bill remained quiet the entire time. What Samuel was saying needed to be put into words if only to exorcise the guilt he felt.

"I guess it would be the best thing if I went to them and . . . and asked them both if they would come home."

"It might be a good start. Your Rena is a fine girl. I'd take it into consideration if she found something good in a man. It just might be there."

"I think I'll go out there."

"She's at Quinn's house?"

"Bad as it is, there's where she is."

"I take it she intended to stay."

"That's what she said . . . firmly."

For the first time Bill smiled. "Yes, sir, I'd say she's a real fine girl."

"Sheriff Horton," Samuel grinned, "I voted for you and supported your last election. I have a feeling I'll do the same for the next one." Samuel stood up and shook Bill's hand. "Thanks, Bill. I just wish I'd been told."

"It had to be a well-kept secret."

"Well, maybe I can repair the damage I've done. Good night."

" 'Night, Samuel . . . and good luck."

Samuel left the sheriff's office, unsure of himself and what he planned to do. He only knew he meant to have his daughter back no matter *what*. That, he was certain, would take unconditional acceptance of Quinn. And he intended to concentrate on that thought . . . all the way to Quinn's house.

After Michael and Hannah had gone, Rena and Quinn had little to do but talk. Neither of them was prepared to face people and they wanted to share their time together to get to know each other better. They had made love and shared a wild passion, but now it was as if each of them had to open the dam of emotions.

Quinn sat, relaxed in the one comfortable chair in the house with Rena nestled on his lap. They talked of an uncertain future and all the hopes they had for it. For Quinn it was still a dream, but Rena's enthusiasm was becoming contagious. For the first time in his life he was actively grasping for the brilliance of a future that he could only see through Rena's eyes.

They were so engrossed in each other that no sound from outside penetrated their world.

The knock on the door was repeated several times before it drew Quinn's attention. He frowned. No one he knew would be visiting him. Quinn was tense knowing that Rena was here and that trouble could be just outside the door.

He rose slowly, depositing Rena on her feet and pushing her behind him. He wasn't sure what lay ahead, but he meant to protect Rena.

"Who is it?" he called out.

"Rena! It's me." Samuel's voice echoed through them like an electrical shock.

"Father!" Rena gasped. She and Quinn exchanged a completely befuddled look. This certainly was the last thing either expected.

"He's probably come with the sheriff and a couple of deputies to drag you home."

"Don't open the door."

"Rena, you can't let your father stand out there begging. We'll just have to try and talk some sense into him."

"Quinn . . . don't let . . ."

"Rena . . . you're here to stay as long as there's a breath in my body. Let's answer the door and get this over with. We have to at least find out what made him change his mind and come back."

Quinn walked to the door and drew it open. For a second Samuel and Quinn stood looking at each other in silence. Then Rena walked to them and stood beside Quinn.

"Father, if you've come to take me home, you've wasted your time."

"No, Rena," Samuel said calmly. "I've come to talk to you . . . and to Quinn. May I come in, please?"

Quinn was sure it was just a ploy to get Rena's sympathy, but Rena wasn't so certain.

"To talk to us?"

"Yes. I . . . I think it's time we had a talk. I have a feeling we could work this out if we just talked reasonable."

It finally reached Quinn the Samuel's voice and attitude were much different.

"Come in," Quinn said, and stepped aside to let Samuel enter. When he closed the door, he turned to face Samuel. "Well, Mr. Brenden, just what is it you wanted to say."

"Well . . . to start, I'm sorry. Sorry I didn't listen to you both when you tried to talk to me before, and sorry both I and the entire town have misjudged you, labeled you, even persecuted you. I'm sorry I didn't know all the truth."

Rena caught her breath while he spoke and tears welled in her eyes. Even Quinn found it hard to speak.

The three stood in a paralyzing silence for several minutes. Then it was Rena who crossed the few feet between them and threw herself into Samuel's arms.

* * *

Patrick, Hannah, Michael, and their friends sat around Patrick's table and talked till late into the night. Even when the boys drifted off toward the hotel to get some sleep, Hannah and Michael were still too excited to sleep.

Patrick had to smother a yawn more than once before Michael laughed. "Patrick, go on up to bed and get some sleep."

"I'll take the couch in the front room. Each of you can have one of the rooms upstairs."

"You will not," Michael said firmly. "You sleep in your own bed. Hannah can have the other room. I'll be comfortable on the couch. I've slept on worse, believe me."

Patrick's eyes sparkled as he looked at the two people he'd grown to care so much for. " 'Course I wouldn't mind staying up to chat with you a little longer."

"Don't make any sacrifices to your comfort on my account," Michael said with wry amusement. "You can just trundle off to bed."

"Thanks. I think I'll do just that. Good night, both of you."

Hannah went to Patrick and kissed his cheek. "Good night, Patrick, sleep well. And thank you."

"Good night, Hannah. Bless you."

When Patrick was gone and his steps had faded into silence, Hannah moved across the room. Neither of them spoke. Michael simply held her close and savored the pleasure of peace and Hannah at the same time.

"Michael?"

"Um hum?"

"Are we going to stay here after we're married?"

"I thought we'd keep Patrick's cabin for a while . . . unless you have something else in mind?"

"No, not really."

"I think it's better if we stayed close to home for a while."

"We . . . we've never made any plans."

"I guess this is not the time to make plans, Hannah. We said one day at a time and that's how it's got to be. It's the only way we can make it . . . one day at a time."

"Oh, Michael," Hannah breathed softly, "I love you so much, it scares me."

"Why scared?"

"Because there isn't just you and me anymore. We're a part of each other. If something does go wrong, it's going to tear away a part of me. Michael . . ."

"Shh, Hannah, I know. But don't look ahead. Let's just grab all we can. Let's just hold today and see what happens." He kissed her gently, holding her against him and feeling the rapid beating of her heart.

But soon the kiss escaped his control and grew in intensity until both were drowning in the pure sensual sensations.

Reluctantly Michael broke the kiss, holding Hannah a little away from him.

"You'd better go on up to bed now. I don't think we can push Patrick's friendship too far."

"I suppose not," Hannah agreed. "I wish . . ."

"Wish what?"

"That this was our home. That we could lock that door and shut the world out and forget everything except each other."

"Sounds good to me. For a while we can make that little place Patrick loaned me into a sanctuary."

"How long . . ."

"Hard to tell. I'd say Jonas has gone for reinforcements and to find out what the senator has planned. Maybe . . . a couple of weeks . . . a month. It's impossible to say."

"Then we'll make it a lifetime."

"It's what I plan to do, love. It's what I plan to do." Michael replied softly as he bent to kiss her again. He realized that every moment Hannah was with him was going to make it that much harder for him to try to control the fierce need that was eating at him.

He took her shoulders and turned her around. "Go to bed, before this gets past my ability to handle. I'll see you in the morning."

She recognized the truth and no longer argued. She left Michael and walked up the stairs without looking back.

Michael eyed the couch, which was a good four inches shorter than he was. The bed and Hannah seemed more inviting than ever. It was going to prove to be a long, uncomfortable night.

By two o'clock in the morning Michael's supposition proved to be right. He and the couch had done battle for as long as he could stand it. He admitted defeat and retreated to spread his blanket on the floor where he could stretch out.

Memories of the prisoner-of-war camp in which he'd been incarcerated flooded back. Then, he would have been grateful for a blanket and a dry wood floor.

As close to comfortable as he was going to get, he finally drifted into a light sleep.

Never one to sleep deeply and each nerve trained to react to adverse situations, Michael heard the sound even though it was barely a whisper. He sat up abruptly, reaching for the gun that always lay close. He faced the doorway.

Moonlight touched the room with a misty-pale glow, just light enough so forms could be discerned. The one that stood in the doorway was one that had been engraved in his mind long ago.

"Hannah . . ." He whispered her name as if unsure she wasn't just a figment of a dream he was having.

But she didn't speak. Instead, she loosened the ties at the throat and waist of the nightgown whe wore and shrugged it from her body. It slid silently to the floor.

Michael laid the gun aside automatically. He found it difficult to draw in a deep breath and felt his pulse begin to pick up a ragged, throbbing beat. Hannah walked across the floor and dropped silently down on the blanket beside him. Still neither spoke. There were no words either could utter that would give a voice to the emotions that filled the air around them.

Then she was in his arms, her warm mouth seeking his and her soft body nestling against him, and words were no longer important. Nothing in his world seemed as important as holding her warm, curved body close and immersing himself in the joy of loving her.

When Michael awoke to the bright rays of the early-morning sun, Hannah was gone and he wasn't too sure he hadn't dreamed the whole thing, conjured it up from his own need.

He rose from his makeshift bed and put his pants on. It was just after dawn and he was pretty certain no one else was up. He walked to the kitchen doorway, lured by the sudden and pleasing scent of coffee. Obviously someone was awake. When he came to the doorway, Hannah was at the table.

"Good morning," she smiled at him across the brim of her coffee cup.

"Morning," he grinned as he leaned one shoulder against the doorframe. "You're not given to walking in your sleep, are you?"

"Me?" she questioned innocently. "Not that I know of."

"I had a very strange . . . but very welcome dream last night."

"Oh?"

"I think I had a ghost in my bed."

"Maybe it *was* a dream."

"She was a remarkably lovely ghost."

Hannah rose and came to him to slip her arms about his waist. She stood on tiptoe and kissed his cheek.

"You're as bristly as an old bear. You need a shave. Come on and have some coffee." She tried to move away but Michael held her.

"So, you don't walk in your sleep? My nocturnal visitor must have been someone else."

Hannah laughed softly and gave him a look that was such a combination of wickdness and seductiveness that Michael had to laugh, too.

"Michael Cord, pity you if I ever find another woman in your bed. If she's not a ghost, then she might find herself becoming one very quickly. You, my tall, handsome friend, are all mine and don't you forget it."

"Hannah, if I ever had doubts baefore, they were sure wiped away last night. Tomorrow will be the answer to my dreams. There will be no more ghosts. I want you where I can reach out and touch you."

"Tomorrow. It seems the hours are so long."

"Well, let's do something with today to help them pass a little faster."

"What do you have in mind?"

I owe a lot of people a personal thank-you for their part in trying to help me. Doc Simpson, the undertaker, and Sheriff

Horton, to name a few. Let's go into town and see them. Then we could take a ride out and look over what will be our temporary home. It needs a lot of work."

Hannah agreed enthusiastically.

"I'll go get cleaned up and maybe we can have a little breakfast, then let Patrick know where we're going."

"I'll start breakfast. I have a feeling Patrick's not a man who sleeps away half the day."

As if in answer, they heard footsteps on the stairs and in a few moments Patrick appeared.

"Good morning." He smiled warmly at them both. "Did you both sleep well?"

"Yes, fine." Hannah cast Michael a quick, threatening look when she saw the devilment dance in his eyes.

"This house is really an old one, isn't it, Patrick?"

"Yes. It was here years before I was. Why?"

"You know how old houses are. I could have sworn there were ghosts flitting about. Contented ghosts, it seems . . . benevolent."

Patrick saw Hannah's flushed cheeks and he knew there was more meaning for her in Michael's words than for him. But the warmth of the teasing was not lost on him. For these few minutes they were happy, and that alone made the day brighter for Patrick.

Hannah explained what their plans were for the day.

"Good. Tell Sheriff Horton I'll see him later."

"We will. Is there anything you need? Michael and I could stop at the mercantile if you like."

"No . . . nothing." Patrick was looking at Michael as he answered.

Michael smiled.

"Strange how good just the ordinary everyday things sound. Going to town, visiting friends. It's almost as if . . ."

"Michael . . ." Hannah said softly. "Don't."

"You're right . . . today it is," Michael nodded. "I'm going to get cleaned up. I'll be back as quick as I can. If I'm going to town, I need breakfast first. If Hannah's anything like my sister Allison, town could be an all-day excursion."

They ate a hearty breakfast, and Patrick insisted Hannah and Michael go on, that he was quite used to cleaning up after himself.

Michael hitched the horse to Patrick's buggy. If they meant to carry anything home, it would be hard riding separately.

It was a very nice, sunlit, and warm day, so Michael drove slowly. He was caught up in the pleasure of "ordinary" things—Hannah beside him and the ability to move on the street with no man facing him at the other end with a gun in his hand.

For the first time in a long time he relaxed his guard. He allowed his usual alertness to waver and gave this total concentration to Hannah.

They moved slowly down Crawford Street, then crossed to Brown. The Grand Hotel intruded onto the street so that the street itself had a sharp corner to it.

The Grand was the best hotel in town and, as far as its owners were concerned, one of the best in the state. It stood three stories high and had a wide front porch that ran the entire length of the structure on which guests could spend a sunny afternoon seated in one of the many cushioned wicker chairs that were scattered along it.

"It's a lovely building, isn't it?" Hannah said. "It reminds me of the old hotel in Denver."

"Yes, it's . . ." He pulled the horse to a halt so abruptly that she had to grasp his arm to escape tumbling forward.

"Michael! What's wrong?" She saw his shocked expression first, but then his face grew pale and his features froze in a look she could not understand. It looked as if he were seeing some terrible apparition.

"Michael?" She spoke his name a second time in question. She'd never seen him this way. "What is it? What's wrong?"

Michael had glanced toward the hotel when Hannah voiced her admiration of it, and as he did, a man stepped out onto the porch, a man he would recognize no matter where he was. Senator Thomas Merrell had come to Virginia City, and Michael knew his temporary reprieve was over.

"Michael, please." Hannah didn't like the way he was staring at the man who stood on the porch. "Is he someone you know? Talk to me, please."

"Yes, I know him."

"He's not . . ."

"Oh, yes, he's here to see me."

"But he doesn't look like . . . like a man who could wield a gun."

"He doesn't have to. Oh, no, he's a gentleman. He doesn't kill. He just hires the scum of the earth to do the dirty work for him."

"That's the senator?" Hannah breathed the words as fear caught her heart in a vice.

"That's the senator. I'm surprised. Some of his plans must have gone wrong to bring him here or . . . he wants to be in on the kill."

"Why now! Why now!" Her anguish tore at him.

"It was bound to happen one day, Hannah. We both knew that. Jonas . . . and God knows how many more, have to be coming around soon."

Michael slapped the reins, urging the horse back into motion again. It would not have been possible for the senator to recognize them in the buggy. But Michael had no doubts that the senator would have all the information he would need about him, where he was and what he was doing. He was pretty certain the senator had just recently arrived, or Mac and the boys would most likely have heard about him or seen signs of a gathering of sorts.

They still had some time, he and Hannah, and he meant to make the best use of it. It was not going to end here before he made sure Hannah's future was secure.

He was so caught in his thoughts that he did not realize Hannah had become very still. He might have been quite shaken to know where her thoughts were and the intentions that were solidifying into a plan.

"Don't worry about him, Hannah. He's not the kind to step out and do anything himself. I can handle whatever he has in mind."

"Michael, why don't we just go and talk to him? Try to reason with him."

"I tried that once, a long time ago. He's not a man who listens. He doesn't reason . . . and he can't handle a blow of any kind without some form of retaliation. Don't even think that way. It's useless."

"I suppose," she said softly. She clutched her hands in her lap, and did her best to control the way they were shaking. Her whole world was slipping from her grasp.

She knew Michael would be very angry should she voice her plans, so she kept them to herself. She knew she could not let her world be shattered without at least attempting to do something about it.

They arrived at the sheriff's office, and Michael helped her down from the buggy.

Bill met them with a smile. "Michael, good to see you. And you must be Hannah." He took her outstretched hand in his. "I'm pleased to meet you, and real sorry for all the grief this must have cost you. I hope you understand that what we did, we did for Michael's good. It didn't work, and I regret that, too."

"You did what was best at the time. I'm grateful that you wanted to help Michael. We've come to thank you . . . and to invite you to our wedding."

"Wedding." He was nonplussed, and cast a quick, surprised look at Michael who smiled.

"Patrick is marrying Hannah and me tomorrow at three. Bill, we'd really like you to be there," Michael said.

"I'd be honored," he replied. "I'd like to be one of the first to wish you both all the happiness in the world. I can't think of two people who deserve it more. I'll sure be there."

When they left, Bill's smile faded. He wondered at the courage of the two who fought such a battle. He really did hope it all worked out, but he knew as well as Michael that Jonas was still around and was reasonably certain Michael would, one day, have to face him.

Hannah and Michael went on to the undertaker's to thank him for his help and invite him to their wedding. Then they spent the balance of the morning purchasing the items Hannah wanted.

Michael seemed to have pushed all the problems away and he teased her into smiles as they did the shopping. His control was not fooling Hannah, who was doing the very same thing. She smiled at his teasing while her heart felt like a lead weight.

When they returned with their bundles, Patrick had already begun setting out some preparations for a light lunch for him and Zeb, tired from a full morning's work.

They made sandwiches and had just sat down when the door opened and Mac and Brad came in.

Both men were grim-faced, and Hannah and Michael had a reasonably good idea what news they brought.

"Sit down, Mac, Brad. Have a bite to eat."

"No, thanks, Patrick. We just ate over at the hotel. I . . . ah . . . I'd like to talk to you for a minute, Michael."

"Sure. What's on your mind, Mac?"

"Ift might be better if we stepped out on the porch a minute. It's . . ."

"It's about Senator Merrell being in town," Hannah said. "Youn might as well sit down, Mac. There's nothing you can tell Michael that I don't already know." She smiled. "But thanks for trying to protect me. I do appreciate it."

"Woman, you sure do beat all," Mac said. He and Brad sat down at the table. "How did you know? I just found out, and from what I can dig up, he only pulled in last night."

"Michael and I went to town today. We saw him on the front porch of the Grand. I suppose he's staying there."

"Yes," Mac nodded. "Jamie and Joey are keeping an eye on the place. Just to see if Jonas pokes his nose around anytime. So far, they haven't made contact."

"Don't worry," Michael said. "They will soon."

"At least we can keep a watch. You won't be in for any surprises. They won't do much until they meet and talk over their plans."

"I'm not going to think about them. Tomorrow's a big day and I'm not going to let them ruin it." Michael's words were firm.

"Good idea," Patrick said. "We can't let things get out of control just because this man came to town."

"No," Hannah agreed. "As Michael said, we're going to take one day at a time from now on. We can handle everything together."

"Well, we're going to get on back and at least let Jamie and Joey know that you're aware of everything. Rest assured, if Jonas comes around you'll know it."

"Thanks, Mac." Michael stood to walk to the door with him. But, when they got there and Mac stepped outside, Michael followed and pulled the door closed behind him. "Mac?"

"Yeah?"

"If Jonas does come around, I'd appreciate it if you could get word to me without Hannah hearing about it."

"Sure. I'm sorry about just now, but she kind of surprised me."

"She has a way of doing that," Michael chuckled. "But I don't want her scared any more than she is already."

"I'll be careful."

"Thanks . . . Oh, by the way, you'll have to let the watch slide tomorrow. I wouldn't want this wedding to go on without you four being there."

"We wouldn't miss it. By rights, we ought to have some kind of celebration party. It ain't right that a lady like Hannah gets married and no one's around to drink a toast or two. Maybe we'll just have to work something out."

"Don't make too many elaborate plans. We don't want to be caught off guard."

"Okay. See you later."

"Thanks." Michael watched them mount and ride away, then returned inside.

Hannah insisted on cleaning up the kitchen and urged them to find something to occupy themselves.

"I'll be fine right here and I can't clean up with men underfoot. Why don't you and Patrick ride out to our 'home' and see what we might need. After all," she smiled seductively at him, "we intend to spend our honeymoon there. I'd like it in livable condition."

"Well, I'll be heading back to the church. I still have lots of work to get done." Zeb turned to go, a bit red in the face after listening to Hannah.

"Yeah, see ya, Zeb." Michael said, then looked over at Hannah. "I hate to leave you alone. Remember what happened last time?"

"This time the door will be locked and I'll be careful to see who it is before I open it. Take the things I bought out to the house and I'll finish up here. You'll be back before dark."

Although both men were reluctant to leave her alone, neither was aware she was desperately manipulating them for a purpose, a purpose that would have set them both off if she'd put it into words.

"All right," Michael agreed. "But I want to hear that door lock click and I want you to promise me you won't open it for anyone."

"I promise. I won't let a soul in this house until you come back." She had not lied, she simply had not stated the fact that she did not promise not to leave the house, only that she would not let anyone in.

Michael had an uncomfortable feeling, but finally Hannah convinced him she really wanted her belongings to be at their temporary home when they got there.

She finally helped load the bundles they had purchased back into the buggy.

Michael kissed her and looked into her eyes, wondering what it was he was so unsure of.

Hannah watched the buggy until she was certain they had not had a sudden change of mind.

Then she went to the door. From a hook beside it she took her shawl and put it around her shoulders. Then she left the house and started down the street with a brisk, determined step.

When she finally reached the Grand Hotel, she paused and looked at it. Yes, she thought, it was time she and the illustrious, and very notorious, Senator Merrell had a long, long talk.

Chapter Eighteen

Michael and Patrick rode along in silence. Patrick glanced at Michael's face occasionally and saw his thoughtful frown.

"What is wrong, Michael?"

"I don't know. I just have this feeling that I've blundered somehow."

"How? It's not possible to blunder when no adverse situation has come up."

"I know. I just feel uncomfortable." He slapped the reins and urged the horse from a walk to a trot.

When they arrived at the cabin, it didn't take too long to unload Hannah's possessions and what few he had, along with the purchases they'd made the day before.

Michael moved automatically, without thought, his mind still tangled in the idea that there was something he'd overlooked, something that was drastically wrong.

They stood on the porch of the little cabin and viewed the area around them. It was obvious no one had been here since their stay, so it was not this that worried him. No, it was a sixth sense that stretched his nerves and sent that expectant feeling whispering through him.

"This is not much of a place to offer Hannah as a wedding present."

"I don't think the place matters to her all that much," Patrick smiled. "The most important thing to her is being where you are."

"She's a remarkable woman, Patrick."

"I can see that."

"She gave up a lot to come here."

"She felt she gained a lot," Patrick countered. "Quit questioning good fortune, Michael. Not many people have the kind of love you and Hannah do."

"I'm not questioning good fortune, it's just that I'm not used to it. Every once in a while I have to check and see if I'm dreaming all this."

"Enjoy the dream."

"It wouldn't be hard to do if I hadn't spotted our illustrious visitor. Hannah and I . . ." Michael paused in midsentence as the answer to his own tension came as clear as spoken words. "Good God! I should have suspected . . ."

"What? What should you have suspected?"

"Hannah. Sometimes that woman is too clever for her own good."

"I don't understand."

"We have to get back to your place right away, and hope to God I'm wrong."

"Wrong about what?"

"Don't you see? Knowing Hannah as well as you do now, can't you see why she was so insistent on you and I coming out here?"

Patrick stood for a minute with a puzzled frown, then a look of shock suddenly filled his eyes.

"She . . . she wouldn't . . ."

"She would," Michael said firmly. "She's *that* angry and *that* determined. Come on, let's get going."

"It's been almost three hours. If she has done what we think, it's too late to try and stop her."

"I just have to make sure she's safe. You don't really know this kind of man. He doesn't have patience or mercy in his makeup."

"Michael, he's a person, despite all else. He can be defeated."

"If he can, I've never found a way."

"Maybe you were running away from your ghosts so long and so hard that you forgot to stop and fight."

"Stop and fight! Every time I tried to stop I had to fight someone . . . I had to kill someone."

"You fought his hired men. Maybe it's time we tried to find a way to stop him."

"There *is* no way."

"You sound more defeated than Hannah ever did."

"Not defeated, just realistic." He turned to look at Patrick. "Neither you nor Hannah have ever looked down a gun barrel pointed at a man who is determined to kill you. Neither one of you ever watched a man die in front of you, knowing it was you that put a stop to his life. Neither of you has had to live with the guilt and the nightmares."

"I'm sorry, Michael. I didn't mean it like that. I know we can only guess what you've been through. We can't change the past, but we want to help with the future."

"I know, I'm sorry, too. I didn't mean to take my fear out on the only people who have helped me. I'm . . . I'm scared, I guess. If anything or anybody took Hannah out of my life . . . I don't know how I could go on."

"Then let's *go* back. Maybe you've made the wrong supposition."

"Yeah, let's go." Michael wanted to agree with Patrick, and say he'd made the wrong guess. But deep in his mind, he knew he hadn't. He knew how far Hannah would go, what she would sacrifice for those she loved. For the first time in a long time he tasted the fear of losing something he knew he could never replace.

Hannah walked directly to the front desk of the Grand Hotel. Her smile was the most devastating she could manage and she held the clerk's eyes with hers.

"May I help you, ma'am?"

"Yes, please. I have a meeting with Senator Merrell, and silly me, I've quite forgotten his room number."

The "loss of memory" seemed to extend itself suddenly to the clerk, who was mesmerized by this lovely creature.

"Ah . . . yes, ma'am. The senator's in suite twenty-seven." He blushed at the warmth of her smile and felt other stirrings that shocked him into silence.

"You are so kind. I'm terribly late, so I'll just dash up and see him. There's no need to send word up. Thank you again." Hannah bathed him in another smile and brushed his hand with hers. Wide-eyed, he watched her walk to the steps with no idea of trying to stop her.

She moved quickly, before the clerk came back to rational thought. She had to laugh, but sobered quickly when she thought of what Michael would have to say about her latest performance.

"Oh, well," she said, half aloud, "he's going to kill me anyhow, so I have nothing to lose!"

She stopped before the white door with the gold 27 on it. She paused to gather both her breath and her courage. Then she raised her hand and knocked.

The auro of power that emanated from the senator struck Hannah full force when he opened the door.

His oratory could sway bodies of powerful men. He had been molded from wealth and power, and well used to using these tools to further an insatiable ambition.

At first Hannah felt a trembling fear shiver through her. But she had only to think of what this man had done to destroy not only Michael's life, but the lives of those men he'd sent to do his dirty work. This man had touched her life with the ugliness of hatred and despair, and all of this soon pushed the fear aside and replaced it with a cold, yet wary determination.

"Yes, young lady," he smiled his warmest chameleon smile. "May I be of service to you?"

"Senator Merrell? May I come in for a moment? You and I have something very important that we have to discuss."

"I'm delighted to invite you in, but since I have not the faintest idea who you are, and I've had no business in this town, it's unclear to me what business we have to discuss."

"May I come in?" Hannah repeated softly.

"Of course." He stood aside and motioned her in with a chivalric half bow.

Hannah stood in the middle of the room with her back to him. She felt like Daniel must have felt when he walked into a den of lions, she thought.

"May I get you something?" He smiled again when he walked across the room to join her.

"No, Senator, this is definitely not a social visit. My name . . . is Hannah Marshall, and I've come to talk to you about Michael Cord?"

She watched his smile freeze into a grimace and his eyes grow cold with a hatred so real it was almost a tangible force. It filled the room, and swirled around them with a malignant blackness that actually made her feel ill.

"So, our brave Mr. Cord has lost his courage and sent his woman to beg for him?"

"Michael needs no one to beg for him, and he would never have me come here. He doesn't even know I am here."

"Your visit will be a useless one. He should have told you I don't give up easily."

"He's told me a great deal about you and your methods. How many men must die before you call an end to this vendetta?"

"Only one. Michael Cord. Until he is as dead as my son, there will be no end to it."

"That won't bring your son back. What will it change if Michael is dead? Why don't you listen to *all* of the truth . . . *all* of the reasons of how and why it happened?"

"Listen to Cord's reasons? I don't need to listen to any reasons. I buried all the truth I need to know and now . . . now I intend to bury Michael Cord. Only this time the grave will be a real one."

"The killing will go on and on, and you don't care."

"This killing will end here. One way or the other, it will end here. I'll see to it."

"It serves no purpose!" Hannah cried. "More than one man will die. You'll destroy so many lives!"

"Let me tell you something, Miss Marshall," Thomas Merrell said. His voice dripped bitterness. "Some years ago I had a life any man would envy. I had a wife, and a son, and a high position. With one bullet Michael Cord took my son from me. My wife grieved herself to death. Now, I have only my power left to fill my life, and with that power I'll see to it that Cord pays dearly."

"How can I reason with you?"

"Don't waste your time."

"Why don't you face Michael yourself?"

"I don't need to talk when I want something done."

"And if Michael kills these . . . men you've hired?"

"I have patience. Cord can sweat, because there is an endless supply of men to do as I wish. His luck can't go on. One day soon, I'll find the right man, one who's a little bit faster. Then, when I stand over Michael Cord's grave . . . then it will all be complete."

"And after that?" Hannah said. "What will you do with all the rest of your years? Your empty, lonely years? What will you say to all the ghosts that wander the halls of your memory? How will you answer for the dark, ugly things you've done and the men who have died because of your dark soul?"

"It's an eye for an eye, and a tooth for a tooth. Consult your Bible, Miss Marshall."

"Is that all there is?" Hannah asked. "The Bible mentions a few other things, like compassion and mercy."

"That is consolation for the weak."

"There has to be a way to stop you," she said grimly.

"Don't consider it," Thomas said calmly. "You are a lovely lady and I wouldn't want to see anything happen to you. Don't get in my way, is the best advice I can give you."

"Michael has more friends than you know."

"Oh, I know that. But you see," his smile was malevolent, "none of his friends will be able to raise a hand to stop him. You see, I've taken the time to study this man well. When it comes down to it, when he's challenged, he won't even consider letting a friend stand in his place. The man is blessed . . . or cursed with a sense of honor and a stiff pride that will never allow it. I know that as well as you do. In fact, I count on it."

He saw the truth of his words reflected in her eyes and his smile was one of satisfaction.

"You know I'm right, don't you? How many times have you said these same words to Michael? And how many times have you seen the stubborn pride that forces him to walk this road?" His voice deepened. "No, my dear . . . one day soon . . . I don't know what the day will be, but the suspense will make the waiting more savory. One day . . . I will see Michael Cord dead."

Hannah could feel the tears sting her eyes. No matter how she wanted to do battle, she knew it was true. He wagered on the one quality of Michael's that she loved, but that would be the weakest, most vulnerable, part of him. And the one thing she could not prevent. Something within her grew as frigid as cold iron. She looked at him with fury that, for a moment, stilled whatever else he meant to say.

"You only understand one thing. Well then, understand this: My revenge will be as brutal as yours. If this goes on . . . if Michael does face one of your men and loses, I'll find a way to see you dead if I have to spend every dime and every moment of my life to do it. If you can hate, so can I. If you can hire men to kill, so can I. Think about it, because I swear . . . I'll find a way."

His smile wavered for the first time. But Hannah had already turned her back and walked to the door.

When she closed the door behind her, she was trembling so, she had to stop and lean against the wall. She could hardly believe what she had said, but she meant every word. She knew *he* had meant every word as well. It was hard to fight the tears of despair. She faced the truth for the first time. Michael meant to stand his ground . . . and eventually it was going to cost his life.

She felt desperation tearing at her.

"The sheriff," she muttered to herself. "He has to be able to do something. He *has* to."

She moved swiftly across the hall and down the stairs. She crossed the lobby without seeing anyone.

Once outside, she raced down the street and burst into Sheriff Horton's office. He was, to say the least, startled. But he was quick to guess her reason for being there.

"Sit down, Miss Marshall. You seem a little upset."

"Upset. That is hardly the word!"

"Is there some way I can help you?"

"Yes . . ." She went on to explain the senator's words and the threat that was hanging over Michael's head. "You've got to put a stop to this!"

"There isn't anything I can do. Patrick had a good idea, it just didn't work. This is a land where the law of the gun still is recognized. If Michael faces a man in a fair fight, much as I'd like to, I can't do anything about it. As far as the senator is concerned," he sighed deeply, "he's a law-abiding citizen with a lot of power. I have no reason to say a word to him unless he breaks a law. And I can't see him doing that. I can't do a thing. My hands are tied."

"This is unbelievable! This man is here to make sure another man dies! Doesn't that mean anything?"

"You have to understand. Coming here is breaking no law. Unless he does, I can't do a thing about it."

Frustration made Hannah too impatient to say any more. As she walked to the door, the sheriff watched her with a hint of pity in his eyes, wishing he could end the ugly situation.

Hannah stood on the boardwalk, trying to gather her thoughts. The sharp sound of an incoming train drew her attention and she watched it chug to a steam-exuding halt.

How she wished she and Michael could just board a train and go away together to someplace where no one could ever find them. She watched the few passengers disembark. Suddenly her attention was caught. Had she seen a familiar face . . . a beloved, dear face? Her eyes lighted with pleasure. Her brother, Terrance, was among a group of other familiar faces that stood on the train platform.

She crossed the street as rapidly as she could, and as she approached the platform, she called out his name.

He spun around in surprise at hearing his name called out in a strange town, then a wide smile lit his face.

"Hannah!" He reached for her and she threw herself into his arms. He hugged her tight, grateful that she seemed well.

When he held her away from him he was so choked with relief that he didn't know whether to express the fear and frustrated anger he had felt or the joy that seeing her now gave him.

For a moment the combination of fear and anger won out. He held her shoulders and gave her a shake. "What the hell did you think you were doing? Do you have even the remotest idea how Ma and Pa are feeling!" He dropped his hands and paced a few steps away from her only to return to scowl down at her. "We've been worried half sick."

"When Emily gets hold of you," Buck added, "I have a feeling your goose is cooked. She's been making a lot of very serious promises about what's going to happen when she gets her hands on you."

"Not to mention the fact that Pa is threatening murder and mayhem. As for me, I don't know what I want to do most, kiss you or strangle you."

"Give me a kiss, dear brother, and both of you can quit growling like bears. I know you as well as you know me, and either of you would have done the same if you'd been in my place,'' Hannah said calmly before her brother's storming face.

Trace chuckled softly as he read the mixed emotions in Terrance's eyes. Hannah know how to handle her brother. In fact, Trace was pretty sure Hannah could handle just about anything.

He watched Terrace's face go from worry and anger to resignation. He'd never been able to understand Hannah and he was pretty sure few people ever lived who would.

Slowly Hannah smiled, and Terrance's lips quirked in return. He didn't want to smile, but the anger was slipping out of his grasp like grains of sand. Hannah laughed softly, then Terrance did, too. Finally he grasped her in a fierce hug.

"You do look fine. God, I'm glad to see you!"

"Terrance, it's wonderful to see you, but what are you doing here? And Trace . . . all of you I . . ."

"Max sent for me. Hannah . . ." Trace said urgently. "Michael, is he here? Is he all right? Are Mac and the others . . ."

"Michael is all right . . . for now."

"What does that mean?"

"I have so much to explain to you all. But the middle of the street is no place to do it. Come on, let's go to Patrick's house where we can talk without interruption."

"Patrick?" Trace questioned.

"Come on, I'll explain." Besides, she thought, Trace might just be able to take Michael's mind off any questions about where she had been if he and Patrick got back before she did.

At the same moment Hannah was greeting her brother, Michael was walking up the steps to Patrick's back door, with Patrick right behind him. When he opened the door, he knew he'd been right. After a quick search, he knew the house was empty.

"You can't be sure she isn't just . . . out!"

Michael gave Patrick a disbelieving look. "Come on, Patrick."

"He can't do her any harm."

"He's like a poison, and Hannah has never faced anyone like him before. She'll be hurt all right, in a way she never expected."

"Be patient for a while. She might be right back."

"You believe that?"

"We have to give it a try, give her the benefit of the doubt."

"All right . . . fifteen minutes."

"Michael . . ."

"Fifteen minutes," Michael repeated firmly.

There was a heavy silence while the clock ticked away the time.

"You're going after her?"

"You bet your life I am." Michael turned toward the door, but before he could open it again, it was opened from outside and Hannah came in. Michael wanted to hug her, kiss her, and strangle her in the same instant.

He was defeated by the spark of love in her eyes and her warm smile. "Oh, Michael, I wanted to get home before you."

"I wouldn't doubt that," Michael said with a dark scowl. "We don't have to ask you where you've been. Patrick and I have a pretty good idea. Hannah, for God's sake, why did you do something so dangerous?"

"There was no danger for me, except to be exposed to the senator's vile character. After all, he couldn't do me harm when there were so many people around. Besides, it gave me the opportunity to bring you home a wonderful gift."

Hannah was suddenly aware that it was Michael's masculine pride that chafed at the idea that she had gone to face his adversary to protect him. She was also aware that his emotions had taken a beating in the past few years. Her love for him was all-encompassing and she intended to overlook what he might say.

"A gift? What kind of a gift?" He was a bit suspicious. Knowing Hannah as he did, the gift could be anything.

Hannah smiled, reached behind her to grasp the door handle, then she stepped aside, drawing the door open. The brothers came face-to-face.

For the first few moments Michael was so surprised he just blinked and stood immobile.

It was Trace who crossed the threshold and grasped his brother in a rough bear hug. In a moment they were laughing and fiercely embracing, pounding each other's backs. After Michael had introduced Patrick, and they had shaken hands with Terrance and Buck, he glanced at Hannah.

"What are you boys doing here anyway?"

"Don't look at me like that, Michael," she laughed. "This time I'm not responsible."

"No," Trace agreed. "Max sent us a message and we came as quick as we could."

"Where is the old bear anyway?" Michael asked. "Didn't he come with you? I can't imagine Max not being in the middle of things."

"I'm not sure. He seemed to have come up with a last-minute plan. One he didn't tell any of us about. He took off with Lee Chu. Said he'd be along soon."

"Trace, how's Allison? I'll bet she's spitting nails because you wouldn't let her come," Michael chuckled.

"Allison is Allison," Trace replied. "You might be surprised about one thing."

"Oh?"

"Our little Allison is engaged to be married."

"Allison? Married?" Michael laughed. "Who's the brave man?"

"Reid Anderson."

Hannah looked at Michael in complete shock. "Michael! How can you say such a thing about your sister? Reid Anderson is a very lucky man."

"That's debatable," he chuckled. "And when *you* get to know Allison like we do, you'll change your tune. You have to have grown up with her to have acquired some defenses . . . although I don't think Trace and I have yet. Yeah," he laughed. "It's *poor* Reid."

"Michael and I are going to have to tell you a few choice stories about innocent little Allison," Trace agreed.

"The way I remember Reid, he was kind of a quiet one, but getting married to Allison is sure going to make for a few changes."

"He had a hard time when he came back from the war. But he's done well with Fallen Oaks. Actually, he's done wonders with it," Trace said.

"And fell into Allison's gentle care when he did. I wonder if he knows yet what he's gotten himself into." Michael smiled, and as Trace went on to praise what Reid had done with Fallen Oaks, Hannah could see the faraway look in Michael's eyes and she could feel his longing for home and family. It made her even more angry at Senator Merrell.

"I have some more good news for you," Trace was telling Michael.

"I can handle all the *good* news you can deal out."

"I think you and I are going to have to find a way to settle this matter and get you home. You have a few obligations that will be calling for your attention one day soon."

"I do?"

"If you're going to be a proper uncle, I think it's time you started practicing. Besides, you need to be a godfather, too."

Patrick was overjoyed. This might be the kind of thing to change Michael's attitude.

Michael's eyes lit with pleasure. "An uncle! You and Jenny . . . God, Trace, that's wonderful! Congratulations."

Hannah had moved close to Michael, and he had put his arm about her, drawing her even closer. This did not escape Trace's notice. It did not escape anyone else's, either.

"I think there are other congratulations to be handed out," Buck said, his eyes sparkling.

"I couldn't agree more," Terrance added, catching Buck's quick glance at Hannah before he spoke.

"At least I hope you've got matrimony in mind, Hannah. When you go after a man, least you could do is make an honest one out of him," Buck grinned. "You're not the kiss-and-run type, are you?"

"Tell me it ain't so, Hannah?" Terrance pretended to be suddenly worried. "You'd plain destroy my faith in human nature. Now consider poor old Michael here . . ."

"Yeah. You wouldn't lead this poor boy astray?"

"Oh, the shame of it," Terrance groaned. "How will we face our parents again if you don't bring home a husband?"

"Terrance Marshall," Hannah laughed. "You two can just stop that right now."

"Besides," Michael chuckled, "you keep on tormenting her and Hannah won't invite you to Patrick's church tomorrow . . . when she and I are getting married."

This did exactly what Michael had planned. It took their attention from her. In fact, it looked as if it totally stunned Terrance to the point that Hannah had to join their laughter. The tables had been neatly turned.

"Married?" Terrance repeated.

"Married," Michael confirmed. "As you so aptly put it, I think it's time for Hannah to make an honest man out of me."

Hannah, who was standing within Michael's embrace, leaned close and whispered softly, "Shall we tell them you agreed to be, Mr. Hannah Marshall?" she said innocently.

She heard his soft chuckle just before his arm tightened about her hard enough to make her gasp. "I have ways to get even, Hannah," he whispered. "Don't push your luck."

After the initial shock, both Terrance and Buck became excited. Trace could only reach for Michael's hand. He'd never felt happier about anything in his entire life. It seemed as if, in a strange kind of way, there was a force being formed, and he was glad for that. Michael had walked alone much too long.

Trace knew there had to be a moment when he could talk to his brother in privacy. There had to be something this newly formed united front could do.

Michael and Hannah were going to get married. The bittersweet courage of this touched Trace. They were casting their lives in the face of fortune.

When Trace glanced at Patrick, he could see the same thoughts reflected in his eyes. Patrick smiled. Then he stepped toward the group.

"I think it's time we invited these weary travelers to sit down and at least offer some food and drink."

"I *am* hungry at that," Trace said.

"I could eat one of my horses," Buck added. "Saddle and all."

"Then please, gentlemen, welcome to my home and make yourselves comfortable. Maybe Hannah would help me rustle up some food."

Soon there was quiet conversation and hopeful ideas, and plans were being tossed back and forth, examined and discarded.

Patrick felt good that Michael's brothers had come. It seemed to brighten his and Hannah's world a bit. Silently he wished there was a way out of this situation without the use of violence. While the conversation swirled about him, Patrick prayed.

*   *   *

Thomas Merrell fumed in virulent hatred when Hannah left his room. She had touched him somehow and he could not admit that, especially to himself. He'd nursed his anguish, his bitterness, and his hatred of Cord too long to let anything stop him now, especially when he knew he was close to success.

He knew exactly where Jonas Holt would be hiding out, so he sent a message to the farm later that afternoon. He was more than certain Jonas would not ride into town until after dark.

Although he had been in hiding, he had a suspicion Jonas would find a way of knowing what was going on. This job had to be brought to an end, and now.

He ate an early dinner in the hotel restaurant, lingering over his coffee and sipping two brandies. He'd hoped Jonas had found a way to send a message. But when he left the restaurant and started for his room there was still no sign of him.

He slipped the key into the lock of his door, opened it, and stepped inside. He shouldn't have been surprised to see Jonas lounging in a chair facing the door, but he was.

"Come on in, Senator," he smiled. "It seems you and I have a little problem to discuss."

Thomas went in, and closed the door behind him.

Chapter Nineteen

St. Louis, Missouri

Maxwell accepted the glass of whiskey from Grant and sat back comfortably in his chair. President or not, Maxwell could see that Grant was still the old Army friend he'd always been.

Lee Chu sat in another comfortable chair a short distance from Maxwell. When he had declined a drink, Grant had laughed.

"I thought staying with old Max here would one day drive you to drink, Lee Chu. But I guess you're made of stronger material than I thought. He hasn't led you astray yet."

Lee Chu smiled his own enigmatic smile. "When traveling in pairs, it is always wise to make certain one is able to keep wits about him. Cannot fall to unwise practice of dlink."

Now it was Maxwell who laughed. "He's right there. One of us usually has to keep the waters calm, and nine times out of ten it turns out to be Lee Chu."

"I'm sure he doesn't appreciate you, Lee Chu. He's an unprincipled ruffian. Now . . . if you were to come to work for me, you'd find the situation much more compatible to your . . . talents."

"Ah, much to my distress, is impossible," Lee Chu said, nodding his head as if he did agree with some of Grant's points. This brought a soft laugh from Maxwell. "One feels gleat responsibility for supplying caution and patience when required."

"I'd like to argue that point with him," Maxwell chuckled, "but I'm afraid he's right. So stop trying to lure my conscience away."

"I'll stop trying now," Grant grinned, "but I'm sure not going to rescind the offer."

Maxwell took a sip of his drink while Grant rose and walked to the window to look out.

"It's been a lot of years, Max."

"And we've both come a long way."

"Yes," Grant said thoughtfully, "and we still have a long way to go Max, we're going to have a lot of trouble cleaning up the mess we started in sixty-one. I have the job now of putting this country back together. I could use help."

"You offering me a job?" Maxwell smiled, but the smile faded when Grant turned to look at him and his eyes reflected his seriousness. Maxwell exchanged a look with Lee Chu. Both of them knew Grant well. He was not a man to ask favors easily.

"Yes . . . I am."

"I . . . I didn't think you were serious."

"I'm deadly serious." Grant returned to his desk and sat down again, folding his hands before him. "I know after the war you felt you had to get your railroad built. I can understand that. But you've built it, Max. Now . . . I need a man—a builder, a man with your capabilities. We need to build more than a railroad, we have to unify and rebuild a whole country."

"One man cannot accomplish all that," Lee Chu said.

"No," Grant said firmly. "One man can't. That's why I need all the help I can get."

"I'd like to but . . ."

"I'm offering you a cabinet post, or at least a carte blanche on whatever you would need."

"I'm sure you'd give me all the support I'd need. But I just can't at this moment."

"Do you mind telling me why?"

"Is obligation to the spirit," Lee Chu said. "One does not neglect to repay debts. It is too heavy a load to carry when one goes to meet his ancestors."

"Obligations?" Grant questioned, the gleam of hope in his eyes.

"Actually, that's why I rushed here when I found you were going to be here. You see, *I* need *your* help."

With a few words from Lee Chu inserted here and there, Maxwell explained his reason for searching Grant out.

"I know how busy you are and that it's asking a lot, but a senator is almost impossible to stop. And Michael has no one to turn to. The senator has seen to the destruction of his reputation. It's a pretty one-sided fight."

"Is vely bad situation when a man has the power to destloy another's life," Lee Chu acknowledged.

"I couldn't agree more," Grant said. "I know Senator Merrell. He's been a thorn in my side. Occasionally we've bucked heads. I'm sure he remembers. I've stung his tail some. I'm not too sure of his character and credibility, and for some reason I don't put this past him. He took his son's death hard, not to mention his wife's."

"I need to stop him from destroying Michael Cord completely."

"He is powerful man," Lee Chu said, "and he does not mind using his power to destroy lives. It is an evil thing to do."

"Umm," Grant agreed. "Power isn't something to be played with. If you're not careful you can end up doing yourself more harm than anyone else." Grant rose again and returned to the window, clasping his hands behind him as he rocked on his heels, deep in thought. The city lay before him unseen and the room was silent. Then, again, he turned to face Maxwell and Lee Chu. "What would you have me do? Remember he is a duly elected senator of these United States."

"I know." Maxwell had read his friend well. "And you and I both know that somewhere along the line he must have done something that we can use as a means of pressure." Maxwell's smile matched Grant's.

"I wouldn't be a bit surprised."

"And I wouldn't be surprised, either, if you already knew where his secrets were buried."

"I might be able to supply one or two," Grant grinned. "I'm just considering the price tag on it."

"I'm an old campaigner, friend." Maxwell's laugh reflected the fact that he knew just what Grant was getting at. "Surely," he added, "you'd do a favor for an old war buddy."

"You'd think so, wouldn't you?" Grant nodded. "But you see, I feel it's kind of . . . reciprocal. I've asked my old friend for a favor and he seems a bit reticent."

Lee Chu was watching the exchange of words with a humorous smile. He knew there was no possible way that these two friends would not help each other. They played an amusing game and Lee Chu, a man of endless patience, had only to wait it out to see the conclusion.

"Reticent!" Maxwell said, as if he were shocked. "Me, reticent? How can you say that? I am a man of infinite cooperation. Why, I was just about to tell you that I'd be happy to offer you . . . say," he eyed Grant thoughtfully, "a year?"

"Two."

"You're a horse thief!"

"Two years and an option to try to convince you to stay on until my tenure in office is over."

"You're a hard man."

"Do we have a bargain?"

"Two years," Maxwell stated. "And I don't think you can convince me to make it four."

"But I can try."

"You can try."

Grant reached across his desk and Maxwell took his hand.

"Now that pleasantlies are over," Lee Chu said, "it is of utmost importance to make decisions. What is to be done? We do not have gleat abundance of time."

"He's right," Maxwell said. "What kind of ideas do you have?"

"Sit down, have one more drink. I'll explain something that might interest you."

The new day promised to be a bright and sunny one. Hannah woke early to the sound of birds singing. She felt comfortable and warm. With a smile she remembered the night before, when she had brought Michael the most satisfying gift of his brother, her brother, and Buck. Now it seemed they were surrounded by people who loved them and wanted to help them.

It was a satisfying thought, but another, even more satisfactory one, followed. Today was her wedding day.

She and Michael had gone into town the afternoon before and found the alteration on the gown had been finished. Now, from where she lay on the bed, she could see it hanging on the back of the closet door.

Today she and Michael would marry and they would take whatever time fate meant for them to have. She refused to think of anything past this day, this hour. She meant to experience all the happiness she could.

Trace and the others had left very late to arrange for rooms at the same hotel where Mac and the others were staying. She, Patrick, and Michael had finally found their way to bed, all three of them so exhausted that sleep came easily.

Voices from below assured her that someone besides herself had wakened early. She rose, put on a robe, and left the bedroom. Barefoot, she came down the stairs slowly, making little noise.

The voices she had heard had been those of Patrick and Mac. They sat at the kitchen table, coffee cups before them, engrossed in their conversation.

"I had the boys help so we could get it all done in a couple of hours," Mac was saying.

"Michael satisfied?"

"Seemed to be. But you know him. He's doing the finishing touches himself."

"I thought he might," Patrick laughed. "He left here before the crack of dawn."

The word "left" tingled through Hannah like the cold touch of a spectral hand. Michael had to finish a job before dawn . . . he had left before she awoke because she might have been unhappy about what he was doing. Just the thought of what things he might be doing made her tremble.

She pushed open the kitchen door and walked in.

"Hannah," Patrick smiled. "Good morning. You're up early."

"It's a beautiful day for a wedding, Hannah," Mac said.

To Hannah both of them looked a bit guilty, but she had no idea why.

"Good morning, you two. Where's Michael?"

"Come and sit down. I've just brewed some fresh coffee," Patrick urged.

"Yeah, and I brought over some of those fresh cake doughnuts

Mrs. Murphy bakes for the restaurant. Have one. They're delicious.''

Hannah poured a cup of coffee and carried it to the table with her. There was no doubt in her mind that these two were hiding something from her.

"Where's Michael?" She repeated the question, holding Patrick's eyes with hers.

But if there was any guilt, Patrick no longer let it show. He smiled. "He said he had an errand to run this morning, but to tell you he'd be back in plenty of time for lunch and for the 'special occasion.' Don't worry, Hannah, Michael doesn't want any problems today."

Hannah suddenly felt the sense of relief, as if a heavy weight had been lifted from her shoulders. She'd been frightened and grasping at the possibilities her fear had formed. She began to wonder if she would taste this kind of fear every time Michael was out of her sight.

She made herself a promise. She would find the strength to face whatever she had to face without complaint. But now it awed her to realize Michael had lived with this deadly, silent fear for years.

She smiled, and both men breathed an inaudible sigh of relief. Neither of them had the answers for the questions they were afraid she was going to ask.

"I'll take one of those doughnuts, thank you," Hannah said as she poured a bit of cream in her coffee.

Grateful that she was not going to put them under pressure, both began to search for any topic of conversation other than Michael.

"Joey and the boys are planning on a little celebration here, Hannah, if you don't mind. Nothing elaborate, just a few of us wanting to wish you well," Mac began.

Hannah looked at him with a smile of true fondness. This man had been her anchor for a long time and she felt there would never be a way ever to express her thanks to him and the three other men who had sacrificed so much for her dreams.

"Nothing would make me happier, Mac. After all, you and the boys are almost my family. I am both proud and pleased that all of you are sharing this day with us."

"I've told Patrick I ought to ride over to Quinn's and see if he and Rena are ready. I'm sure you want a lady here to help you get dressed and all."

"I wish things were better for them," Hannah said. "I'm so happy today, I just wish I could reach out and touch everyone around me and make them just as happy."

"You've reached out and touched Rena," Patrick said. "I don't think she would have done what she has if you hadn't shared some of your magnificent courage with her."

"I hope they're happy. It's so terrible that Quinn knows so little of his past. It must have made him so terribly unhappy."

"Rena is going to make up for that." Patrick reached out and touched her hand. "The past, Hannah . . ." he said gently. "Sometimes it's a thing we just have to learn to deal with, and everyone has to deal with it in their own way. Quinn has to learn to put more stock in the future which he can do something with, and not in the past, which he can't do anything about."

"I suppose you're right. I guess I just wanted everyone I know and care about to be happy today."

"We'll see what we can do about it." Mac's eyes sparkled.

He stood up and stretched. "Well, I guess I'd better move on. By the time I get there and get those two to get a move on, then return, it ought to be time for everyone else to be pulling in." He walked to the door. "I'll see you all later."

When the door closed behind him, Hannah again turned to Patrick. "All right, Patrick, what's going on?"

"Going on? A wedding I hope," he chuckled.

"I think there's more than that going on," she laughed. "You're not going to tell me a thing, are you?"

"I don't have the faintest notion of what you're talking about. If something is going on, no one has confided the secret to me."

"All right, I give up. I think I'll borrow that big tub of yours. I'd like to take a bath and wash my hair."

"I'll put some water on to heat, and bring the tub upstairs for you."

* * *

When Hannah sank down into the warm water, she felt the tension ease and her body relax. This was the first time since she started to follow Michael that she felt so calm.

She allowed herself to think, and to wish that the circumstances were different. She closed her eyes and tried to visualize how it would be if she were home.

She could see her mother's smile as she fussed over the food she could offer guests. She could feel the strength of her father's arm as they walked together down the aisle of the small church in which her parents had been married.

She could hear her sister Emily's happy, teasing laugh. And best of all, she could see Michael, standing tall in the light that streamed from the stained-glass window.

Suddenly she realized she was crying. In surprise she raised her hand to brush the tears from her cheek. For a while she surrendered to them, promising herself that they would be the last sign of weakness she would ever allow. From this moment on she would only think of the time that would belong to her and Michael.

Mac rode slowly toward Quinn's cabin, deep in thought. He, like all of his friends, wished with all their hearts that some power beyond them would change the situation. But there wasn't anything that could.

Jonas Holt would come out of hiding one day soon, meet with the senator and who knew how many other men the senator had gathered.

Mac knew one thing for certain, that there was no one in the group surrounding Hannah and Michael who would not stand and fight with him . . . if there was a way to do that and if they could make Michael see the necessity. Of course, his pride would most likely be the biggest barrier.

When he arrived at Quinn's cabin and knocked, it was only to find no one was home. Puzzled, he got back in the buggy and started for town. Quinn and Rena had to be somewhere. They were the best man and maid of honor, it was his job to find them.

The last place he expected to be successful was at Rena's home.

But word of Rena's return wafted to him on whispers as soon as he arrived in town.

"Rena Brenden and Quinn Wayland," the whispers said, "scandalous . . . brave . . . romantic . . ." There were mixed descriptions from assorted people, but Mac could pick up an undercurrent of envy. There were few young ladies who would not have changed places with Rena if they had the courage to face parents who had long ago let practicality overshadow romance.

When the door was opened Mac faced Rena's father, and was quite unsure of how to handle him.

"Mr. Brenden, I'd like to talk to Miss Brenden for a minute, please. I have a message for her that's very important."

"You're that young friend of Michael Cord."

"Yes, sir, Mac McCarthy. Is your daughter home, sir?"

"Yes, she is." Samuel smiled for the first time, and this made Mac somewhat relieved. "Come in, Mr. McCarthy."

Mac came in and, standing in the foyer, he could hear laughter and voices from the next room. Obviously, whatever damage had been done by Rena's rebellious stand had been repaired.

When Samuel closed the door, he gestured to Mac to come with him. "Come on in, please, we are just discussing some future plans. By the way, Rena told me about the wedding. She says she's to be maid of honor. I wonder if Mr. Cord would be forgiving enough to invite my wife and me. We had hoped for some way to atone both to Rena and to Michael for the way this town has judged . . . or rather *misjudged* both Quinn and him."

"I'm sure Michael and Hannah would be more than pleased if you and your wife came. Actually, the Reverend and the rest of us have planned a small gathering at his home later. I'm sure you'd be more than welcome."

"Thank you." Samuel urged Mac on, and the two entered the living room.

Mac was introduced to Quinn. He was a completely different person than he had imagined from the rumors. He saw change in the depth of his eyes. He'd seen the faces of gunfighters before, but with Quinn there were no tired lines around his mouth and not wary or distrustful looks in his eyes. His smile made him look younger and Mac could see by his relaxed posture that the guarded, defensive barriers had been totally wiped away.

"Mac, it's good to meet you," Quinn said as he rose to shake his hand. "What are you doing here?"

"Running you two down. I'm sure glad that this is where I found you." He grinned broadly when he was introduced to Rena and promptly told not to call her Miss Brenden. "Rena, you sure look happy about something," Mac grinned. "Should I guess?"

"I don't think you need to," Rena laughed. "Why were you looking for us? We were planning on going to Patrick's house a little later."

"I think," Mac grinned, "that Hannah might need someone . . . sort of moral support, you might say. You see, me and the boys, Trace, Michael's brother, and Terrance, Hannah's brother, are the only family she has here. Us being all men . . . well, I guess it might be a little hard on her."

"Oh, that poor child," Sophie said. Her eyes were brimming wells of sympathy. "Do you think she would mind if I came, too?"

"I think she'd probably be real grateful, Mrs. Brenden."

"Good."

"So . . . since her parents are not here," Samuel asked, "who will stand for Hannah's father and give her away?"

"We've all been fighting over it," Mac said. "There isn't a one among us that wouldn't be real proud to do it. But since her brother came, he'll have the honor."

"Poor child," Sophie repeated. "This must be a very difficult time for her. Wouldn't it be better to wait . . . to . . ."

"No, ma'am." Mac's face grew serious. "Hannah and Michael . . . I guess maybe they figure their time is short and don't want to waste it. I think they're right. Every day is too valuable not to take advantage of."

"I agree," Quinn said, as he reached out and took Rena's hand. "Sometimes if you waste something good, you never get a chance to get it back."

"Something ought to be done about this," Samuel said. "Why can no one put a stop to it? If Michael Cord wants to lay down his guns, why doesn't he just do it?"

"Because it's not that easy. All of this . . . well, it's a long story. I don't know if it's my story to tell."

"I wish you would confide in me," Samuel said. "If there is any way at all that I can help, I'd like to."

"Frankly, Mr. Brenden," Mac replied, "I think the kind of help Michael and Hannah need is up to a higher power. Right now it's real important that we make this time as good as we can for the both of them."

"I guess you're right," Samuel agreed. But he was reluctant to let it go. "I'll go and have our buggy hitched."

"Is there anything else I can bring?" Sophie inquired.

"Mother, that cake you baked this morning is quite enough," Rena said.

"How about I bring my crystal punch bowl and make some punch? Sam, why don't you bring some of that wine you had imported last month?"

"Dandy idea. I'll have a half dozen bottles packed." He started from the room, but Quinn was quick to join him.

"I'll give you a hand loading up that buggy."

"I'll see to the cake," Sophie stated firmly. "If I let these men handle it, it might not get there in one piece."

This left Rena and Mac alone. They looked at each other, amused at the sudden excitement and flurry of activity.

"Things have really taken a surprising turn, haven't they?" Rena began.

"Sure have. I'm real glad things turned out so well for you and Quinn, and that your family came around to seeing things your way."

"I have Hannah to thank for that. If anyone deserves a little happiness in her world, it's Hannah Marshall."

"Yeah, you're right about that."

"Mac, what do you think is going to happen?"

Mac sighed and ran his fingers through his hair in frustration. "It's hard to say. The senator's not going to give up and Michael knows it. He'll face whatever comes, when it comes."

"Senator! You mean the person behind all this is actually a senator?"

"Yes, and he has a lot of money and power behind him that he doesn't mind using."

Mac could see that Rena had grasped the reality quickly. This was a problem that was out of their hands.

When Quinn and Rena's parents returned, the entire group headed for Patrick's house.

* * *

Terrance and Michael stood together on Patrick's porch. For a short while they had stood in companionable silence.

"You really made this day special for Hannah, Terrance," Michael said. "In all these preparations, I hadn't thought of who was going to take your father's place. I haven't seen Hannah happier, and I just want you to know how glad I am you got here in time."

"I wish it was different, for Hannah's sake," Terrance replied, "but I'm more than happy to do it. Hannah has always been . . . kind of special. I just couldn't be more proud of her. By the way, how are all the 'arrangements' coming along."

"Nobody's breathed a word to Hannah?"

"And spoil everything for her? Not likely."

"The place looks pretty good, I must say. I think she's in for a surprise."

"Great. And from the sounds inside, I think everybody is getting ready to go on over to the church."

"Who's with Hannah?"

"Rena."

"She been asking for me?"

"Every half hour," Terrance grinned. "You think she might be getting the idea you could have lost your nerve and run out on her?"

Michael laughed. "I tried that, it just doesn't work. Now . . . I couldn't let go of her if my life depended on it. Matter of fact, it does."

Before Terrance could say any more the door opened and Patrick came out.

"Time to go on over to the church," he said. "You ready, Michael?"

"Ready as I'll ever be."

"I'll stay here, Reverend," Terrance said. "I'm giving my sister away, so I'll wait and bring her and Rena over."

"Very good," Patrick smiled at Michael. "Come along. It's time to get this business rolling."

Michael went with the group and Terrance stood alone on the porch. He prayed silently that all of this would work out, but deep inside he was scared Hannah would end up a widow before she was really a wife.

When Michael went into the church and the other guests had found their seats, he drew Trace aside.

"Trace, I need a promise from you."

"A promise?"

"If . . . if something happens to me, I want you to be the one who makes sure Hannah is well taken care of."

"Michael! You didn't have to ask me a thing like that. You know I'd see to Hannah's care. But the best thing for her is to see that nothing does happen to you."

"Don't fool yourself, Trace. One way or another, one day or another, this little dream is going to end. I just wanted to make sure of Hannah's future."

"Well, rest easy, brother. She'll never have to worry about a thing." Trace said the words firmly, but he felt his heart wrench at the bleak idea of such a dark future.

"I guess we'd better go in," Michael said, his voice strained as well. Trace nodded, and they walked into the church together.

Hannah sat before a mirror with unseeing eyes. Her mind drifted to her home, and the warmth and love that had surrounded her there. Suddenly she sighed deeply and forced her mind away from the saddening thoughts.

This was her wedding day and she was not going to cry about things she could do nothing about. She was glad of one thing. The worst of the bruises were gone, and she had begun to look much better.

She had tried to coil her hair sleekly on top of her head but, today of all days, it would not seem to cooperate in any way. So she brushed the thick mass of stubborn russet curls and let her hair hang free. It cascaded in waves and curls to well below her waist.

She sat in just her shift and petticoats, but on the door behind her she could see the beautiful dress. She had invited Alice to the wedding and the party afterward, and the seamstress had graciously accepted the invitation.

When she heard the soft rap on her door, she was surprised. She hoped it wasn't Michael. She didn't want him to see her in this sad mood.

The door cracked open a bit and Rena poked her head around it. "Can I come in?"

"Oh, Rena, of course. I thought it was Michael."

"He's already waiting at the church. I've come to see if I can help you."

"I'd be grateful. I can't seem to arrange my hair."

"Your hair is beautiful just as it is." Rena went to take the dress from the hanger. "Oh, by the way, Terrance is waiting downstairs for you. He said to tell you he never thought he'd have the privilege of giving you away."

"Lord, I'm glad he is here. He's the only family I have right now."

"Come on, let's get this gown on, and I'll fasten it. You must have fifty buttons up the back of it."

Rena lifted the gown and let it fall slowly down over Hannah's head. While she fastened the buttons, Hannah gazed at herself in the mirror. The dress was beautiful, and her green eyes seemed to blaze like emeralds. Her long russet hair only made the brilliance of the dress more alluring.

"Hannah, you're beautiful." Rena stood behind her.

"I'm suddenly so frightened."

"Don't be. You're a very courageous lady. Don't let go now. You have a wonderful life waiting for you. I hope you find happiness . . . Oh, I brought you something." Rena reached into her pocket and drew out a small bottle of perfume and a single strand of pearls.

"I think the pearls will be just right . . . and," she giggled, "I think Michael will enjoy the perfume."

Hannah blushed, but accepted the gifts graciously.

"Well . . . I guess I'm ready."

"Then let's go down and join Terrance. If I'm not mistaken, I think I hear organ music from the church already. I'm sure that's Patrick's way of telling us to hurry."

They left the room together, and when Hannah came downstairs, Terrance watched her walk toward him with a glow of loving pride in his eyes.

He had one hand behind his back. When Hannah stopped beside him, he withdrew it and handed her a bunch of freshly picked wildflowers.

"I couldn't let the bride go without some flowers. They're not the best, but they're beautiful nonetheless."

"Oh, thank you, Terrance." Tears came to her eyes as she stood on tiptoe to kiss his cheek.

"Be happy, Hannah," he said softly.

"I will."

Terrance extended his arm to her and she tucked her hand under it. The three of them walked the distance to the church.

Patrick stood before the small pulpit, and next to him stood Quinn, Trace, and Michael. Michael laughed to himself. For a cool, steady-handed gunfighter he was amused to find he was actually shaking.

Then, the strains to the "Wedding March" began and the double doors of the church were opened. From that moment on Michael forgot everything else except the vision that was walking toward him.

With Rena in front of her and her brother at her side, Hannah felt a bit shaky herself. Then her eyes met Michael's and she knew this was the most perfect day of her life and one she would always remember.

Chapter Twenty

The church was small, and had been carefully built by the people who had first settled the town. The pews and the floor had been polished smooth by the many people who had moved through the vaulted room.

Huge windows lined each side of the narrow structure, and through them the late-afternoon sun sent its brilliant beams. The addition to the church, finally getting under way, lent the scent of fresh-cut wood.

Hannah walked slowly toward Michael, and as she did, the sunlight caught her, turning her to an ivory-and-flame vision. Michael felt his breath catch and a heavy constriction in his chest, as if his heartbeat had quickened. She had given . . . no, *was giving*, so much to him in return for so little. Stability in his topsy-turvy world. Something to hold on to.

Fleeting visions of their short time together flashed through his mind and he thought of the many facets that made him love her. Her humor and courage were immense, but it wasn't that. It was a fleeting thing he could not put his finger on. He wished with everything he had that he could share enough time with her to answer that question.

For Hannah the moment was just as mystically sweet. Michael seemed so . . . so tall and strong. When she stopped at his side and looked up at him, she could see herself reflected in his eyes.

The words Patrick spoke echoed in the hearts of the two people who faced him. To love and to cherish . . . to hold to one another in the face of adversity . . . to love and honor . . . forever.

"I now pronounce you man and wife. What God hath joined together let no man put asunder." The last words reached everyone present. Patrick smiled at Michael. "You may kiss the bride."

Michael turned to Hannah. He saw the love and the trust deep in her eyes, and a feeling of deep humility caught him so poignantly that it brought the sting of tears to his own eyes. He took her in his arms gently, and the kiss was deep and one of such an intense hunger that Hannah could hardly bear it.

"I love you, Hannah," he whispered.

Then they were suddenly amid a crowd of well-wishers who were delightedly shaking Michael's hand and kissing Hannah.

"Come to my house, one and all," Patrick invited. "Let's have a grand celebration."

They followed Patrick from the church and made their way to his house, where the celebration began in earnest.

For a while all outside problems remained at the door, unwelcome in this group of people who had been united in the most unique of ways.

There was laughter and a great deal of tormenting of Michael and Hannah, who took it all in good spirits. Still, Michael was only biding his time until he could get Hannah safely away. He had worked from before dawn to create something special for her. He had little to offer a bride on her wedding night, but he'd tried. Now he wanted to share the haven he'd fashioned with her.

There wasn't a person present who could not read his anxiety with some amusement.

Zeb came to Michael's side and paused for a few minutes, as both men watched and enjoyed Hannah's happiness. "You sure are a lucky man," he said quietly.

"Thanks, Zeb. I quite agree."

"I want to wish you all the luck in the world, Lieutenant Cord. If anyone deserves it, you sure do."

"Thanks again, Zeb."

Michael was fighting his frustration and watching Hannah in

animated conversation with the Brendens when Trace paused beside him and spoke softly.

"It seems to me this party could go on all night."

"Yeah," Michael said.

Trace chuckled. "Everybody's having such a good time that it wouldn't surprise me none. Now, if you were quick and clever, you could slip out with Hannah."

"If I could get her alone for a second."

"Faint heart never won fair lady. Whatever happened to my enterprising brother?"

"Damn if I know," Michael laughed. "But I think I've just reached the end of my patience."

"I thought so," Trace grinned. "So I had Joey slip out and harness Patrick's buggy. It's ready and waiting."

"Thanks." Michael clapped his brother's shoulder and moved resolutely toward Hannah.

When Michael came up behind her and put his arm around her, he never knew that she breathed a silent sigh of relief. For the past hour she'd been trying to figure a way to excape with him.

"We have to get out of here," he whispered as be bent close. "Ready?"

"Yes." Her voice was breathless. Then Michael took her hand and they moved swiftly toward the door. Patrick, well prepared for this, opened the door just as they reached it, watched them pass through, closed it, and smiled at the devilishly grinning men whose way he barred.

Hannah was laughing when Michael helped her into the carriage and climbed in behind her.

It was a cozy ride to the cabin and she snuggled close to him. "I can't believe all this. It's like a dream."

"It is that," he agreed. "A dream I never thought would ever come true."

"Michael?"

"Um-umm?"

"Where were you all day? You were gone long before I got up, and I never saw you until it was time for the wedding."

He turned and looked down at her. Then he grinned. "Have I had a chance to tell you how absolutely beautiful you are? When

I saw you coming down the aisle, I had the feeling I couldn't get my next breath."

"You're dodging my question."

"I guess I am."

"Michael!"

"Are you going to be a nosey wife?"

"I most certainly am," Hannah stated firmly.

"Well, I guess you'll have to learn a little patience, because that's one question I don't intend to answer right now."

"You were up to something."

"That I was," he agreed amiably. "It's a surprise, so don't ask."

"I can see," she said with a soft, threatening laugh that should have warned him, "that you are going to be difficult." She moved closer, pressing against him, then rested her hand on his thigh.

"Hannah . . . behave."

"I am," she said seductively. She leaned toward him and kissed his cheek, brushing her lips softly across his skin.

"C'mon, Hannah," Michael laughed. "I don't want to stop this buggy right here, but I will if you keep on like that."

"Then tell me your secrets," she replied, her hand slipping upward.

"You don't play fair."

"All's fair in love and war."

"We're almost home. I promise, I'll tell you as soon as we get there."

Satisfied, she sat back in the buggy and removed her hand. "Hey," he said, "I didn't say you have to move so far away." This brought her back to snuggle against him.

When they pulled up in front of the cabin Hannah was surprised to see the windows glowing with mellow light. She looked quickly at Michael who only smiled like a Cheshire cat keeping the secret of vanished cream.

He helped her out of the carriage and started toward the door.

"Aren't you going to care for the horse and buggy."

"A little bit later."

When they got to the door, Hannah reached for the handle, only to find Michael's hand staying hers. She looked up at him questioningly.

Without answering her unspoken questions he swept her up in his arms.

"Welcome to your first home, Mrs. Cord."

"Mrs. Cord," Hannah repeated softly.

She reached to unlatch the door and Michael pushed it open with his foot. As he stepped across the threshold, Hannah looked about her in total awe.

What had been a dirty, roughly supplied cabin had been transformed. Someone had cleaned it thoroughly. But what was more surprising was that in one corner a huge, four-poster bed had replaced the cot. At each side of it a small table with an oil lamp burning low was placed. The bed was already made up with a thick comforter and several pillows. Hannah looked up at Michael.

"Wherever did you get that? Patrick never had anything like it in his house."

"Somehow I knew you'd ask that. The only thing that matters is if you like it. It took me and the boys nearly the whole day to get this place clean and get that set up."

"But where did you get it?"

"Oh, I just had the boys help me scout around until I found it."

"Where?"

"Does that matter?" He was dodging and she knew it, which intrigued her more than anything else. She'd never seen him off balance.

Michael was shaken, because she had gone straight to the point and asked the one question he'd hoped not to answer. He slid her feet to the floor, but kept his arms around her. Then he bent to kiss her deeply.

"It isn't important," he said softly. "There's a bottle of wine on that table and a couple of glasses. Let's try it. It's time to get more comfortable."

But her arms remained around his neck. "Michael Cord," she smiled wickedly, "if you want to use it, you'd better tell me where you got it."

"You are one stubborn woman," he protested. But he knew he wasn't about to continue with an evening he'd been dreaming about unless he did tell her. Of course, once he told her, it was debatable just how the evening would go on. "All right. I got it at Rosie's."

"Rosie's?" For a minute Hannah looked puzzled, then understanding dawned in her eyes and she didn't know whether to laugh or be angry. Her innate sense of humor won out. "A . . . a brothel! You bought my wedding bed from a brothel!" She was choking on her laughter.

"Look, Hannah," he tried hastily to explain, "it was the only decent bed in town. The store would have had to order one, and that would have taken weeks."

"And," her lips twitched, "how did you know this bed was there, and that it was the only good one in town?"

"Now look . . ." he started to say, beginning to see the laughter dancing in her eyes for himself. "You're a witch."

"But you didn't answer the question," she replied, but now the humor of the situation was obvious.

"I asked the boys to . . . ah . . . check around."

"Oh, I'll bet they did." Hannah could not contain her laughter any longer. The idea of Michael having his friends check the local brothels for a bed was too much to contain.The laughter was contagious. Michael wrapped his arms around her and both dissolved in the humor of the situation.

"Do you think I could possibly tell my parents," Hannah gasped, brushing tears from her eyes, "that I spent my wedding night in a well-used bed, procured from a brothel?"

"Please don't," Michael choked back his laughter. "I'm pretty sure they *wouldn't* understand."

"Oh, Michael Cord," she giggled, "you sure do add spice to a lady's life." She put her arms around his waist and pressed close to him. "I'm so glad you came into mine."

"I am, too," he said seriously. "I'd hate to have missed you." He bent to kiss her, slowly and leisurely, tasting her lips and savoring the way her willing warmth reached to envelop him.

When he released her mouth, he looked down into emerald pools of melting love. She had a way of looking at him that pushed every other thought from his mind but her. He could feel his pulse race and his body stir awake as if touched by an electrical current. He was safe in assuring himself that there never would come a time when he would not want Hannah, not want to keep this loving, heated look in her eyes. He cupped face in his hands and gently kissed both eyelids, then gazed for a long moment at the woman he thought more beautiful and precious than any other he'd ever known. There was an exotic quality about her. Those amazing green eyes were framed by the thickest lashes, darker than her glowing russet hair.

He kissed the tip of her fine, straight nose, and then the corner of her full, soft mouth, where it turned up in the hint of a smile.

He could feel the tension within her, like the low hum of a honeybee, motionless but full of quivering excitement. Hannah stood with her eyes closed, content to feel the warmth and taste of him.

He watched the pulse at the base of her throat begin to beat. Then he kissed her mouth again. This time he opened his own and sought entry with his tongue. He felt her shiver and her lips part to accept him.

The effect was tantalizing, and he felt her tingling response. Hannah paused to look up at him for a moment. Then she silently turned around and stood with her back to him and reached up to lift the heavy weight of her hair.

Wordlessly, with trembling fingers, he began to undo the buttons down the back of her dress. She smiled to herself when she thought she heard a soft, muttered curse as a stubborn button refused to cooperate with his shaking hands.

When the dress finally slipped to the floor, Hannah still stood quietly. Michael's arms came around her, drawing her back against him, feeling the softness of her body mold against his. He bent to kiss her bare shoulder, while gentle gingers slid the strap of her underslip down.

His fingertips traced the curve of her shoulder and brushed the length of her arm. Then, slowly, with a whispered touch, he drew his hand back up her arm, pausing to gently caress the firmness of her breast.

She shook with a tingling spasm that sensitized every nerve with quickened expectation. He savored her softness and the elusive scent she wore, and she enjoyed the way her senses were attuned to him . . . his warm, muscled body, the pleasant, clean scent of him. He kissed her mouth, her neck, nipping lightly at her flesh and making her quiver.

But Hannah was no longer satisfied with accepting this magic, she wanted to return it as well. She turned in his arms and, with trembling fingers; began to remove his clothes, while he grasped the opportunity to rid her of the few thin pieces of material that stood between them. Then they stood, warm body to warm body, barely touching.

"God, Hannah," Michael rasped. "Do you have any idea how beautiful you are and how much I want to make love to you?"

"Yes, Michael, yes," Hannah breathed. "Make love to me. Make me forget that there's a tomorrow."

He bent and lifted her gently in his arms and took the few steps to the bed.

When they lay side by side on the bed, Hannah felt the fiery excitement claim her, a heightened awareness of every sensation. Every place his body pressed against hers, a tingle coursed through her; his hands touching her, his arms around her, the length of his body against hers, and the hardness of his manhood throbbing against her.

Michael groaned with the need that filled him to be inside her. But this night would not be rushed if he could help it. This night had to be perfect.

Michael could hear her whispered sigh as he tasted the curve of her breast, then caught one in his mouth and suckled the nipple so deeply that she moaned. Raw desire pierced her, but he had no intention for it to end here. He roamed her flesh with heated lips, letting his tongue savor the unique taste of her, and she almost cried out as he tasted even deeper the warm depths of her.

Her hands caught his shoulders, kneading them, forcing them away, only seconds before drawing him to her to delve even deeper. The warmth of his tongue as it probed the most sensitive spot shot spikes of excitement through her. She was so sensitive, her reaction so powerful, that it was almost unbearably stimulating. She did not hear herself cry out his name, but he did, and it was as arousing as the touch of her hands urging him to deeper possession.

She pressed up to him, losing herself in the sensations coursing through her body. For both of them all feeling was turned inward.

There was no reality, no tomorrows, no fears, only the rising intensity of their senses.

Hannah had abandoned herself completely to the fierce need to hold him inside her, and for Michael it was matched equally to his.

She felt him enter her and tried to rise up to meet him, but he was holding her immobile, refusing to let her make this exquisite pleasure end.

He moved slowly, forcing himself deep inside her, feeling her warm, moist sheath close about him, then withdrawing with a slow, sensuous move.

Pulsing with the sensations of his movements, she felt the fullness of him, then his drawing back and filling her again. Until she was beyond feeling anything else.

Her complete response built the flame in him even higher. He could feel his rhythmic response to her need, and though he wanted it to last, he was losing what control he had over the situation.

In the mellow glow of lamplight their bodies, glazed with perspiration as they moved in unison, both gave and took so fully that sight, sound, and place were completely forgotten.

A glowing ball of fire seemed to be expanding within both of them. It grew and grew until it exploded, sending rippling sensations coursing through them.

He caught her cry of completion with his mouth against hers, and groaned in compliance with the miracle of sensation.

Then they were still, drawing in ragged breaths and clinging to each other until their careening world righted itself.

Hannah held him close, welcoming his weight, feeling a blending between them that was more than just a physical joining. It was as if two separate spirits had been molded into one.

"I'm too heavy for you," he whispered. He tried to move, abut she had clung to him that one precious moment more.

"I don't mind." Her voice was a soft breath against his skin.

Michael rolled to his side, pulling her close. "Hannah . . . Hannah, I love you so much. I don't know how I existed in that lonely, dark world before you."

When she looked into his eyes, she knew the depth of what he was trying to express. There were no words she could say that would have been half as expressive as what they had just shared.

"I promise you," she replied, with a catch in her voice that betrayed unshed tears, "that you'll never be lonely again. Not as long as there's a breath in my body."

The kiss they shared was one of gentle promise.

"That wine is still cool. Do you want a glass?" he asked.

"Yes."

She watched him as he rose from the bed and walked to a nearby table to pour them each a glass. He carried the glasses aback to the bed and handed one to her. Each took a sip. Then he bent to brush her lips with his, tasting the wine on hers.

"Has anyone told you, Michael Cord," her voice was mellow, "that you are absolutely beautiful?"

"Not hardly." He laughed, but his face flushed slightly with pleasure. "This battered face and scarred body can hardly be called beautiful."

He lay down beside her, resting on one elbow and holding the glass with the other.

Hannah reached out and lightly traced the scar on his hip. He watched her face, absorbing every line, every flicker of emotion that crossed it. She heard his swift intake of breath as she bent and brushed her lips across the scar. When she lifted her head to meet his gaze, she smiled. Michael took the glass from her hand, placed them both on the table beside him, then reached and drew her into his embrace.

For a while they lay in silence, content to hold each other.

"Well, I have the answer to one question," Hannah said.

"One question? What?"

"I've always wanted to know what made Rosie's and places like that so popular."

She could hear his soft chuckle. "It isn't the bed, my love, and nobody that frequents Rosie's has ever found anything like you in their bed."

"No?" She was pleased.

"No, nothing as beautiful, and certainly nothing as exciting. I think we'd better keep this bed."

"For our house one day?" she said cautiously.

"Yes," he finally answered. "For our house one day."

Both knew that what they were saying was the part of their dream that might never be there.

"Michael?"

"Umm?"

"Tell me about you . . . when you were a boy, I mean. You and I have never really had all that much time to talk."

He laughed softly. "I was the ideal child. Quiet, obedient, and a picture of decorum."

"Of course." Her laugh matched his. "And if I believe that, you could sell me the moon."

"Hannah! How can you doubt me?"

"Maybe," she looked up at him impishly, "because even I know you better than that."

"As a boy . . ." he mused thoughtfully, "I guess I was a boy like any other. I was born between Trace and Allison, and I used to think I was misused by fate. Trace . . . well, I thought he was perfect, and Allison," he paused to laugh again. "Allison was Allison. If there was a heart in the vicinity; she owned it. Trace was hard to live up to."

"But you didn't resent him?"

"No . . . he made that pretty hard to do. He was always there to help over the rough spots, always leading the way, except . . ."

"Except?" Hannah could feel his body stiffen slightly.

"Except for the war. That was something even Trace couldn't fix. From that time until now, everything went downhill." For a minute he was caught in the past and enclosed in the old pain.

Hannah rose on one elbow and bent to kiss him. "Don't go back, Michael," she breathed. "There's only tonight to remember. Let's promise to keep only the good things and forget the rest."

"There's only tonight," he repeated. Then he drew her to him and wrapped his arms about her so fiercely, she could barely breathe. The kiss was of such intensity that Hannah could only hold on to him while she seemed to dissolve within. Michael was washing away the past in the magic of her love and for she that was grateful, since it was the best promise he could give.

The kiss, fierce at first, dissolved into something much warmer and seeking. Again the mellow lamplight bathed the lovers in its glow while they shared the mutual joy that fill the room.

*   *   *

At the same moment Michael and Hannah had closed the door of their sanctuary, the sound of the shrilling train whistle echoing in town heralded the arrival of the last evening train.

When it came to a stop with a hiss of steam and screech of brakes, it was to let the only two passengers disembark.

Allison looked around while Reid saw to the baggage. When he came up to stand beside her, he was smiling.

"What are you smiling about?"

"The baggage man asked me where I wanted the baggage taken since there are only two hotels in town. I told him only the best would do, and he told me which one that was."Allison had to respond to his amusement and his attitude that assumed he knew her so well. "It's the Grand Hotel, and it's not too far from here. Do you want to walk, or shall I arrange some transportation?"

"It's a nice evening. Let's walk. It will give us a better look at the town."

Reid agreed, and they started toward the Grand Hotel. Once they were standing before it, both could see it was a very elaborate place. When they questioned the clerk as they checked in, there were no guests named Cord, nor any of the others.

Allison's eyes narrowed at the clerk, who smiled when they signed for adjoining rooms. The look was frigid enough to wilt his amusement, and when he looked at Reid, the cold and somewhat threatening look dampened anything he might have said.

"There's another hotel in town. Can you tell me where it is?" Reid asked.

"Sir," the clerk was abjectly remorseful. Besides, this kind of thing could cost him his job. "The accommodations at the Grand are the best the town has to offer. Surely . . .

"No, no. We're looking for some friends. If they're not here, they must be at the other hotel."

"Reid . . ." Allison said. "Why don't you go on over and check while I finish seeing to our rooms?"

"Good idea. I'll be back in a few minutes."

When Reid did return, it was to explain to Allison that Trace and the others were registered at the hotel but that there was no sign of anyone.

"They said there was some kind of a celebration going on at Reverend Carrigan's home."

"Reverend Carrigan? Have you heard that name before?"

"No."

"I wonder why Trace and the others would have business with the local pastor," Allison said thoughtfully. "You asked about Michael?"

"Just the hotel clerk. He seemed a little shaken up with the idea that Michael is still here in town."

"Why would he be shaken up?"

"I don't have any idea. It was more the way he acted than anything he said."

"What did he say?"

"Something about Michael seeming to have nine lives, and no wonder he was the preacher's friend. None of it made much sense to me. But this preacher, whoever he is, is closely connected to both your brothers . . . What do we do now . . . wait for Michael and Trace to get back to the hotel?"

"No . . . no, I think it's time for us to go to a party."

"Allison, you can't just barge into someone's home." Reid could have bitten his tongue after he spoke. He should have known better. One did not *tell* Allison Cord she couldn't do something. "C'mon, Allison," Reid protested at the gleam in her eyes.

"Come with me or not, Reid." her smile was brilliant. "I'm going to find out where the pastor lives then *I'm* going to a party." She turned and walked away. There was no doubt in his mind that she would do what she intended. He followed, muttering under his breath.

"Trace and Michael are going to kill me . . . they're going to kill me."

As they approached Patrick's house, then walked up onto the porch, the sound of laughter assured them, whatever the party was for, it was still going on. Reid knocked.

Trace happened to be standing nearest to the door. Still smiling at something someone had said, he took the step or two to the door and opened it.

For a second he couldn't quite grasp the fact that it was Allison who stood before him with a somewhat upset Reid right behind her.

"Close your mouth, Trace," Allison laughed as she breezed past him. "It's really me." Trace closed both his mouth and the door, but the look he cast Reid was not a happy one.

"I'm sorry, Trace," Reid said quickly. "But you should have known that if there was a problem in the family, Allison sure wasn't going to be kept out of it."

"You should have kept her at home."

"You want to give me some suggestions as to how? If I hadn't come with her, she would have gone alone. Which way would you have chosen?"

Trace shook his head and gave a sigh of helplessness.

"I thought you'd understand," Reid said.

Trace introduced Allison and Reid to Patrick and to the others, with the exception of the men she already knew. Jamie and Joey's welcome was warm. They had all grown up together and they understood Allison pretty well.

Mac's smile was warm, but he was as wary as Trace. This was ceertainly an unforeseen circumstance.

Allison acknowledged the introductions with her usual Georgia charm. Within minutes Patrick was among the number who fell to her smiling expertise. Trace and Reid watched with fascination. She'd turned that charm on them much too often for them not to appreciate its power.

"Well, this is quite a little gathering," she said. "What's the occasion?"

There was a silence so pregnant with explosive force that one could have heard the proverbial pin drop. Allison looked at Jamie and Joey, who suddenly found something quite interesting about the boots they wore.

Mac silently groaned and turned his back so that he would not meet her eyes. Brad was just as involved in something else.

By this time a very alert Allison was a good bit more than suspicious. She turned to her brother.

"Trace?"

"What?"

"What do you mean, *what?* Has the cat gotten everyone's tongue all of a sudden?" She paused, and then it dawned on her that one very important person was missing. "Where's Michael?"

"Uh . . . he's not here," Trace said lamely.

"Obviously. You found him, didn't you?"

"Well . . . yes, we did."

"Then where is he?"

"Actually this party was for him."

"It's not his birthday. If it's a party for finding him, why isn't he here?"

"Oh . . . well . . ."

"What kind of a gathering is this anyway? You ladies are dressed so beautifully. It looks like you all were having a celebration."

"We were," Trace said.

By this time a deep suspicion was dawning in her eyes.

"Michael's wedding," Trace added.

"Michael's wedding," she repeated. Then the look in her eyes turned to one Trace had seen too many times before. "Michael got married?"

"This afternoon," Trace confirmed.

Mac, Jamie, Joey, and Brad wished heartily they were somewhere else. Quinn and Rena seemed amused at the situation. Patrick was still unsure of what was going on. But Reid and Trace were quite sure the roof was going to fall in on their heads. Allison smiled . . . sweetly, which worried them more than anything else.

"Trace Cord, you mean you let me put off my wedding until we could rescue Michael, then you casually stand there and say he got married today. You all couldn't have wired and told me! I'm the last guest expected at my own brother's wedding?"

"It wasn't exactly like that, Allison," Trace protested.

"Oh?" Her dimpled smile reappeared, and Reid and Trace exchanged a helpless look. "Suppose you tell me how it was."

Trace was going to do his best to explain. But he was pretty sure he wouldn't want to be in Michael's shoes when Allison got hold of him.

Patrick was now smiling to himself. He'd caught a glimpse of what must be the relationship here, and it amused him to watch this group of tall, strong men melt like wax in the hot sun before a sweet-speaking woman who, Patrick was sure, had a will like iron . . . and a love just as strong.

Chapter Twenty-one

Even though they all realized Allison accepted everyone's explanations and still worried about Michael and what could happen, there was an unspoken uncertainty. They all had a pretty good feeling that somewhere along the line all of them, including Michael, were going to pay a price.

"Well, Allison . . ." Trace began. "Since we're all at the same hotel, why don't you and Reid join us there."

"Don't be clever, dear brother." Allison sparkled with amusement. "First, I have no wish to stay in the second best hotel, and second, I won't be rendered useless by sitting under your thumb. I'm not staying in that hotel when I can be of some help at the Grand. Besides, from all you've told me, I think having a couple of us staying closer to the senator might be better."

"That man and those he gathers around him are too dangerous for you to be playing games with," Trace was quick to protest.

"I'm not playing games. This man wants to kill Michael. We know now that he has to make contact with . . . with those dreadful men. Having one of us close enough to see who comes and goes might be beneficial. Reid will be with me, so I won't be in any danger. We can watch, Trace . . . I can do that much."

"I know you want to help, Allison, but for God's sake . . ." Trace began to argue.

"Trace . . ." Patrick interrupted. "She just might be right. You know it has occurred to me," he smiled, "that you and your brother are certainly connected to a fine breed of women."

"Why, thank you, Patrick," Allison laughed at Trace's face which was a reflection of Reid's.

"Don't worry, Trace," Reid said. "I kind of agree with Allison. We might be of some help, and I'll do my darndest to keep her from doing anything drastic."

"I'd like to scratch his eyes out," Allison added.

"You see," Trace laughed, "she doesn't need encouragement. All right." He held up both hands as if to ward off Allison's retort. "All right. Go back to your hotel and see what's going on there. You don't know what he looks like, though."

"Maybe I've never seen him," Allison replied, "but I bet I'll be able to pick him out of any group. We've seen his kind before, haven't we, Trace?"

"I guess you're right again."

"Then I think we ought to get on back to the hotel," Reid said.

"I don't know," Allison replied, seeming to appear thoughtful. "Maybe we ought to take a little ride and go out and congratulate my dear brother."

"Allison . . ." Trace chuckled. "If you escaped my wringing your neck, I can assure you you wouldn't escape Michael doing it."

"It would serve him right."

"Maybe so," Reid laughed, "but, out of my own desire to protect myself, I don't think I can go along with that." He turned to grin at Allison. "You might not be afraid of your brothers, my love, but *I* am. Let's go back to the hotel."

"All right, you win. But I'm not finished yet."

"I don't doubt that for a minute," Reid agreed.

Amid well wishes and advice, fears and worry, Allison and Reid left for the hotel. The party soon began to dissipate. After a while, Patrick was left alone with Trace, who had told the others to go on back to the hotel. He needed this moment with Patrick to really hear the entire story.

"So . . ." Patrick finished the entire tale. "Michael and I thought it a really splendid idea if we masterminded his death and burial to convince those men that their search was over."

"How did the plan fall apart? How did they find out the truth?"

"I don't know. I only know the cowardly way they set about letting us know they knew." He went on the explain what had happened to Hannah. Trace was shocked, and his fury blazed anew.

"You mean they attacked Hannah!"

"Yes, beat her rather severely. Michael was more than angry. I won't state it for a fact, but I'm pretty sure that he went after . . . and killed the man who did it."

"Yes," Trace said softly, "but this is one time I agree with him. I'd have done the same."

"Taking a life has never made your brother happy before, and it didn't this time. It only made his life darker. Murder is never the answer to anything. This kind of thing is the reason he's has spent so many years the way he has."

"I suppose you are right in a way, Patrick. But, you see, men like that, they don't understand forgiveness, or turning the other cheek. For them, the gun is what rules."

"Then, maybe it's up to all men . . . and particularly strong men, like you and your brother, to find a way to bring an end to such actions."

"How?"

"I don't know," Patrick smiled. "I'm just a small-town preacher. That's up to you."

"Thanks," Trace chuckled. "I'll see what I can do."

"The best thing you and Michael can do is to unite with your family again and start your lives over."

"I wish there was a way over this mountain. I wish it could all just go away. One man. It's hard to believe one man can cause all this grief."

"Well, it may be hard for you to believe it right now, but miracles do happen."

"It would take one, and you'll pardon me, Patrick, but they seem to be in short supply lately."

"Oh?"

"What does that mean *Oh?*"

"Your brother has escaped the senator's wrath so far. He's found a lovely girl to share his life. His family and friends have gathered around him. What do you call a miracle?"

Trace gave this a bit of thought, then nodded with a wry grin. "Come to think of it, I guess you're right. The odds against any of these things happening must be pretty big. I hope you're right about more miracles. We need a big one now."

"Well, Trace, my boy, trust me. They come in all sizes." Trace looked into Patrick's eyes and saw a faith there as awe-inspiring as the man himself, and he was surprised that he began to wonder if Patrick just didn't have contact with a force much bigger than random fate.

Reid and Allison walked back to the Grand Hotel slowly, caught in the tangle of the situation. Allison was much quieter than usual, and Reid was uncertain about the cause. Was it worry about her brother . . . or was her agile mind on the man who had brought them all to this.

"A penny for your thoughts?" Reid asked quietly.

"What? . . . Oh, I was thinking about Michael. How difficult it must be. He has Hannah now, and I know that makes him happy. But in the back of his mind he must be thinking about . . . either killing more men, or being killed himself."

"I feel kind of sorry for Hannah, too. Lord, the next few days are going to be frightening for them."

"I suppose it's a bit late for dinner. I'd hoped to at least try and find out what this man looks like."

Reid took his watch from his vest pocket and snapped it open. "When we get to the hotel I'll try to put out some strategic feelers. A few coins to the servants can get you a lot of gossip."

"Gossip?"

"Allison, when a man as influential as a senator comes to a hotel, every servant not only knows what room he's in, but what he's been doing since he got here. You'll get more information from the hired help than from anyone else. At least I can get a description."

Allison squeezed his arm and pressed close to him. "I knew I was picking the right man," she laughed.

"Allison . . . I want you to understand something."

"You're so serious suddenly."

"Yes, this time I am serious."

"All right . . . what?"

"There isn't anything you might want, or anything you might want me to do, that I wouldn't try. Anything except one thing."

"What?"

"I'm not going to let you walk into any real danger." To Allison's surprise, he stopped and looked down at her, and she realized the firm strength of him. "I happen to love you very much, and because of that I brought you here. But there's a limit to how far I'll let you go. I can't let anything hurt you . . . not even *you*."

"Reid, I . . . "

"No, listen to me. We never talked much about my past, my marriage . . . my loss. I can only tell you that the cost I paid then and the pain I'm still getting rid of, is something I can't afford to have happen again. I know how you feel about your brothers. I even know how devastated the war left you when you thought you'd lost them both. But I won't let that blind you. You see, I know how you Cords can often be so single minded. But you have to decide if you really love me. Because, if you do . . . then I want my place in your life, and that place doesn't include standing by and letting this situation do you any harm."

"Quite a long speech, Mr. Anderson." Allison regarded him quite seriously. "I guess the war did scare me. For a long time my brothers were all I had. Do I love you, Reid? Yes. I guess I haven't told you that often enough to convince you, and for that I'm sorry, too. And I guess I've not only been a little blind, but I've taken advantage of your love for me. For that, I'm sorry, too." She put her hand on his arm. "And my consideration for all the hurts you've had has been lost in my desire to have my own way. I won't make that mistake again. Because I do love you, and losing you or having you walk away from me would be the worst thing I can imagine. I'll be careful, Reid, and I won't walk into danger unless I'm holding your hand."

"That's what I needed to hear," he smiled. "So we'll go into this little problem together. No heroic actions on your part. Is that a promise?"

"That's a promise," her smile answered his. "And I promise to tell you I love you more often. You are a strong and very special man, and when all this is over, I intend to prove to you for the rest of my life just how important you are to me."

Again she took his arm, and they started to walk. The silence between them was comfortable.

Allison was surprised and also pleased to find out that beneath Reid's acquiescence to her will was a man who had an unbendable, and perhaps formidable, will of his own. She also made a silent promise. It was time to learn more about this man she was going to marry. It had just occured to her that there was a depth to him that she'd never known. It was an intriguing thought.

Reid, too, was contemplative. The sudden thought of harm coming to Allison, and her unique ability to put herself in the midst of it, had unnerved him. In the beginning, it was the knowledge that Allison would not be happy until she was reunited with Trace and Michael. But now she knew danger lurked on the horizon.

He'd been away, waging a war, when fate had taken his wife and son from him. For a long time he had tried to hide his sorrow in a bottle. He was quietly aware of the debt he owed Trace and Michael Cord, and he would have been willing to pay any price ... unless that price endangered Allison. This was the line he drew and he'd had to make it clear to her. He was surprised at her promise to cooperate. That was certainly uncharacteristic for Allison Cord. He wondered what she was thinking. But if he'd known, it might have surprised him.

They arrived at the hotel and walked into the lobby when the clock chimed ten. There were few people besides the clerk behind the desk. Two were gentlemen, seated in comfortable chairs reading the evening paper. Another two were seated before the large front window, engaged in a game of chess.

While Reid walked to the desk to check that their baggage was safely in their rooms and to get the key, Allison stood in the center of the room, waiting and looking around her. As she turned slightly to face the polished wood door of the bar's entrance, a man suddenly filled it. He paused in the doorway only for a few minutes, but Allison could feel a tingle up and down her spine.

This man exuded the aura of power. His eyes focused on her at once and she could feel the heat of them as he regarded her.

He made a half bow, smiled slightly, and walked a short distance into the lobby where he stood to remove a cigar from the inside pocket of his jacket. He snipped the end, placed the cigar in his mouth, then slowly and deliberately lit it.

Her eyes were so caught on him that she paid little attention to the man that exited the bar behind him and started for the hotel door.

Only when the first man's eyes flicked toward the second, then away, did the second man attract Allison's attention. The contact caught her attention just in time for her to see them exchange a meaningful look. She had no idea who the second man was, but he gave her a feeling of unease. She was reasonably certain of one thing, that the first man was the infamous Senator Merrell.

Reid appeared at her side at the moment, his gaze following hers. Then he took hold of her arm in a firm, unrelenting grip. "Our rooms are ready."

If Allison suspected this was the man they sought, Reid was even more suspicious. And he intended to make sure the didn't do or say the things he saw relected in her eyes. She sighed, nodded, and moved toward the steps with him.

Thomas watched the lovely creature walking away from him with the tall young man at her side. There was something oddly familiar about her, but he couldn't put his finger on what it was.

She had registered interest, he had seen it in her eyes. He was used to seeing such looks in the eyes of women. His wealth, power, and charm had brought more than one innocent to his bed.

The question was, why was the young man with her so protective? Unless, Thomas smiled, unless he sensed a challenge to his possession.

He walked to the desk, to greeted effusively by the night clerk. "Can I be of any help to you, Senator?"

"Yes. The young couple that just went upstairs. Are they married?"

"No, sir. I believe not. They have adjoining but separate rooms."

"How did they register?"

"Both rooms are registered in his name."

"Which is?"

"Reid Anderson."

"Where does he come from?"

"That I don't know, sir. He put nothing but his name in the book."

"I see." Thomas's curiosity was piqued. He fully intended to cross paths with this young lady again, preferably when her very efficient-looking guard was not around. But right now he had another, more important, meeting.

He left the hotel and went down the street. He knew quite well be was a man who was easily noticed, just as he knew any visitors coming to his hotel would be noticed as well. He'd arranged a clandestine meeting near the edge of town, and when he'd finished hiring a closed buggy, he drove toward it.

Crossing the covered, wooden bridge thart marked the border of town, he pulled the buggy to a halt. Minutes later a man joined him in it.

"Senator," Royal Dane said in a clipped voice. "Is it time to get this show goin'?"

"No, not yet. There's something else I want to talk over with you."

"Oh?"

"You ever tangle with Jonas Holt?"

"Come close once. He was pretty good. That's why I was kind of surprised at you hiring me. You don't mind hedging your bets, do you? What's the problem?"

Thomas turned to look at Royal. "He is." The words were precise and final . . . and Royal knew exactly what he meant. Jonas had become more of a liability than an asset.

"When?"

"I'll tell you when."

"It will cost you double."

"We won't quibble about price. If he decides to cross me, I want you ready."

"I'll be ready."

Thomas nodded. There was very little more to be said. A few seconds later the buggy was on its way back to town with its solitary passenger.

Jonas moved cautiously toward the stable. He didn't want to tangle with Cord and his host of newly arrived friends, not yet. The senator had warned him to be cautious. They would play the game out according to the senator's timetable.

He, too, had cast a fleeting glance toward Allison, and had been nudged with the same touch of familiarity, but had shrugged it off. He had other things to concern him. He'd always been a man to attack a problem head on, preferably with a gun. This cat-and-mouse game was not one he was choosing. He was harboring a special hatred for Michael Cord now, and meant to see him lying in the street at his feet.

He considered their first meeting again, for no matter what amount of confidence he tried to portray, the senator had a way of unnerving him. Still, he had his purpose and he would see it to an end—no matter what he had to do to accomplish it . . . and no matter who got in his way.

The senator had made his views clear.

"Jonas . . ." Thomas had said. "I'm glad to see you. But I think you'd better give me an explanation. Cord should have been dead by now."

"For a while we thought he was,"

"I don't understand."

"Well, hold your horses. This is a real interesting story and I need a drink or two."

"I have a bottle in that cabinet. You can drink here."

"You don't have to take chances."

"I haven't gotten where I am by taking chances. And by the way; I had a visitor not long after I arrived," Thomas said as he poured the drinks.

"Oh?"

"Hannah Marshall."

Jonas smiled, too. His memories of Hannah were quite different. "She's a nice little piece, isn't she? Hammond had quite a time with her."

"Hammond . . . and you made a pretty good mistake. I want Cord. Pushing her didn't bring him out."

"No?" Jonas said softly. "Hammond's dead. Somebody beat him all right, and it looks like he was forced to draw on someone."

"Michael Cord."

"Damn right. I'd say the man was pretty fast. I'm going to draw against him if it's the last thing I ever do."

"Not yet. I want him to know when, and how it's going to happen."

"How are you going to do that?"

"Tension . . . suspense. You wait. Before too long Cord will come to me. I want to make it very clear to him, before he dies, that I will be here to see his blood soak into the street. He'll come to me."

"You're sure of that."

"Absolutely."

The senator had been sure then, and he'd seemed just as sure tonight. They had sat over drinks and discussed the rumors and whispers that had eventually reached his ears.

"It seems Cord has gathered more friends . . . and it seems he's well protected," Thomas said.

"Won't do him much good. You say the word and I'll find a way to call him out. He's not the kind of man to take to someone else doing his fighting for him. You give the word and I'll get to him."

"Then I'll be giving you the word soon. I want to be there to watch."

"Fair enough."

"Come again tomorrow. By that time I will have some strategy worked out."

"Strategy?"

"Michael Cord obviously is not interested in doing battle. I'm going to figure out a way to make sure he does."

Jonas had agreed. Now he returned to the deserted Madison Ranch. During the long, quiet night his thoughts remained with Michael.

Reid had seen Allison to her door, but before she went in, he took her arm and turned her to face him. She was grateful for his strong presence and the deep love reflected in his hazel eyes. Her own eyes grew moist, and when he saw the crystal blue of them shimmering, he bent to kiss her lightly.

"I'm sorry you had to run across him," he said softly. "You're much too good to be touched by anything like that. I had a pretty good idea who he was. I knew you did, too."

"I think I knew as soon as he looked at me. He's . . ." Allison
shivered. "Unbelievable."

"Allison, please unlock the door between our rooms. If there's
any difficulty I want to be able to get to you."

"What kind of difficulties?"

"I don't know. I'd rather be safe than sorry. I took the rooms
under my name, hoping no one would connect you to Trace and
Michael. But if they do, you're in a bad position."

"All right. I'll unlock it. But I don't understand."

"I don't either. It's just a feeling. I'm sure he has no way of
knowing you're Michael's sister, but if he did, it might be something he'd try to take advantage of."

Allison was about to deny this, but the remembered look in the
senator's eyes made her realize Reid could be right.

"Reid, the man who came out of the bar behind the senator . . ."

"Yeah?"

"Were they together? I mean . . . I got the strangest feeling.
You don't think that could be Jonas, do you?"

"I don't know. I was so busy watching the senator I didn't notice
him. I didn't like the way he was looking at you."

"Maybe he's just a rich old man who has a taste for young
women."

"Maybe." Reid grinned, and put his arms about her. "I've got
a taste for this pretty, young woman, too." He pulled her gently
to him and kissed her lightly, knowing if he made the kiss any
deeper, he'd be hard put to keep the door between them closed.
"Get some sleep and don't worry. I'm sure," he chuckled, "Michael is in very little danger tonight, and Trace and the others
won't go looking for any either."

"I'll try."

"You know," his smile was teasing, "since your brother got
married here, do you think it might give you a little enthusiasm
for a short engagement and a quick wedding for us?"

Allison put her arms about him and nodded. "It might at that,"
she replied with sparkling eyes. "After all," she added quietly,
"except for Jenny, all my family is right here. Just maybe you
could convince me . . . if you tried."

Reid had always been shy with Allison, only because he still felt the memories of the little girl next door. But this was no little girl in his arms now and the shyness was dissipating rapidly.

In the empty hallway, he again bent to kiss her. Only this time the kiss had no touch of shyness about it. This time Allison was given a small glimpse of the momentous passion Reid had held in check with more effort than she could have surmised. It was a glimpse the opened the door to sensations she had only dreamed of.

An awareness tingled through her, centering a coil of expectant delight within, and as the kiss deepened, she felt the uncoiling send a sudden explosive current through her

Allison, never one to deny a truth, accepted this revelation with sensuous enjoyment. Her body molded itself to his, her arms held him close to her while her mouth softened and parted beneath his. She wanted this newfound pleasure . . . she wanted Reid and did not bother to deny it.

It was Reid who suddenly grasped the last frayed bit of his control. He shook himself mentally, realizing in another minute he would have been past good sense.

He held her away from him, seeing with the eyes of a man who'd experienced sensual passion before. Her heavy-lidded eyes and parted lips combined with her flushed cheeks were enough to tell him that what she was feeling as an echo of what boiled inside him.

"Reid . . . " Her voice was soft as velvet. His name was more a revealing statement than a question.

"Lord, I wish we were home." He tried to laugh to cover the taut nerves and aching need that set his body on fire. "Or else I wish . . ."

"Wish?"

"Never mind. I think you'd better go in." She started to protest, but he interrupted. "Please, Allison, go. I'm not made out of iron and I want you so bad, it's going to cost me a night's sleep anyway. Just . . . go on in."

"All right," she agreed quietly. She turned from him without another word and went to her room.

Inside his own room, Reid closed and locked the door. A second later he heard the bolt on the adjoining door click. The door between them was unlocked. All he had to do . . . He shook his head. It wasn't fair. Allison was a novice at passion, she was alone, she was vulnerable. He gave himself every logical argument he could find and it all did very little to assuage the hunger that had begun to gnaw at him. It was going to prove to be another long, long night.

Reid laughed at himself. He assured himself that he deserved a reward for courage well above and beyond what a normal man could hope for.

He was right about another thing. His body awakened, every sense he had alive and sensitive, kept him from lying down and going to sleep.

So he lay with his hands folded behind his head and let his imagination do what his rigid control forbade his body from doing.

He did not hear Allison pacing the floor, nor was he aware of the moment she slipped out of her clothes and put on a nightgown.

Allison brushed her hair while she studied her face in the mirror. A playful flirt she may have been, but Allison had never felt anything like the sensations she had just experienced in Reid's arms.

She loved Reid. There had never been any doubt of it in her mind. But was she just a bit afraid? She shook her head negatively.

She had just sensed the reason Hannah had come to Michael across all these lonely miles. She understood now the way it must have been between Trace and Jenny.

And finally she realized that she was not a little girl who had to hide behind rigid formalities. Reid loved her. She did not doubt that, either. They were miles and weeks from home. It was not only that she had felt his need for her, it was like an awakening that she felt her need for him.

She rose from the chair and extinguished the lamp in her room Still, moonlight cast it in pale-gray-and-black shadows.

When her eyes had become accustomed to it, she walked slowly to the door that stood between them. She tried it carefully, making herself a bargain. If his side had still remained locked she would do nothing. If it was unlocked . . . then this was something meant to be. Her hand trembled as she put a small amount of pressure on the door handle. It clicked softly . . . and swung silently open.

Reid was caught up in his own imagining, and for several minutes he thought Allison was just a part of it. Then reality brought him upright.

She didn't speak, and he couldn't seem to. She walked to him, sliding her arms around him and feeling his enfold her.

"Allison . . ." His voice was a ragged sigh. "Are you sure? Do you know what you're doing?"

She looked up at him, and he could read the absolute assurance in her eyes. "I've never been more sure of anything in my ife."

When he kissed her now, she knew with a finality that she was right.

Reid was a gentle man, a man who had known the heights to which a caring man could lift a woman. He meant to see to it that this was not a night Allison would ever regret.

His touch was tender, each caress accompanied by a desire to give her all that she would want. The night went from lonely and quiet, to the most perfect of moments. And Allison went from girl to woman on the wings of a love that seemed enchanted to her.

The night passed and day broke. A warm and sunlit day. And all those tied together by the thin strands of fate waited. But there was no sign of pressure from the senator, who spent most of the day in his room. There was no sign of Jonas, either.

This beautiful day turned into another, then another, and again nerves began to stretch toward the breaking point.

By the end of four days Patrick sent word through Mac for everyone to come to his house. Something needed to be done.

But before the meeting was to occur, Allison and Trace were to come, at separate times, face-to-face with the forces that had, for so long, turned Michael's life into a nightmare. For Allison, it happened when she was alone.

When she had awakened in Reid's bed, in his arms, she had searched her mind for regret and found none. She was happy in her choice, and, she thought, more contented than she had ever been in her life.

Reid had awakened to find her smiling at him, and his heart had filled with his love for her. They had made love in the early-morning sunlight that filled their room. Then, later, they had gone down to breakfast. Only to find that the senator was sitting few tables away.

When he saw her again, he bowed slightly and smiled. He made no overtures, but in his subtle way, he had already set about trying to find out who she was.

Reid was annoyed, but he wanted no confrontation. "We can't start anything, Allison. We have to keep things calm and not antagonize him. If Jonas and Michael don't meet each other, our good senator won't be able to do any harm."

"How long can this go on?" Allison demanded angrily.

"Until we make him see how useless his vendetta now is. We have to be a strong force, if we're going to win. But," he reached across the table and took her hand, "we will win, and we will go home."

Consoled by his words, they spent the balance of the day close to the hotel. Both of them wanted to see if the man Allison had thought was with the senator would return, still suspicious that he was the elusive Jonas Holt.

The morning of the third day Reid asked Allison if she would stay in their room while he spoke with a few men in the various saloons. "I can describe him to a few people and they can hopefully put a name to him."

"All right."

"You agree too easily," he laughed. "Are your fingers crossed behind your back?"

"No. I'll be good and stay right here in the hotel. I promise."

"Thanks, Allison," he said quietly. "I don't want to be scared for you. There's no way I can keep my mind on what I'm doing."

"I'll be right here," she said as she went to him and put her arms around him. "I don't want to stand in the way of anything to defeat this man. I want to go home. To go home with you, marry you, and make enough babies to keep Amanda happy for another generation."

"If I needed incentive, that would be the best you could give. I'll be back as soon as I can. Maybe, if you're a good girl, I'll find out where Michael and Hannah are, and we can try to find a way to see them."

"Wonderful!" She was excited. "He deserves to have his 'honeymoon' interrupted. Besides . . . I want to see him so badly."

"Remind me, when we get married, to take you as far away from those brothers of yours as I can. I don't know if I'm prepared to handle this family all in one lump."

Allison laughed, and Reid kissed her and left. Soon bored, Allison decided that going down to the restaurant and having a cup of tea would not exactly be placing herself in any real danger.

When she walked into the restaurant, it was nearly empty. She found a small table in a rather secluded corner and ordered.

When she looked up, after putting a spoon of sugar in her cup, it was because a shadow had fallen over her table. Thinking it was a waiter, she glanced up with a smile. But she was looking up into Thomas's cold eyes and smiling face.

"Hello," she said, a bit too haltingly for her satisfaction. She wanted nothing to reveal her aversion.

"Are you alone, Miss . . . ?"

"No, I'm expecting someone," she replied. She knew he was seeking her name and she had no intention of giving it.

"Ah," he said. "Your young . . . friend. I was quite sure I saw him leave the hotel a bit earlier. Perhaps I was wrong."

His innuendo that she and Reid were more than friends somehow sounded unclean coming from him. And the fact that he must have been keeping track of them made her even more nervous.

"I'm sure he'll be right back," she replied coldly, hoping the chill in her voice and attitude would dissuade him. But it only made him chuckle softly.

"No . . . I don't think so. And I think I have something to say that might interest you. My name is Thomas Merrell. And . . ." he smiled a chameleon's smile, "do I detect a delightful Georgian accent?"

She tried to keep her face expressionless, and again he laughed softly. She was deliberately ignoring his question. Then he drew out a chair and sat down opposite her. "You really are quite a lady."

"I have not invited you to join me," she replied stiffly, "and your name means little to me. It's hardly a formal introduction. So if you will excuse me please, I should like to enjoy my tea."

"Quite interesting," he said softly. "You are a great deal like your brothers . . . Miss Cord."

Chapter Twenty-two

Allison felt the shock pierce her. She put forth a monumental effort to keep herself under control. Still, she knew he sensed her tension and her aversion. Her head tilted up proudly and brilliant sparks lit her eyes. This man had put her brother through hell and she did not intend to let him intimidate her. She held herself sternly and forced a brittle, cold smile. Then she spoke calmly, as if he were of small importance.

"If you know who I am, then why are you here? You must understand you're unwelcome at my table."

"Of course. But I'm only going to be here for a minute. Just long enough to tell you how fruitless the . . . ah . . . gathering of your forces will be."

"I don't know what you're talking about."

"Of course you do," he chided gently. "Your acting abilities have become a bit faulty." He bent forward and patted her hand as one would do to a wayward child. She jerked it away. "You see . . . there are men . . . several men, who are going to see to it that Michael Cord never leaves this town alive."

"Why?" Allison demanded through clenched teeth. "Why are you doing this dreadful thing?"

"I? I, my dear? I'm doing nothing. I shall be no more than an innocent bystander. Actually, it will be fascinating. The first time

I've ever seen a . . . what do you people in this wilderness call it . . . a gunfight."

"This is monstrous."

"I quite agree. Gunfighting in the streets. I do suppose one day this area will be more civilized. But," his eyes glimmered viciously, "until then . . . men will be killing men."

"This is not that kind of a situation and you know it."

"I do?"

"It's you . . . you're doing the killing, and it's not *men* it's *one man*. How can you do this?"

"Shall I tell you, my dear," he said, his voice growing as cold as his eyes. "Shall I tell you how your brother destroyed two lives?" He went on to explain the reason for his vendetta to Allison, and for the first time in her life, Allison looked into the eyes of relentless insanity.

Her face grew paler with every word, when she realized there could be no end to his relentless persuit.

"You've brought your man here," she said angrily. "I'm sure he was that . . . that awful-looking thing who was with you the other night. What will you do," her voiced cracked on her fury, "if Michael kills him?"

Thomas chuckled mirthlessly. "Let me tell you about the differences in the mental workings of the man who likes to kill and the man who doesn't. You see . . . when the men who can't bear killing is forced to, it eats at them. They break easier. They find that killing destroys something within them. They find they can't kill again. It weakens them. They run. On the other hand, the man who likes to kill has an edge. He's the kind of man who will be the eventual winner. But," he smiled again, "in case he is not, I have others . . . plenty of others."

"Michael does not fall into either category," Allison lifted her chin proudly. "He's the kind of man you don't understand at all. A man of honor and pride. No, you don't understand Michael. He won't fight your man. We won't let him."

"Oh, but you're wrong again, I see the pride in your eyes. It's in his as well. I count on it. You see . . . his pride won't let him have all his family and friends protect him. No . . . he'll fight . . . and I can wait. I've waited a long time. A few more days won't make any difference."

Allison rose to her feet so suddenly, her chair fell back and crashed to the floor. Her eyes blazed with the intensity of her outrage.

"I'll stop you." She said the words with vengeance. "Somehow, someone has got to stop you."

"No, my dear, I think not. You see, I'm not the one who will raise a hand. Even when I have the satisfaction of seeing him dead. I can't be touched." His voice lowered. "Think about that. There was no one there to stop Michael Cord from taking my son's life . . . and there will be no one here who can stop his from being taken."

"And that's where you're wrong. I see it so clearly. You did not love your son, he was your obsession. Now, to ease your guilt, you lay the blame elsewhere. You're a man who's dead inside, a man who has nothing but worthless vengeance to fill his dark, ugly life. But that's not so with Michael. Michael has love in his life, and we'll find a way, because we stand together, and you . . . you will always be alone!"

She turned from him, her body rigid, and left him watching her retreating figure with a grimace that was a rare combination of hatred . . . and grief.

Trace kept his eyes open for any overt sign of trouble, as did all the others. He found a few free minutes and went to pick up a few things. It was early morning and very few people were on the street.

He'd just started past an alley when he heard his name spoken with a vicious hiss. He turned to see Jonas Holt, hand hovering close to his gun and one shoulder braced against the building. Trace was completely aware of who he was and what he was. He took a step toward him.

"Don't push it, Cord. You're not the one I'm after, and I have no intention of crossing with you."

"You're making yourself scarce," Trace smiled. "Jonas Holt, isn't it?"

"Yeah," Jonas chuckled. "But not scarce, just patient. I'll move when the time is right."

"Why don't you just leave it? You're not going to get to Michael.

There's too many of us to stop it. One way or the other, the senator—and you—are going to regret you started this."

"You want it to end," Jonas chuckled. "It will . . . in time. For now," he shrugged, "I can wait."

"Let Michael alone," Trace said coldly.

"My, my, little brother need big brother's protection? One of the Cords is a coward maybe?"

"You wouldn't understand a man like Michael."

"I hear he went and got married," Jonas grinned. "Too bad. That's sure one pretty woman to be left a widow. Who knows," his voice grew cold. "I might have to console her a bit."

"You ever touch Hannah again and you won't be able to handle the trouble you ge."

"I'm real scared," Jonas laughed.

"Why don't you take a message for your boss. Tell him he's not man enought to come out into the open and fight like one." Trace's voice grew taunting. "Tell him to stop sending animals to do a man's job."

Jonas's face froze into a mask of fury. Then he realized Trace was deliberately pushing him to end it here.

"Oh, no, friend," he smiled again. "In time, I'll get the one I want . . . the way I want. He can't help it. Those guns of his weigh more than you will ever know. No . . . I'll wait . . . and I'll be there at the right timne." He deliberately turned his back on Trace, who realized just how dangerous Jonas Holt really was . . . Michael's guns weighed too much. The weight would be the thing that killed him. this plagued his mind as he walked back to Patrick's house, and a new idea began to form.

Patrick poured coffee for the mengathered around his table. To his surprise Trace had shown up early, a lot on his mind. Within an hour or two Mac, Jamie, Joey, Brad, Terrance, and Buck arrived.

Before the men were expected, Trace had told Patrick about his confrontation with Jonas, and the idea that had been bred from it.

"So, that's my idea," Trace had said, once he had explained the few things he'd spent so many hours thinking over.

"Your brother has that much courage?" Patrick said, his voice tinged wigh wonde.

"I think he does."

"I guess there is only one way to find out for sure. When Michael gets here . . ."

"No, when Michael *and Hannah* get here. This time I think she should have something to say about it. It's their lives and future together. It will take two of them to decide."

"Of course."

"I know it's going to be difficult for the both of them. But knowing Michael like I do, and realizing what this could mean, I think Hannah will be a supporter of my idea."

At that moment the other group of men came in. They gathered around the table.

"I haven't seen one sign of Jonas Holt," Mac said.

"Well, I did," Trace replied. "I had a nice little talk with our friend. He's a cold man with no heart and no conscience at all."

"You talked to him!" Brad said in surprise.

"I said my piece. I just don't think it did a whole lot of good."

"That's one man I'd love to get my hands on," Mac said, anger, unusual for him, in his voice.

"You stay out of his range, Mac," Trace said quickly. "Taht man is real fast with a gun and you're not that breed. Give him a lot of space if you do see him."

"Yeah," Mac agreed reluctantly. "But to have a few minutes alone with him . . . no guns involved, would give me a whole lot of pleasure."

Again footsteps sounded on the porch and the door opened to admit Quinn, whose first question was about Michael and Hannah.

"Any work, Trace?" Quinn asked.

"No, nothing. Where's Rena?"

"She had to go to her parents' place . . . something about planning our wedding," he grinned. " I don't want to interrupt that. Did you get word the Michael?"

"Yeah, he'll be here. Before he comes, I'd like to try out an idea on you."

"Shoot," Quinn replied, then laughed at Trace's wry expression.

Again, Trace explained his idea and watched Quinn's brow

furrow in concern. "Hell, Trace, that . . . that's sure asking a lot of a man."

"I just think it's one of the few chances Michael might ever have. At least I'm going to suggest it."

"We'll all have to be pretty well on our guard," Terrance added. "It takes only one mistake and . . ."

"Yeah, Terrance," Joey said, "but you don't know Michael. He's not likely to make that mistake." "Not if he really sets his mind to it," Jamie agreed.

"I think," Buck said, "that if Michael does concede to do this, he's going to have to have the cooperation of the sheriff and a few other ment."

"You're right," Trace agreed. "It will take a little effort on the sheriff's part. He'll have to make it clear to the senator and, through the senator, to Jonas. Once he makes the situation clear, it's only a matter of waiting it out."

"I'd be sweating blood," Mac added.

"Michael has a lot of support," Trace said grimly, "and he's strong enough to do it."

"Let's hope all of us are right." Patrick spoke quietly. "I, for one, think Trace has chosen a very wise way, a way that might bring the situation to an end."

"I guess," Trace added thoughtfully "it all depends on Michael now. Michael . . . and Hannah."

When Reid first came back to the hotel, he was counting his blessings, for it was obvious Allison had done just as she had promised and stayed put. He unlocked his door, expecting to use the adjoining door to reach her. He was surprised to find her in his room. But what surprised him more was to see her pacing the floor like an angry lioness in a cage. For a second he could only gape at her. He'd seen Allison in many states of emotion, but he'd never seen her like this.

"Allison!" He spoke her name in total shock. "What happened? Did someone come here?"

"I really never knew, I never understood what Michael was going through until now. I don't know how he has stood it. He must have felt such despair. I can't bear it. I have never felt the urge to kill anyone until today. But if I'd had a gun I would have shot him!"

"Shot him? Shot who? What in God's name happened?"

Allison came to him. "Hold me for a while . . . please," she said as she pressed against him.

As his arms enfolded her, he could feel her entire body shaking. Now his own alarm began to grow. Allison was not as much angry as she was frightened. He should have known. Battle was her way of handling fear.

"Who was here? Did anyone touch you?"

"No. No one was here. No one touched me. Not physically anyhow."

"I don't understand."

"I promised you I wouldn't leave the hotel, and I didn't. But the rooms were so confining. So I decided a cup of tea might help."

"You went downstairs."

"Yes, to the restaurant."

"And?"

"He was there." Her voice was scathing.

"He? Who?"

"The senator." She looked up at him with her eyes filled with shock. "Reid, he is a monster, a smiling, ugly, evil monster. But he is so . . . so powerful. I don't think, even during the war, that I was ever as afraid as this."

Allison inhaled a deep breath and went on the explain all that had been said. "But it wasn't just *what* he said, it was . . . his eyes and his voice, and . . . and all the things he didn't say."

"I think it's time I get you out of here and to some safer place."

"No! Michael and Trace, they need us here!"

"Michael and Trace would be the first ones to want you clear of all this."

"That's why you're not going to tell them."

"Now just a minute!"

"Reid, both of them have enough of a problem on their minds. I have you, and I'm safe with you. He'll never be able to do this kind of thing again. And, maybe it's best that I really understand what Michael has been up against."

"What about me, Allison?"

"What?"

"I said, what about me. Don't you see, I'm scared to leave you alone."

"I won't be alone. We'll stay together. It's not me he wants to harm. Reid, I know it's going to be hard for both of us. But . . . we have each other and together we can do what's needed. If we leave here and join the others, will, it's like we're hiding. I'm too angry for that. I don't know how he'll ever be stopped, but Michael and Trace don't need me to worry about when they try to do it."

"I suppose you're right. All right," he agreed reluctantly. "But I want you close to me from now on."

Allison had just begun to get over her fear and regain her confidence. "Oh, yes, Reid," she said softly as her arms tightened about his neck and drew him to her. "I intend to stay so close to you that you just won't be able to take a breath without feeling me in your arms."

"Sounds fine to me." Reid smiled for the first time since he'd returned. "You know we have to go over to Patrick's house?" he said softly.

"Yes . . . we will," she murmured, "later."

Amid soft, whispered endearments, deep and prolonged kisses that sent their senses spiraling, and much fumbling with buttons, they found each other again and made love with a furious passion that seemed to soothe away any other emotions.

It was some time before they left the hotel and started toward Patarick's house, quite unaware the Thomas stood above them at his window, curtains drawn aside so that he could watch their progress.

When they walked onto Patrick's porch it was to hear the surprising asoud of laughter. After exchanging a look, they knocked.

The door was opened by Jamie, who was still laughing. "Hi, Allison, come on in."

"What's so funny?" Reid asked as they entered the house and closed the door.

For a moment here was an embarrassed struggle for sobriety, and Mac fought the laughter that was easily seen in his eyes.

"We were . . . discussing . . . ah . . . "

"What?" Allison laughed, growing suspicious.

"Trying to figure out how long it's going to take Michael and Hannah to get here," Trace said.

Most of them tried their best not to laugh, and Allison had an even deeper suspicion that much more had been wagered on than a matter of timing.

Reid, too, had amusement dancing in his eyes, enough to make even Allison blush at the knowledge that they could have arrived much sooner. "What is going on, Reverend?"

"Trace has a couple of pretty good ideas that might just work."

"Only it's going to take every member of this group to make MIchael listen to reason and cooperate."

"Sounds like it's something he isn't going to agree with, or like," Reid said.

"You're right there," Trace agreed.

"Trace . . . " Allison spoke up. "If you know it's something Michael isn't going to agree to, how can you suggest it?"

"Because, kitten, it's the only . . . no, the last and very desperate idea we can use."

"What is it?"

"Sit down, you two," Patrick interjected. "Have you eaten lunch yet?"

"No, we gat a late start," Reid said, keeping his eyes from Allison.

"Allison was always one to like her sleep," Trace agreed.

"Well, would you like to eat?" Patrick inquired.

"I'm not really hungry," Allison replied. "I want to hear about this idea Trace has."

"I'll just take some of that coffee, if you don't mind," Reid said.

When he accepted the cup and pulled up a chair beside Allison, who'd sat next to Trace at the table, Trace went on to again explain his thoughts.

At first they were shocked. But after explaining his logic, both began to wonder if it just wouldn't work.

"It has to stop somewhere," Trace went on, "and no matter how you look at it, no matter how much the bunch of us would like to take as much of this situation on and protect Michael, in the end, it's Michael and Hannah who have to do this."

"Lord it's dangerous," Allison breathed.

"Yes," Trace agreed. "But is it any more dangerous than what Michael has been liveing through for the past few years?"

"No, I suppose not," she replied. "Poor Hannah. This is going to be very hard on her."

"You're right, kitten," Trace agreed, "and I've given that a lot of thought. But now that we know the fiber Hannah is made of, it's not hard to imagine her taking this in stride."

"Yeah," Terrance agreed. "Hannah won't let much get to her. She was always like that, even when she was very young. Me and Emily, we'd fight and argue about things with Ma and Pa. but Hannah, she'd just set that stubborn chin of hers and, in her own quiet way, go on and do just what she wanted."

"Some mixture, she and Michael," Trace laughed. "He was always the kid who could laugh most things off. I'll admit he's changed a bit."

"What's been going on in his life would change any man," Terrance agreed. "Killing a man in a war is one thing. Facing down a man on the street is another."

"I do wish I knew how he was going to accept this idea," Patrick said. "He's a very proud man."

"Well, Patrick, there's pride . . . and then there's pride." Quinn spoke for the first time. "Sometimes too much pride can cause more harm than good."

"Yes . . . I guess you're right," Patrick said quietly. For a few minutes there was an introspective silence. Each man thought of what he had and why he would not want to change places with Michael.

The morning after the wedding Michael awoke to the first gray-black dawn.

The cabin lay in shadows, and the bed felt to him like an island. Warm and safe from the outside world. Hannah lay with her back to him, her russet hair spread on the pillow. Very gently he rolled to his side and fit his body against hers spoonlike. He placed his arm across her, nestling her to him. He buried hs face in the mass of her scented hair and lay still, listening to her rhythmic breathing and savoring the feel of her in his arms.

The only thought he would allow in his mind now was the desire to hold time at bay, to keep this precious moment for as long as he could. He didn't want to think of the tomorrow that had to be faced.

No matter what everyone else thought, searching in desperation for a way out, he knew that in the finality of it all he would have to stand and face as much as the senator was able to throw at him. He knew this just as he knew it was inevitable that one day, the man who was a second quicker than he was would come along. It had to be.

He thought of Jonas Holt. This was one of a breed of men he knew and understood. Relentless. Once Jonas's mind was set to face Michael in a gunfight, nothing would make him veer from that path.

It seemed, no matter which way he turned, he was bound to hurt Hannah. Hannah . . . His arm involuntarily tightened around her. His love for her welled up in him so suddenly and so fiercely that he caught his breath. Hannah, precious, loving Hannah, who, he knew, would give her life for him.

Thoughts of her blended in rapid moving pictures through his mind. Hannah, laughing up at him, her green eyes glowing. Hannah, her hair reflected sunlight. Hannah, a lover who could make his head spin, his senses explode, and his heart nearly cease to beat.

He closed his eyes, welding this memory to the others. Her skin was so warm and soft. And then there was the elusive scent that was Hannah . . . Beneath his hand he could feel the steady soild beat of her heart.

"I love you, Hannah," he whispered. "I love you so much."

Her voice startled him. "And I love you, Michael."

"I didn't know you were awake." She turned in his arms and smiled at him.

"I've been awake for a while, but I felt so warm and comfortable, I hated to move."

He kissed her, teasing his lips across hers. "Mrs. Cord," he said. "Mrs. Michael Cord . . . Mrs. Hannah Cord. No matter how you say it, it sounds like music to my ears."

"Even though I had to chase you half across the continent to get you to marry me?"

"That's something I'll never understand, unless you're a lady who doesn't know when she's well off."

Hannah slid her arms around him and moved against him. "Oh, I know when I'm well off," she said seductively. "Right now I couldn't feel better about who I am and where I am. I'm where I want to be."

"I wish I could change things, Hannah. Give you a nice home, raise a family with you."

"I thought we weren't going to let any regrets intrude."

He laughed. "You're right, we did make a promise, didn't we? One real special one. To love, honor, and, if I'm not mistaken, the word 'obey' popped up in there at one time."

"It did mention something like that. You have some command, oh lord and master?" She laughed. "Some special thing I'm supposed to obey."

"I sure do."

"I'll get up and see to it right away. Just give the order."

"The order has nothing to do with you getting up, that's for certain," Michael chuckled as he tightened his arms around her. "Matter of fact, I don't see any reason in the foreseeable future for us to abandon this absolutely heavenly bed."

"You plan on staying in bed . . ."

"Indefinitely," he stated firmly.

She had no arguments, and his seeking hands were already exploring and stirring his senses and hers.

Making love to Hannah, Michael found, was always a unique experience. No matter how often he touched her, it seemed more perfect, more exciting, and more fulfilling.

Later they dressed and walked into the depths of the woods, learning other interesting facts about each other. They talked, sharing the past, the days of childhood and fun. The good days and the bad. Building a barrier against an uncertain future.

That night they put together a small meal and sat on the floor in front of the small, rough fireplace to eat it.

They both felt complete, enough for each other. Both were willing to pretend the world began and ended here.

The hours melted into days, and Michael was not surprised when the outside world intruded in the form of Mac, who unwillingly brought the magic time to an end. Patrick had asked them to come to his house for a meeting.

The next morning both tried to do their best to keep the pretense alive. But the strain in Hannah's voice hurt Michael.

"Do you want any coffee?" she asked, her eyes shifting from his.

"No, we'll have some at Patrick's," Michael answered.

"All right. I'll be ready in a while," Hannah began as she started to walk past Michael. He caught her arm and turned her to face him.

"We knew . . ."

"I know." Her voice was a broken whisper. "I'm not going to cry. I'm . . ." The tears on her cheeks belied her determination. Michael took her in his arms and rocked her against him. But a moment later Hannah stepped back and brushed the tears from her face. "I think we'd better go."

Michael watched her walk away from him and had no words that could have expressed the pride he had in her. They rode toward Patrick's house in silence.

The group was becoming tense, and conversation was sporadic and trivial. When they heard the sound of someone arriving, a tone of expectancy filled the room. Allison was the one who could not contain her enthusiasm a moment longer. She ran to the door and pulled it open. Michael had just reached the bottom step of Patrick's porch when, with a cry of his name, she threw herself into his arms. He hugged her in a fierce bear hug, spinning her around.

"Michael! Oh, Michael, I'm so glad to see you!"

"It's been a long time, kitten. How are you?" Michael asked as he stood her on her feet.

"I'm fine now that we're all together again. Hannah, it's wonderful to see you again. Come on in, you two. Everyone's here and I have some delicious news to tell you." She looked at Michael. "And I've got a lot of other things to say to you, too, my dear brother."

"Oh oh," Michael laughed. "Am I in some kind of trouble?"

"You bet you are," she replied happily as the three walked into the house together.

They were welcomed enthusiastically, and laughter filled the air when Hannah found a small bit of revenge against Jamie, Joey, Brad, and Mac.

"I must thank you boys," she said.

"Us?" Mac said innocently.

"Thank us for what?" Jamie asked, walking neatly into her clutches.

"Why, for all your research, and devotion, and hard work. I'm sure you had to put in a lot of time testing the quality of that fine piece of furniture you provided."

Jamie and Joey, shy to begin with, turned a fiery red. Brad struggled with a choked laugh and Mac laughed outright. Trace and the others were dumbfounded.

"My, my," Allison said, thickening her drawl with pretended innocence. "I do declare you two are blushing."

"Would you like to let us in on the joke?" Trace questioned. He was amused first of all because he'd never seen either Jamie or Joey quite so embarrassed.

"Aw, c'mon, Hannah," Joey complained.

Hannah had to laugh, and they realized she was not going to reveal where they had gotten the bed.

"It's my secret, I'm afraid," she said. "But one day you'll have to share the secret of just how you got your 'friends' to part with it."

"You not ever going to let us forget that, are you?" Mac grinned.

"Not on your life. Just wait. Your day is coming," Hannah said sweetly. "I promise you."

"If I get married, I'm elopin'," Jamie said at once. "I ain't taking no chances."

"This sounds more interesting by the minute," Trace added.

"What's more interesting is what this meeting is all about." Michael looked at Patrick.

"No," Allison interrupted. "I think there are a few other 'interesting' things that have to be taken care of before we get down to business."

"Like what?" Michael walked into her trap a second before Trace could utter a signal of danger.

"Like," Allison smiled at him, "Mr. Michael Aloysius Cord, why you all went and got married without even sending me a wire?"

Hannah gave a delighted laugh and her eyes filled with a promising glow of future torment. "Aloysius?" she repeated with a giggle. "Michael Aloysius Cord." Her voice broke as the laughter would no longer be restrained.

"Michael *Aloysius* Cord!" Mac nearly shouted while others broke up in laughter. Michael scowled at Allison, who took one step closer to Reid. Patrick could not help but laugh at Michael's chagrin and Hannah's silvery laughter. Even Trace was enjoying the situation until Allison turned her sparkling eyes in his direction.

"And you, Trace *Chauncey* Cord. You're no better than he is. I don't know what Mama would have to say to you two. I . . ."

She was interrupted when the group, to Trace and Michael's discomfort, burst into gales of laughter.

"Aloysius!" Jamie roared. "And Chauncey! Oh, Lord, this is rich."

"Jamie . . ." Joey was nearly in tears. "Can you just see the boys at home when they hear this?"

"Yeah," Jamie replied, "and just think about it. When Michael has a son, he can always call him Aloysius!"

"Or Chauncey Aloysius!" Brad joined the fun.

Quinn was trying his best to restrain his laughter, but his face was a suspicious shade of red and his shoulders shook.

"I think," Mac said, brushing the tears of laughter from his eyes, "that this is so wonderful we ought to make it complete. How about it Michael . . . Trace . . . What's Allison's middle name?"

Both brothers looked thoroughly put out and desirous of throttling Allison should she get out of Reid's abnormally close proximity. Now it was Allison who laughed.

"Mama didn't give me a middle name. She wouldn't do that to me. She always liked me best anyhow."

"Allison Cord," Trace said. "One more word and I'm . . ."

"Okay, Trace, okay," she laughed. "As long as you let me be the one to tell them the most important news from home."

"News? What news?" Michael asked.

"That Jenny and Trace are going to have a baby."

The excitement she expected the news to cause didn't appear.

"Shucks, Allison," Mac said. "That's not news. We all know that already. You better think of something better than that. Old Michael here is going to be a godfather."

Hands on hips, Allison gave Trace a look of utter frustration. "Trace Cord, how could you do such a thing?"

"Well, if you remember right," Trace included Allison and Reid in the same look, "you two were supposed to stay home."

"Now, you'all knew . . . or should have known, that I'd never be able to do that." Her teasing smile faded. "I had to know you," she reached to touch Michael's hand, "and Michael were safe."

"I know, kitten. Even using those unmentionable names is forgiven. We're all together. Let's see what can be done."

"We have some ideas we'd like to talk to you and Hannah about," Patrick said, looking at Michael.

"Ideas?" Hannah asked quickly. She was the one more anxious than anyone else to grasp any thought or idea that could give them a glimmer of hope. Michael was not quite as quick, nor quite as easy to convince.

"Actually it was pretty much Trace's idea. It might be easier for him to explain it."

"So, what's on your mind, Trace?" Michael asked.

"The sheriff was one of the men behind your and Patrick's original plan?"

"Yes. He was pretty quick to get to the scene, tell everyone I was dead, and get me hauled away before anyone was wise to it."

"What does he have to do with this?" Hannah was fast to question.

"I don't think the town or the senator is going to swallow the same thing twice," Michael smiled.

"No. No one expects him to. But he could be a liaison between Michael and Jonas Holt."

"How so?"

"Michael . . . it's time you took those guns off and began to live a normal live."

"That thought has crossed my mind a time or two," he said grimly. "But I don't stand much of a chance of doing that and living any longer than the time it takes for the others to find out."

"I don't think so," Trace said.

"How do you figure that?"

"It's a truth, Michael," Trace said gently, "that it's not men who kill, it's guns. Think what would happen if the sheriff makes it clear that you not only will be unarmed, but that any move made against you will be considered against the law and that he'll lock any offenders up at once and have a trial where the senator's name will be branded as harshly and publicly as possible. Senators can handle many things, except a public exposé."

"No!" Hannah said sharply. "He can't go out on that street alone and unarmed. They'll try to get him to fight the moment they see him!"

"Not if one or two of us are with him all the time until the senator gets the message."

"Want me to find the flaw in that for you, Trace?" Michael asked gently.

Trace nodded.

"Time doesn't mean much of anything to this man. If he doesn't do it now . . . well, he can outwait me, you, the boys, the sheriff, anyone. He's a man with more patience than any other person I've ever met."

"I know this would be hard on you and on Hannah. Hell, it's hard on all of us to see you in this kind of mess. But, somewhere along the line you've got to make a stand."

"You think that's never entered my mind?" All present in the room were silenced by the tone of Michael's voice. "The last time I took a stand I killed a boy about twenty-two. I couldn't convince him to let the few hundred dollars the senator paid him go. Want me to tell you how many more there were before that?"

Hannah reached for Michael's hand. "No, Michael, please . . . don't."

"I know how hard it would be," Trace said. "I know how much pride you'll have to swallow to refuse to fight. But even Jonas Holt wouldn't take the chance of being tried and convicted, and Senator Merrell does not want the world to know what he's doing. That threat and your now being surrounded by so many people promising to make it clear will hold him off."

"For how long?"

"One step can lead to another. We'll find a chink in the man's armor. Once we do, we'll bring all this to an end. All you have to do is be patient until we find a way. All you have to do," Trace said softly as he reached out to place a hand on his brother's arm, "is to take off those guns . . . and to trust us."

The brothers' eyes met. Memories passed between them. Memories of a trust built from childhood. Hannah felt as if her heart was being torn in two. She was terrified. With a soft cry she ran to the door and left. Michael followed and the room was left in silence.

Hannah stood on the porch and looked out over the area with eyes so blurred with tears, she couldn't see anything. She did not turn around when she heard the door open again, then close. Michael came up behind her and took hold of her shoulders. He drew her back against him and wrapped his arms around her.

"I don't know if I can stand it," she whispered.

"You can do what you have to do. That's the kind of lady I married. That's the woman I love more with every beat of my heart."

She turned swiftly. "You're going to do it, aren't you!"

He cupped her face between his hands and held her eyes with his. "Not if you don't agree to it," he said gently. "It's us or nothing, Hannah. Please believe that."

"Do you really believe it could work?"

"I don't honestly know."

"But you think it's worth trying?"

Michael dropped his hands, turned, and walked a few steps from her. "You don't know how tired I am of running from him. I have you, and for the first time in years . . . maybe . . ."

She rushed to him and flung herself into his arms. "I'm being selfish. I should have been the first one to see that Trace is probably right. But all I can see is . . ."

"I know. But maybe Trace was right about one thing. It is guns that kill. It's going to be hard on the pride to be protected as if I'm ten, but . . . if it works. Maybe Trace can find his weak spot. Maybe we'll win after all. Then," he took hold of her shoulders and looked again into her eyes, "we could go home, Hannah . . . home."

"Home," she repeated, struggling to find a smile and to stop the fear from bubbling forth. "All right, Michael. If . . . if this is what we need to do, then we'll do it."

"I think, maybe it is what we need to do."

"They'll try to force you to put those guns back on."

"If they want me to reach for something," he tried to laugh, "I'll reach for you instead."

"Make sure you do. I'll be there," she said softly.

"I know." His voice was a whisper as their lips met in a deep, blending kiss.

They returned to the kitchen together and faced the supense-filled room.

The sheriff was more than quick to agree with Patrick, who explained everything to him. It was Bill's idea, and one that Patrick was more than grateful for, to talk to the newspaper.

"Old Jacob Marley is a man who can be trusted, and so is Samuel Brenden. That's a club the old senator will understand. A newspaper is as strong as a gun any day. I'll go talk to them, Patrick, starting with the newspapers first. I think the senator's in for a very big surprise. Tell Michael to stay put for another day. At least until I get my warnings made."

"I'll tell him."

"Patrick?"

"What?"

"I hope this works."

"So do I, and so do a lot of other people."

Sheriff Horton took his hat from a peg behind the door, buckled on his gunbelt, and left for the newspaper offices. From there he would go directly to Thomas Merrell. Patrick walked in another direction. He went to the church, where he knelt, folded his hands, bowed his head, and prayed.

Chapter Twenty-three

Even though his control was perfect and his demeanor calm, there was an intensity of rage in Senator Merrell's eyes such as Bill Horton had never seen before.

"I think you have taken the ramblings of this . . . wild gunfighter to heart, Sheriff. Otherwise you wouldn't be presenting such an obnoxious ultimatum to me. I am a senator of one of the largest of these thirty-seven states."

"Look, Senator," Bill said, "I wired back to St. Louis, to check on the death of your son. That part of the story is true. The men who came here to kill Michael Cord are as real as death. This is my town and you're not the power that can make a circus out of it. There are two pretty good newspapers here with the full intent of spreading this story and your involvement in it all over the country. Scandal can eat a man in politics alive. Now, I'm warning you. I've seen to Michael Cord taking off his guns. If anything should happen to him, it would be murder. In that case, I'll trail down the perpetrators and see to it that one of the biggest trials this century has ever seen is played on every newspaper from here to the East Coast."

"You're making a big mistake, Sheriff Horton."

"I don't think so. This vendetta has got to end and it's got to end now. Let me remind you that there are going to be a lot of witnesses. An armed man against an unarmed man would make one hell of a story.''

As the sheriff closed the door behind him, Thomas's rage broke to the surface. The glass of brandy he had calmly sipped from was smashed against the wall, leaving amber liquid running down to pool on the floor.

He paced the floor, hardly able to contain himself. He'd never bent before anyone's power. His profound sense of his own power and superiority had never allowed it. He had always achieved any goal he had set for himself no matter what means he had to use. Now, the one thing he wanted most was being thwarted by a small-town sheriff and the clan that had gathered around Cord.

He feared ugly publicity, had used it as a tool so often himself that he knew the extent of the harm it could do. The last thing he wanted was for this, to rouse enough interest across the country that it piqued the investigating ability of other newspapers.

His hands were still shaking from his anger as he poured another glass of brandy and tossed the fiery liquid down. No, he had to use his head and not let this insatiable need and deep anger to blind him and force him into doing something he might pay a high price for.

Either this night or tomorrow night, he knew Jonas would make his appearance. He also knew Jonas was not going to be too happy. Jonas was always an uncertain equation in his plans. Always volatile and unpredictable. He was the killer, and that's what Thomas had needed.

As the day wore on, plan after plan was born, only to be eliminated in the face of the same barriers—Michael's friends, the sheriff, and the possible effect of any newspaper stories. He had to think of a way, but as of midnight he still had not succeeded in doing so.

When he heard the soft rap on his door he was still unprepared to contain the ugly force he knew stood outside his door.

Jonas did not react with the same outward rage at the news as Thomas did. But the frigid eyes told Thomas volumes, and those volumes annoyed him.

"You can't just call him out on the street if he's unarmed and has all those friends around him to testify to the fact. This could blow up into something too hot for either of us to handle.''

"You sound real scared, Senator," Jonas sneered. "What's the matter, can't you stand being in the line of fire?"

"Use your head, Jonas, instead of your gun. This is a bigger problem than you think. You'll have the law on your back until they bring you in and hang you."

"There ain't nobody going to bring me in, and I'm not going to have my neck stretched. If Cord draws against me, I'll kill him. I'm faster than him and he knows it. That's why he's hiding behind anything he can. To keep from facing me."

"Don't be a damn fool," Thomas said. "To draw against you he has to be armed, and he is not going to do that."

"That takes more guts than even the great Michael Cord has. I can force his hand."

"How?"

"He's not that tough. If I accuse him of being a coward, he'll strap those guns on again."

"You have to be a fool if you believe he's a coward. He won't do it, Jonas, and if you try, you might just find yourself warming a jail cell. The sheriff meant business. You corner Cord and the sheriff, and those friends of his, not even counting the newspaper people, will be right there to pick up the fight. I'm not going to lose everything because you can't use your brain."

"You going to let him get away with it?"

"No. No, I'm not. But brute force is not what we need right now. We need caution and a lot of thought. You lay low. Let this rest for a few days. Let them relax their guard and think they've won. When the time is ripe, I'll come up with a plan."

"If you think I'm going to sit out there all this time and do nothing, you're crazy."

"Go over to Sutterville for a few days." Thomas reached into his pocket and withdrew a roll of bills. He extracted several and handed them to Jonas. "Have a few drinks, find a girl or two. Relax. Believe me, I'll come up with something soon."

"That's more like it," Jonas grinned.

"I'll get word to you when the stage is set."

"You really are a puzzle, Senator. Why not just have me gun him down from an alley some dark night? No one would ever know who did it, or why. It's simple."

Thomas wanted to tell Jonas what a fool he really thought he was, but he knew it would be of no use.

"No, Jonas, it can't be like that. I want to be there. I want to watch his eyes when that bullet finds his heart. I want to see him lie in the street and die. We'll do it my way."

Jonas shrugged. "It's a waste of time, but you're paying the price. Send word when you're ready."

"I'll do that," Thomas replied. He watched Jonas leave, for the first time trying to consider how he could eliminate Jonas Holt from his life when Cord was dead. He had just begun to realize Jonas could be a weight he couldn't afford to carry around.

Michael knew he had to eventually test his newfound, temporary freedom; he just wasn't as certain it was going to work as some of the others seemed to be.

Besides that, when he took off the guns and holster, whose weight he was well used to, he felt a bit naked and uncomfortable. Hannah knew he hadn't slept. The night after the sheriff had given the ultimatum to Senator Merrell, she had wakened in the wee hours of the morning to find the bed empty, and no sign of Michael in the cabin.

Alarm had brought her quickly to her feet. Clad only in a nightgown, her feet bare, she raced to the door. She flung it open, and relief made her dizzy. Michael stood, one shoulder braced against the wooden porch support. He turned when he heard the door open.

"Michael?"

"I didn't want to wake you, I just couldn't sleep."

Hannah came to him, and he reached out an arm to enclose her. She rested against his side for a minute in silence. She knew where his thoughts were, knew that habit had forced him to try to face them alone.

Michael had lain awake long after Hannah, sated and relaxed from their intense lovemaking, fell asleep in his arms. His world had gone through so many dramatic changes lately that he couldn't quite cope with, or trust, all the good things that seemed to be coming his way. He was more than half certain that if he fell asleep, he might wake up and find all this had been just a wonderful and elusive dream.

Tomorrow he would put this new freedom to the test. He realized that scared him. He, more than anyone else, knew the breed of man Holt was. Was it possible to stop him by any other means than a gun? He wasn't too sure about all the things Bill had said to Senator Merrell, but he'd soon find out how effective the plan was going to be.

He pushed self-pity away. He had known full well that this moment had to come. His only regret was the time he would not be able to share with Hannah if the plan didn't work.

He realized he would be pressured by Jonas, challenged, and he wondered if his courage went far enough to be able to accept that and do nothing about it.

This kind of vulnerability was entirely new to him, and it was pretty hard to swallow. A moment of weakness had nearly overwhelmed him, and he was prepared to refuse the situation when the door opened. He turned to see Hannah framed in the doorway.

There were no recriminations. She simply made it clear, by coming into his arms and holding him, that she already knew and shared his fears.

"Cold?" he questioned softly.

"No," she replied, pressing closer to him. "Michael?"

"What?"

"It's all right to be afraid sometimes. Just remember you're not alone."

"I know, Hannah." He kissed the top of her head and drew her closer to him. "Some habits are hard to break." He'd not denied he'd been afraid.

"I love you, Michael," she whispered. "We have hope, and that is so much more than we had before. It will work . . . it has to work."

"Sure, sure," he soothed. "It will work."

Hannah looked up at him. "You were making plans, weren't you?"

"Not really. Nothing I wouldn't have talked over with you first." He held her face between his hands and kissed her deeply. "What do you say we go into town tomorrow?"

"We have to . . ."

"I know, I know. We have to have a troupe of bodyguards with us. In fact, I have a feeling there are a couple of friends camping out in those woods."

"You know . . ."

"Lord, Hannah, I do know. But I'm not used to being tied to someone's apron string. If things are as the sheriff says, you're witness enough."

"No! I won't let you do this, Michael. We agreed, and pride or no pride, we'll stick to our agreement, at least for the first time. Please."

"All right, all right, don't get upset. Quinn and Rena ought to be good company."

"Yes, and later we can go to Rena's parents' house. Mr. Brenden has wanted to see you. His paper is one of the two that are supporting us."

"You keeping this wayward boy off the streets?" He smiled.

"Any way I can," she responded, her smile matching his. "I know we have to prove this, Michael, but we don't have to do it all in one day."

"You're a remarkably good liar," he chuckled. "Remind me to never cross you. You can outmaneuver the quickest cardsharp on the Mississippi."

"All right. I'll admit I'm scared silly about testing this. And I'll admit I don't want you on the street any longer than necessary. But can I help it if I happen to love you enough that I want you safe?"

"No more than I can help being grateful," he said gently. "And loving you." With the moonlight reflected in her eyes and her very close, soft, and intensely inviting presence, Michael was forgetting about the problems surrounding them, at least for this precious time. Without another word, he bent to lift her into his arms. When he kicked the door shut, it was with a determination to shut the world away for as long as he could.

But the next day was more of a surprise to Michael than anyone. Except for the stares of the people who still could not believe this man they had seen killed was actually walking their streets, the town was quiet.

There was no sign of Jonas anywhere, and neither Hannah nor Michael was aware that from behind the window of one of the small restaurants, Thomas watched with eyes as cold as death.

There were no problems . . . and still Michael's nerves began to tingle, a sensitive reaction that he had depended on the past few years to keep him alive. It took every effort he had to ignore it.

Several hours spent at the home of the Brendens completed the shift in Samuel's attitude. He'd been wrong about Quinn, and he'd been wrong about Michael Cord. This was not a man, like so many had labeled gunfighter, not what his reputation proclaimed. This was not a man who killed for the love and excitement of killing.

Neither Hannah nor Michael realized how tense they had been until they returned home. Only then did Hannah realize she was trembling, and even Michael's hands were not too steady.

But the next day proved so uneventful, and, when all of them came at Patrick's invitation to dinner, Michael was feeling reasonably good. Of course, he knew that the final mountain had not been faced. It sat, quietly ensconced in the Grand Hotel.

No one knew that Michael had now considered his own plan. If the mountain wanted to remain immobile . . . he would go to it. It was time. His only problem was, that no one around him, especially Hannah, was going to let him out of their sight long enough to do so.

He listened to the laughter of those around him . . . and made his plans in silence. Allison kept the lively banter going, and Reid began to wonder if it wasn't mostly out of a kind of raw fear.

"It's going to work!" Jamie was elated. To his mind, every day without event made it more secure.

"We've a long way to go, Jamie," Mac cautioned.

"I think the senator took the sheriff's threat real serious," Brad said. "Maybe he just figured it was too much to go on with and called Jonas off."

"I'd like to believe that," Michael said.

"We can hold out as long as he can," Trace replied. "He has obligations he can't stay away from forever. And I intend to see that the threat follows him right back to Washington. If he's scared of the newspapers here, think of the damage some of the scandalmongers can do to him there.''

"We might have just put a stop to this once and for all,'' Patrick smiled.

"If that man leaves here,'' Rena said firmly, "I'm going to throw the biggest party this town has ever seen.''

"What about Jonas?'' Buck asked.

"If the senator has called him off and leaves town, Jonas will get the idea he has no pay and no support for this little job. What purpose would he have to kill Michael?'' Trace asked.

Michael made no answer, he merely smiled. No one in the room knew what breed of man Jonas Holt was. He would face the senator himself, make it clear to him that no matter what was done he had no intention of drawing a gun against another man. The entire group seemed anxious now for the problems to be held at bay. They blended with their good humor as best they could, because Michael was deep in thought . . . and Hannah knew it.

Michael and Hannah rode slowly toward the small cabin the two of them had come to consider home. At Patrick's insistence they used a buggy, and Jamie and Brad rode beside them, planning to make sure they were secure before they left.

"What's on your mind, Michael?''

"On my mind? I don't have any idea what you're talking about.''

"You've been bogged down in deep thought almost the whole evening.''

"It's nothing really. I guess unwinding from all this has me on edge yet.'' He put one arm around her and pulled her close. "But I'm not so on edge that I don't appreciate my bride. That, my sweet, is enough to put any red-blooded man into a 'bog of deep thought.' ''

"Then let's hurry and get home, Mr. Cord. Maybe I can . . . unboggle your thought.''

Michael laughed and kissed her soundly, then urged the horse into a trot. When they arrived, he unharnessed the horse and hobbled it where it could graze and said good night to Jamie and Brad. Then he and Hannah entered the house.

She responded to his amorous intent, never letting him know that she was still a bit suspicious. She laughed with him and made love to him, hoping she was enough to balance what black thoughts were still lingering in his mind.

Michael refused to let sleep claim him. He had something planned and he meant to see it out. The moon was high in the night sky when he slipped from the bed and quietly dressed.

When he reached the edge of town, he circled around it and tied the horse in the shadows and walked to the hotel.

Hannah had already mentioned the room number, so Michael had no need to reveal his presence to the hotel clerk.

When he paused by the door, he saw a band of light beneath it. The senator had not found sleep easily, either. Michael knocked.

For almost three days Thomas had seethed, watched, and searched for the right plan. He had devised and discarded more than one. In the face of the very thing a politician with a not too savory past hated to face—adverse publicity, he had realized that what was done would have to be done as if it no longer had a connection to him.

He would have to make it appear that he had surrendered to their pressure. Yes, he thought, it would have to look as if it were all Jonas's fault. The only question was *how.*

But the how didn't really worry him. He would find a way. He was an experienced, and in his estimation, a very fine actor. Let them believe he was defeated, subdued. Let them enjoy their euphoria. He would still win.

His plan was simple. He would pay Jonas off and force him to leave town. Then he would give his finest performance and capitulate to their demands. He would inform the sheriff and all concerned that he, too, was going home. But there was another hand, with another gun, and there was a force that the Cords and their entourage had not reckoned with . . . what they would do in the defense of each other. Yes . . . he knew Michael Cord and all those around him. Michael Cord would bend to his will if it meant the protection of those he loved.

He went downstairs to the restaurant for a leisurely dinner and a drink or two before he retired. He would speak to Jonas tomorrow and give him some extra money to sooth his ego.

Jonas had always been a subtle threat to him. Although he had held his own in their confrontations, some deep-embedded fear of this man's unsteady emotions made him nervous. He could handle a man who used his wit and his will to do battle, but the uncertainty of this man's mental stability made him uneasy. Thomas liked to have control of those around him, and deep within he wasn't too sure of that control with Jonas. He left the restaurant and went upstairs. He had left a lamp burning, because he did not like to return to a dark room. When he slipped the key into the lock and swung the door open, he was shocked to find Jonas seated in a comfortable chair.

"I don't like you slipping in and out of my room. I'll send for you if I want you. Besides, you should still be in Sutterville."

Jonas uncoiled from the chair like a lethal snake, his eyes cold and suddenly deadly.

"I don't need to be 'sent for,' like somebody's servant. I come and go as I please. I'm getting damn tired of waiting around. I think it's time to get this thing over with."

"Sit down, Jonas. Have a drink. We have some things to discuss."

"About time you came up with a plan," Jonas said. But he didn't sit down, and Thomas grew tense. He would not sit down himself and let Jonas tower over him, but standing face-to-face was too much like a confrontation, and he couldn't deny the twist of apprehension in the pit of his stomach. He had to bring this situation to an end as fast as he possibly could.

"I've made some changes in my plans."

"Oh? Just what kind of changes."

"I think I have to take a different approach to this Cord situation. I've given it a lot of thought. I think they are much too aware of your presence. Even though you've been out of sight a few days, it's you they're expecting trouble from. So . . . I've decided we have to change that."

"Have you now?" Jonas replied in a calm and very casual voice which should have warned Thomas that this was not quite so simple.

"Yes. I know I offered you a substantial sum of money, and I intend to pay you despite the fact that you needn't complete the job."

"Now that's downright charitable of you." Jonas's voice chilled a bit more and his eyes narrowed as he regarded Thomas. "And just who's going to do this little job in my place?"

"I've hired Royal Dane. He's here in Virginia City. I have not told him who is his target, or what the situation is, but I will soon."

"I know Royal real well," Jonas laughed softly. "Just where is he?"

"He's at Maguire's Boarding House, but what does that have to do with anything?"

"Might just drop by and say hello."

"On your way out of town, you can do just that," Thomas replied angrily.

"Maybe," Jonas chuckled. "But I think I'll stay for another day. Might just drop by and see old Royal."

"What are you planning! I won't have . . . !"

The words were cut short when, in one swift move, Jonas grasped his shirtfront and jerked Thomas toward him. With the same move, he drew his gun and touched the barrel to Thomas's now shocked and sweating face. The man of power, used to wielding the fate of others, was not a man of courage when faced with his own possible death.

"You won't have or not have nothing. I'm a hell of a sight faster than Royal . . . and I'm faster than Cord, too. Now I don't know what kind of game you're playing, but I came here to kill Cord, and I intend to do just that before I leave. To make sure you understand . . . I'm going to fix it so you don't get any more ideas about someone besides me doing it."

"You can't! You damn fool, you'll ruin everything. Jonas, for God's sake, listen to reason."

"I'm tired of sittin' around, just listening to reason. Cord killed Hammond, I came here to kill him, and that's what I intend to do. Now it looks to me like I have to prove a little something to you. You just sit tight, Senator. I'll be back tomorrow and we can make plans to get this little job done."

He pushed Thomas aside and left the room, leaving Thomas shaking, and for the first time scared enough to realize he had created a monster over whom there was no longer any control.

*   *   *

Jonas walked with slow, deliberate steps toward Maguire's Boarding House. His eyes had become twin points of frigid ice. The senator had touched the fury embedded in him, and now it sought the only kind of release he knew . . . violence.

He stood outside the boarding house, and in a voice loud enough to carry within, he called out, "Royal Dane!"

He, like all men of his breed, knew Royal would answer the summons. He was right. Within a few minutes the door opened and a man walked out. He stood, hands hooked nonchalantly in his gunbelt, and smiled at Jonas.

"Well, well. If it ain't Jonas Holt. I thought this territory had seen the last of you. What's on your mind, Jonas?"

"You. It seems you hired out for a little job, a job that belongs to me."

"So you say. Seems the boss found a better man. Why don't you ride along before you bite off more than you can chew?"

Royal was a short, compact man. His eyes were a frosty shade of blue and his hair white with a short, square beard to match. He might have been overlooked in a crowd until one looked directly at him and caught the full force of his deadly personality. Royal had been responsible for the deaths of over twelve men. He was afraid of nothing and no one.

"I'll give you the same chance. Ride out of here," Jonas replied.

Both men's eyes narrowed, their hands lowered to hover close to their guns, and their bodies grew tense with expectation.

"Don't make a mistake, Jonas." Royal's voice lowered and grew more cautious.

"You leavin'?"

"Not without doin' what I came to do."

"You're the one makin' the mistake. Be better to cut and run now . . . else you might stay permanent."

"Quit your jawin', Jonas, and get to it." Royal's voice had the sharp edge of deadly intent.

The time to talk was finished. Both men stood immobile, as if silently contemplating each other. But inside, their nerves coiled tight, and breath seemed regulated to a timed beat.

Their eyes locked, seeking to recognize that flicker of movement in their depths that would herald the slightest move.

When it came, it was a flash . . . a blur of movement so swift it came between breaths. The guns seemed to appear like magic in the hands of each man. Both guns barked. But in the end it was Jonas who walked away from the body sprawled in the street. He chuckled to himself. It was Senator Merrell's move.

Thomas wiped the perspiration from his brow and tried to gather his resources. It would be better in the long run if Royal Dane killed Jonas. That way there would be no connection between him and Royal.

Still, he had to make a plan that would make his position certain. He had to find a way to force Michael Cord to put his guns on of his own volition. He also had to find a way to hold off Cord's horde of supporters and force them to leave. He had to find their most vulnerable spot.

His nerves were frayed, so he had a drink, then decided to get some air before he retired. He had just stepped back into the hotel when the bustle of excitement seemed to fill the lobby.

He, like the other onlookers, waited expectantly. Eventually a man came in, flushed with news.

"There's been another gunfight. Down at Maguire's Boarding House."

Thomas sat frozen, not wanting to seem to be inordinately interested. But he could have struck the man for not saying who got shot . . . who was dead!

But it was soon obvious that the man only knew of the action and not the names of the men involved. He was about to try to find out himself when a few words were spoken that confirmed his worst thoughts.

"One of 'em . . . the dead one . . . seems he was a boarder at Maguire's. Nobody, not even the sheriff, knows why. But there was a couple of bystanders and they say it was a fair fight."

Royal Dane was dead! Thomas felt the initial frustration. But he was not a man to panic or not to be able to come up with an alternative plan. And it looked like that alternative plan had to include Jonas Holt. He just had to keep control, and to figure out how to detach himself from Jonas so he would not be the condemned one when the situation was finished.

As he returned to his room, he made himself a promise. Once this was over, he was going to find a way to rid himself and the world of Jonas Holt.

Once in his room, he settled himself in to do some deep thinking.

He allowed himself to drift back into time, to the day that he lost all that he felt was worth living for. His position, his career, had been secondary to his almost obsession for his wife and the only child she would ever be able to give him. They were his possessions, his veneer of civility, and Michael Cord had taken them from him.

His whole world, his plans, his wealth, every move he made had been for Scott. Until the day they had come to him. Come to him and told him that all the light and breath of his life had been taken away. With one bullet, in one explosive moment, Michael Cord had taken his son's life—and his own—away.

It had all been, Scott's friends had told him, because Cord had stolen a woman Scott had wanted. Because Scott was rich and charming and had the world at his feet, a cold man like Cord had been jealous. The jealousy had turned to violence when Cord had found Scott and Marie together. He had challenged and killed Scott. As far as Thomas was concerned it was murder, and he would not rest until he witnessed Michael Cord dying in the dirt at his feet.

He sighed deeply and reached in his pocket to remove a picture he always carried, of himself and Scott, arms around each other and laughing into the camera.

"It has taken a long time, Scott. I have pursued this man across a continent. But this time I will finish it. I promise you, my son. I will finish it."

His gaze was so intent, his thoughts so focused, he did not hear the first rap on the door. Only when it was repeated did it draw him back to reality.

A reality that was again shattered when he saw Michael Cord standing in the doorway.

Chapter Twenty-four

The train that left St. Louis for Virginia City was not an ordinary one. It carried over fifty military men, fifteen secret service men, and a group of others whose identities were never revealed for political purposes. None of the four cars carried ordinary passengers. The last car was also unique. On the back platform rail, red, white, and blue bunting was hung. Over that was the seal of the man who occupied it.

Within the car, Maxwell Starett sat at a small, square table with a fascinating hand of cards, a full house. Nearby sat Lee Chu, who had watched this contest with the utmost interest.

Behind Lee Chu, in a plush seat near the window, Stewart sat looking out at the passing scenery. He was a bit more than disgruntled, he was mystified as well. Mystified, and yet totally intimidated and admiring of the man who sat across the table from Maxwell.

President Grant had his sleeves rolled up, his tie loosened, and a cigar clamped between his beard-covered cheeks. He was glaring balefully across the table at Maxwell, who smiled benignly.

"You son of a sea cook, I'll be damned if you'll bluff me out of this one," Grant said, joyfully belligerant. He'd not had so much fun since the war ended and he'd taken the oath of office.

"I have two hundred dollars on that table that says you'll have to call to find out," Maxwell laughed.

Grant took a deep drink of the whiskey that half filled the glass that was placed at his elbow. It had fascinated Lee Chu to see how much whiskey Grant could consume without even showing it.

Stewart glanced at Grant. He still could not quite believe what had seemed to happen so quickly. Grant had cast him that 'I'll stand for no interference' look and told him they were changing their plans.

"But, sir," Stewart had argued, "our schedule . . . our plans. We'll be so far behind. People are expecting . . ."

"So, we're behind. Being President," Grant had roared his hearty laugh, "makes it pretty damn hard for anyone to argue with you. All will be forgiven, Stewart, trust me on this. Too many people want too many favors to even pretend to be angry with me."

"Sir . . ." Stewart had tried to make sense of it. "Think of the security risk! This is dangerous."

"Stewart . . ." Grant had clapped him on the shoulder so hard he had nearly staggered him. "After the war I've been through, I understand that if a man finds a way to kill me, all hell won't stand in his way. I've fought side by side with this man and he protected my back more times than I care to count. If I pay it back this once, it's worth it. Did you send all the wires?"

"Yes, sir," Stewart said with resignation. When Grant was in this mood, there was no stopping him. And as a matter of fact, there was no stopping Grant no matter *what* he wanted to do.

Now they were on their way to Virginia City with the strangest set of men, and Stewart didn't know why except that they were friends.

"All right, I call," Grant said. "What do you have?" He gazed at the cards Maxwell laid on this table with a remarkably gloating laugh. "By God, you got me again. I'd swear you cheat somehow."

"I don't cheat," Maxwell laughed. "You just don't play poker very well."

Grant had to laugh in response, and even the usually silent Lee Chu smiled with amusement.

Grant rose from his seat and stretched to relax his tight muscles.

They had been playing poker for several hours. Then he took out his pocket watch, snapped it open, and cursed mildly.

"No wonder I feel like I could eat a horse, it's past seven o'clock. Stewart, go tell them to get that meal on."

Stewart left the car and went into the next, still wishing Mr. Maxwell Starett had never entered his life. He liked things precise. Schedules, once formed, should never be deviated from. Grant was the most nonconforming, unpredictable man he'd ever known . . . and he would have given his life for him.

Grant and Maxwell exchanged a glance as Stewart left, and both smiled.

"Your secretary seems a bit disgruntled," Maxwell grinned.

"Stewart thinks he's ordained to run my life," Grant responded with a throaty chuckle. "He thinks I should mind my p's and q's, and be on time at all times. It's his job and one day, when he retires, I bet he'll have a lot of stories to tell his grandchildren. I'm making them better for him, that's all."

"I can't begin to tell you how grateful I am that you decided to do this. It's one man's life, and I know you have much greater responsibilities."

"I'm not doing it for you," Grant replied with a serious demeanor that puzzled Maxwell for a minute. "I'm doing it to impress Lee Chu. Maybe he'll finally realize that I'm such a powerful man that he'd be better off with me."

"Am afraid is still impossible," Lee Chu said mildly. "One can see your perfection, so is unnecessary to need care. On other hand, Mistah Maxwell is a man of great imperfections and needs continued assistance."

"Thank you very much, Lee Chu," Maxwell said dryly.

"Dinner is ready, sir," Stewart said as he stuck his head back in the door.

Maxwell and Lee Chu rose to join Grant, who was promptly followed by three very impressive-looking bodyguards. This was necessary but something Grant did not relish.

As they ate, the two men talked again of the past they had shared, and Lee Chu enjoyed what he saw. These two would have all that was necessary to save Michael Cord . . . if they got to him in time.

*   *   *

Thomas stared at Michael for a second, too surprised to react at once. Then the reality of it awakened his consciousness. He backed up a step and smiled a smile that could have chilled the coldest of ice.

"Well, well. Mr. Cord. To what do I owe this very dubious pleasure?"

"I want to talk to you."

"Oh, by all means. Come in, come in." Thomas might have smiled and acted the host, but he was not only curious, he was somewhat amazed that, knowing his hatred forhim and his pursuit of him, Michael would come here at all. "Whatever you have to say, say it quickly, because it will mean very little anyway." He gave Michael a swift persual. "I see the sheriff was right. You have taken off your guns. How long do you think it can last?"

"A lifetime."

"Don't put much faith in that."

"I think the sheriff has explained about murder to you. I don't think you'd be so foolish."

"I can wait. Somebody will do it."

"I've been thinking for a long while about the explanation you must have gotten about what happened."

"A perfect explanation," Thomas snapped angrily. "You killed my son. What more explanation do I need! Killed him in cold blood."

"That's what I thought," Michael said wearily. "You've been sold a bill of goods that put you on this bloody rampage."

"Please," Thomas said derisively, "is this the best you can think of? If it was different, why did you run?"

"I was . . . it was a mistake. The war had . . . done its share. I guess I wasn't exactly in control of the situation."

Thomas watched Michael for a moment, a dark frown on his face. "If it's sympathy you want, you have come to the wrong person."

"I'm not after your sympathy. The only reason I came was to give you the truth, and to tell you that I will never again put those guns back on."

"The truth," Thomas sneered.

"Yes, the truth, whether you want to hear it or not. Your son was not the angelic boy you thought he was. He was a spoiled child. But even he didn't want this fight. He was pushed into it by his so-called friends, who were out for an evening's amusement." Michael went on to tell Thomas exactly what had transpired that fateful day. "He died because he wouldn't listen to reason any more than his father would. He was drunk and asking for a problem. But even during the worst of it, I would never have killed him. But he left me little choice. Like a coward he drew his gun when Marie was between us, thinking it would stop me. He never, in his drunken state, thought that he would kill her . . . or that he was forcing me to defend myself."

"You're trying to tell me Scott killed Marie!"

"That's the way it happened."

"You've said your piece. I don't believe a word of it. My son's friends were good boys. They wouldn't have forced him to fight, and especially to fight if he was drunk, which I don't believe, either. I think there's little left to be said."

Michael sighed. "I suppose you're right. I just thought there might be one last chance to tell you the truth. You may not believe me, but that is what happened that night. You try to ignore it if you can, but no matter what you say or do, you can't change the truth. This, at least, has never been on my conscience. You've sent men against me. Their lives aren't on my conscience any longer, they're on yours. I'm going to live my life from now on in peace, and that peace means I'll never pick up my guns again. From now on, as Sheriff Horton and the newspapers have said, it's up to you. They'll do as they've said they would. I'm doing now what I know is right. I'm not going to kill a man again, and you don't have the power to change that."

Thomas stood quietly, only his eyes revealing the fire that burned within him, eating his soul and destroying reason. "Can I not?"

"No, because you are not the breed of man who can fall from grace. You're not the breed of man who can pay the price for what you do. You need others to do that. No, I think you know when it's time to end it."

"I loved my son," Thomas said softly. "Did you know my wife grieved herself to the grave because of what you did." His voice dripped venom. "Tell me, Mr. Cord, do you have someone that close to you . . . someone you love with every breath in your body. Maybe it'stime you learned what that kind of loss is like.''

Michael's face paled a bit, and he could feel something deep within him grow hard like a core of steel. For a second he almost felt his control slipping.

"I don't need to learn what that kind of loss is like. I've had my share of trouble. But I will tell you this. No man who is a man fights his battles with the innocent.''

"Ah . . . the innocent. I've heard it gossiped through the town that the 'ghost' of Virginia City has taken himself a bride.''

Michael felt a sickening fear. They could try to reach him through Hannah. She was his weakest point.

"If you think that disaster wouldn't follow you from here to Washington, give it another thought." He inhaled deeply. "Hannah won't be out of the sight of me or my friends until this is finished. Don't ever think of touching her again.''

"I've made no threat. Your . . . friends have made their positions clear. I see everything as being up to you. How can I be to blame if you choose to put your guns on again and fight? That is your choice, not mine.''

"That will not happen . . . and this 'ghost' has a very normal mind. I can take care of my own. Don't doubt that.''

"I see no point of us threatening each other. What you decide to do is your choice. I no longer have any choices.''

Michael doubted that Senator Merrell had truly backed away from anything. But he at least had found out if the truth would have any effect on the situation. Now he knew all the truth in the world made little difference to a man too blind and full of hate to accept it. He had to make one point clear. As he walked to the door and opened it, he turned to face Thomas.

"Your man, Jonas, is fast . . . real fast,'' Michael said calmly. "But, I'm faster. You made me that way. Keep that in mind . . . I'm faster." He left, closing the door quietly behind him.

Michael knew, as soon as he grew close to the cabin, that he was going to be facing a problem. He'd left the cabin in darkness and now a light flickered within. Hannah was awake.

His mind set on bringing the truth to Thomas, he had assured himself that he would be home long before the time came to rise. There was not yet even a hint of dawn in sight.

He walked across the porch and opened the door.

Hannah was seated Indian fashion in the middle of the bed, and the lamp glow reflected in her eyes matched the flame that was burning from within. It was balanced evenly between a furious anger and an even more controlled fear.

"Where have you been?" The question was asked softly, much too softly. "Out for a relaxing midnight ride?"

"I rode over to see the senator." Michael said it bluntly, first because there was little use to try and deny it, and second because lying to Hannah was not only something he never intended to do . . . he wasn't too sure he'd get away with it if he tried! Hannah was silent while she attempted to digest the shock of this news. "It had to be done sometime, Hannah. I needed to know if he knew the truth about how his son really died."

"And did he?"

"No, he didn't."

"And you enlightened him."

"Yes . . . at least I told him the truth. He just didn't believe me."

"Did you really expect him to?"

"I don't know. I just felt it had to be done."

"So you slipped away in the middle of the night and scared the living heavens out of me." Her voice was rapidly scaling up, as control seemed to be slipping from her.

"There was nothing to be frightened about," he replied, and sensed at once that he'd chosen the wrong thing to say. She fairly leapt from the bed, and in a moment stood inches from him.

"How dare you say a thing like that to me! How much do we have to go through before you realize I'm frightened every time you're out of my sight? How can you act as if you're alone in all this! You're not playing fair, Michael!"

"Are we having our first fight?" He tried to make the statement sound amusing to take the edge off her fear, but it didn't work.

"You bet we are!"

"Come on, Hannah. It's not as bad as all that. It was a mistake, I'll admit. But . . ."

"Not as bad as all that! We've got a relentless man out there who would pay any price to see you dead. I wake up, hoping to find you safe, and instead I find you gone! How was I to know you weren't dead or lying somewhere hurt and alone! Are you trying to tell me I should have just turned over and gone back to sleep?"

The past few years, Michael had lived on the edge. His marriage was too new for him to be able to adjust to the fact that someone else really knew and shared his fears. He was not used to someone sharing, to someone walking the edge with him, holding his hand and offering a haven of support. Hannah's words crashed against him with an almost physical force.

"I'm sorry. I didn't mean for it to seem that way. If I made a mistake it was only because I was as scared for you as you must have been for me. Like I said before, old habits are hard to break. I have to ask you to forgive my inconsiderate stupidity with a promise that it won't happen again."

"I'm too mad to forgive you so easily." Her anger faded before the fact that he was here, he was safe, and he was contrite.

He saw the forgiveness in her eyes long before she could voice it. He put his arms around her and drew her close. "I can fight this now with all the strength I get from you. I can't fight you, Hannah, because I love you and need you too much . . . and because I know your anger is justified. I just . . . well, I'm not used to reaching out to another person. Can you understand?"

Still reluctant to let go of her unspent anger, she sighed and nodded. But Michael refused to let her move out of his arms. She looked up at him and saw the tenderness there. This man, who had been so brutally hurt, could be so gentle. It melted her last reserve of anger.

"I didn't mean to be so angry. It's just that, when I woke up and you weren't there, I was so scared."

"I know. I guess it's going to be hard for me for a while, and if I hurt you along the way, I don't mean to. Don't let go, Hannah," he whispered against her hair. "That's one loss I couldn't take."

Tears pooled in her eyes, and she clung to him. "I won't." Her voice caught. He lifted her chin with one hand and bent to kiss her tear-moistened mouth. The fire of their past contact gave way to a deeper, yet gentler possession. And when Michael took her to their bed it was not with the fire of hungry new love. It was an awakening to a deeper and more meaningful expression. It was a forging not only of bodies but of spirits as well.

As they came together, Hannah could see that Michael, too, wept. For the beauty of it washed over them like the soft waves of a peaceful sea. Both had found their haven for any of the storms life would throw at them.

Later, they drifted off to sleep, enclosed in an embrace. The last thing Hannah heard was the sound of the solid beat of Michael's heart, combined with the distant sound of a train whistle.

Maxwell and Grant were both still awake in the wee hours of the morning. Lee Chu, who to Grant never seemed to sleep, provided hot tea almost before they asked for it.

"Thank you, Lee Chu," Grant said, as he accepted the cup of steaming liquid.

"Quite welcome." Lee Chu's wise eyes looked closely at him. "Make special tea every night for Mistah Maxwell. Perhaps could give herbs to cook . . . would bling much welcomed sleep."

"I'd appreciate that, Lee Chu. I don't have the faintest remembrance of the last time I got a really good night's sleep." He sighed as he sipped the tea and stretched his booted feet out before him. "This office," he said grimly, "is not quite all it's cracked up to be."

"It's quite a responsibility," Maxwell agreed. "I know I wouldn't want it. How soon do you think it will be before we get to Virginia City?"

"My engineer says in about another half hour."

"Lord, I hope we're in time."

"We'd better be," Grant said grimly. "I had Stewart wire for a complete, updated report on Thomas Merrell's activities . . . a private report. The senator's even more unscrupulous than I thought."

"He'll be hard to stop."

Grant grinned. "No, he won't be hard to stop. I know every breath he's taken in the past ten years, from the ladies he keeps in assorted places to the suspicious defense contracts . . . coupled with some bank deals, I'd like a closer look at. No . . . he won't be hard to stop."

"You'd destroy him?"

"Oh, no, absolutely not," Grant laughed aloud at this. "A strong man with a lot of power is a good tool." He winked at Maxwell. "I'll just let him know what I can do with it. From tomorrow on, Senator Thomas Merrell belongs to me."

"It's hard to believe that a man who has as much as he has could carry on such a vendetta."

"I know all about that, too. I suppose Michael explained a great deal of it to you already though."

"Well, pretty much just the situation that made him run."

"The senator has been blind, both to his own failings and to the son he was so obsessed with. You see, I think he had high aspirations for the boy . . . the presidency, when he was groomed enough. Scott as President, with him standing behind it pulling the strings. I don't think it was just the death of his son. I think Michael killed his poisonous dream . . . and that, a man like Senator Merrell can never forgive. He got drunk on power. He wanted more."

"A man like that running the country!" Maxwell mused thoughtfully.

"Could cause more havoc and destruction than any war ever did. So you see, Max, I'm glad you brought him to my attention. I've been caught in the web myself, and I've overlooked too much."

The shrill sound of the train whistle brought them out of their deep conversation.

"We're here," Grant said, as he rose to his feet. Stewart opened the door and stood just inside.

"Mr. President?"

"Yes, Stewart, what is it?"

"I have some information that I have to discuss with you in private."

"Excuse me, Max."

Maxwell nodded. "If you don't mind, Lee Chu and I will step out on the back platform. Since we're pulling into Virginia City, maybe we can get a closer look at it."

"I'll be finished here shortly and we'll move fast once we arrive. Much as I'm enjoying myself, I can't remain here too long."

"Of course. We'll be ready to do whatever you say, when you say the word."

Lee Chu accompanied Maxwell to the back platform and they watched the town appear as the train pulled into the station.

There was no one who knew of the train's arrival except the two men on duty at the station, and they were not only awed, they were entirely intimidated by Grant's protective guard as they made sure the perimeter of the area was placed under heavy guard. They were told to remain in the station, that the balance of the night passed in complete silence.

Thomas awoke from an unremembered dream in a cold sweat. He had to think for a minute to figure out what had really awakened him. It had been the shrill sound of a train whistle. It had seemed to echo in his dream like the scream of a banshee.

He suddenly felt the darkness around him like a potent, dark force. It seemed to urge him from the bed, and he lit a lamp quickly, breathing a relieved sigh when the room flooded with mellow gold light.

Still, he felt an oppressiveness that made him certain he would not be able to find sleep again. He sat in a chair near the window and looked out on the darkened, deserted streets of the town.

He saw the sheriff cross the street, making his usual nightly rounds, and the indignity broiled within him. This man had had the effrontery to try to thwart his plans! Well . . . he intended to see that *he* was the one who would be thwarted.

Since word had come to him that Royal was dead he'd faced the fact that Jonas was the only way. He had known Royal's speed and he was certain if Jonas beat him, he would be fast enough to beat Michael Cord as well.

He had met again with Jonas, and their plan was one that would work. It would be Cord who would come for Jonas. It would be Cord who would force Jonas into a fight. And when Michael Cord was dead, there would be no one to proclaim him guilty, for it would be obvious to the law and to the citizens of Virginia City that the entire fight was forced by Michael Cord.

It was a matter of timing. By dawn the plan should be set into motion.

Patrick, too, was drawn from sleep by the train whistle, and deep within him, the fact registered that there had never been a train through at this time of the morning. But he was too drugged with a relaxed sleep, a sleep he had not enjoyed for a long time.

Trace and the others stirred, too, but did not awaken. The railroad had been their home for a long time, so the whistle of the train was not unusual.

Only Sheriff Horton, who had just checked the last of the doors of the banks and shops, had started back to his office and paused with a puzzled frown.

No trains came through at this hour, and this was another of his responsibilities. To make sure unusual things were thoroughly examined. He started to walk toward the station.

But just as he crossed the street he could see there was an unusually large group of men, not only scattered over the train platform, but surrounding the train as well.

"Must be somebody pretty damn important," he muttered. He started across the street, but had barely gotten halfway when he was spotted. Three men disengaged themselves from the group and started toward him. They met in the center of the street.

"Evening, gentlemen," Bill began. He smiled, but he saw very little humor in the narrowed and observant eyes of the three. "I'm Sheriff Horton. This train is a bit unexpected. Mind telling me what's going on?"

"Brady," one of the men said to a second. "Go on back and tell him we got an unexpected visitor. See what he wants to do about it. Don't forget to tell him it's the sheriff."

"Yes, sir." The second man detached himself and loped toward the train.

"Somebody real important, I take it," Bill grinned, but there was no humorous response. Whoever this passenger was, he thought, these men take their protection of him real serious.

"Yes, sir. Real important."

"You stopping here a while?"

"I don't know, sir."

"You picking up or leaving people off?"

"I don't know, sir."

Bill really was puzzled. There was not a doubt in his mind that the man he was talking to was quick, astute, and intelligent. He could read it in his eyes. It was just as obvious that until he got orders to do so, he had no intention of telling anyone anything.

Bill inhaled a deep sigh. He was a patient man. He was also too smart to start an altercation before he knew what he was walking into. Besides, these men looked much too serious to suit him. And to top it off, the way he figured, he was outnumbered by about fifteen to one . . . as far as he could see. This train was an armed camp. He waited.

After a short, and very silent, wait, he could see the second man returning with the same loping trot.

"He said to bring the sheriff on in. He wants to talk to him."

"Now just a minute." Bill was becoming annoyed. He was not at the beck and call of some rich, arrogant businessman. This was his town and he damn well expected some answers.

"Please, sir," the first man said. But his crisp-no nonsense attitude made Bill sure he wasn't really asking for any favors. He motioned Bill toward the train. "There will be no trouble, if you will please just come with me." Bill could also hear that the last sentence was more a subtle threat than a request.

"All right." He was more curious than annoyed. He walked to the platform and followed the first man into the train, aware that the others were right behind him.

The first paused at the door to block Bill's way. "I'm afraid, sir, you shall have to leave your gun outside . . . and we shall have to search you."

"I'm a sheriff, for God's sake! Not some assassin. Who the hell is this man anyway?"

"Your gun, sir," the man repeated.

Bill did not really believe he was in any danger, but he was highly annoyed as he unbuckled his gunbelt.

Once they had made sure he had no other weapons, the first man swung the door open and let Bill precede him into the train car.

Bill might have been amazed at the plush comfort of the car. He might have been upset at the mystery that surrounded it. But none of these emotions could compare to the combination of shock, awe, and disbelief as he gazed at the three men in the room.

One was a Chinese gentleman, the second man looked like the very successful businessman he had expected. But the third. . . !

The third was a man whose face he'd seen, a man whose reputation he knew, a man who demanded respect from every person around him. Bill broke his silence for one shocking moment.

"Good God . . . it's . . ."

"This is Sheriff Horton, Mr. President," the first man said. "Sheriff Horton, this is the President of the United States."

"Good morning, Sheriff Horton," Grant said, as he motioned Bill closer. "Come in, come in. You are just the man I want to see. Have a seat and a cigar. I think you and I have a lot to talk about."

Dazed, Bill sank into the offered chair. He accepted the cigar with a trembling hand. He knew he had to listen, for it had become impossible to talk.

Chapter Twenty-five

The day began slowly, this warm morning in Virginia City. Stores began to open with awnings dropped into place and sidewalks swept. The sounds of an awakening city . . . the rattle of harnesses as wagons and buggies began to move.

Very few noticed the train that sat silently at the station. Nor did they notice the four men who left it and started to walk toward the Grand Hotel. Only when a few pedestrians recognized their sheriff among them did they pause to speak or to watch. There was something mysterious and very powerful about the men, and it roused deep curiosity.

When they reached the Grand Hotel, Sheriff Horton continued on toward Reverend Carrigan's house while the other three entered the hotel.

The clerk watched wide-eyed, with no thought of hampering the movement of the three, as they passed his desk and started up the stairs.

Thomas Merrell rose early. It was habit, and it was also tension. If all his plans went well, the problem would be finished today.

He had met with Jonas just before dawn and they had laid their plans out carefully. Now . . . he had to wait and let Jonas play the game out.

When the knock sounded on his door, he was completely surprised, but was certain it could be nothing too important. He was smiling when he opened the door, but the smile faded as he recognized the men who stood before him.

"Brady, Tucker, Stevens . . . What are you doing here? I thought you three were the President's shadows. How did you manage to get this far away from him?"

"Actually, Senator Merrell," Brady said, without a trace of a smile, "we're not very far away. The President's train arrived in Virginia City last night. He's quite interested in speaking with you, sir. If you wouldn't mind accompanying us . . . please."

Thomas's smile was weak, and he had no idea why he should feel a tingle of apprehension so sharp that it made him perspire. Then another thought came to him.

"How did he know I was here . . . or where I was staying?"

"I'm sorry, sir, but the President has not asked us to contribute any information. He simply requires your presence as soon as possible."

"I'll drop by after I've breakfasted."

"I'm sorry, sir, but our orders are to accompany you . . . now."

"I see." Thomas was clever enough not to cross words with these men, and ambitious enough not to cross words with the President. He knew that once Grant's eye was on him, especially in anger, the scrutiny could make him quite uncomfortable. "I'll go with you right now."

There was no conversation as they walked toward the train, but Thomas's mind was humming. What could the President be doing here, and just why would he know where he was staying and more important . . . how did he know he was here?

Maxwell and Lee Chu had left the train even earlier and started toward the Settlers Hotel. Sheriff Horton had been the one to tell them where Trace could be found. Lee Chu was regarded with some interest as they passed.

Patrick and Trace were seated at Patrick's table having coffee. Unable to sleep, Trace had walked to Patrick's house to talk over the situation, looking still for any flaws in the plan.

"I'm sure this is going to work. It's been a few days, and Michael has been coming and going freely. It looks like you've won," Patrick said.

"I won't believe it is working until Senator Merrell has left town and I'm certain that gun of his is gone as well," Trace replied.

"One step at a time. Bill has made it pretty clear to him, and I think the senator knows he meant it."

"Yeah." Trace sipped his coffee thoughtfully.

"But you still have some uncomfortable feelings?"

"I don't know why. Don't ask me for reasons. It's just," Trace shrugged, "I don't know."

"Well, it's been a long, hard time. I hope for the sake of your entire family that it's over once and for all."

"It's that Jonas Holt. He's not really the kind of man to listen to reason."

"He can't get anywhere with a sheriff watching his every move and Michael unarmed. Try to relax, Trace."

"I suppose you're right," Trace laughed shortly. "I'm pretty sure Michael's just as tense as I am, though."

"I suppose he is, but I think that you will all be going home soon. I shall miss every one of you, especially Michael and Hannah. Michael has become almost like a brother to me."

"It's been so long since he's seen home. Still, I'm sure it's going to be difficult for him to go. I'm sure his gratitude is deep. Maybe," Trace grinned, "he'll call on you to come visit and baptize their first child."

"I hope so," Patrick laughed.

The sound of footsteps made both of them turn toward the door.

Mac and the others were surprised yet very delighted to see Maxwell and Lee Chu. Smothered with questions, Maxwell had to quiet them before he explained.

The entire group was shocked and only Mac could voice it. "You mean, you actually brought the President of the United States out here? Boy! Remind me to always keep you on my side. You go all out for a friend."

"Thanks," Maxwell grinned. "Where's Trace?"

"I'll go get him," Joey said quickly. He was gone only a few minutes, when he returned to announce that Trace wasn't in his room. "Bet you a dollar he's at Patrick's house," he said. "Want me to go get him?"

"No. I want to meet this Patrick Carrigan anyway. From what Mac here has just told me, everyone involved owes him a debt."

"That's true," Mac said. "I'll walk over with you."

"Hell, we'll *all* walk over with you," Jamie said. "I want to see Trace's face when you tell him what kind of help you got."

"Well, the Prsident is sending for our friend Senator Merrell about now. I'd say in a matter of a couple of hours we should all be celebrating together. C'mon, boys,let's go and let Trace know this little set-to is just about over."

The happy group set out at a brisk walk and took very little time to get to Patrick's house.

Maxwell knocked, and the door was opened by Trace, who had a swift moment of surprise, then a pleased smile and a handshake for Maxwell.

Welcomed enthusiastically into the house, Trace made quick introductions.

"Max, I'm glad you're here, and, Lee Chu, it's sure good to see you again."

"Mistah Tlace, seem plenty happy. Has been good occurrence, I plesume?"

"Well, we're putting up a damn good fight."

"Come, sit down," Patrick said. "We'll tell you all that's going on."

"You do that," Mac said with a wide smile. "And when you're done, we'll tell you about the nice little gift Max has brought."

"Gift?"

"Oh, just a little something to use as insurance," Maxwell said nonchalantly.

At this, Trace had to laugh. He'd worked with Maxwell Starett much too long not to recognize the very satisfied look on his face, not to mention the pleased grins on the others' faces.

"Okay, Max, let's hear about your little gift."

"Let me tell him, Max." Mac was too excited to contain his enthusiasm.

"Go ahead, tell him."

"Trace, when you and your family get rescued, you sure as hell get rescued good. In his own special train, sittin' right down there at the station, is no other than the President of the United States!''

Trace's face registered as much shock as Patrick's.

"The . . ."

"Yes, sir," Jamie grinned. "The President!"

"I don't believe this!"

"Well, believe it," Maxwell said. "Because not only is it true, but he's got enough on the senator to make sure he never tries something like this again."

"Then it's over," Trace breathed. "It really is over."

"Someone has to go get Michael and Hannah right away. Those two need some good news."

"Let me go," Mac said.

"C'mon, Mac," Brad protested. "The four of us came out here with Hannah. I think all four of us should go."

"Great," Trace said. "We'll feed Lee Chu and Max. I guess, for the first time, we can celebrate."

Mac, Jamie, Joey, and Brad left at once, while Maxwell and Lee Chu were invited tosit down and eat, and to fill them in on all the details.

"So that's how it is, Trace," Maxwell finished. "Grant and I are close friends. I decided to go and see him. It was a last chance."

"But it worked."

"He sent for Senator Merrell this morning. I'd say by now the good senator has had the wind taken from his sails. The whole mess is over."

"Thank God," Patrick whispered.

"Yes, thank God," Trace repeated. But deep within, some nagging thought kept the euphoria he wanted to share a bit subdued. He'd never really feel Michael was safe until the senator spoke the words himself.

Thomas Merrell felt as if something within him had been crushed. He sat with Grant in the train car, and he sat now immobile, frozen for the ultimatum he had received.

Oh, he had denied it, then he had tried to justify it, then he had tried to stand firm. Only then, in a quiet voice, did Grant reveal all the points of pressure he had that would destroy Thomas.

"I'm not out to destroy your career," Grant smiled. "I think that is a waste. I need all the help I can get for the things I plan to do. But . . . if this man has any problems, if this is carried any further," Grant's voice lowered, "I'll see to it you will never hold a public office again . . . not even as street sweeper. That I can promise you."

"That's blackmail! You're the President of the United States for God's sake!"

"And you are a duly elected senator who has misused your office to the point of treason. You disgust me. To use your office . . . your power, to do a thing like this. Well, as you were so prepared to use it, so am I. I keep my promises . . . trust me. And if you want to keep your office, call off this travesty. Call it off . . . or pay the price for it."

The last words were said with such finality that Thomas knew there was no question that he meant it.

"All right . . . all right." The last two words were a deadened whisper.

"I think it would be wise once the problem is settled to everyone's satisfaction and the celebration I'm sure everyone concerned will have is over that you return to Washington with me. You and I," Grant said, with satisfaction, "have a great deal to talk about. You can attach your private car to the end of my train."

Thomas was beaten and he knew it. He has wielded power too often not to recognize the fact that Grant was not bluffing. His own weakness would not allow him to surrender all he had.

"I'll give you time to make it clear to your . . . friend, that this little game is over once and for all. I shall make it a point to contact the Cords over the years to make sure things are running smoothly. And once I'm out of office, I intend to take enough evidence with me so there will never be a repetition of this affair . . . ever." Grant took his watch from his vest pocket. "It's nearing ten o'clock. I'll give you until dinnertime tonight to . . . tie up this loose end. I expect you back here by seven."

Thomas could only nod. He felt as if all the air had been sucked from his lungs and his heart had been crushed with a huge vise. He left the train and walked like a man in a daze toward town and the back room of the saloon located amid its red-light district.

He knew Jonas had returned from the ranch and waited for him there.

Jonas was seated at a round table, which was stained with marks from the hundreds of whiskey glasses that had rested there. He looked up when Thomas walked in. Thomas was aware of the stares of the parlor girls and other patrons. He was just as aware of Jonas's first startled look before he motioned to the girl who sat next to him to leave.

"Well, Senator," Jonas grinned. "You takin' to slummin'?"

"I'm in no mood for your dubious wit, Jonas. I've come to pay you what I owe you and to tell you to get out of town. The party's over. I've called the whole thinig off. I won't need your services any longer." Thomas reached into his pocket and took out a roll of bills, peeling off what he owed Jonas and tossing it on the table.

Jonas looked from the money to Thomas . . . then he smiled. "Is that so? What gave you religion all of a sudden?"

"That's none of your affair. The point is, I hired you to do a job. I don't want the job done now, and you've been paid . . . so nobody loses."

"You think it's that simple?"

"It *is* that simple. I want you to get out of town."

"You paid me off, Senator. That means I ain't your man anymore. What I decide to do is my own affair."

Panic struck Thomas. Jonas could not go off and face Michael Cord now. Surely Grant would think he was responsible. It would ruin his entire life.

"What good does it do now? Cord has too much protection. Be smart. Take your money and go."

Jonas stood slowly, then walked the few steps to face Thomas. There was an ugly humor in his eyes.

"Your right, Senator, you paid me off. Now, I'll do what I want, and what I want is to see Cord dead. And I'll see him dead before I leave this town."

"You can't, you fool! You'll ruin us both!"

Jonas was not a fool, he knew from the look in Thomas's eyes that there was a great deal more to this. He was used to reading men's eyes.

"Looks to me like you're scared," Jonas said thoughtfully, and the flushed look on Thomas's face and his evasive eyes told Jonas his words hit close to the mark. "You are scared, aren't you?" He said the words like a revelation. Then he laughed. He threw back his head and laughed uproariously.

When the laughter died, he looked at Thomas with the predatory look of a man who finally had the upper hand. "No . . . I'm not lettin' go. You be the coward, not me."

"Coward, no. Do you want me to tell you what you're up against?" He went on to explain the presence of President Grant. "You kill Cord and the world will fall on your head. He's unarmed and he won't put his guns back on. Try that and you'll have the Federal Army in your lap."

"Unarmed . . . so, I'll challenge him. He'll put his guns back on."

"Damn you!" Thomas said in exasperation. "Don't you see that won't work, either. Give it up, Jonas . . . just give it up!"

"No," he said firmly. "Get out of here, Senator. I have some planning to do."

Jonas was pleased when he saw Thomas crumbling before him. It gave him a sense of power he had never felt before.

"Jonas . . . you can't. Don't you see . . . you can't!"

"The one who can't see is you. Look at it this way. I want to take Cord . . . and what happens to you because of that doesn't matter one little bit to me. So you might as well get out."

"I'll tell the sheriff . . ." Thomas began, but then paused. It didn't matter what he said, he would get his share of the blame.

He could see disaster coming and he was completely helpless to stop it. He turned and walked out with Jonas's soft laughter following.

When he'd gone, Jonas sat down to consider what had been said and what barriers stood in his way. No, he could not challenge an unarmed man. No, he could not afford to have the military on his trail. But he could defend himself. He could kill Michael Cord . . . when Michael Cord challenged him.

"Rena, this chicken is the best I've ever eaten," Quinn said as he reached for his fifth piece of fried chicken.

"I'll second that," Michael replied. "I think I've eaten enough for two men."

"You're right about that," Hannah agreed dryly. "I have a feeling it's going to be hard to keep you fed."

"Oh, I wouldn't say that." Michael laughed as he reached across the table to touch her hand.

The four had enjoyed a comfortable lunch together while Quinn and Rena shared their wedding plans. They had finally been able to laugh about the unique way they had met.

"I have to have a fitting on my gown today, Hannah," Rena said. "I wish you would come along. Oh, and by the way, you were right. Alice is really a wonderful seamstress."

"I suspect she has done wonders on your gown, too. I should love to go with you to see it."

"Not by yourselves," Michael said firmly.

"Michael, I wouldn't be alone," Hannah protested. "I'll be with Rena."

"And with my mother," Rena laughed. "Who is the fiercest protector a girl could have."

"You're still not going into town alone," Michael repeated. "It's just the kind of opportunity Jonas would like."

"Michael's right," Quinn agreed. "Much as I could do without sitting in a dressmaker's shop, I will. Until this situation is resolved completely, you two aren't going anywhere without us."

"This situation can go on for a long time. Trace, Mac and the others can't hang around here forever. Then, only the sheriff, Rena's father, and his friend will be any barrier. I just can't see old Jonas not trying to find his way around that," Michael argued.

"We've said this before, Michael," Hannah added, "but it bears repeating. One day at a time."

Michael was about to speak again when the arrival of others was heralded by the sound of approaching horses. Michael and Quinn were on their feet at once. Michael moved swiftly to the window, only to smile. "It's Mac . . . and all the boys. From the hurry they're in, I'd say they had some news."

Hannah was the first to the door, and she flung it open before the group had a chance to knock. She felt the first tingle of excitement when she saw their smiling faces.

"Mac?" Hannah and Michael spoke the question almost in unison.

"I've got the best news ever," Mac said happily. "It's over, Michael . . . Hannah. It's over."

"What are you talking about?" Michael demanded.

For a minute all four tried to explain what had occurred, but the confusion was so much that they finally had to give up. Reluctantly the others turned the explaining over to Mac.

The more he talked, the more wonder appeared in Hannah and Michael's eyes. Finally, the true import of it broke through. Hannah turned to Michael, who laughed softly and held out his arms. She threw herself into them and was lifted from her feet in a fierce hug. He spun her around laughing in delight, and her laughter joined his.

When they could finally control the excitement, the boys found themselves inundated with a million questions. They answered as best and as fast as they could.

"So Max is here?" Michael asked. "And Lee Chu, he's with him?"

"He sure is," Mac said. "As clever as he's always been, and just as much in control of old Max as ever, too."

"The President," Hannah said in awe. "It's so hard to believe."

"Max is a remarkable man," Michael laughed. "I'm not surprised. He's the kind of man who would go to that length to help. I guess for the first time, I can breathe a free breath." He smiled down into Hannah's eyes. "It's over," he kissed her lightly. "Let's go thank the men responsible."

"That sounds like a good idea to me."

When they arrived at Patrick's house, Maxwell and Michael embraced. For a second, words were caught in constricted throats.

"Max, you can always pull a surprise out of your hat, can't you?"

"Whatever it takes, Michael, my friend," Maxwell laughed. "Whatever it takes. Come to think of it, you and Hannah pulled a bit of a surprise on me. I prayed to find you alive, I had no idea I'd find you married. I'm glad things worked out all right. I wish you every happiness."

The knock that sounded on the door was a shock to everyone. As far as they knew, all concerned parties were gathered here, in Patrick's house.

Patrick opened the door to find Brady, solemn and unsmiling as ever, accompanied by Stewart, who looked just as put out.

"The President would like you to come to the train," Stewart said. "He's decided to join you in celebrating."

Everyone was overwhelmed. From despair and fear they were suddenly lifted to a plane of euphoria.

"I don't have anything to wear to meet a President!" Hannah gasped. "I can't go like this!"

"Hannah, you look fine," Michael soothed, but it didn't do much good.

"We'll stop by my house," Rena said. "I have enough clothes in my closet for three of us. Besides, I have to cancel my fitting today. I most certainly am not going to be trying on a dress when I have a chance to meet the President."

"I don't blame you," Hannah replied. "Thank you so much, Rena."

"I'll get Allison and Reid," Trace said. "They should be here for the celebration."

The group then left, first for Rena's house, then for the train.

It turned into a perfect celebration, with the participants approximately awed, Stewart as usual fretting about the delay, and Grant was relaxed and at ease for the first time in a long time.

Senator Thomas Merrell sat in his darkened room, seeking a way out of his dilemma.

Jonas Holt seemed to have vanished, and after a day of searching, Mac, Jamie, Joey, and Brad returned to assure Hannah that Thomas Merrell must have done as the President had ordered.

Hannah and Michael felt the real freedom to be able to come and go as they pleased. They enjoyed every second of it.

Two uneventful days passed. Assurance grew that the blackest episode in Michael and Hannah's life had finally ended.

Hannah watched Michael change before her eyes. The grim, silent man seemed to vanish and the laughing, teasing man who appeared in his place was a delightful revelation to Hannah, who had never seen this side of Michael.

For the same two days Thomas never left his hotel room. His

mind grew blacker, his anguish deeper. His eyes dimmed and his face paled.

The third morning dawned clear and bright. Hannah had finally coaxed Michael into realizing they were safe and that she could come and go with more freedom. It was his sensitive spot. He found it hard to let her out of his sight.

"But this time I promised Rena I'd go for that fitting with her. And you promised Trace and Patrick that you'd join them and the President for a farewell lunch."

It was against every sense Michael had, yet he could never find a way to battle Hannah when she was set on doing something. She had a way of making him surrender that was very difficult to fight.

"All right. But you be careful."

"I will. Come on, I'll ride as far as Patrick's house with you."

Even Patrick tried to reassure Michael. Still, when Hannah left to go to Rena's, he was less than happy about it.

Hannah and Rena stood in the small fitting room. Rena had just tried on her gown and Hannah had declared it a masterpiece.

Both were relaxed and laughing when Alice appeared, white-faced, at the curtained door. Both women looked at her in surprise.

"Alice?" Hannah questioned, as she started to take a step toward her. Suddenly, the seamstress was roughly pushed into the room.

Hannah's face grew pale. There was no difficulty in recongizing Jonas Holt.

"What do you want?" she said angrily. "You're a fool to cause any problems."

Jonas laughed. "I'm not going to cause any problems. We're just going to take a little ride, you and me."

"I wouldn't cross the street with you," Hannah said furiously. Her fear was a blackness inside. She realized Michael's awareness had been honed to a sharp edge. He must have sensed that the situation was not yet complete.

"You will," Jonas said calmly, "if you don't want to see your two friends die right here." The gun moved slightly toward Rena and Alice.

"All right, all right."

"You," he pointed to Rena, then tossed a folded piece of paper at her. "You take this message to Cord." Rena picked up the paper with trembling hands. "And you . . ." His attention went back to Hannah. "Out the back door. I have horses waiting. If you have anyideas, forget them unless you want some innocent bystander to pay for it."

Hannah glared at him, filled with a combination of anger and fear, knowing that this would bring Michael into Jonas's grasp.

"C'mon," he motioned with his gun, "and don't try anything funny."

Hannah moved ahead of him, but Jonas was very careful, and she had no opportunity to do anything.

When they'd gone, Rena grasped the message in her hand and raced from the room. She meant to race all the way to Patrick's house, but he and Michael had had lunch with Trace and the President, and were on their way home when she met up with them. Michael had only to look at her face and he knew.

"Hannah." He half groaned the name.

"Jonas . . . he came through the back door," Rena gasped. "He left you this message."

"Michael?" Patrick questioned as his face grew pale. Michael didn't answer. He read the note with a grim face.

"Michael, let me get Sheriff Horton," Patrick pleaded. He recognized the look in Michael's eyes.

"No!" Michael finally looked at Patrick, who was struck an almost physical blow by the deadened and murderous look he saw there. Without saying another word, Michael turned and left the house.

"Patrick?" Rena said.

"Rena, you go the hotel and tell Trace and the boys. I'll go and get the sheriff. It's certain he's supposed to meet Jonas some-

where. We just have to find out where before . . . Hurry, Rena,
hurry.''

Michael rode back to the cabin at breakneck speed, the rage in
him so dark, it filled every corner of his mind. He cursed himself.
He had let down his guard, he had again ignored the intuition
that had always kept him alive.

Visions of Hannah when she was so badly beaten made every
moment a nightmare.

As he reached the cabin, he dismounted before the horse even
came to a complete stop. Inside, he went to a peg behind the
door where his guns hung. Taking them from the wall, he buckled
them on.

Finally he stood for a minute and, with slow deliberation, gathered his control. Hannah's life depended on it.

Jonas would want him angry, frightened, and off guard. It would
slow his hand and Michael knew that. It took every effort he had
to regain the calm, cold control he'd had. He meant to kill the
spector of Jonas Holt once and for all.

Jonas watched Hannah carefully as they waited for Michael. The
place had been carefully chosen and would take any searchers
quite a long time to find. By that time Cord would be dead. Jonas
was seriously contemplating taking Hannah with him when he
left the territory. She would be fun for a while.

He watched the hatred broiling in her steady gaze. Yes . . . he
would enjoy her, especially since he knew she had been Michael
Cord's woman.

Within his hotel room a despairing and defeated Thomas Merrell
walked to a dresser and slid open a drawer. The only answer he
could find was there before him.

Michael rode with the fury of the damned. There was no way he
could have told Trace or any of the others. Hadn't Jonas's note

made it clear. If he caught sight of anyone other than Michael coming, Hannah would die right there.

When he rode into the clearing several miles from town, it seemed empty. He stood in the middle of it.

"Jonas! Jonas Holt, you black-hearted coward. I'm here. Come out and show yourself."

From the edge of the wooded area surrounding them, Jonas walked slowly, one hand close to his gun and the other holding Hannah by the base of the neck.

"Michael!" Hannah cried. "He'll kill you." Her terror was for him and Michael felt torn with the need to see her safe.

"No, Hannah, he won't," Michael said, in a voice much too calm to suit Jonas. He needed to remove Michael's edge. With a malicious jerk he pulled Hannah close to him and kissed her roughly. She struggled, but Michael's eyes were riveted on Jonas. He'd cleared his mind to make room for what he had to do. Aware that Michael wasn't reacting in the way he'd expected, Jonas knew the time was now. He gave Hannah a rough push and she fell to the ground.

A heavy silence filled the air as the two men regarded each other. Each was totally immobile . . . breathless . . . waiting.

Within his darkened hotel room, Thomas sank into the valley of darkness. He reached into the drawer and withdrew a gun. He walked to the chair by the window. There he sat down and after a long moment . . . he put the barrel of the gun to his head.

The sunlight sparkled across the meadow, where two men faced each other in a duel of control and speed. The very air seemed to tingle with expectancy.

Hannah was afraid to look and just as afraid not to. The air seemed to be too thin to even breathe and her heart pounded so furiously she felt it might burst.

With a speed that would have amazed any onlooker, both men drew the guns that hung low on their hips.

But at that very same moment, as two shots echoed through the morning air, a third shot was fired.

Thomas Merrell slumped forward as the gun fell from his lifeless hand. Jonas Holt jerked as the bullet from Michael's gun found its mark, while the shot Jonas had fired kicked up a splatter of dirt between Michael's feet.

Then, for another breathless moment, all was still. Hannah jumped to her feet and raced to Michael to throw herself into his arms. She cried his name over and over until it was silenced by his fierce kiss and the iron-hard arms that crushed her to him.

Only then, when the relief that had been almost a pain had passed, Michael held Hannah away from him.

Slowly and deliberately, holding her eyes with his, he unbuckled his gunbelt. With a heave, he tossed the guns as far from him as he could.

"I'll never put them on again, Hannah. I swear. I think . . . it's time to go home."

Hannah had no words. She simply went to him and put her arms about him . . . raising her face to accept the kiss that was a seal against yesterday and a promise for tomorrow.

Epilogue

Six Months Later
Eatonton, Georgia
Patrick was the only passenger to step down from the train, and he was enthusiastically welcomed by Trace, Michael, and Joey.

Patrick was amazed at the change in the brothers. Both seemed to have had a weight lifted from them and they smiled easier. They were joyfully enthusiastic to see him.

"Patrick! It's wonderful to see you again," Michael laughed as he shook Patrick's hand.

"And I must say, Michael, it's good to see you. You look well and happy."

"I've never been happier. I'm a Georgia boy, born and bred, and I can't seem to manage too far away from my roots."

"Trace . . ." Patrick extended his hand.

"Welcome, Patrick. Allison will be pleased. She was anxious to make sure you were at the wedding."

"You look reasonably contented."

"I am. And I want you to meet my son, Richard, named after my father. Born one month ago today."

"Wonderful! Wonderful!"

"Well," Joey chimed in, "it could have been better."

"Better?" Patrick was puzzled.

"Well, see, Rev, me and Jamie kind of figured a man should give his son his name. Now it was bad enough he didn't name the boy Trace Junior . . . but he could have given him some part of his name. We was plannin' on takin' little Chauncey fishin' and . . ."

"Joey. . ." Trace said with a threatening smile. "You just whisper that name at the wedding and it gets back to me, I'm going to take you for a little walk behind the shed."

"Shucks," Joey grinned. "You're too danged happy to get mad."

The whole group laughed at this, and Trace was the first one to admit that was the truth.

"Come on, Patrick." Michael picked up his satchel. "Everyone's waiting to see you. The wedding's tomorrow, so the whole house will be in a state of confusion. Jenny's family is all here, and Mr. and Mrs. Marshall."

"And Allison, how is she?"

"Allison? She's never in a state of confusion. It's Reid who me and Trace are feeling sorry for."

"Come now," Patrick chuckled. "It can't be as bad as that."

"Well, no," Trace grinned. "But don't let the brat know we don't think that or she'll be pretty hard to live with."

Patrick couldn't have been more pleased to see the happiness in the two men who'd struggled so hard for it.

"Rena and Quinn arrived about a week ago," Michael offered.

"I thought they might. Quinn is doing quite well now with the newspaper. He had to take a trip to St. Louis, so he and Rena decided to come straight here."

"They're settled at Fallen Oaks. The house hasn't seen such a party since before the war."

Patrick could feel the atmosphere as they rode up the wide circular drive. He could see the remarkable beauty of the home itself.

They had barely stepped down from the carriage when the front door opened and Jenny, Allison, and Hannah came out, their smiles bright and welcoming.

"Hannah, my dear." Patrick kissed her cheek and embraced her. "You look radiant."

"Thank you, Patrick. I'm so glad you're here."

"As am I, Patrick," Allison said. "It wouldn't have been the same without you."

"I wouldn't have missed it for the world."

"Patrick, this is my wife, Jenny," Trace said.

"Jenny . . . it's a pleasure. I do hope I'll get to see that son of yours who's put such a sparkle in your husband's eyes."

"He asleep right now, but I'm sure he'll soon be up and controlling the whole household. Come in and let us offer you some refreshment."

Patrick followed them into the spacious and very beautiful home. He soon was fed and pampered until he felt as if he were in the bosom of a home filled with love that they were anxious to share with him.

Dinner was an affair filled with laughter, and Patrick found an immense joy in dandling Trace's young son on his knee. By the time it was time to retire, Patrick felt as if this home was almost his.

Fallen Oaks was filled with guests, and more were arriving by the minute. The house itself blazed with light, and gay music could be heard through the open windows.

Today Allison Cord had been married, and the wedding had been one of beauty and perfection. The show of family unity had been admired by many.

But now it was time to laugh and to dance. Allison, in Reid's arms, began the first waltz, and soon the celebration had begun in earnest.

Michael and Hannah stood together with Patrick, Joey, and Jamie. They watched Reid and Allison dance by, and soon Trace and Jenny.

"Michael, they look so happy," Hannah said. "Jenny is absolutely beautiful, and that son of hers, he's even more ravishing."

"Isn't he?" Michael agreed. "I swear he knows me."

"He should . . . you've been hovering over him like a papa bear even since we came home."

"He sure has," Joey agreed. "Seems to me he's got a real soft spot for babies."

"Yeah," Jamie agreed. "Ought to have a couple of his own, twins maybe. Since Trace wouldn't use those fine names, somebody ought to take advantage of them."

"You're right. Aloysius and Chauncey. Sounds good, doesn't it?"

"Good Lord," Michael laughed. "I wouldn't commit a crime like that against an innocent baby. Come on, Hannah, let's dance, before these two give you any ideas. Allison's the devil in this house. Maybe you ought to talk that idea over with her."

Hannah was laughing as Michael put his arm around her and they moved out onto the floor.

"Those two devils are not ever going to let me and Trace live those names down," Michael chuckled.

"Where did they come from?"

"My mother was very proud of a couple of rambunctious ancestors. Trace and I got stuck with their names. Good thing she relented and gave us different first names."

"You wouldn't consider handing it down to your own son, would you?"

"Good Lord, no! Anoysius stops with me."

"I'm relieved to hear that."

"Oh," Michael laughed. "You have no fondness for the illustrious name of Aloysius?"

"Hardly." Hannah's laugh bubbled from her. "What I would like," she smiled up at him, "is for him to be called Michael Cord Junior."

For a second what Hannah had just said did not register completely in Michael's mind. But when it did, among all the swirling dancers, he abruptly stopped where they were.

"Hannah, what are you saying?"

"Oh." She looked innocent. "That Trace and Jenny seem so happy, and . . ."

"All right, no games. I think you were just trying to tell me something important."

"You mean . . . that you and I are going to have a child?"

"Lord, Hannah," he breathed softly, adoration written on his face. He caught her face between his hands and kissed her, while the dancers continued to move. "Thank you," he added gently.

"You're quite welcome," she laughed softly in pleasure. "Don't you think we should be dancing? Everyone's staring."

But instead of dancing, he grasped her hand and walked off the floor and out onto the balcony. There, beneath a star-studded sky, with the soft strains of the waltz filling the air, Michael took her in his arms. This time the kiss was deeper.

"It's true then?"

"Yes, it is."

"I never thought a wonderful night like this would ever happen. I never thought I'd ever be so happy. I love you, Hannah Cord . . . more than I ever thought it possible to love anyone."

"I know . . . and you deserve all the happiness you can have. I hope your son gives you all your dreams."

"My son . . . yes, but my wife . . . you are the one who has given me my life. It seems as if everything is complete."

"Then let's share our news with the rest of the family."

"Not now, not tonight. Tonight is ours alone."

Hannah smiled. There were no words left. They had battled so hard and now the battle was done. Now the future lay before them, and it appeared brighter than either had imagined. Again she moved into his arms and returned his kiss with one of promise. Their future began with this night and both were secure in the fact that whatever came, they would be facing it together.